ROME'S FALLEN EAGLE

Robert Fabbri read Drama and Theatre at London University and worked in film and TV for 25 years. He was an assistant director and worked on productions such as *Hornblower*, *Hellraiser*, *Patriot Games* and *Billy Elliot*. His life-long passion for ancient history inspired him to write the *Vespasian* series. He lives in London and Berlin.

Also by Robert Fabbri

THE VESPASIAN SERIES

TRIBUNE OF ROME
ROME'S EXECUTIONER
FALSE GOD OF ROME

Coming soon ...

MASTERS OF ROME

SHORT STORIES

THE CROSSROADS BROTHERHOOD
THE RACING FACTIONS

ROME'S FALLEN EAGLE

ROBERT FABBRI

CORVUS

First published in trade paperback in 2013 by Corvus,
an imprint of Atlantic Books Ltd.

10 9 8 7 6 5 4 3 2 1

A CIP catalogue record for this book is available from the British Library.

Hardback ISBN: 978 0 85789 744 2
Trade paperback ISBN: 978 0 85789 745 9
E-book ISBN: 978 1 78239 033 6

Printed and bound by
CPI Group (UK) Ltd, Croydon, CR0 4YY

Corvus
An imprint of Atlantic Books Ltd
Ormond House
26–27 Boswell Street
London
WC1N 3JZ

www.corvus-books.co.uk

For my sister, Tanya Potter, and her husband, James, and their three lovely daughers, Alice, Clara and Lucy.

P.S. For those who wondered what resulted from my dedication in the last book, you'll be pleased to know that Anja said yes!

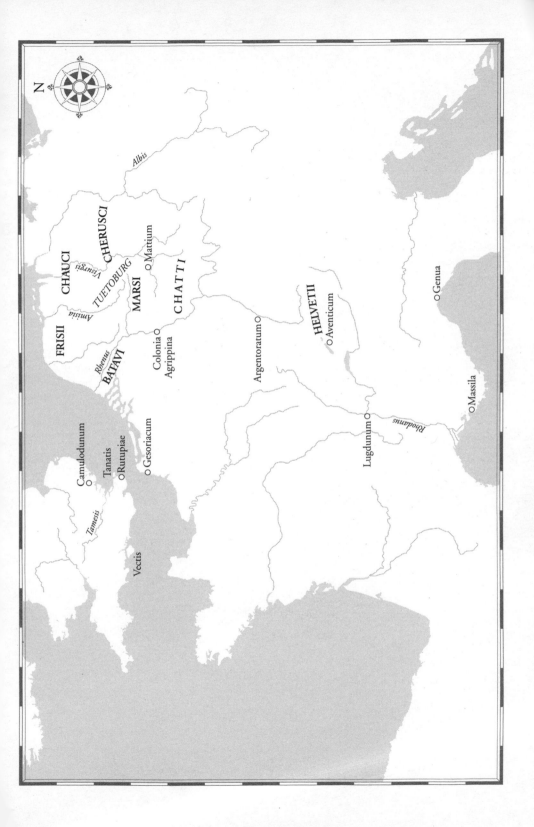

PROLOGUE

ROME, 24TH JANUARY AD 41

THE RIGID, WIDE-EYED grin of a gaudily painted, comic-actor's mask leered out at the audience; its wearer skipped a short jig, the back of his left hand pressed to his chin and his right arm outstretched. 'The wicked deed that causes you *all this* distress *was* my doing; I confess it.'

The audience roared with laughter at this well-delivered, purposely ambiguous line, slapping their knees and clapping their hands. The actor, playing the young lover, inclined his mask-obscured head in acknowledgement of the appreciation before turning to his partner on the stage, who wore the more grotesque, gurning mask of the villain of the piece.

Before the players could continue the scene, Caligula jumped to his feet. 'Wait!'

The ten thousand-strong audience in the temporary theatre clinging to the northern slope of the Palatine Hill turned towards the imperial box, jutting out on supporting wooden columns at the exact centre of the new construction.

Caligula copied the actor's pose. 'Plautus would have wanted the line delivered like this.' He skipped the jig perfectly whilst imitating the mask's broad grin, opening his sunken eyes wide so that the whites contrasted markedly with the dark, insomniac's bags beneath them. 'The wicked deed that causes *you all* this distress was *my* doing; *I* confess it.' As he finished the last syllable he brought his left hand up from his chin to rest on his forehead and melodramatically threw back his head.

The audience's mirth was even more vigorous than at the first rendition, loud and raucous – but forced. The two actors held their bellies and doubled up in unrestrained hilarity. Caligula

10

came out of the pose, a sneer on his face, and, throwing his arms wide, turned slowly to the left, then to the right to encompass the whole audience in the semi-circular construction, bathing in their adulation.

Standing at the very rear of the theatre, within the shade of one of the many awnings rigged over the precipitous seating, Titus Flavius Sabinus looked down at his Emperor with disgust from beneath a deep hood.

Caligula swept up an arm, palm towards the audience; they quietened almost instantaneously. He sat down. 'Continue!'

As the actors obeyed his command a middle-aged man wearing a senatorial toga, seated at Caligula's feet, began to shower kisses on the young Emperor's red slippers, caressing them as if they were the most beautiful objects that he had ever seen.

Sabinus turned to his companion, a pale, thin-faced, auburn-haired man in his thirties. 'Who's the unashamed sycophant, Clemens?'

'That, my dear brother-in-law, is Quintus Pomponius Secundus, this year's Senior Consul, and that's as close as he'll come to expressing an independent opinion whilst he's in office.'

Sabinus spat and gripped the hilt of his sword, concealed beneath his cloak. The palm of his hand felt clammy. 'This hasn't come a moment too soon.'

'On the contrary, this is long overdue. My sister has been living with the shame of being raped by Caligula for over two years now; far longer than honour dictates.'

Down on the stage a hearty kick by the young lover up the backside of his newly arrived slave sent him tumbling to the ground and the audience into a fresh fit of laughter that grew as the players then proceeded to chase each other around, with many trips, turns and near misses. In the imperial box Caligula gave his own demonstration of comedy running, chasing his lame uncle, Claudius, up and down, this time to the genuine amusement of the crowd, who never failed to appreciate a cripple being mocked. Even the Emperor's sixteen full-bearded German Bodyguards, lined up across the rear of the box, shared in the enjoyment of the hapless man's degradation. The two Praetorian tribunes standing to either side of the enclosure made no effort to reprimand their subordinates.

'Are you really going to make that buffoon emperor?' Sabinus asked, raising his voice against the escalating mirth as Claudius' weak legs gave out and he sprawled onto the floor.

'What choice do we have? He's the last of the adult Julio-Claudians. My men in the Praetorian Guard won't accept the restoration of the Republic; they know that'll lead to their disbandment. They'll mutiny, kill me and any other of my officers who stand in their way; then they'll make Claudius emperor anyway.'

'Not if we assassinate him as well.'

Clemens shook his head. 'I can't in honour order his death, I'm his client.' He indicated the two Praetorian tribunes in the box and lowered his voice as Caligula, tired of humiliating his uncle, retook his seat and the audience settled back down to watching the scheduled entertainment. 'Cassius Chaerea, Cornelius Sabinus and I have agreed that Claudius must become emperor: it's our best hope of surviving this. We've had discreet negotiations with his freedmen Narcissus and Pallas – as well as Caligula's freedman, Callistus. He's seen the way things are going and has thrown his lot in with the Claudius faction; they've promised to try and protect us from any vengeance that Claudius would be honour bound to exact for killing a member of his family, even though he'll be the beneficiary – a very surprised one.'

'Claudius doesn't know yet?'

Clemens raised an eyebrow. 'Would you trust that garrulous idiot with such a secret?'

'And yet you would trust him with the Empire?'

Clemens shrugged.

'I say he should die.'

'No, Sabinus, and I demand your oath to Mithras on that. We could have done this a couple of months ago but we delayed so that you could get back to Rome to strike the blow and satisfy your honour. Jupiter's tight sack, I've already exposed another conspiracy to the Emperor in order to ensure that it will be us who will have the pleasure of killing him.'

Sabinus grunted his assent, well aware that he was in no position to argue. For the two years since the rape of his wife, Clementina, and his appointment as legate of the VIIII Hispana by the perpetrator of that outrage, he had been stationed with his legion on the northern frontier in the province of Pannonia, cut off from Rome. He had been forced to wait until Clementina's brother, Clemens, one of the two prefects of the Praetorian Guard, had identified a group of his officers disaffected enough with Caligula's deranged behaviour to risk their lives in an assassination attempt. This had proved to be a lengthy process – as Clemens' coded letters had informed him – owing to his men's understandable reluctance to share treasonable thoughts; if they misjudged their confidant they would have been immediately executed.

The tipping point had come the previous year after Caligula had returned from a half-hearted punitive expedition to Germania and an aborted invasion of Britannia where the legions had refused to embark on the ships. He had humiliated them for their insubordination by making them collect seashells, which he paraded through the streets of Rome in a mock triumph. Having alienated the army he had then proceeded to do the same to the Senate and the Praetorian Guard, making himself absolutely friendless, by announcing his intention to move the Empire's capital from Rome to Alexandria. This had caused consternation amongst both the officers and the nine thousand rank and file of the Guard: they feared that they would either be forced to relocate to the unpleasantly hot province of Egypt or, worse, be left behind to rot into irrelevancy so far from the Emperor who gave purpose to their existence.

United in their fears for their future, the officers had hesitantly begun to share their unease with one another. Clemens had soon been able to recruit the tribune Cassius Chaerea, whom he had long suspected of harbouring murderous intent towards the Emperor who constantly mocked his high voice. Chaerea had brought his close friend and fellow tribune Cornelius Sabinus into the plot as well as two disaffected centurions. With the conspirators finally in place, Clemens had kept his promise to

Sabinus that he would be the one to strike the first blow and had written informing him that all was ready and he should return to Rome in secret; Sabinus had arrived two days earlier. Since then he had remained hidden in Clemens' house; not even his brother, Vespasian, nor his uncle, Senator Gaius Pollo, whom he could see seated next to each other near the imperial box, knew of his presence in the city. Once the deed was accomplished he would return to his posting. He was confident that he could leave unnoticed and that the alibi he had given the junior officers he had left in command of his legion in winter quarters was secure: that he had been visiting his wife and two children, who were staying, out of Caligula's reach, with his parents in Aventicum in the south of Germania Superior. This way, Clemens had reasoned, if there were to be any vengeance meted out to the conspirators by the incoming regime, Clementina would just lose her brother and not her husband as well.

On the stage below the plot had resolved to a happy conclusion and the characters were exiting to a wedding feast through a door in the *scaenae frons*, the two-storey scenery fronted with columns, windows, doors and arches. Sabinus pulled his hood further over his face as the final player turned to address the audience.

'To all our friends here, we would gladly extend an invitation to join us; but though enough is as good as a feast, what is enough for six would be poor fare for so many thousands. So let us wish you good feasting at home and ask, in return, your thanks.'

As the audience burst into applause the German Bodyguards parted to allow a tall man, shrouded in a purple robe and sporting a gold diadem around his head, into the imperial box. He bowed to Caligula in an eastern fashion, putting both hands to his chest.

'What's he doing here?' Sabinus asked Clemens in surprise.

'Herod Agrippa? He's been here for the last three months, petitioning the Emperor to extend his kingdom. Caligula's been toying with him, making him suffer for his greed. He treats him almost as badly as he does Claudius.'

Sabinus watched the Judean King take a seat next to Claudius and exchange a few words with him.

'Caligula will leave to take his bath soon,' Clemens said as the applause started to die down. 'On the way there he wants to hear a rehearsal of a group of Aitolian youths who are due to perform tomorrow. Callistus has had them wait above us in front of Augustus' House just by the entrance to the passage that leads directly to those steps by the imperial box. You can get to there through that exit.' He pointed to the extreme left of the gates that ran along the rear of the theatre; it was shut. 'Knock on it three times, then wait a beat and repeat the signal. It's guarded by two of my men, both centurions; they're expecting you and will let you through. The password is "liberty". Put your neckerchief over your face; the fewer people who can identify you the better if the worst comes to the worst. Chaerea, Cornelius and I will escort Caligula out of the box and then up the steps. As soon as you see us leave, make for the passage and walk down it; we should meet about halfway. I'll delay his German Bodyguards by ordering them to prevent anyone following us up, so we'll have a little time but not much; strike him as soon as you can.' Clemens held out his right arm.

'I will, my friend,' Sabinus replied grasping it. 'It'll be a blow straight to the neck.'

They held each other's gaze for a moment – the grips on one another's forearms firmer than they had ever been – then nodded and parted without another word, both aware that this day may be their last.

Sabinus watched Clemens enter the imperial box and felt calm spread through him. He cared not whether he lived or had died by the close of the day; his one concern was to avenge the brutal and repeated rape of Clementina by the man who had set himself up as an immortal god over all men. Today that false god would taste the limits of his immortality. Clementina's face, as she pleaded with him to save her from her fate, burned in his mind. He had failed her then; he would not do so now. He gripped his sword hilt again; this time his hand was dry. He breathed deeply and felt his heart beating slowly and steadily.

A troupe of acrobats took to the stage and began hurling

themselves around, spinning, tumbling and cartwheeling, only to be met by a disinterested rumble of conversation from the audience, no matter how high or far they leapt. All eyes were on the Emperor as he prepared to leave.

Sabinus saw the Germans salute Clemens as he barked an order at them. Cassius Chaerea and Cornelius Sabinus moved from their positions and came to stand behind the Emperor's chair. The Senior Consul showered one last passionate fall of kisses on the beautiful red slippers, only to be kicked aside by the objects of his adoration as Caligula stood up.

The crowd cheered, hailing Caligula as their god and Emperor; but their god and Emperor did not acknowledge them. Instead, he looked down at Claudius and lifted his chin to examine his throat, passing his finger across it like a knife; terrified, Claudius twitched and drooled over his nephew's hand. With a look of disgust, Caligula wiped off the saliva on Claudius' grey hair and shouted something, unheard over the din, into his uncle's face. Claudius immediately got to his feet and lurched out of the box; the Germans parted for him, and he disappeared as fast as his weak legs could take him. Sabinus stayed focused on Caligula, who then turned his attention to Herod Agrippa and with a couple of bellows sent him, bowing obsequiously, from the box. Caligula threw back his head, laughing, and then mimicked Herod Agrippa's fawning exit, much to the amusement of the crowd. Having milked the comedy value from the situation he swept from the box, slapping Chaerea's arse on the way. Sabinus watched the tribune tense and his hand begin to go for his sword; it stopped mid-movement when Clemens caught his eye, and fell back to his side with fingers flexing as he and Cornelius followed Caligula to the steps. Just before Clemens left the box his eyes flicked up to Sabinus and widened slightly; he strode past the German Bodyguards, half of whom followed him to block the steps to the public whilst the imperial party climbed them, leaving the Consul, nursing his bruised face, watched over by the eight remaining Germans left guarding the imperial box.

All was set.

Sabinus turned and made his way along the rear of the last row of seating to the gate that Clemens had indicated. Pulling up his neckerchief, he put his knuckles to the wood and gave the signal; within an instant a bolt slid back, the gate opened a fraction and he was staring into the dark, hard eyes of a Praetorian centurion.

'Liberty,' Sabinus whispered.

With a slight inclination of the head the centurion stepped back, opening the gate; Sabinus walked through.

'This way, sir,' a second centurion, his back already turned, said as the first closed and bolted the gate.

Sabinus followed the man along a paved path climbing gently up the last few feet of the Palatine; from above a close-harmony dirge drifted down. Behind him he heard the rhythmic clacking of the first centurion's hobnailed sandals as he followed.

After thirty paces they came to the summit. To his left Sabinus could see two Praetorian centuries, clad in tunics and togas, standing at ease next to the Aitolian youths rehearsing their melancholy hymn in front of what remained of the imposing facade of Augustus' House. Once an architectural study in elegance combined with power, it was now disfigured by the series of extensions that Caligula had added. They snaked their way forward, each more vulgar and ill-conceived than the one before, and cascaded down the hill to the Temple of Castor and Pollux at the foot of the Palatine, which now – sacrilegiously in the secret part of many people's minds – served as a vestibule to the whole palace complex. It was to the closest of these extensions, just ahead of him, that the centurion led Sabinus.

Taking a key from his belt, the centurion unlocked a heavy, oaken door and pulled it open, noiselessly on goose-fatted hinges, to reveal a wide passageway. 'To the right, sir,' he said, stepping aside to allow Sabinus past. 'We'll stay here to prevent anyone following you down.'

Sabinus nodded and passed through; sunlight washed in from regularly spaced windows on either side. He swept his sword from its scabbard beneath his cloak, pulled a dagger from his belt and strode forward; the hard slapping of his footsteps reverberated around him off the whitewashed plaster walls.

After a few dozen paces he heard voices from around a bend to the left; he quickened his pace. From the theatre below came another burst of laughter followed by applause. Sabinus approached the corner; the voices were close. He raised his sword and readied himself to strike as soon as he made the turn. Swinging sharply left he pounced forward. He felt his heart leap in his chest as a shrill shriek greeted him and he stared into two terrified eyes set in a long, down-turned face; mucus oozed from a pronounced nose. Claudius' cry died in his throat as he gaped at the sword pointing directly at him and then back at Sabinus. Herod Agrippa stood stock still, his face frozen in fear, next to him.

Sabinus pulled himself back; he had given Clemens his word not to kill Claudius. 'Get out of here, both of you!' he shouted.

After a moment's dumbfounded delay Claudius lumbered off, twitching and muttering, leaving a pool of urine behind him. Herod Agrippa, breathing deeply, stooped and stared up, under the hood, at Sabinus' concealed face. For a moment their eyes met; Herod's widened slightly. Sabinus made a threatening gesture with his sword and the Judaean pelted off after Claudius.

Sabinus cursed and prayed to Mithras that it was not recognition that he had seen in the King's eyes. Voices from further down the corridor drove the worry from his mind; one of them was most definitely that of Caligula. He retreated around the corner and waited as the voices grew closer.

'If those Aitolian boys are sweet-looking I might take a couple to the baths with me,' Caligula was saying. 'Would you like a couple, Clemens?'

'If they're sweet-looking, Divine Gaius.'

'But if they're not then we can always have Chaerea; I'd love to hear that sweet voice moan with ecstasy.' Caligula giggled; his companions did not join in.

Sabinus surged around the corner, sword raised.

Caligula's mirth faltered; his sunken eyes went wide with fright. He leapt backwards; Chaerea's strong hands clamped onto his upper arms, pinioning him.

Sabinus swept his sword through the air; it sliced into Caligula's flesh at the base of his neck. Caligula shrieked; a gobbet of blood slopped onto Chaerea's face. Sabinus' sword arm jarred and he lost his grip as the blade wedged, abruptly, into the collarbone.

There was a moment of shocked silence.

Caligula stared down, eyes gaping, at the sword embedded in him and then suddenly burst into manic laughter. 'You can't kill me! I'm still alive; I am a g ...' He juddered violently; his mouth froze open, mid-laugh, and his eyes bulged.

'This is the last time you'll ever hear my *sweet* voice,' Chaerea whispered into his ear. His left hand was still grasping Caligula but the other was now hidden. Chaerea jerked his body, forcing his right side forward, and the tip of a *gladius* burst through Caligula's chest; his head jolted back and he exhaled violently, spraying a fine crimson mist into the air. Sabinus tugged his weapon free and pulled down his neckerchief; the false god would know who ended his life and why.

'Sabinus!' Caligula croaked, blood trickling down his chin. 'You're my friend!'

'No, Caligula, I'm your sheep, remember?' He thrust his weapon, sharply, low into Caligula's groin as Clemens and Cornelius both drew their swords and plunged them into the stricken Emperor from either side.

With the bitter joy of vengeance, Sabinus smiled as he rolled his wrist, twisting the blade left and right, shredding the lower intestines, and then forcing the point forward until he felt it break through the flesh between the base of the buttocks.

All four assassins wrenched back their swords simultaneously; Caligula stood unsupported for a moment before crumpling, without a sound, to the floor into Claudius' pool of urine.

Sabinus stared down at his erstwhile friend, hawked and spat a globule of phlegm at his face and then pulled his neckerchief back up. Chaerea aimed a shuddering kick at Caligula's blood-seeping groin.

'We must finish it,' Clemens said quietly, turning to leave. 'Hurry; the Germans will find the body soon, I told them to wait for a count of five hundred to stop anyone following us up the steps.'

The four assassins walked briskly back up the corridor. The two centurions were waiting by the door.

'Lupus, bring your century into the palace,' Clemens ordered as he passed them. 'Aetius, keep yours outside and don't let anyone in. And get rid of those caterwauling Aitolians.'

'Did Claudius and Herod Agrippa see you?' Sabinus asked.

'No, sir,' Lupus answered, 'we saw them coming and stepped back outside until they'd passed.'

'Good; get going.'

The two centurions snapped salutes and doubled off through the door towards their men. From back down the corridor came guttural shouting.

'Shit!' Clemens hissed. 'Those bastard Germans can't count. Run!'

Sabinus burst into a sprint and flicked a look over his shoulder; eight silhouetted figures appeared from around the corner; their swords were drawn. One turned and ran back in the direction of the theatre. The remaining seven began to chase them.

Clemens crashed through a door and led them on up a set of marble steps, through a high-ceilinged room full of lifelike painted statues of Caligula and his sisters and on into the palace. Turning left they reached the atrium as the first of Lupus' men were coming through the door.

'Form your lads up, centurion,' Clemens shouted, 'they may have to kill some Germans.'

At a sharp order from Lupus a line was formed as the Germans raced into the atrium. 'Swords!' Lupus yelled.

With the precision expected of Rome's élite soldiery the eighty swords of the century were drawn in ringing unison.

Hopelessly outnumbered but maddened by the murder of the Emperor to whom they owed absolute loyalty, the Germans screamed the war cries of their dark-forested homeland and charged. Sabinus, Clemens and the two tribunes slipped behind the Praetorian line as, with a resounding clash of metal on metal that echoed through the columns of the room, the Germans crashed into the Praetorians with their weight fully behind their shields. They slashed with long swords at the heads and torsos of the unshielded defenders. Four went down immediately under the ferocity of the attack but their comrades held the line, punching with their left arms in lieu of shields and stabbing with their shorter swords at the groins and thighs of their assailants, whose numbers quickly dwindled. Soon five of their companions were lying dead or dying on the floor, and the last two Germans disengaged and ran headlong back the way that they had come.

A shrill female voice cut through the clamour. 'Just what is going on here?'

Sabinus turned to see a tall woman with a long, horse-like face and pronounced aristocratic nose; she held a child of about two years old in her arms. The girl's young eyes stared greedily at the blood wetting the floor.

'My husband will hear of this.'

'Your husband will hear nothing, Milonia Caesonia,' Clemens informed her coldly, 'ever again.'

For a moment she hesitated; then she drew herself up and looked Clemens in the eyes; defiance burned in hers. 'If you mean to kill me too then my brother will avenge me.'

'No he won't. Your *half*-brother, Corbulo, thinks that you've brought shame and dishonour to his family. If he's sensible he'll get his legion, the Second Augusta, to swear loyalty to the new Emperor; then, when he's served his term as legate, he'll come back to Rome and hope that the stain on his character that you have left will be forgotten in time.'

Milonia Caesonia closed her eyes, as if acknowledging to herself the truth of the statement.

Clemens walked towards her with his sword drawn.

She held up the child. 'Will you spare Julia Drusilla?'

'No.'

Milonia Caesonia clutched her daughter tightly to her breast.

'But as a favour to you I will kill you first so you don't see her die.'

'Thank you, Clemens.' Milonia Caesonia kissed her child on the forehead and set her down; she immediately started to wail, holding her arms up to her mother and jumping up and down to be picked up again. After a few moments of being ignored she flew at her mother in a frenzy, tearing at her *stola* with sharp nails and teeth.

Milonia Caesonia looked down with tired eyes at the screaming brat at her feet. 'Do it now, Clemens.'

Clemens grasped her shoulder with his left hand and punched his sword up under her ribs; her eyes bulged open and she exhaled softly. The child looked at the blood seeping from the wound and, after a moment's incomprehension, started to laugh. Clemens gave one more thrust and Milonia Caesonia's eyes closed. He wrenched his sword out and the child's laughter died. With a squeal of fear she turned and scampered off.

'Lupus! Get that monster,' Clemens shouted, laying Milonia Caesonia's body down.

The centurion sprinted after the small figure and caught her within a few paces. She lashed out with her nails, drawing blood on his arm, as he lifted her, before sinking her teeth into his wrist. With a cry of pain, Lupus grabbed her ankle and held her, struggling and screeching, dangling upside-down at arm's length.

'For the sake of the gods, finish her!' Clemens ordered.

A shriek curtailed by a sickening crunch made Sabinus wince.

After a quick look at his handiwork Lupus tossed the lifeless body aside to land in a crumpled, broken heap at the base of the bloodied column.

'Good,' Clemens said, sharing the relief that everyone in the room felt at the sudden quiet. 'Now take half of your men and search the eastern side of the palace for Claudius.' He pointed at a Praetorian optio. 'Gratus, you take the other half into the western side.'

With smart salutes Lupus and Gratus led their men off.

Clemens turned to Sabinus. 'I'm going to find where my drooling idiot of a patron has hidden himself. You should go now, my friend, it's done; get out of the city before this becomes public.'

'I think it already has,' Sabinus replied. The good-humoured noise that had emanated from the theatre below had now turned into uproar.

Sabinus squeezed his brother-in-law's shoulder, turned and ran out of the palace. Screams and panicked cries filled the air as he raced down the Palatine.

People had started to die.

PART I

❧ ❧

Rome, The Same Day

CHAPTER I

VESPASIAN HAD ENJOYED the play despite the Emperor's constant interruptions; *The Pot of Gold* was not his favourite by Plautus but the dual-meaning dialogue, misunderstandings and slapstick chases as the miserly protagonist Euclio tries to hang onto his new-found wealth always made him laugh. The problem he had with the play was that he actually rather sympathised with Euclio's desire to part with as little money as possible.

The troupe of young male acrobats currently leaping about the stage did not enthral Vespasian in the way they did his uncle, Gaius Vespasius Pollo, seated next to him, so, as he waited for the next comedy to commence, he closed his eyes and dozed peacefully, thinking of his young son, Titus, now just over a year old.

Vespasian woke with a start as a harsh, throaty cry cut through the half-hearted applause for the acrobats as their act reached a tumbling finale. He scanned his eyes over the heads of the audience for the source and cause of the yelling. Twenty paces to his left, a German Imperial Bodyguard came racing out of a covered staircase; his right hand was raised and covered in blood. He sprinted, shouting unintelligibly in his native tongue, towards eight of his colleagues guarding the entrance of the imperial box, recently vacated by the Emperor. The audience close by stared at the man in alarm as he brandished his blood-soaked hand in the bearded faces of his comrades.

Vespasian turned to his uncle, still applauding the scantily clad youths leaving the stage, and stood, tugging at the sleeve of Gaius' tunic. 'I've a feeling that something bad is about to happen. We should leave immediately.'

'What, dear boy?' Gaius asked distractedly.

'We need to go; right now!'

The urgency in his nephew's voice made Gaius heave his corpulent body to his feet, pulling a carefully tonged curl away from his eyes and casting one last look at the disappearing acrobats.

Vespasian glanced nervously back over his shoulder as the German Bodyguards drew their long swords simultaneously. Their combined bellows of rage silenced the crowd nearest to them; a hush spread in a wave until it encompassed the entire audience.

The Germans held their swords aloft, their faces contorted with rage, the roar dying in their throats. For an instant the hush, deep and tense, enveloped the whole theatre; all eyes fixed questioningly onto the nine barbarians. Then a sword flashed and a head spun through the air, spiralling blood that fell in heavy drops onto the people gawping up in open-mouthed bewilderment at the macabre missile spinning over them. The body of the decapitated spectator – a senator – spewed forth gore for two or three heart-pumps, sitting upright and motionless, drenching the horrified people surrounding it. It slumped forward onto a wide-eyed, uncomprehending old man – also a senator – twisting round in the seat in front; a sword slammed into his gaping mouth, the point exploding through the back of his skull without his eyes changing expression.

For another half-heartbeat there was complete stillness; then a single scream of a woman, as the head landed in her lap, shattered the moment and unleashed a cacophony of terror. The Germans swept forward in a blur of flickering iron, carving their way indiscriminately through the crowd, leaving in their wake the limbs and corpses of anyone too slow to join the immediate stampede away from them. In the imperial box the Senior Consul gazed stupefied at a snarling barbarian bearing down on him before leaping over the balustrade at the front and falling, arms and legs flailing, onto the backs of the panicking mob below.

Vespasian thrust his uncle forward, pushing aside a screeching matron, and headed for the nearest gangway leading down between the aisles of seating, towards the stage. 'Now's not the time for good manners, Uncle.' As he shoved his way down through the crush, using his uncle's bulk as a battering ram, he caught glimpses of the mayhem all around. To his left, two senators went down under a hail of slashes. Behind him, three maddened Germans hacked their way through the surging mass, in a welter of blood, closing in on them. Vespasian caught the eye of the leading swordsman and felt his concentration fixed upon him. 'Senators seem to be their main target, Uncle,' he yelled pulling his toga from his right shoulder so that the broad, purple senatorial stripe would be less visible.

'Why?' Gaius shouted, treading over an unfortunate who had gone down in the crush.

'I don't know, just keep pushing.'

With their combined body weight and downhill momentum they managed to heave their way away from the trailing Germans who had become entangled in the dead and dying. Bursting out into the relatively uncongested *orchestra*, between the seating and the stage, Vespasian risked another backwards glance and was shocked by the havoc just nine armed men could wreak amongst so many defenceless people. Bodies littered the seating and more than a few wore bloodied senatorial togas. He grabbed his uncle's arm and broke into a run; he pushed his way up a short flight of steps, onto the stage and moved, as fast as Gaius could waddle, towards a bottlenecked arch in the scaenae frons on its far side, crammed with desperate people. Joining the scrum they jostled and sweated their way through, struggling to stay upright, feeling the soft flesh of those not so fortunate beneath their feet, and eventually surged out of the theatre onto a street running along the base of the Palatine.

The crowd streamed out to the right as, from the left, came the pounding, even steps of three centuries of an Urban Cohort advancing at the double. Vespasian and Gaius had no choice but to be swept along by the torrent whilst all the time easing themselves across to the edge. As he felt his left shoulder brush the wall, Vespasian looked out for a turning.

'Ready, Uncle?' he shouted as they approached the opening to an alley.

Gaius huffed and wheezed; he nodded his head, beads of sweat flowing down his wobbling jowls. Vespasian yanked him left and they escaped the panic-driven flood.

Vespasian almost tripped over the corpse of a German Imperial Bodyguard lying across the alley's mud-splattered floor as they tore up its length. Just before the end they hurdled another German, bald but with a long blond beard, sitting leaning against the wall, grasping the stump of his right arm trying to stem the flow of blood; he stared down in horror at the severed hand, still clutching a sword, next to him. At the mouth of the alley Gaius caught his breath whilst Vespasian quickly looked around. To his right a man hobbled away, head down. Blood ran down his right leg from under his cloak; he held a sword slick with gore.

Vespasian ran to the left towards the Via Sacra. Gaius lumbered after him, slowing with every rasping breath.

'Hurry, Uncle,' Vespasian called over his shoulder, 'we must get back to the house in case this spreads throughout the city.'

Gaius came to a halt, hands on his knees, gasping. 'You go ahead, dear boy; I can't keep up. I'll head to the Senate House; you go and see to Flavia and young Titus. I'll join you once I have any news of what's happened.'

Vespasian waved a hand in acknowledgement and raced off to be with his wife and young son. He turned onto the Via Sacra, heading to the Forum Romanum, as two centuries of the Praetorian Guard came clattering down from the Palatine, away from the screams and anguished cries that still emanated from its north slope. Vespasian was forced to wait as they crossed the Via Sacra. In their midst, carried in a chair, sat Claudius, twitching and drooling, with tears streaming down his face, pleading for his life.

'Lock and bolt the door,' Vespasian ordered the young and very attractive door boy who had just let him into his uncle's house, 'and then go around the house and make sure that all the outside windows are closed.'

The lad bowed and raced off to do as he had been bidden.

'Tata!'

Vespasian turned, breathing deeply, and smiled at his thirteen-month-old son, Titus, as he hurtled across the mosaic floor of the atrium on all fours.

'What's the matter?' Flavia Domitilla, Vespasian's wife of two years, asked, looking up from her spinning by the atrium hearth.

'I'm not sure, but thank the gods that you're safe.' Vespasian picked up his son and kissed him on both cheeks in relief as he walked over to join her.

'Why shouldn't we be?'

Vespasian sat down opposite his wife and bounced Titus up and down on his knee. 'I don't exactly know but I think that someone has finally—'

'Don't excite the child so much; his nurse has just fed him,' Flavia cut in, looking disapprovingly at her husband.

Vespasian ignored his wife's plea and carried on the rough ride. 'He's fine; he's a sturdy little fellow.' He beamed at his giggling son and pinched a chubby cheek. 'Aren't you, Titus?' The child gurgled with delight as he pretended to be riding a horse and then squealed as Vespasian jerked his knee suddenly to the left, almost unseating the miniature cavalryman. 'I think that someone has finally assassinated Caligula, and for Sabinus' sake I pray that it's not Clemens.'

Flavia's eyes widened, excitedly. 'If Caligula's dead then you'll be able to release some of your money without fear of him killing you for it.'

'Flavia, that's the least of my concerns at the moment; if the Emperor has been assassinated I need to work out how to keep us all safe during the change of regime. If we're going to persist in this folly of choosing an emperor from the heirs of Julius Caesar then the obvious successor is Claudius, which might work out well for the family.'

Flavia waved a hand dismissively, ignoring her husband's words. 'You can't expect me to always live in your uncle's house.' She indicated the homo-erotic art work littering the atrium and the lithe, flaxen-haired German youth who waited on them discreetly by the *triclinium* door. 'How much longer am I going to have to endure looking at all this, this ...' She trailed off unable

28

to find the right word for Senator Gaius Vespasius Pollo's taste in decor and slaves.

'If you want a change join me on my trips to the estate at Cosa.'

'And do what? Count mules and fraternise with freedmen?'

'Then, my dear, if you insist in staying in Rome, this is where you live. My uncle has been very hospitable to us and I've got no intention of throwing his generosity back in his face by moving out when there's plenty of room here for all of us.'

'You mean you've got no intention of taking on the expense of having your own house,' Flavia retorted, giving her spindle a fractious twist.

'That as well,' Vespasian agreed, giving Titus another full-blown gallop. 'I can't afford it; I didn't manage to make enough extra money when I was a praetor.'

'That was two years ago. What have you done since?'

'Managed to stay alive by seeming to be poor!' Vespasian looked sternly at his wife, immaculately presented with the latest coiffure and far more jewellery than he thought necessary; he regretted that they could never see eye to eye about finances. However, the fierce independence in her large brown eyes, the allure of her full breasts and the pregnant swell of her belly – under what seemed to be yet another new stola – reminded him of the three main reasons why he had married her. He tried the reasonable approach. 'Flavia, my dear, Caligula has executed a lot of senators just as wealthy as me so that he could get his hands on their money; that's why I keep my money invested in the estate and therefore out of Rome whilst living in my uncle's house. Sometimes being perceived as poor can save your life.'

'I wasn't talking about the estate; I'm thinking about that money you brought back from Alexandria.'

'That is still hidden and will remain so, until I'm certain that we have an emperor who is a little less free with his subjects' property; and their wives for that matter.'

'What about their mistresses?'

A series of hiccups from Titus followed by a stream of partly digested lentils splattering onto Vespasian's lap came as a welcome distraction. Conversations with his wife about money were never enjoyable, especially as they always led on to the subject of his keeping a mistress. He knew it was not that Flavia was sexually jealous of Caenis but rather that she resented what she imagined he was spending on his mistress while she, his legitimate wife, felt that she was deprived of some of life's comforts; the chief amongst which was her own house in Rome.

'There, what did I tell you?' Flavia exclaimed. 'Elpis! Where are you?'

A comely, middle-aged slave woman bustled into the room. 'Yes, mistress?'

'The child has been sick on the master; clean it up.'

Vespasian stood and handed Titus over to his nurse; the lentils slopped to the floor.

'Come here, you young rascal,' Elpis cooed, taking Titus under the arms. 'Oh, you're the image of your father.'

Vespasian smiled. 'Yes, the poor little fellow will have a round face and just as large a nose.'

'Let's hope he'll have a larger purse,' Flavia muttered.

A loud rapping on the front door saved Vespasian from having to respond. The attractive doorkeeper looked through the viewing slot and then immediately pulled the bolt back. Gaius dashed through the vestibule and into the atrium, his body wobbling furiously under his toga; his curls were now lank with sweat, sticking to his forehead and cheeks.

'Clemens has assassinated the monster. Reckless idiot,' Gaius boomed before pausing to catch his breath.

Vespasian shook his head regretfully. 'No, *brave* idiot; but I suppose that it was inevitable after what Caligula did to his sister. I just thought that after two years his sense of self-preservation would have re-established itself. Thank the gods that Sabinus isn't in Rome, he would have joined him; I heard them make a pact to do it together and I would have been honour bound to help. Clemens is a dead man.'

'I'm afraid so, not even Claudius would be stupid enough to let him live. He's been taken to the Praetorian camp.'

'Yes, I saw. After the madman we get the fool; how long can this go on for, Uncle?'

'As long as the blood of the Caesars lasts and, I'm afraid, Claudius has it pumping around his malformed body.'

'The fool was begging for his life, he didn't realise that they were just keeping him safe until the Senate proclaimed him emperor.'

'Which should be very soon. Get that sick off your tunic, dear boy; the Consuls have summoned a meeting of the Senate in one hour at the Temple of Jupiter on the Capitoline.'

Progress up the Gemonian Stairs to the summit of the Capitoline Hill had been slow, clogged as they were not only with members of the Senate answering their Consuls' call but also teams of slaves heaving many heavy strongboxes, the entire contents of the treasury, for safekeeping up to the Temple of Jupiter, the most sacred building in Rome. At the foot of the stairs, in front of the Temple of Concordia in the Forum, the entire three Urban Cohorts stood to, with orders from Cossus Cornelius Lentulus, the Urban prefect, to guard against any attempt by the Praetorian Guard to retrieve Rome's wealth. Across from the Forum, on the Palatine, the temporary theatre stood silent, dead bodies still strewn about its empty seats.

Eventually over four hundred senators were assembled in the dim, cavernous chamber. The business of transferring the strongboxes went on around them as the Consuls sacrificed a ram to their host deity.

'This could turn nasty,' Gaius whispered to Vespasian as Quintus Pomponius Secundus, the Senior Consul, inspected the auspices, assisted by his junior colleague, Gnaeus Sentius Saturninus. 'If they've brought the treasury up here they must be thinking of defying the Guard.'

'Then we should get out of here, Uncle; Claudius becoming emperor is inevitable.'

'Not necessarily, dear boy; let's listen to what people have got to say before jumping to any rash and maybe dangerous conclusions.'

Satisfied with what he saw, Pomponius Secundus declared the day auspicious for the business of the Senate and took the floor; the bruise on his face that he had received from Caligula earlier was now swollen and discoloured. 'Conscript Fathers and fellow lovers of liberty, today is the day when our world changed. Today is the day when the man whom we hated and feared in equal measure has finally been brought down.'

To emphasise the point he nodded towards the statue of Caligula standing next to the sedentary statue of Rome's most sacred god; a group of slaves pushed it from behind and the image of the late Emperor crashed to the marble floor, shattering into many fragments. A mighty cheer from the senators echoed around the chamber. For a moment Vespasian remembered the good-natured, vibrant youth he had known and regretted the loss of a friend, before the memories of the monster he had become returned and he began to cheer along with the rest.

'Today is the day,' Pomponius Secundus continued, raising his voice above the celebrations, 'when all of us who so fearlessly opposed the tyrannical regime of Caligula can, once again, call ourselves free men.'

'I wouldn't call kissing Caligula's slippers in the theatre this afternoon fearless opposition,' Gaius muttered as this statement was greeted with more cheering. Judging by the looks on many faces Vespasian guessed that his uncle was not the only person to hold that opinion.

The Senior Consul pressed on, unaware that some of the cheers were, now, ironic. 'The Praetorian Guard has taken it upon itself to try and impose a new emperor on us: Caligula's uncle, Claudius. Conscript Fathers, I say no! Not only does Claudius stutter and drool and stumble in a way that would bring dishonour to the dignity of government but also he is not known to, and therefore not loved by, the legions. We cannot allow the Praetorian Guard to force an emperor like this onto us; if the legions of the Rhenus or Danubius decide to nominate their own more martial candidates we could face another civil war. As free men we should choose one from our number as the new Emperor to rule in conjunction with a loyal senate. He should be a man acceptable to us, the legions and the Guard. He should be …'

'You, is what you're trying to imply,' Gnaeus Sentius Saturninus, the Junior Consul, shouted as he got to his feet, jowls and belly quivering. He raised an accusatory finger at his colleague and then cast his piercing blue eyes around the temple. 'This man would have us replace the known tyranny of one family with the unknown tyranny of another; is that what free men do? No!' A rumble of agreement met this assertion and Saturninus took as statesmanlike a pose as his flabby figure would allow, with his left arm folded across his body, supporting his toga, and his right down at his side. 'Conscript Fathers, today we have a historic opportunity to take back our ancient powers and become once again the legitimate government of Rome. Let us rid ourselves of these Emperors and return to the true freedom of our forefathers, a freedom so long denied us that very few here present have savoured its taste; a freedom that belonged to a time when the eldest men here were mere boys: the freedom of a Republic.'

'Keep your face neutral, dear boy,' Gaius hissed in Vespasian's ear. 'Now is not the moment to be seen to have an opinion.'

Almost half of the assembled company broke into enthusiastic applause and cheering but a goodly minority scowled and muttered to one another; the rest stood and watched impassively, preferring, like Gaius, to wait and see which faction was more likely to prevail.

Gaius tugged at Vespasian's elbow, pulling him back through the crowd. 'We would do well to remain as inconspicuous observers until this matter has been decided, one way or the other.'

'At which point we'll profess our loyalty to the winning side, eh, Uncle?'

'It's a sensible course of action that has a far higher survival rate than rashly cheering for what one believes in.'

'I quite agree.'

The cheering began to subside and the ex-Consul, Aulus Plautius, took to the floor.

'This should be telling,' Gaius muttered, 'Plautius has a knack of staying in favour.'

Vespasian gave a wry grin. 'He has a knack of changing sides, you mean.' Almost ten years previously, Aulus Plautius had managed so survive being a supporter of the doomed Sejanus by leading the demand for his erstwhile benefactor's death.

'Conscript Fathers,' Plautius declaimed, pulling his broad shoulders back and puffing out his muscular chest; the veins on his thick neck bulged. 'Whilst I can quite understand our two esteemed Consuls' differing opinions and can see that each in its own way has merit and is worthy of discussion, I would remind the House that one thing has been overlooked: the power of the Praetorian Guard. Who can stand against them?' He picked out the Urban prefect, Cossus Cornelius Lentulus. 'Your Urban Cohorts, Lentulus? Three cohorts of almost five hundred men against the nine cohorts of the Guard, each nearly a thousand strong? Even if you added the Vigiles to them you would be outnumbered three to one.'

'The People would join us,' Lentulus retorted.

Plautius' lip curled disdainfully. 'The People! And what would they use to fight against the élite force of Rome? Eating knives and meat cleavers with baking trays for shields and stale bread for sling shots? Pah! Forget the People. Conscript Fathers, however much it offends your *dignitas* to hear this, I put it to you that, pragmatically, the matter is out of your hands.'

Vespasian looked around from his position at the rear of the gathering to see that the unpalatable truth in Plautius' words was sinking in.

Plautius' eyes hardened as he too saw that his argument had traction. 'This is what I suggest, Conscript Fathers: that we send a delegation to the Praetorian camp to meet with Claudius. We need to ascertain whether he really wants to be our Emperor and, if he does, how he intends to rule? If he doesn't, and he can be persuaded to refuse the Guard's offer, whom would they accept in his stead? Because I can tell you this for sure: the Guard will not accept a return to the Republic.'

The senators were silent as the last word echoed around the chamber until it was finally lost, like the vague memory of a pleasant dream that disappears upon waking to the reality of daily existence.

'We should leave immediately,' Vespasian whispered in Gaius' ear, 'and present ourselves to Claudius.'

'And what if the Senate persuade Claudius to step down? Where would we be then? It's too soon to make a decision; we stay with the flock.'

Vespasian frowned, doubt clouding his thoughts. 'At this point whatever we do is dangerous; we should take a gamble on the most likely course of events.'

'Would you gamble with the lives of your wife and child?'

Vespasian did not need to think about the answer. 'No.'

'Then stay anonymous; don't make a decision until you have all the information.'

The Senior Consul stepped forward, his demeanour now subdued. 'I am forced to agree with the ex-Consul and suggest that we nominate a deputation representing the full dignity of this House; all Consuls and praetors, past and present, should go.'

There was a murmur of assent.

'Very good, Consul,' Plautius jeered, 'and who should head this delegation?'

'Naturally as Senior—'

'No, not naturally at all; you'll just be seen as a prospective candidate for the job and not impartial. This has to be led by someone who, although he has senatorial rank, is not eligible to be emperor or even consul. It must be someone whom Claudius considers to be a friend so that he won't feel that he's being bullied or manoeuvred. In short it cannot be anyone here present.'

Secundus looked puzzled. 'Who then?'

'King Herod Agrippa.'

Night had fallen by the time the Judaean King had been found and summoned before the Senate. Torches and sconces had been lit in the temple making its polished marble interior a place of dancing light, far brighter than during the day. The sedentary statue of Rome's guardian god watched over the deliberations. If Jupiter's stern face had been able to register emotions it might have taken on a look of contempt as it looked down on the depleted gathering. Over the last couple of hours, now that it was apparent that the Guard had the upper hand, many of the senators who had openly supported a restoration of the Republic had suddenly remembered urgent reasons to hurry to their country estates outside Rome. Vespasian and Gaius had stayed, safe in the knowledge that they had, as yet, expressed no opinion.

Herod Agrippa's dark eyes glinted with amusement as they looked around the remaining senators from either side of a beak-like nose. 'I'm very happy to head your delegation, Conscript Fathers; you honour me by your invitation. However, I fail to see what it can achieve.'

'We wish to know Claudius' mind,' Pomponius Secundus replied testily. 'Perhaps he would be willing to refuse the Guard's offer of making him emperor.'

'He tried to do that but has been persuaded otherwise.'

'By the Guard at the points of their swords?'

'No, Secundus, by me.'

'You!' Pomponius Secundus almost choked and had to slap his chest as he stared with disbelief at Herod Agrippa sitting serenely before him in his gold-embroidered, purple robe and kingly golden diadem.

'Well, someone had to.'

'Someone did *not* have to,' the Senior Consul exploded, 'especially you; a greasy little, eastern client king who can't even bring himself to eat pork like any self-respecting Roman should.'

'I think that was the final bit of information that I needed to make a decision, Uncle,' Vespasian said out of the corner of his mouth.

Gaius nodded his head sagely. 'I've just become an ardent supporter of Claudius. I always thought that he was the best man for the job, a natural leader.'

Herod Agrippa remained unruffled by this outburst. 'This greasy little, eastern client king – who, by the way, enjoys pork very much – took it into his own hands today to save your idiotic necks because I could see that the outcome was inevitable; unlike some people. I followed Claudius to the Praetorian camp and I was there when the Guard proclaimed Claudius emperor. However, Claudius thought it unconstitutional for the Guard to elevate him to the Purple—'

Gnaeus Sentius Saturninus jumped to his feet, bursting with latent Republican indignation. 'It's absolutely unconstitutional, only the Senate can do that!'

Herod Agrippa smiled placidly. 'Yes, that was Claudius' view, even though the Guard proved otherwise by killing one emperor and replacing him with another. Claudius was very keen – insistent even – that the Senate should proclaim him emperor immediately he was taken to the camp; he wanted his elevation to have at least the appearance of it being requested by this House. He waited for hours but heard nothing from you. Instead you sat up here on treasury strongboxes, scheming and plotting – what about, he could only guess. However, he knew that one thing was for sure: the fact that you hesitated to make him emperor meant that you didn't want him.'

'We never said that,' Pomponius Secundus stated flatly.

'Don't demean yourself by lying to me. Every word of what has been discussed up here has recently been reported to Claudius by a few senators, including one of the praetors, anxious to stress that it was nothing to do with them but, strangely, begging for his forgiveness anyway.

'From my understanding of it the only one of you who has come out of this reasonably well is Aulus Plautius.' Herod smiled thinly at the gathering as each man tried to remember exactly what positions he had held in the debates that afternoon. 'Once your silence had deafened him for a few hours, Claudius decided that it might be best, for his own safety, to step down before things started to escalate into an armed confrontation. I persuaded him not to, arguing that that would be akin to signing his and all your death warrants; his freedmen agreed. So he accepted the Guard's acclamation and showed his thanks by promising a donative of one hundred and fifty gold aurei per man.' There were soft whistles of incredulity. 'He now feels very safe and intends to stay as emperor. Face it, gentlemen, by your failure to take the initiative and quickly accept the inevitable you have allowed the Guard and Claudius to create a very nasty precedent: from now on the Guard can make emperors and the emperors will pay handsomely for them to do so. You've just lost what little power remained to you.'

Cossus Cornelius Lentulus, the Urban prefect, got to his feet. 'I've heard enough, I'm taking the cohorts to swear loyalty to Claudius.'

'You can't do that,' the Junior Consul called, 'they're meant to be protecting the Senate.'

'From what? The Senate has just become irrelevant,' Lentulus barked. 'And even if the Guard were to come to attack the Senate with an emperor at their head do you think my men will fight? Bollocks they will.' He turned and walked out.

Gaius looked at Vespasian; they came to a swift mutual agreement. 'We'll come with you, Lentulus,' Vespasian called as he and Gaius stood up.

There was a chorus of similar calls as the senators rose to their feet.

Following the Urban prefect to the door, Vespasian glanced at Herod Agrippa who frowned as their eyes met; then a half-smile of understanding seeped over his face.

As Vespasian passed, the Judaean King turned back to Secundus. 'Would you still like me to lead that delegation, Senior Consul?' he asked innocently, above the noise.

Pomponius Secundus scowled at him and stormed from the temple.

The streets of Rome were almost deserted as the Senate led the Urban Cohorts up the Vicus Patricius towards the Viminal Gate, beyond which was situated the Praetorian camp. As one of the main brothel streets in Rome, its pavements would normally be crowded at any time of the day or night; but this evening business was very slow. There was not even a single cart or wagon, forbidden to enter the city during the day, rumbling along the road taking advantage of night-time delivery hours. The common people of Rome had mostly locked their doors and closed their shutters as they waited for the power struggle to be played out so that life could get back to normal and they could be safe in the knowledge that somebody – and they cared not who – was in charge of distributing the grain dole and financing the games.

Passing under the Viminal Gate, Vespasian took a deep intake of breath; before them, a hundred paces away, lined across the front of the Praetorian camp, stood three cohorts of the Guard in full arms. The burnished iron of their helmets and scale armour and the bronze of the rims and bosses of their oval shields reflected the guttering torchlight. At their centre, on a raised dais, sat the new Emperor; the few senators who had already offered their allegiance to him stood to either side.

On the dais, behind Claudius, Vespasian recognised Claudius' freedmen, Narcissus and Pallas, as well as Caligula's erstwhile freedman Callistus; all three wore citizens' plain white togas.

'I'll go first,' Herod Agrippa told the two Consuls who were showing a reluctance to go forward although each was escorted by twelve lictors bearing fasces, the bundle of rods tied around an axe symbolising the magistrates' power.

The Consuls both nodded and, despite the loss of dignitas, allowed themselves to be preceded by a client king.

Upon drawing closer, Vespasian could see an amused look play on Narcissus' pudgy face as he stroked his oiled, pointed black beard with a stubby hand, heavy with bejewelled rings. He had always served Claudius, and Vespasian knew that he had been responsible for keeping his master safe during the reigns of Tiberius and Caligula by encouraging him, although little encouragement was needed, to play the fool; for him, today was the vindication of that policy. Pallas, tall, slim and full-bearded, betrayed, as ever, no emotion; he had served Vespasian's late patron, the Lady Antonia, but upon her death had transferred his allegiance to her son Claudius, as the eldest surviving male in her family. Vespasian tried but failed to catch his eye, hoping that their past acquaintance, friendship even, would still count for something. The shaven-headed, wiry Callistus was not so well known to Vespasian although he had met him on a few occasions, firstly as Caligula's slave and then as his freedman. How he had transferred his loyalty to Claudius before Caligula's assassination, just in time to save himself, Vespasian did not know. It did not, however, surprise him, as the one thing he did appreciate about the three men who now stood behind the Emperor was that they were all consummate politicians; not public demagogues but private intriguers with a subtle and accomplished understanding of imperial politics.

When Herod Agrippa was ten paces from the dais a sharp command followed by the deep rumble of a *cornu*, the horn usually used for signalling on the battlefield, led to three thousand blades being simultaneously unsheathed. The Consuls stopped abruptly.

'The Senate and the Urban Cohorts have come to swear allegiance to the Emperor,' Herod Agrippa shouted and then swiftly stepped aside.

'And ab-b-bout time,' Claudius yelled at the senators; saliva sprayed from his mouth and his left arm shook uncontrollably as it gripped the arm of his curule chair. 'I wanted you to make me e-e-e-emperor in a constitutional manner; instead we have a situation whereby my first issue of coinage is going to have my head on the front and "emperor, thanks to the P-P-P-Praetorian Guard" on the back and not "thanks to the Senate and People of Rome". Why did you delay? Didn't you want a cripple for your emperor?'

'That never crossed our minds, Princeps,' Pomponius Secundus lied.

Claudius held up his right hand and Narcissus unravelled a scroll and, after a small pause for effect, started reading: '"Not only does Claudius stutter and drool and stumble in a way that would bring dishonour to the dignity of government but also he is not known to, and therefore not loved by, the legions."' Narcissus lowered the scroll and his eyebrows raised a fraction as he met Pomponius Secundus' bewildered gaze.

Claudius turned to a senator, in his early thirties, standing close to the dais. 'That is what he said, isn't it, Geta?'

'It was, Princeps, word for word,' Gnaeus Hosidius Geta replied, looking smug. 'I was ashamed that a consul of Rome could state such untruths about ...'

'Yes, yes, that's e-e-enough. No need to overdo it, praetor.' Claudius jerked his attention back to the mortified Consul. 'Can you think of one reason why I should not have you executed? In fact, can anyone think of one reason why I shouldn't have the whole S-S-Senate executed?'

'Because you wouldn't have anyone worthwhile left to dominate, Princeps?' Herod Agrippa suggested.

There was a moment's stunned silence before Claudius exploded with laughter. 'Ah Herod, you do cheer me up, my friend.'

Herod smirked and bowed extravagantly, his hands upon his chest.

Claudius acknowledged the gesture and then turned back, his face set rigid again with displeasure, to the Senior Consul. 'As to the army n-n-not knowing or loving m-m-me, you are mistaken. I am the brother of the great G-G-G-Germanicus; they will love me as they loved him because I will love them as he did. I will ...' Behind him Narcissus subtly pressed a hand on his shoulder and Claudius immediately fell silent. Pallas bent down to whisper in his ear.

'I think we're getting a foretaste of what is to come,' Vespasian mused. 'But at least we can still consider Pallas to be a friend.'

Gaius frowned. 'Let's hope so, although past friendships can't always be counted upon when the political landscape changes. How are you with Narcissus? Has he forgiven you for cashing that bankers' draft of Claudius' whilst you were in Alexandria?'

'He owes me a couple of large favours but I assume that cancels one of them out.'

Claudius nodded at his freedman as Pallas stood back up, having given his advice, and then struggled to his feet to indicate that the impromptu audience was at an end. 'I shall retire to bed now; you will attend me tomorrow at the second hour and lead me to the Forum where you will announce your unanimous decision to endorse the will of the Guard; then you will swear

41

allegiance to me in the Senate House. I expect all of you to be there. Now go!'

Claudius was helped down from the dais by Narcissus; Callistus and Pallas tried to outdo one another in courtesy by offering the other the honour of being next down the steps before descending together. The senators and the Urban Cohorts broke out into a series of 'hail Caesars', whilst the Guard, in two swift motions, sheathed their drawn swords and then snapped to a resounding attention.

Claudius disappeared into the ranks of his now very wealthy Praetorians and the senators turned to go.

'Well, that went as well as we could have expected,' Gaius observed.

Vespasian grimaced. 'I don't think that we can expect too much favour from the new regime. We should have gambled, like Geta and those others, and got here to offer our loyalty before we were forced to. Once the Guard supported him it was inevitable, as Herod Agrippa said.'

'I'm so glad that you appreciate my wisdom,' a voice oozed from just behind Vespasian's ear.

Vespasian turned and looked into the cold smile on Herod Agrippa's face.

'Claudius' freedmen appreciated it too; so much so in fact that they're going to recommend to Claudius that he confirms me in my kingdom and makes a couple of very lucrative additions to it. Would you like to know why?'

Vespasian shrugged. 'Do we need to?'

'You don't need to, but it just might interest you all the same. You see, not only have I helped Claudius secure his position for the present, thereby making his freedmen very influential; but I've also advised Narcissus and Pallas on how to hang onto their power by instituting a new precedent to discourage the Guard from making a habit of changing emperors. Did you see your friend Clemens in his rightful place as Praetorian prefect next to the Emperor? Or for that matter his tribunes, Cassius Chaerea and Cornelius Sabinus? No, of course you didn't.'

Vespasian was unimpressed. 'They signed their own death warrants by killing Caligula.'

'Of course, although Claudius unwisely wanted to spare them, reward them even; especially after they claimed to have done some deal with Narcissus and Pallas, brokered by that weasel Callistus. Naturally Narcissus, Pallas and Callistus have denied all knowledge of this because, as you have just intimated, it wouldn't do to have people assassinating emperors and surviving. However, my refinement was to take it a step further.' Herod Agrippa paused for a moment of self-appreciatory reflection. 'The second Praetorian prefect, Lucius Arruntius Stella, who wasn't part of the plot, has also been arrested. I suggested to Narcissus and Pallas that perhaps it would be a good thing if, in future, the prefects realised that an important element of their duties is to keep an eye on their colleagues. Narcissus and Pallas thought that was an excellent idea and so Stella is going to be executed along with all the conspirators.' Herod Agrippa thrust his face closer to Vespasian's and looked at him with mock innocence. 'And by the way, I intend to make sure that it will be *all* of them.'

CHAPTER II

CAENIS LAID HER head on Vespasian's chest and traced the outline of his well-toned pectoral muscles with a slender finger, working her way slowly down his stomach. 'It's an empty threat, my love; there's no way that Herod Agrippa can link you to Caligula's assassins.'

Vespasian kissed her full, black curls, savouring their sweet scent, and then stared up at the dim, whitewashed ceiling of their bedroom. They lay in the house that Antonia, Caenis' former owner, had gifted her, along with her manumission, on the day she opened her veins. The first rays of dawn seeped into the room as, outside, a dove cooed – a soft, reassuring sound. He took a deep breath and sighed. He had not had any sleep in the few short hours they had been in bed: too troubled about what Herod Agrippa had meant. 'Sabinus is married to Clemens' sister; that links me strongly to him. Perhaps Herod is just speculating.'

'Why would he do that?'

'Vengeance for Antonia having him imprisoned six years ago; it was Sabinus who read out her evidence to the Senate.'

'Then he should take his revenge on Sabinus.'

'Sabinus is hundreds of miles away; perhaps he feels that his younger brother will do.'

'That's not revenge, it's just malice.'

Vespasian grunted with satisfaction as her hand moved even lower, massaging and kneading gently. 'I also witnessed his humiliation in Alexandria and told the then prefect of Egypt, Flaccus, about his illegal stockpile of grain.'

'How would he know that it was you who told Flaccus? Besides he's had vengeance for his lost grain two years ago; it was his damning letter to Caligula supporting the Alexandrian Jews' embassy complaining about Flaccus that got him executed. No, my love, this is nothing but an empty threat.' She began working her hand more vigorously whilst playing on a nipple with the tip of her tongue.

Vespasian found himself relaxing for the first time since his confrontation with Herod Agrippa. 'Now that Caligula is finally dead,' he murmured, stroking her hair, 'it will be safe for you to go out in public.'

'Perhaps I prefer staying in.' Caenis' attention left his nipple and she began to kiss her way down his chest.

Vespasian pushed back the blankets and adjusted his position. In the thin dawn light her smiling, blue eyes gleamed as she looked back up at him, working her way ever lower.

A soft knock on the door interrupted her progress.

'Mistress?' a voice quietly called.

'What is it?' Caenis replied, not attempting to hide her irritation at the interruption.

'There's a man here to see the master.'

'Can't it wait?'

'No, he says it's urgent.'

Caenis looked back to Vespasian. 'Sorry, my love, perhaps we should reconvene later.'

Vespasian smiled ruefully. 'It wouldn't have taken long.' He swung his legs over her and sat on the side of the bed. 'Tell him I'm coming,' he called out, grinning at Caenis; she giggled. 'What's this man's name?'

'He said to say it's your friend Magnus, master.'

'Didn't interrupt anything did I, sir?' Magnus asked with a look of false concern on his battered, ex-boxer's face as Vespasian sauntered into the atrium fastening his belt.

'As a matter of fact you did; something rather enjoyable.'

'I expect most things that go on in that room are enjoyable.'

Vespasian smiled at his friend. 'Only if Caenis is involved, which she was.'

'Yeah well, I'm sorry to have curtailed her involvement, however deep it was, if you take my meaning?'

'I do and you're wrong, we were involved in a different way.'

Magnus' eyes widened with delight. 'Ah, a nice early morning wash, how kind of her. Well, your ablutions are going to have to wait for later. We've got to get round to your uncle's house.'

'Why?'

'I'm afraid we've got a big problem, sir; it's Sabinus.'

'Sabinus is in Pannonia.'

'I wish that he was, but I'm afraid he ain't. I've just left him; he's here in Rome.'

A look of dismay crept over Vespasian's face; now he understood the true meaning of Herod Agrippa's words.

'At your Crossroads Brotherhood's tavern!' Gaius boomed in horror. 'What in the name of all the gods is he doing there? He's meant to be in Pannonia.'

Magnus shrugged. 'Yes, but he's not, sir. He turned up a couple of hours ago, weak and wobbly as a drunk Vestal from loss of blood from a nasty wound to his thigh.'

'How did he get that?'

'I don't know; he's been dropping in and out of consciousness since he arrived. I called the doctor we use in these situations – he don't ask too many questions – and he's cauterised the wound and stitched it up. He says that with food and rest he should be fine in a few days.'

Gaius slumped down into a chair by the fire in the atrium's hearth and reached for a calming cup of hot, sweet wine. 'The young fool took part in the assassination, didn't he?'

Vespasian paced nervously to and fro. 'Why else would he be here in Rome without telling us? And if he was trying to keep his part in it secret, then he's failed. Herod Agrippa knows, I'm sure of it, and, as we know, he bears no love for Sabinus.'

Gaius took a sip of his wine. 'Then we need to get him out of Rome as soon as possible.'

'Where to, Uncle? If he's condemned he can't go back to his legion in Pannonia and they'd find him on one of our estates. He's safest at the moment with Magnus. What we need to do is ensure that he's not condemned.'

'And how can we do that?'

'By taking advantage of the new system of government. You saw it in action last night; it's Claudius' freedmen who rule him.'

'Of course!' Gaius looked relieved for the first time since being dragged from his bed to hear the bad news. 'I'll send a message to Pallas to say that we need to see him as soon as possible after the ceremony this morning. We'll find out then whether we can still count upon his friendship.'

The people of Rome turned out in their hundreds of thousands to witness their new Emperor receive the oath of allegiance from his now loyal Senate and the Urban Cohorts. That they had regularly laughed at him previously and mocked his malformed body as he was publicly humiliated by his predecessor was now conveniently forgotten by most of the masses crowding in and around the Forum Romanum and along the Via Sacra. However, neither Claudius nor those surrounding him had overlooked the ridiculing of the past, and so the entire Praetorian Guard was stationed along the procession route. They were dressed in full military uniform rather than in togas – their normal attire when on duty within the boundaries of the city – as a reminder to the citizens that it was military power that had elevated Claudius and it was military power that would keep him in his position, and that power was not to be mocked. The sensibilities of the Senate and People of Rome had taken second place to the need to preserve the dignitas of the new Emperor; anyone suspected of making fun of him was dragged away for a thorough lesson in how quickly a man could develop a limp and start drooling uncontrollably.

Resplendent in freshly chalked, gleaming white togas bordered by a thick purple stripe indicating their rank, the Senate led the procession. Their numbers had swelled back up to over five hundred as those who had left the city the day before had hurriedly returned in the hope that the Republican sympathies they had expressed would be forgotten – or at least overlooked – by the new Emperor once they had sworn loyalty to him. The senators walked with slow dignity, looking neither left nor right, holding their heads high and with their left arms crooked before them supporting the folds of their togas. Each eligible magistrate was accompanied by the requisite number of fasces-bearing lictors to add to his stature. Military crowns, won whilst serving in the legions for acts of bravery, were worn by every man entitled to them.

Preceded by twelve lictors, Claudius was borne in an open sedan-chair by sixteen slaves at shoulder height so that all could see him. Behind him, travelling recumbent in a horse-drawn carriage, strewn with cushions and garlanded with flowers, came his wife, Messalina, heavily pregnant but brought out of her confinement for the parade. Her daughter, Claudia Octavia, travelled with her; only eighteen months old, she seemed bewildered by the occasion.

Following them, marching in slow-time, crashing their hobnailed military sandals down hard on the paving stones to the blaring of *bucinae*, came the Urban Cohorts.

Surrounding Claudius and Messalina were three centuries of the German Imperial Bodyguard, sauntering rather than marching, with their hands on the hilts of their swords behind their flat oval shields and keeping their pale blue eyes fixed on the crowd. Long-haired, full-bearded, be-trousered and each over six feet tall, their barbarian looks presented a striking contrast to the otherwise ordered and very Roman pageant.

The multitudes chanted and cheered themselves hoarse, waving brightly dyed rags or racing-faction colours in the air as the slow procession passed. They lined the streets, crowded the steps of temples and public buildings, balanced on the bases of columns, clung to the pedestals of equestrian statues or heaved themselves up on to window ledges; small children sat on their fathers' shoulders whilst their more nimble elder siblings scaled any vantage point too small or precarious for an adult.

It seemed that every one of the common people of Rome, free, freed or slave, was there to welcome the new Emperor, not because they particularly disliked the old one or that they particularly liked Claudius; it mattered not to them who was in charge. They had come because they still remembered the games, largesse and feasts that accompanied Caligula's accession and they wished to earn, through their rapturous support of the new incumbent, a repeat or maybe even a surpassing of that profligate display of generosity. There was, however, a sizeable minority in the crowd with longer memories; they hailed Claudius not in his own right but as the brother of the great Germanicus, the man whom many wished had succeeded Augustus to the Purple.

Claudius, for his part, sat as composed as he could in his chair. He acknowledged the ovation of the crowds with jerking waves and sudden nods, occasionally dabbing his chin with a handkerchief to stem the flow of the drool that, along with his nervous tic, was far more pronounced, betraying his excitement at receiving, for the first time in his fifty-two years, public acclamation.

Messalina ignored the crowd. She kept a firm arm around her small daughter and with her other hand gently caressed her swollen belly. She stared straight ahead towards her husband with a self-satisfied expression on her face.

The procession eventually neared the Senate House in front of which, in an outrageous breach of all precedent, stood Narcissus, Pallas and Callistus.

Doing their best to ignore the affront, the Consuls mounted the steps and positioned themselves to either side of the open doors, ready to welcome their Emperor. The rest of the Senate spread out, in order of precedence, on the steps, leaving a path to the doors for Claudius.

The imperial chair came to a halt at the foot of the Senate House steps.

'This should be interesting,' Gaius commented to Vespasian as the sweating slaves stopped and made ready to lower it. It swayed slightly.

A look of panic swept across Claudius' face and he gripped the chair's arms.

Vespasian half closed his eyes. 'I can hardly bear to watch; I don't know how they got him up there but it must have been in private. I don't think that they've thought about this part.'

'Wait!' Narcissus almost shrieked above the din. Claudius looked gratefully at him, twitching almost uncontrollably.

Narcissus mounted the steps and spoke briefly to the Senior Consul. Secundus' face tensed, he drew himself up and glared at the freedman in outrage. Narcissus muttered a few more words and then raised his brow questioningly, staring with steely eyes at the Consul.

After a few moments Secundus' shoulders sagged, he nodded almost imperceptibly; he descended the steps towards Claudius and looked up at him. 'Princeps, there is no need for you to step down to us; we will take the oath here on the steps of the Curia.'

There was stirring and muttering all around Vespasian and Gaius. How dare a jumped-up freedman humiliate the ancient governing body of Rome thus? But no one dared step forward to complain.

'There's still one thing that we can take heart in, dear boy,' Gaius muttered as preparations got under way to take the auspices. 'However much Claudius' freedmen seek to draw power to themselves, Claudius will always need members of the senatorial order to command his legions and govern the provinces. Narcissus, Pallas and Callistus can never take that away from us.'

'Perhaps, but who will decide who gets those posts, them or the Emperor?' Vespasian glanced over to where Pallas stood, but the freedman's face, as always, remained neutral.

The auspices were taken and, unsurprisingly, the day was found to be eminently favourable for the business of Rome. The will of the Senate, that Claudius should be emperor, was heralded around the Forum to tumultuous cheering; then the oath of loyalty was administered to the Senate and the Urban Cohorts. This was followed by a proclamation that all the legions of the Empire should swear their loyalty to the new Emperor.

Then the speeches started.

By the time the final speaker drew to a long-winded close it was well past the eighth hour of the day and everyone just wanted to get home. Claudius made a short speech of thanks, announcing seven days of games to rapturous applause, and then the procession turned about and headed back towards the Palatine. The only things that had marred the proceedings had been the early, unscheduled, departure of Messalina and the collapse of one of Claudius' chair-bearers, neither of which had surprised anyone.

The imperial cortège disappeared up the Via Sacra and the huge crowd began to disperse, talking animatedly of the coming games.

'Another expensive time for the treasury coming up,' Gaius reflected as he and Vespasian jostled with their peers to get down the Senate House steps.

Vespasian smiled ruefully. 'It'll be cheaper than buying the Praetorian Guard.'

'But that was a sound investment as I think you'd agree, gentlemen.' Vespasian and Gaius turned to see Pallas; he put a hand around their shoulders and added quietly: 'But perhaps not enough to ultimately secure Claudius' position. Walk with me, my friends.'

Pallas led Vespasian and Gaius away from the Senate House, attracting many an envious stare from the mass of senators seeing two of their number so openly favoured by one of the new powers in Rome – however far beneath them in status they considered him to be.

'Rest assured that I would've found you two today without you sending me that note, Senator Pollo,' Pallas informed them once they were out of earshot of anyone of importance.

Gaius inclined his head, acknowledging the favour. 'That is good to know, Pallas; but please, call me Gaius in private as we are friends, are we not?'

'We are friends, although not of equal social standing.'

Vespasian looked Pallas in the eye and added: 'Or of equal influence.'

Pallas gave a rare half-smile. 'Yes, Vespasian, I'm afraid that you're right, my influence is going to be considerable; I am to be the imperial secretary to the treasury.'

Gaius was dumbfounded.

Vespasian looked at Pallas in disbelief. 'But there is no such post!'

'There is now. You see, gentlemen, Narcissus, Callistus and I have had plenty of warning of this change of government and time to plan how our patron could best be served. As you two are amongst the few people in Rome to know, he is of reasonable intelligence – if somewhat chaotic – but harbours both an over-inflated opinion of his own talents and a dismissive view of those of others. He is therefore, more than anything, inconsolably bitter about how he has been mocked and overlooked.'

'But Caligula made him consul,' Vespasian pointed out.

Pallas raised a thick eyebrow. 'As a joke; although I think everybody, especially his mother, was surprised by how well he carried it off. The point is that he's now distrustful of everyone who has not supported him in the past, which is most people in Rome, with very few exceptions.'

Gaius slapped Pallas on the back. 'The most notable of whom being his freedmen, I presume?'

'Exactly, Gaius. And when the Senate refused to declare Claudius emperor immediately – an eventuality that we freedmen had foreseen – he knew for sure that he could never trust them. At that point it was easy to persuade him to implement our plan.'

'Bypass the Senate?' Vespasian queried as they wandered into Caesar's Forum, dominated by a huge equestrian statue of the man who once tried to impose his will upon Rome.

'We prefer to call it: centralising government. From now on all decisions will be made by the Emperor.'

'With the help of those closest to him,' Gaius added.

'Naturally the business of running the Empire is too great a burden for one man, so that is why his loyal freedmen will assist him: myself in the treasury, Callistus in the law courts and Narcissus ... well, Narcissus will be in charge of his correspondence.'

Gaius understood immediately. 'Access to him, in other words; which means that he'll have power over foreign and domestic policy, as well as appointments and ...' Gaius paused and looked meaningfully at Pallas, 'and appealing to the Emperor on life and death issues?'

Pallas nodded slowly.

'So you can't help us with our problem?'

'Not directly, as much as I would like to be able to, for all the courtesy you and Vespasian have shown me in the past. Narcissus, Callistus and I have agreed not to interfere in each others' spheres of influence; and, although I can't see that being adhered to over the years, it's best to keep to that agreement for as long as possible. Sabinus' life is out of my hands; you have to go to Narcissus.'

'We could appeal directly to Claudius.'

'That would be impossible and, besides, it wouldn't be wise. Claudius doesn't know of Sabinus' part in the assassination and it would be best to keep it like that. This morning, Herod Agrippa told Narcissus and me – with far too much glee for my taste – that he now knew that the masked assassin whom he and Claudius had met in the passage was Sabinus. He'd realised it when he saw your eyes, Vespasian, in the Senate yesterday, it jogged his memory.'

'We look so similar, why didn't he think that it was me?'

'Because when the assassin spoke he didn't have your Sabine accent, so it had to be your brother as it's well known that he disguises his origins. For obvious reasons we thought that was impossible but he was convinced. He insisted that we should find him and have him executed tomorrow along with all the rest. If we didn't then he would go to Claudius.'

'He could've just gone straight to him.'

'That wouldn't have suited his purposes. He's interested in power as well as revenge; he desperately wants Claudius to trust him and leave him to his own devices in his kingdom. We are counselling against that. Herod hoped that we would refuse his demand and then he could go to Claudius and tell him that his freedmen were protecting one of his nephew's killers, thereby making him seem a more faithful adviser than us. However, Narcissus disappointed him and agreed; I then had no choice but to do the same.'

Vespasian and Gaius looked at Pallas aghast.

'You're going to be responsible for having Sabinus found and executed?' Vespasian almost shouted.

Pallas remained calm. 'I didn't say that, I said that I agreed to do so. I had no choice once Narcissus knew his identity; I had to be seen as co-operating with my colleague. Had Herod Agrippa just come to me, I could have made a very real threat that would have kept his mouth shut; but he didn't, so we must work with the situation as it is.

'Now, I've done nothing to help find Sabinus even though I can guess where he is. We know that he was wounded; two of the German Bodyguards survived their foolish attack on Lupus' century and withdrew and waited until they saw one of the assassins leave the palace complex. They followed him, waylaying him at the foot of the Palatine. The assassin killed one and wounded the other. Callistus had the wounded man questioned; thankfully he didn't see his face but he claims to have cut the assassin's thigh open; Sabinus must therefore still be in Rome.'

Vespasian put his hand to his forehead. 'I saw him! It was as we came out of the alley, Uncle; a man was hobbling away. That must have been Sabinus. I decided to go in the other direction because he was armed.'

'It's as well that you did,' Pallas said. 'Had you met there and taken him home he would be sitting in a cell by now. Now that Narcissus knows it was Sabinus, he's had your house, Gaius, and Sabinus' house on the Aventine as well as Caenis' house searched this morning during the ceremony.'

'He's done what? How dare he!' Gaius exploded.

Vespasian wondered anxiously how Flavia and Caenis would have reacted to having their privacy violated; he was not looking forward to having to give either of them an explanation.

'Times have changed, Gaius,' Pallas said quietly. 'Narcissus dares because he has the power to do so and also because he must; there is more than just a man's life at stake here. We cannot allow Herod Agrippa to gain Claudius' unwavering trust. Since Caligula gave him his kingdom three years ago he has started to repair the defences of Jerusalem, making it one of the most formidable cities in the East. He has sworn to Claudius that it is to defend Rome's interests against the Parthians; Claudius believes him and has reconfirmed him in his kingdom. But we all know that Jerusalem's defences look west as well as east and we all know, too, what the Jews think about Roman rule. If Judaea rebels then the flames of that revolt could spread throughout the East, fanned by the Parthians who are hungry to have access to Our Sea again, denied to them since Alexander's time. We have to undermine Claudius' trust in Herod Agrippa so that eventually we can topple him. We can't begin to do that if he tells him that we are sheltering one of Caligula's killers.'

Vespasian could see the logic of it, however distasteful. 'So what can we do, then, Pallas?'

'Firstly you need to move Sabinus from where I guess he's hiding, at Magnus' Crossroads Brotherhood's tavern. It won't be long until Narcissus remembers your family's relationship with him; I've done nothing to remind him of that fact. You should take him to your house, Gaius; it should be safe there now that it's been searched. The only hope we have of Narcissus sparing Sabinus is if it is never known that he took part in the assassination.'

'But what about Herod Agrippa?' Gaius asked.

'He can be dealt with; I can assure you of that. Fortunately we can rely upon Herod Agrippa preferring power over revenge.'

Vespasian pulled his teeth over his lower lip. 'At least we only have Narcissus to convince; he does, after all, owe me at least one favour.'

'I know, and he also owes Sabinus; a fact that I reminded him of this morning.'

'Thank you for that at least, my friend,' Vespasian said with genuine feeling.

Pallas shrugged. 'It's not the only way in which I have been able to help. During our discussions, over the last month or so, on how best to secure our patron's position, your names have both come up; Sabinus could still be of use to us. But first Narcissus has to be manoeuvred into a position whereby he feels that he can spare him.'

'You mean that Sabinus could buy his life with a favour?'

'We shall see. I've made an appointment at the second hour tomorrow for you to see Narcissus. I think that you should surprise him by taking Sabinus along too.'

CHAPTER III

THE SUN WAS beginning to set and their long shadows preceded Vespasian and Gaius as they walked east along the crowded, tenement-lined Alta Semita towards its junction with the Vicus Longus on the southern slope of the Quirinal. Here, at the apex of the junction, stood a three-storey building that Vespasian had passed many times but had never entered: Magnus' Crossroads Brotherhood's tavern. It was used as the base from where the South Quirinal Crossroads Brotherhood, of which Magnus was the leader, ran their business of protection for the local traders and residents. It also housed the shrine to the Crossroads lares whose worship was the Brotherhood's main responsibility and the original reason for their existence.

The plain wooden tables and benches outside were empty apart from two hard-looking men whose job, Vespasian guessed, was to waylay travellers who looked wealthy enough to afford the protection of the Brotherhood as they passed through their territory; just as his family had been waylaid upon their arrival in Rome, over fifteen years ago, when he had been a lad of sixteen.

With a nod to the two men, he and Gaius stepped through the low door into the fug of the noisy parlour. The talking instantly died down and all eyes turned to them.

'Venus' pert arse! I never thought I'd see a couple of senators walk through that door, and both ex-praetors no less,' Magnus exclaimed with a grin, getting up from a table in the corner. His companion, an old man with a saggy throat and gnarled hands, stared with milky, sightless eyes in the rough direction of the new arrivals. Magnus put a hand on his shoulder. 'Have you ever seen a senator in here before, Servius?'

Servius shook his head. 'No, and nor will I ever.'

'Yeah, too right, brother.' Magnus slapped Servius on the back and walked over to Vespasian and Gaius. 'Follow me.'

The floor was sticky with spilt wine and their red, senatorial shoes clung to it as they walked. A low, quizzical muttering accompanied their progress through the room.

'We need to move him, Magnus,' Vespasian said as they passed through the door next to the amphora-lined bar at the far end of the room.

'What, now?'

'As soon as it's completely dark.'

'He ain't that sprightly at the moment.'

'I'm sure, but Narcissus knows he's wounded somewhere in Rome, so it won't be long until you have a visit. Who else knows he's here?'

Magnus started to climb an uneven wooden staircase. 'Only Servius, my second in command, Ziri, and then Sextus and Marius; they were on guard last night when Sabinus crawled in.'

'Good, they can help us move him. Is there a back way out?'

Magnus looked over his shoulder and scowled at his friend, humorously.

'Sorry, silly question.'

'There are three, actually,' Magnus informed him, leading them down a dark corridor. At the end he opened a low door. 'Welcome to what I call home, gentlemen,' he said, stepping inside.

Vespasian and Gaius followed him into a dimly lit room, no more than ten feet square, with a table and two chairs on one side and, on the other, a low bed. Sabinus lay in it, asleep; his face was pale, even in the low light. Ziri, Magnus' slave, sat on one of the chairs.

'How is he, Ziri?' Magnus asked.

'He's improving, master,' the wiry, brown-skinned Marmarides replied, indicating to an empty bowl on the table. 'Look, he ate all that pork earlier.'

Sabinus stirred, woken by the talking. He opened his eyes and groaned as he saw his brother and uncle standing behind Magnus. 'You shouldn't have come.'

'No, you idiot, *you* shouldn't have come!' Vespasian exploded, the tension of the last few hours welling up from deep inside him. 'What the fuck do you think you were doing? You were safe in Pannonia, and Clementina and the kids were with our parents, why didn't you just let it be and allow others to commit suicide?'

Sabinus closed his eyes. 'Look, Vespasian, if you've come here just to shout at me for avenging my honour then you can piss off. I kept you out of it; I purposely came in secret so that you would not have felt obliged by our blood-tie to aid me.'

'I realise that and I'm grateful; but I feel obliged by our blood-tie to tell you that you're nothing but a horse's arse and unless you're fucking lucky you'll be nothing but a *dead* horse's arse.'

Gaius stepped between the two brothers. 'Dear boys, this'll get us nowhere. Sabinus, how are you feeling because we need to move you? Narcissus' men are looking for you all over Rome.'

'Herod Agrippa recognised me, then?'

'I'm afraid so.'

A faint smile touched Sabinus' lips. 'The oily bastard; I'll bet he's having a lovely time telling anyone who'll care to listen.'

'Fortunately he's too busy playing politics with the information; we've still got a chance to save you.'

'Save me? You mean they've executed the others?'

'They will tomorrow.'

'But Clemens had a deal.'

'Don't be so naïve, Narcissus was never going to stick to that.'

'But Pallas?'

'Pallas is the one person who's helping us but there's nothing he can do for Clemens and the rest, it's public knowledge that it was them. They're dead men.'

Sabinus sighed. 'They should be praised, not killed.'

'I'm sure Narcissus is praising them quietly to himself all the time; but he's going to kill them anyway. Now, dear boy, we should get going soon. Magnus, get your lads.'

Magnus nodded and left the room.

'What's going to happen, Uncle?' Sabinus asked, hauling himself up unsteadily onto his elbows.

'First we're taking you to my house and then tomorrow morning you're going in front of Narcissus and, however distasteful it may seem to crawl to a freedman, you're going to beg him for your life.'

Gaius knocked on his own front door; it was sharply opened by the very attractive young doorkeeper. 'Tell Gernot to put a brazier in a spare bedroom and then have the cook prepare some soup,' Gaius ordered the young lad.

The boy looked up at his master with frightened eyes. 'Master, we've had the ...'

'Yes, I know, Ortwin, the house has been searched. Don't worry; there was nothing that you could have done to prevent it. Now go.'

Ortwin blinked and ran off through the vestibule; Gaius eyed with appreciation his slave boy's short tunic, revealing, as he ran, what it should have concealed, before turning back to the cross-roads brothers in the street. 'Bring him in, Magnus.' He looked at Vespasian. 'Flavia must not be told the truth, dear boy; obviously I wouldn't know, but I'm told that women are prone to gossip amongst themselves.'

Vespasian chuckled. 'Of course not, Uncle, I understand. However, there's no explanation that will fit the facts.'

'Then don't try to give her one.'

Vespasian marvelled that his uncle could feel that it was that simple.

'Careful with him, lads,' Magnus warned Marius and Sextus. 'An arm each around his waist, then ease him up.'

'Arm round the waist and ease him up,' Sextus repeated, as always slowly digesting his orders.

Marius nodded. 'Right you are, Magnus.'

Vespasian watched with concern as Marius and Sextus hauled Sabinus off the handcart they had used to transport him as Ziri steadied it. Sabinus grimaced as the two crossroads brothers supported him and he stood upright on his left foot. A trace of blood had seeped through the heavy bandaging on his right thigh as a result of the rattling journey along the Quirinal. Aided by the brothers he hobbled painfully through the door.

'Take the cart around the back, Magnus,' Vespasian requested, 'we'll need it tomorrow.'

'What about us, sir? Will you be needing an escort in the morning?'

'Yes, can you and the lads be here at dawn?'

'We'll be here,' Magnus confirmed as Ziri turned to wheel the handcart down the side alley.

Vespasian walked through the vestibule and into the atrium to be confronted with a sight he had never before witnessed: his wife and his mistress in the same room. They both looked less than pleased; Gaius was nowhere to be seen.

'Just what has been going on?' Flavia demanded, her voice shrill with indignant outrage. 'We've both had our houses forcibly entered and our bedrooms searched by men who have worse manners than them.' She pointed an accusatory finger at Sextus and Marius who were helping Sabinus down onto a couch. 'Then Sabinus is carted in here, more dead than alive, when he should be, by rights, a thousand miles away. And when I demanded an explanation from your uncle he took one look at me and ran off into his study.'

Vespasian was not surprised that Gaius had retreated. Flavia reminded him uncomfortably of his mother and he felt a deep sympathy for his father whom he had witnessed facing this sort of tirade many times in his life. An unpleasant thought flashed across his mind: had he married Flavia because she *had* reminded him, without him realising it, of his mother? He glanced at Caenis, standing so incongruously next to Flavia, and judged from her expression that he could expect little support from that quarter.

'Well, Vespasian? We're waiting.' Flavia persisted, putting an arm around Caenis.

Vespasian winced at the sight.

'What have you done to have caused our privacy to be so rudely intruded upon?'

Remembering the satisfying results that had followed his father taking the offensive in these situations – admittedly rather belatedly in life – he resolved to do the same. 'This is not the time for shouting and recriminations, woman. And there'll be no explanation! See to it that Sabinus' room is being made ready and then tell the cook to bring him some soup.'

Flavia put a hand on her swollen belly. 'I could have miscarried with all the stress; I will have an expl—'

'You'll get nothing, woman! Make sure that Sabinus is settled. Now go!'

Flavia started at the force of the dismissal and then, sharing a brief look of mutual sympathy with Caenis, turned and walked briskly from the room.

'Caenis, see to Sabinus' bandaging; it needs changing,' Vespasian ordered, far more curtly than he had intended.

Caenis opened her mouth and then shut it immediately as Vespasian shot her a warning look; he did not want to shout at her and she understood. She walked over to Sabinus who was by now lying, propped up with cushions, on the couch; the look on his pale face told of just how much he had enjoyed witnessing the colliding of his brother's complicated domestic arrangements at first hand. Sextus and Marius stood next to him, clearly unsure of where to look or how to escape.

'Thanks, lads,' Vespasian said, his equilibrium returning. He reached into his purse and pulled out a couple of sesterces apiece for the brothers. 'I'll see you tomorrow.'

'Thank you, sir,' Marius mumbled, heading for the door. Sextus grunted something unintelligible and followed him out; neither looked Vespasian in the eye.

'The stitches have held,' Caenis observed, examining Sabinus' wound, having removed the bandage. 'It just needs swabbing with vinegar and a fresh dressing; I'll go and get some.'

She left the room, keeping her eyes to the floor.

Vespasian sank into a chair and wiped the sweat from his brow with his toga, leaving a white stain of chalk.

Sabinus looked at him, too weak to do more than chuckle. 'I take it that was the first time that all three of you have been in the same room?'

'And the last, I hope.'

'Unless it's in your bedroom, perhaps?'

Vespasian glared at his brother. 'Piss off, Sabinus!'

Any more comments on the subject were curtailed by Gaius poking his head around his study door. 'Have they gone?'

'Yes, Uncle, but they'll be back.'

Gaius quickly retreated behind the door.

Vespasian reached for a jug on the table next to him and poured himself a large measure of undiluted wine. He took a long sip and savoured the taste, with his eyes closed, wishing that what he had just witnessed was not true.

Unfortunately, a short while later, it was reconfirmed: the sound of two sets of footsteps came from the *tablinum* at the far end of the atrium. Vespasian took an extra-large slug of his drink. Flavia and Caenis walked in together; Flavia with a bowl of soup and a loaf of bread and Caenis with a bottle of vinegar and fresh bandages.

In silence they ministered to Sabinus together, until his bowl was empty and his wound re-dressed. They then called for a couple of slaves to help them take him to his room.

When they returned they stood before Vespasian, still slumped in his chair, nursing his second cup of wine.

'I shall go home now,' Caenis said quietly.

Flavia looked contrite. 'I'm sorry, husband, you were right to refuse to tell me anything. Caenis has guessed what has happened ... why Sabinus is in Rome; and he did the right thing by Clementina. I know you would have done the same.'

Caenis walked past Vespasian to the door, laying a hand softly on his shoulder as she did so. She took her cloak from a hook in the vestibule, slung it around her shoulders and then looked back. 'We both understand the importance of keeping this secret. We won't say a word about this ever, Vespasian, not to anyone; will we, Flavia?'

'No, my dear, we won't; never a word.'

'I hear that you found yourself in a bit of a tricky situation last night, sir,' Magnus said conversationally as he accompanied Vespasian and Gaius down the Quirinal the following morning. His breath was faintly visible in the early morning air; a light drizzle fell from a heavy, grey sky.

Vespasian looked disapprovingly over his shoulder at Sextus and Marius pushing Sabinus, whose face was concealed under a deep hood, in the handcart. 'I thought that it was only women who gossiped about the domestic woes of others.'

'Don't blame the lads; I heard all the shouting from outside so I asked them what was going on when they got out.'

'It was a fearsome sight, my friend,' Gaius opined, blanching at the memory. 'One irate woman is bad enough, but a brace of them? Intolerable!' Gaius shook his head, sucking the breath in between his teeth. 'They were both standing there, fire in their eyes, bonded by a mutual sense of violation, with all past hatred and jealousy between them put aside, to face their common foe. Utterly hideous! Luckily I had some urgent correspondence to deal with.'

'You mean you ran away, Uncle.'

'Dear boy, it's not my business to deal with your overly complicated domestic arrangements; especially when they're united in an unnatural alliance of vengeance. That takes the sort of resolve found only in men rash enough to believe that they can go into a negotiation with nothing to bargain with.'

'As you're just about to do, senator,' Magnus pointed out.

Gaius grunted uneasily and Vespasian smiled to himself despite the truth of Magnus' observation. They had, indeed, nothing to offer Narcissus in return for Sabinus' life; nothing, apart from the hope that he, Narcissus, would remember the two debts that he owed them. Ten years previously, Vespasian and his brother had kept the secret of a coded, treasonous letter, written in Claudius' name – and with his connivance – by his deceased freedman Boter. They had shown it only to Claudius' mother, the Lady Antonia; she had it read to a mortified Narcissus. He had vowed to keep a firmer hand on the affairs of his malleable but overly ambitious patron. Narcissus had expressed his gratitude to the brothers for their discretion in the matter – it was information that in Tiberius' or Sejanus' hands could have meant the banishment or execution of Claudius and the end of Narcissus' career. He had promised to repay the favour when he could.

The second debt was a more ignominious memory and Vespasian still felt the shame of it. At the Lady Antonia's behest he and his aristocratic friend Corbulo had murdered Poppaeus Sabinus, who had been financing Sejanus' successor, Macro's, bid for power. The deed had taken place in Claudius' house, with Narcissus and Pallas' help, during the exchange of Claudius' debt of fourteen million denarii to Poppaeus for seven of his valuable estates in the province of Egypt. Claudius had been left very wealthy, retaining both the debt marker and the seven estates. This was the favour that Vespasian hoped Narcissus would repay. Although Narcissus had acknowledged his obligation to him at the time, Vespasian knew that there was no way that he could force the issue as it was completely deniable – for they had made it seem Poppaeus had died of natural causes.

These thoughts played around Vespasian's mind as they trudged up the Palatine, in foreboding silence, until they arrived at the front of the palace complex.

Vespasian was shocked by the sight that greeted them: in the open space before the building, now very cramped owing to Caligula's ill-considered extensions to Augustus' once grand house, milled hundreds of senators and equites, stamping their feet and hunching their shoulders in the miserable weather. 'What are they all doing outside in the cold?' he wondered. 'The atrium can't be full yet.'

'All of Rome wants to know how they stand with the new regime,' Gaius suggested. 'Magnus, stay here with Sabinus and the lads, we'll go and see what's happening.'

Vespasian and Gaius eased their way through the disgruntled crowd, offering greetings to rivals and acquaintances, until they saw the cause of the impasse: arranged in front of the main doors was a century of Praetorians, still, outrageously, in full military uniform. In front of them were four desks manned by imperial clerks to whom senators and equites alike were giving their names to be checked against a list of people due to be admitted that day. The look on the faces of those who had been turned away told of the indignation and humiliation felt by those of the highest classes being refused access to their Emperor by mere slaves.

'Not even Caligula went this far,' Gaius fumed quietly. 'In fact, he positively welcomed people coming to greet him every morning.'

'That's because, being an immortal, he had no fear of assassination.'

Gaius and Vespasian turned round to see Pallas who had once more managed to catch them unawares.

'Good morning, gentlemen,' he said, again putting an arm around their damp shoulders. 'I've been waiting for you in order to help Sabinus circumvent Narcissus' new admittance policy. Where is he?'

Vespasian pointed through the crowd. 'Back there with Magnus in a handcart; he can't walk too well.'

'I'll have my men take them through a side entrance.' Pallas signalled to a couple of clerks waiting on him to come closer. After a brief muted conversation, during which Pallas seemed to reiterate a particular point, they went off on their errand. 'They'll take him to my new quarters where he can wait until the interview. Now we should get you through.'

'Is this going to happen every day?' Vespasian asked as they moved towards the nearest desk.

'Yes, only those with appointments will get through and then they will be searched for weapons by the Praetorians.'

'Senators searched?' Gaius huffed.

'Julius Caesar would have done well to follow that policy,' Vespasian observed, trying to lighten his uncle's mood. 'If he had we might be living in a different world today.'

Pallas remained expressionless. 'I very much doubt it.'

Half an hour later, having finally got through to the expansive and imposing atrium – designed by Augustus to overawe foreign embassies with the sombre dignity and majesty of Rome – Vespasian was surprised by how few people were waiting to be seen. Their quiet conversations were almost inaudible above the splatter of the central fountain and the slapped footsteps of an excessive number of imperial functionaries walking to and fro with wax tablets and scrolls. He was relieved, however, to notice that in the two days since Caligula's assassination most of the more vulgar decor that had so pleased the brash young Emperor had been replaced by the original, more subtle but exquisitely manufactured furnishings, ornaments and statuary that he had so admired when he had first seen the chamber.

'I will leave you here, gentlemen,' Pallas said, indicating to a pair of chairs either side of a table, beneath a much idealised statue purporting to be of Claudius. 'You will be called in due course. One of my men will alert me as you go in and I will bring Sabinus. Good luck.'

'Thank you, Pallas,' Vespasian said, offering his arm, 'for all your help.'

Pallas stepped back. 'I can't take your arm, my friend, not in public. If Narcissus hears of it then he will think of you more as my man, not his. For your sake you should cultivate him now; he's the real power here; Callistus and I are secondary.' He turned to go, before adding quietly: 'However, Claudius is only fifty-two and has a good few more years to live.'

A slave offered them a tray of assorted fruit juices as they sat down and watched Pallas disappear through the columns.

'I'm beginning to think that we might have been better off under Caligula,' Gaius said, taking a cup.

Vespasian kicked his uncle's shin under the table as he selected his drink and waited for the slave to leave. 'Careful what you say, Uncle. We're loyal supporters of Claudius, remember? That's the only viable option at the moment. At least he's not setting himself up over us as a god.'

Gaius smirked. 'Even if his favoured freedman is beginning to act like one?'

Vespasian looked away so as not to laugh and saw an unwelcome sight walking through the main doors: Marcus Valerius Messala Corvinus, the man who had, by abducting Clementina and delivering her to Caligula, knowingly set in motion the train of events that had led to Caligula's assassination and his sister, Messalina's, rise to empress. His striking, patrician face had an expression of immense satisfaction on it as he strode through the atrium as if he owned the place.

Vespasian had first encountered the man whilst serving as a quaestor in Cyrenaica and they had become enemies. Now he turned his head to avoid being seen; but too late.

'What are you doing here, bumpkin?' Corvinus sneered, looking down his long, aristocratic nose. 'I can't imagine that there are any positions for foolhardy country boys who enjoy abandoning their social betters to slavers and losing over a hundred men in the desert.'

Vespasian got to his feet, his jaw rigid. It was true that his venture against the desert-dwelling Marmarides tribe had been foolhardy – he had undertaken it solely to impress Flavia – but he did not like being reminded of the fact. 'My family still have a score to settle with you for what you did to Clementina, Corvinus.'

'Really? I should say we're equal.'

'Not after what Caligula put her through.'

'Would it help to know that it was mainly business? Although, I will admit there was a sweet mix of pleasure in it as well; I knew that the only person who stood a good chance of assassinating Caligula would be one of the Praetorian prefects. So Clementina was just perfect to have my revenge on you and to goad Clemens into clearing the way for my sister to become empress. Your idiot brother even unwittingly told me where she was; I was surprised he didn't join with Clemens in the assassination – or is he happy being a dishonourable cuckold?'

'You don't want to make it any worse.'

'An empty threat, bumpkin. I'll speak to you any way I want; Messalina's empress now and if you want my advice you should consider us square.'

Vespasian opened his mouth to argue as a clerk cleared his throat next to them. 'The imperial secretary will see you now, sirs.'

Corvinus creased his nose as if he had trodden in something unpleasant and then turned on his heel and strolled away, seemingly without a care.

'Follow me, sirs,' the clerk said, turning to go.

'That, my dear boy,' Gaius whispered, 'is a very well-connected man whom you'd be wise to steer clear of.'

'Thank you, Uncle,' Vespasian snapped. 'But I think that I've got more pressing issues to worry about at the moment; Sabinus' life, for example.'

CHAPTER IIII

A WAY FROM THE atrium, the palace seemed almost completely deserted. They passed the occasional imperial functionary in the high, wide corridors as they snaked their way deep into the complex. The overcast day allowed for very little light or heat to enter through the few, high-set windows and the atmosphere was chill and gloomy; the clacking of the hardened leather soles of their red senatorial shoes echoing around them made Vespasian feel that he was being led to a place of incarceration rather than to the centre of power.

Eventually the clerk stopped outside a grand set of double doors; he knocked on the black lacquered wood.

'Enter,' a familiar voice ordered languidly.

The clerk swung the heavy door open, slowly and soundlessly, and then ushered Vespasian and Gaius into a room, predominantly decorated in deep red, awash with flickering golden light.

'Good day to you, Senators Pollo and Vespasian,' Narcissus crooned from behind a sturdy oaken desk littered with scrolls; he did not get up. Five chairs were placed opposite him in a semi-circle; the left-hand one was already occupied.

'Good day, imperial secretary,' Vespasian and Gaius replied, almost simultaneously.

Narcissus indicated the slight, shaven-headed man already seated. 'Do you know my fellow freedman, Callistus?'

'Our paths have crossed,' Vespasian confirmed.

Callistus nodded briefly to them. 'Senators.'

'Please, have a seat,' Narcissus offered.

They walked forward. In each corner of the room, standing in front of a curved, polished bronze mirror, was an identical silver candelabrum. All had ten arms and were set on four legs ending in perfectly formed lion's feet; each was as tall as a man, and gave out a beautiful golden light.

Gaius and Vespasian took the two central unoccupied chairs and sat stiffly on the hard wooden seats; Narcissus evidently did not want his interviewees to feel comfortable. The scent of his lush pomade enshrouded them as they sat.

The freedman considered them for a while with his extravagantly ringed fingers steepled, resting against full, moist lips protruding from a neatly combed beard. He cocked his head slowly as if to get a better view; two weighty, gold earrings rocked gently, glistering in the magnified candlelight. Behind him rivulets of rain trickled down the outside of a window, crisscrossed with lattice work supporting the individual, almost translucent, glass panes. Next to it, a heavy curtain blocked the draught from a door leading to the outside world.

Vespasian had not seen Narcissus up close for two or more years and he noticed new lines of stress etched into his wellfleshed, fair-skinned face. He was also evidently greying as there were tell-tale signs of dye staining the skin around his hairline.

Vespasian and Gaius sat in uncomfortable silence as they were scrutinised, unsure of whether it was their place to open the conversation or not.

A merest hint of amusement flickered across Narcissus' ice-blue eyes as he sensed their unease; he linked his fingers and gently laid his hands on the desk. 'So what is a life worth?' he mused, almost rhetorically. He let the question hang in the air for a few moments before gazing directly at Vespasian.

'That depends on who is buying and who's selling.'

The corners of Narcissus' mouth rose slightly and he nodded almost imperceptibly. 'Yes, Vespasian, market forces are always at work, especially in the commodity that we're trading in at present. That's why I find myself in such a delicate position in this case. There have been prior investments made by both parties in this deal and I'm forced to admit that one outweighs the other.'

Vespasian tensed inwardly; was Narcissus remembering his debts? A knock at the door ruptured the silence; Vespasian almost jumped.

'Ah!' Narcissus exclaimed with interest. 'That will be the arrival of the object of our bargaining. Enter!'

Vespasian frowned; how did Narcissus know of Sabinus' presence? Gaius shifted uncomfortably in his seat, which was too narrow to fully support his ample behind.

The door opened and Pallas walked in; Sabinus followed, supported by Magnus.

'Secretary to the treasury, how good of you to bring the masked assassin.'

If Pallas was surprised that Narcissus was expecting them it did not show on his face. 'I am glad to be of service in clearing up this matter, imperial secretary.'

'Of great service, my dear Pallas, please stay,' Narcissus urged, his voice brimming with overly genuine entreaty. 'I have had five chairs put out.'

Pallas inclined his head. 'It would be my pleasure, my dear Narcissus; I wouldn't wish to upset your seating arrangements.' He took the chair between Gaius and Callistus.

Vespasian was confused: who was surprising whom? Or were the freedmen acting and this meeting had been planned in advance?

Narcissus looked over to Sabinus, pale and resting on Magnus' shoulder. 'Our surprise visitor: the legate of the Ninth Hispana; and so far from his posting. Or ex-legate to be more accurate, which is a pity really as my people in that legion tell me that Camp Prefect Vibianus and Primus Pilus Laurentius are very impressed by you, but no matter. I guessed it was you when one of my agents saw a hooded man being taken secretly into Pallas' apartments earlier. Well, well. Please sit down, ex-legate; you, out of all of us, look like you most need a chair.'

'Thank you, Narcissus,' Sabinus said, hobbling to the chair next to Vespasian.

'My title is imperial secretary,' Narcissus reminded him coldly.

Sabinus swallowed. 'My apologies, imperial secretary.' Magnus helped him down.

Narcissus put a finger to his lips in thought and then shook it gently at Magnus. 'The redoubtable Magnus of the South

Quirinal Crossroads Brotherhood; of course, that's where you were hiding, Sabinus. Why did I not think of that?' He turned to Pallas. 'But you did, I'm sure, esteemed colleague; or did Magnus' involvement with this family slip your memory too?'

'Evidently not, Narcissus.'

Narcissus nodded slowly. 'You just forgot to share it with me. Well, we can all be a little forgetful at times; but no matter, Sabinus is with us now. I assume that you've managed to get him here unnoticed.'

'Apart from us, only Caenis and Vespasian's wife know that he's here in Rome, and they will keep that secret,' Pallas confirmed.

'And my two lads, sir,' Magnus put in, 'and my slave, but they're all loyal.'

'I'm sure they are, Magnus, but they're also irrelevant; as are you.' Narcissus waved a hand. 'You can go.'

Magnus shrugged, then turned and walked out; the clerk followed him, closing the door.

Narcissus played with the point of his beard, ruminating for a few moments in the silence. 'I imagine that you've been thorough, Pallas, and have ensured that Herod Agrippa doesn't go sneaking to our patron, undermining us if we keep this between ourselves?'

'Sabinus and I have just had a short conversation with our eastern friend. I told him that I was minded to block the addition of the two tetrarchies that he's asking to be incorporated into his kingdom on the basis that it would be a considerable loss of revenue to the imperial treasury which, after Caligula's excesses, we can ill afford. I then asked him to look carefully at Sabinus and tell me if he was convinced that he was the man he'd seen just before Caligula was assassinated.'

Narcissus pretended to look interested. 'And?'

'Regrettably, after further consideration, he now feels that he has made a mistake. He thinks that we may never know who that man was.'

'I see, so Sabinus could now be considered innocent; admirably done, dear partner.' Narcissus flicked a look to

Callistus as if to gauge his thoughts. His face was unreadable to Vespasian but Narcissus seemed to gain some insight; he nodded cogitatively and then arranged a couple of scrolls on the desk in front of him. 'So, to business, gentlemen. I recommend that we confine ourselves to straight talking; I think we all know each others' positions. So let me begin. Sabinus, were you the masked man who took part in Caligula's assassination?'

'No.'

Narcissus pointed vaguely to Sabinus' right thigh. 'Lift up your tunic.'

Sabinus glanced at Pallas, who widened his eyes a fraction; he slowly revealed the bandaging.

'I'll ask you again. Were you the masked man who took part in Caligula's assassination?'

Sabinus hesitated for a moment before conceding the point. 'Yes, imperial secretary.'

'You may drop the formalities now that we are all old friends together.'

'Indeed, Narcissus.'

'Good. Your comrades are due to be executed as soon as I command it. I have delayed it until today so that they can spend a few last hours with their wives and children. I've allowed that because I am not insensible to the fact that they have done my patron, me and indeed the whole of Rome, especially its treasury, a great service in ridding us finally of Caligula. However, they must die for obvious reasons. And, at the moment, despite Pallas' best efforts to clear you, you may well be joining them.'

Sabinus lowered his head.

Vespasian felt his guts tense.

Narcissus picked up a scroll and rolled it in his hands. 'I don't know whether you're all aware that the conspirators had a deal with Pallas, Callistus and me to protect them against any retribution, in return for declaring Claudius emperor. They kept their side of the bargain but only the most naïve fool would expect us to keep ours.' He glanced at Pallas and Callistus.

'It would be a recipe for instability,' Callistus stated.

Pallas nodded once in agreement.

'Quite so,' Narcissus concurred. 'However, the great advantage of this deal was that we have been able to prepare, for the past few months, for our patron's elevation. My agents have been busy, sounding people out, ascertaining how they would react to a drooling cripple who has been the butt of countless jokes, becoming emperor.' He unravelled the scroll. 'This is a condensation of the reports from my agents in the Rhenus legions and it does not make for comforting reading.' He perused the contents for a few moments as if to remind himself. 'It's not good at all; nor is that one.' He indicated to the second scroll in front of him. 'That is from the Danubius. In short: the officers think of Claudius as a laughing stock and the men are at best ambivalent – even though he's the brother of their favourite, Germanicus. And I have no reason to think that anyone here in Rome thinks any differently.'

'Nonsense, Narcissus,' Gaius protested. 'We are great admirers of Claudius; his knowledge of law and history …'

'Spare me the platitudes, Gaius,' Narcissus cut in, waving the scroll at him. 'I said that we would be straight talking. Do you really want Claudius as emperor?'

Gaius' mouth fell open, his jowls wobbling.

'Well?' Narcissus pressed.

'It's not ideal,' Gaius conceded.

'No, it's not ideal for most people. But it is for me.' He looked at his colleagues. 'As it is for Pallas and Callistus.'

'It suits us perfectly,' Callistus confirmed.

'And what's more, it's a fact: Claudius *is* emperor,' Pallas stated.

'Yes, he is.' Narcissus almost purred with pleasure. 'But the question is: how do we keep him there? We've bought the Guard, so in Rome Claudius is safe. But what if the legions on the Rhenus mutiny as they did on Tiberius' ascension? Civil war? A breakup of the Empire? Or perhaps both. That cannot be allowed to happen. So how do we secure our malformed patron in his office?' Narcissus' eyes slowly came to rest on Vespasian.

In a moment of clarity, Vespasian now saw that the three freedmen had been acting in concert over a different matter. This was never going to be a meeting about saving Sabinus' life; there was much more to it than that. Narcissus' look told him that this was about his, Vespasian's, role in securing the new regime. Pallas had merely used the opportunity to try and add Sabinus to whatever was about to be negotiated. In removing the threat of Herod Agrippa's testimony he had given Narcissus a face-saving way of sparing him even though he had admitted his guilt. He now saw where they were heading. 'Make the army respect him, perhaps even love him. He needs a victory.'

'Exactly; and he needs it soon.' Narcissus rolled up the report and discarded it to one side as if it offended him. 'But where?'

Silence filled the room so that the marching stamp of a small column of men outside the window could be clearly heard.

After a few moments, Sabinus brought himself out of his morbid introspection. 'Germania is out of the question since Varus lost the Seventeenth, Eighteenth and Nineteenth Legions there. The border is now set on the Rhenus; it would be hard to persuade the legions to cross it and, even if they would be willing, it would not be a quick victory.'

'No, it wouldn't,' Pallas agreed easily. 'Nor would any attempt to annex the lands north of the Danubius be the work of just a year or two.'

'And the legions refused to embark onto the ships when Caligula attempted to cross to Britannia,' Callistus said as if he was reciting from a well-rehearsed script.

'There's nothing worth having south of our provinces in Africa,' Narcissus carried on almost seamlessly. 'We are planning to annex Mauretania, further west; Suetonius Paulinus has been given that task and, as a reward for his timely declaration of loyalty, the Emperor has made Hosidius Geta legate of one of the legions under Paulinus' command.' Narcissus paused for a moment in thought, as if a fact had just occurred to him. 'But it is of little value and would hardly be a martial feat. Not really deserving of a triumph, although I'm sure the Senate will vote Claudius one, which he will, of course, modestly refuse.'

'We could always annex Thracia.'

'Indeed, my dear Callistus, but where's the glory in that? And in the east, Armenia has a Roman client king on its throne. So all that leaves is Parthia.'

Pallas nodded, taking up the reins of the argument without a pause. 'However, Lucius Vitellius fought a successful campaign there a few years ago and for the moment we have a settlement that is working in our interests. So we should forget going east and, anyway, if we did go that way it's too great an area to hold without committing the sort of resources that we just cannot afford. So that only leaves one financially viable option.'

'Yes, Pallas, you are so right. It only leaves Britannia,' Narcissus said slowly. 'But this time we do it properly. Callistus, please.'

Callistus cleared his throat. 'When my former patron, Caligula, was planning his haphazard attempt to invade Britannia, I played a major role in co-ordinating all the various elements. I know that an invasion of Britannia is eminently possible. And it has three great advantages: firstly, we've already put the entire infrastructure in place; this will save us millions.' He twitched one corner of his mouth at Pallas in what Vespasian assumed was his equivalent of a self-congratulatory beam; a suggestion of a raised eyebrow signalled Pallas' approval. 'We already have a disembarkation port, Gesoriacum, filled with granaries, warehouses, workshops and supply depots; the Gallic provinces are very fertile, so we will have ample supplies with which to fill them. There are still a goodly amount of ships up there, although nowhere near the thousand or so that we'll need, but that will be addressed by our senior general on the northern coast, Publius Gabinius Secundus, the Emperor's personal friend.

'Secondly, we have two exiled British Kings, Adminios and Verica, currently here in Rome asking us to restore them to their thrones; this gives us an air of legitimacy and pro-Roman local rulers once we're successful.

'And the third great advantage is that the chief city in the south of the island, Camulodunum, is no more than a hard summer's campaigning from where we would land. Claudius could have his victory within one season.'

'If the legions don't refuse to embark,' Pallas reminded everyone.

'*If* the legions don't refuse to embark,' Narcissus repeated. His gaze now wandered to Sabinus.

'How do you propose to make them this time, Narcissus?' Sabinus asked, interested, his present dilemma seemingly forgotten.

'That's how you and your brother now have the chance to save your life, my friend. Had it not been for Pallas' adroit handling of your predicament – albeit behind my back – you would have been a dead man.' He paused and gave Pallas a fleeting look of disapproval that carried far more weight than the minuscule movements of the facial muscles outwardly conveyed. 'However, I now find myself free to give you this opportunity in payment for the debt I still owe you for the discretion you showed over my patron's foolish letter. Will you take it, not knowing what it is, or would you prefer to die with the others?'

Vespasian glanced at his brother, relief flooding through his body. Gaius exhaled as if he had been holding his breath for the entire meeting.

It was an easy question for Sabinus. 'I'll take it, Narcissus, whatever it is.'

'Good. Palagios!'

The door opened and the clerk walked in. 'Yes, imperial secretary.'

'Are the prisoners ready?'

'Yes, imperial secretary.'

Narcissus rose. 'Come with me, Sabinus; Vespasian, you'd better help him.' Pulling back the curtain, he opened the door and stepped through.

Vespasian and Sabinus followed him out into a small court-yard, grey with drizzle. Six men knelt at its centre before a wooden block; each guarded by a Praetorian with a drawn sword under the command of a centurion. The closest prisoner raised his auburn head and smiled in resignation at the brothers, his pinched face more pallid than ever.

'Proceed, centurion,' Narcissus ordered, 'there will be no one else added to their number. Centurion Lupus first.'

'Yes, imperial secretary.'

As Lupus was led forwards to the block Sabinus grabbed Narcissus' arm. 'You can't make me watch my wife's brother's execution.'

Narcissus glanced down at the hand grasping his arm and removed it. 'You are in no position to make demands, Sabinus; unless, that is, you wish to demand to join them.'

Vespasian placed an arm around his brother's shoulders and pulled him away. 'There's nothing to be gained by arguing.'

Lupus knelt before the block, placing his hands upon it as the Praetorian guarding him touched the back of his neck with his blade; Lupus tensed as the weapon was raised, hunching his shoulders close to his head. The sword flashed down; Lupus screamed in agony as it embedded itself in the base of his neck, severing his spinal column but not his head. Paralysis was almost instantaneous and Lupus slumped to the ground, bleeding profusely but still alive.

Narcissus tutted. 'I would expect a Praetorian centurion to be able to hold himself with a little more dignity and extend his neck when faced with death.'

As Lupus' limp body was stretched out with his head over the block, his eyes staring in agonised terror, Vespasian glanced at Clemens; he held himself calmly as the executioner brought down his sword a second time and struck off Lupus' head in an eruption of spurting gore.

'That's better,' Narcissus commented as the headless corpse was dragged away from the block, leaving a copious trail of blood across the wet paving stones. 'I think we should have Prefect Clemens next, let's see if he can do better.'

Sabinus stiffened, the muscles in his cheeks pulsating as he struggled to keep himself under control. Vespasian kept his arm firmly around his shoulders.

Narcissus turned to the brothers. 'Do you know, I think you were right, Sabinus, it would be wrong for me to make you watch Clemens' execution. I think that the perilousness of your situation would be far better stressed if you performed the deed yourself.'

'I can't execute Clemens!'

'Of course you can; if you don't I'll have him execute you before he's despatched.'

'Do it, Sabinus,' Clemens called as he was led to the block. 'If I'm not to be allowed the dignity of suicide by this double-crossing, oily Greek freedman then I would rather die at your hand than have the humiliation of a mere ranker taking my life.'

Sabinus shook his head, tears welling in his eyes.

'You have to, brother,' Vespasian whispered. 'Narcissus is making you do this to emphasise the power that he has over us; either submit to it or die.'

Sabinus heaved a huge sigh, holding his head in both hands. 'Help me over there.'

Vespasian supported his brother as he hobbled over to Clemens, kneeling in front of the blood-drenched block. The Praetorian offered his sword, hilt first; Sabinus took it and stood over his brother-in-law.

Clemens looked up. 'Tell Clementina and my wife that you did this because I wanted you to; they will understand and be grateful that you made my death less of a humiliation.'

'I will, Clemens. Thank you for giving your sister to me; she is a good wife and has made me very happy; I'll always keep her safe.' Sabinus hefted the sword in his hand, judging the weight.

Clemens nodded and mouthed: 'Avenge me.' He then placed both hands on the block and stretched his neck. 'Watch over my children.'

With one continuous motion, Sabinus raised the sword above his head and swept it down, the muscles in his arm bulging with the exertion, to cleave through flesh and bone with a wet, crunching impact and a crimson explosion. Clemens' head was propelled forward by the force of the spraying blood; it hit the ground and rolled once, coming to a halt facing Sabinus and Vespasian. For a moment the eyes stared at the brothers, life still in evidence, before a final beat of the heart sent a surge of blood slopping over them, blinding them for the last time.

Sabinus dropped the sword with a metallic clang that rang around the silent courtyard.

Vespasian averted his eyes from the macabre sight and saw Narcissus, the man who had gained so much from Clemens' actions and yet had betrayed him, give the faintest smile of satisfaction before he turned and walked back inside. 'Come, brother, it's done; you have acknowledged Narcissus' power.'

A third body was heard hitting the ground outside as Vespasian retook his seat but he knew better than to let his contempt for Narcissus play on his face. He looked briefly at Sabinus; his brother was having less success at controlling his emotions.

Narcissus noticed it too. 'Whatever you think of me for having you execute your wife's brother is irrelevant, unless, of course, I ever suspect that you are doing more than thinking. If that becomes the case then I will reverse this decision that I've been manoeuvred into and I shall make sure that you are not the only one who suffers.' He glared at Sabinus and then slowly cast his eyes over Vespasian and Gaius as the threat hung over them. 'But enough of this; back to business. What do we require of you both? Now that Pallas seems to have got his team back together again, I think that he had better explain, as it was his idea originally.'

Vespasian looked at Pallas, realising that his help had not been totally altruistic. Pallas caught his eye but showed nothing as from outside came the sound of another killing blow. 'Thank you, Narcissus, for the recognition,' Pallas began. 'A month ago, after we'd decided to resurrect Caligula's idea to conquer Britannia, we began thinking about how to make the army respect Claudius enough to get four legions and the equivalent number of auxiliaries to invade an island for him, that the superstitious amongst them – which is virtually all of them – consider to be haunted and rife with spirits. My colleagues were considering paying a bounty, which, to me, was out of the question; so I was looking for a cheaper option. Then I remembered Caligula's other idea of emulating his father, Germanicus, who restored the army's pride after Varus' disaster in the Teutoburg Forest; he won their love forever by pushing back into Germania six years later, and recapturing the Eagles of the Eighteenth and

Nineteenth Legions. Caligula wanted personally to find the third Eagle that fell in that battle but did not have the patience to see it through.

'However, I recalled the enthusiasm with which the announcement of this plan was greeted and I realised that had Caligula succeeded he would have been so popular that the army would not have refused to embark for Britannia. So I thought: why shouldn't Claudius do the same?' He looked along the row to Vespasian and Sabinus as a dull thump indicated that the fifth prisoner had met his end. 'Obviously Claudius couldn't do it himself but someone could do it in his name; then I remembered how you two had gone to Moesia and found and extracted that hideous weasel-faced priest. And there we have it.'

Vespasian and Sabinus looked in disbelief at Pallas, the horror of Clemens' execution momentarily put to one side. 'You want us to find the Seventeenth's lost Eagle?' Vespasian gasped eventually, unable to believe that anyone other than Caligula could be mad enough to suggest it thirty-two years after its capture.

'Yes,' Narcissus confirmed. 'If we can resurrect Rome's fallen Eagle in Claudius' name then we will have the army on his side and they will embark on those ships and they will invade Britannia. Claudius will have his victory; and his place, and, more to the point, ours, will be secured.'

'And if we do this then I keep my life?' Sabinus asked carefully.

Narcissus smiled faintly, devoid of humour. 'No. If you *succeed* in this you keep your life; although I rather think that if you don't succeed you'll probably lose it anyway in the attempt.'

'I expect you're right. But why should my brother be going too?'

'You miss the point, Sabinus,' Vespasian said, looking around at the three passive-faced freedmen. 'This was all decided before Caligula was killed; we were both always going to go.'

'Whether we wanted to or not?'

Narcissus inclined his head. 'Whether you wanted preferment or not under this regime, would be a better way of looking at it, but yes. And now you have no choice if you want that unfortunate misunderstanding about who was the man behind the mask to be cleared up.' He paused as another sword blow sounded outside, followed by the final body collapsing onto the blood-wetted stone.

Vespasian shivered. Gaius shook his head sorrowfully and rubbed the back of his neck. The centurion bellowed at his men to pick up the heads and drag the bodies away.

Narcissus pursed his lips. 'Well, that's over with. They were good men if somewhat naïve; you did well not to join them, Sabinus – today at least.' He turned to Vespasian as if nothing of import had happened. 'I will repay the debt that I owe you for managing to leave my patron so wealthy after that business with Poppaeus – I think you'll agree that cashing the bankers' draft in Alexandria pays for the other?'

Vespasian forced his mind away from the image of Clemens' dripping head being held up by its auburn hair; he nodded.

'So to even our score, I – or rather the Emperor – will confirm you as the legate commanding the Second Augusta based at Argentoratum on the Rhenus.'

'But that's Corbulo's legion.'

'Indeed, but whoever heard of an ex-consul becoming a legate? Caligula gave it to Corbulo, rather than give him a province to govern, to humiliate him for daring to complain about the way Caligula exhibited Corbulo's half-sister naked at dinner parties. In view of his semi-fraternal connection with Caligula's wife, we feel it better that he returns to Rome and I'm sure he will be grateful to be relieved of a position that he certainly considers beneath him. You will replace him.' He picked up a scroll and proffered it. 'This is the Emperor's mandate confirming your appointment. Will that be acceptable?'

'Yes, Narcissus,' he replied. Normally such news would fill a man with excitement and pride but all Vespasian could think of was Clemens' decapitated body being hauled away outside.

'Good. The Empress was very keen that her brother, Corvinus, should have the commission but fortunately there is now a vacancy for him with the Ninth Hispana; I wonder how he'll measure up to the expectations of the camp prefect and the primus pilus.'

Sabinus stiffened on his chair and the muscles in his jaw clenched.

Narcissus glanced at him briefly, his lips twitching in a shadow of a mirthless smile. 'No doubt my agents will tell me.' He picked up two more scrolls from his desk and handed them to Vespasian. 'These are the orders for you and Corbulo, both signed by the Emperor. You will present yours to the Governor Galba when you get to Argentoratum; he will make the necessary arrangements. Give Corbulo his orders personally. You will proceed there with Sabinus as soon as possible; as legate you'll be free to use the resources of your legion and its attached auxiliaries to help your brother find this Eagle. My advice would be to start your search at the Teutoburg Forest.'

'You're toying with us, Pallas,' Vespasian accused as soon as the doors to Pallas' suite of rooms, on the second floor, were shut against inquisitive ears roaming the corridor beyond. 'That meeting was not set up to bargain for Sabinus' life; it was all about your ambitions and my role in fulfilling them.'

'Both of your roles in fulfilling them,' Pallas pointed out, gesturing to his steward to bring wine. 'I need both of you to go. This is my idea, so my reputation with the Emperor rests upon it. I can't afford it to fail.'

Vespasian was incensed. 'So if you hadn't had a use for Sabinus, you would have left him to his fate?'

'Dear boy, calm yourself,' Gaius advised, slumping down onto a couch placed haphazardly just beyond the doors. 'It doesn't matter how it was managed or what Pallas' motives were, the end result is what counts; Sabinus has got a reprieve.'

Sabinus sat down next to him and rested his head in his hands, breathing deeply as the relief flooded through him in a delayed reaction.

'Yes, but only just. Nar—'

'"Just" is good enough, Vespasian!' Sabinus snapped, glaring up at his brother from beneath his eyebrows. 'I can even take the humiliation of Corvinus being given my command because I know that I have a chance to survive and have my revenge.'

Vespasian collected himself. 'Yes, I know; but Narcissus seemed to be ahead of us. We didn't surprise him by bringing you; instead he surprised us by knowing that you were coming.'

'Oh, but we did surprise him,' Pallas said, taking two cups of wine from the returning steward and proffering one to Vespasian.

Vespasian took it and downed a good measure. 'Did we? I saw a man in full control of the situation.'

'Of course,' Pallas replied smoothly, taking a sip of wine. 'That's because he likes to think that he always is. I purposely told my clerks to let his agent see Sabinus come in here so that he had time to get used to the surprise and regain, in his mind, the upper hand. I know Narcissus very well and I know that if Sabinus had just come through the door of his study unannounced, then, despite how well I'd covered up his part in the assassination, Narcissus would have executed him anyway because he would have felt outmanoeuvred. Narcissus only spared him because he thought that he'd outwitted me; he gave me Sabinus' life as a sort of consolation prize.'

Vespasian took another gulp of wine as he turned this over in his mind. 'Why didn't you tell us that that was what you were doing, instead of just having us sit there not knowing what was going on?'

'Because, my friend, I needed Narcissus to see the confusion on your faces, otherwise he would have guessed what was happening. If he hadn't believed that he had genuinely outwitted us, Sabinus would now be dead.'

Vespasian sighed, exasperated by how Claudius' freedmen played mind-games with one another from behind their neutral expressions. He looked around for a seat and realised how sparsely furnished the room was.

'Forgive me,' Pallas said, 'I have just moved into this suite this morning; it's still being refurbished to my taste. Please follow me, gentlemen.'

Pallas led them through three high and spacious chambers looking out over the Circus Maximus to the Aventine Hill beyond, shrouded now in a damp mist. Slaves were busy arranging furniture, polishing ornaments and erecting a couple of statues of Greek, rather than Roman, origin. Vespasian could see that Pallas planned to make himself very comfortable. At the far end of the third room Pallas opened a door and ushered them into a study whose walls were lined with boxed, wooden shelving containing hundreds of cylindrical book cases.

'Please,' he said, bidding them to be seated, before going to the far right-hand corner and retrieving a case. He slipped out a scroll and spread it on the desk; it was a map.

'This is Gaul and Germania,' Pallas said, placing an inkpot on one side and a wax tablet on the other to keep the scroll from rolling up. 'The two military provinces on the west bank of the Rhenus, Germania Inferior to the north and Germania Superior in the south, provide the buffer from the lost province of Germania Magna on the east bank.'

Vespasian, Sabinus and Gaius peered at it; there was not a great deal of detail to take in.

'As you can see, the Rhenus is clearly marked, as are the legions' camps along its western bank.' Pallas pointed to each one, from north to south, with a well-manicured finger and stopped at one halfway down the river. 'And this is Argentoratum, where the Second Augusta is stationed.' He then traced his finger a good way north and east. 'And this is the site of Varus' disaster, in the homelands of the Cherusci.'

Vespasian looked more closely; there was no marking beneath Pallas' finger. 'How do you know?'

'I don't exactly, but from the reports we have from twenty-five years ago when Germanicus and his general Caecina found the decayed bodies of our men strewn through twenty miles of forest, this is our best estimation.'

'How are we meant to get all the way there?' Sabinus asked. 'Walk in with a whole legion and invite the bastards to have a repeat show?'

'I don't think that would be altogether sensible,' Pallas observed with the merest hint of condescension in his voice.

Sabinus bristled but refrained from a riposte.

'The Eagle is not going to be there any more,' Vespasian said, suspecting that he was stating the obvious but feeling that it should be said anyway.

Pallas nodded. 'In all probability not; but Narcissus is right, it's the best place to start. It's more than likely it's in the homeland of one of the six tribes that took part in the battle under the leadership of Arminius, to give him his Latin name. The Eighteenth was found with the Marsi and the Nineteenth with the Bructeri. So that just leaves the Sicambri, the Chauci, the Chatti and Arminius' own tribe, the Cherusci.' As he named the tribes he pointed to their homelands marked with their names. 'However, an Eagle is a potent and valuable trophy for these people and worth fortunes in trade, so there is no guarantee that it has stayed in one place.'

Vespasian looked at the seemingly endless lands over the Rhenus that extended to the end of the map and wondered how much further east they went and who or what was out there. 'So we go to the battle site – but what then, Pallas? This is your plan; you must have had an idea when you formulated it.'

'Arminius was murdered by a kinsman who resented the power that he had accumulated. After his death the confederation of tribes that he had brought together disintegrated. He did, however, leave a son, Thumelicus, he must be twenty-four now; if anyone can tell you where to look it would be him.'

'And he's in the Teutoburg Forest?'

'We don't know. Germanicus captured his mother, Thusnelda, whilst she was heavily pregnant with him. After they had been paraded in Germanicus' triumph, two years later, they were exiled to Ravenna. The boy was trained as a gladiator and fought bravely enough to win the wooden sword and his freedom. After that he disappeared; in all likelihood he went back to Germania and to his tribe, the Cherusci.' Pallas pointed vaguely to the huge area east of the Rhenus. 'If he's still alive then he's probably somewhere out there and that's why the Teutoburg Forest is the best place to start.'

'So if we find this man, who may be dead, he might tell us where his father, whom he never met, might have hidden the Seventeenth's Eagle.'

Pallas shrugged.

The brothers looked at each other and immediately burst into incredulous laughter.

'There must be more that you can tell them, Pallas,' Gaius said, studying the sparse map and sharing his nephews' unease.

'I have told them all we know; if we knew any more, then the Eagle would have been found by now.'

'They might as well have sent you to find Venus' hymen,' Magnus muttered as they walked back down the Palatine in the deepening dusk.

'At least we'd know then where not to look,' Vespasian observed gloomily. 'As it is, it could be anywhere across the Rhenus.'

'Kept by any one of those tribes,' Sabinus added.

His face was hidden by his hood but Vespasian could tell by the tone of his voice that he was scowling; and well he might. They had spent the rest of the daylight hours going through Pallas' library reading anything that they could find on Germania and the tribes that inhabited it, as well as accounts of the battle of the Teutoburg Forest; none of it had made for very comforting reading: a land full of dark forests watched over by strange gods and inhabited by tribes who gloried in the masculine pursuits of battle and honour and yet held their women in highest regard. The one thing that united the tribes was their mutual antipathy and distrust for each other. It seemed that the Germanic code of honour would not countenance one tribe holding hegemony over another, so they were constantly fighting.

'At least you'll have the chance to visit your parents on the way,' Gaius suggested, trying to lift the mood. 'And you'll see your wife and children, Sabinus.'

'If we have time.' Sabinus' mood was not to be lifted.

'What are you going to do with Flavia and young Titus, sir?' Magnus asked.

'Leave them here,' Vespasian said. 'I can't imagine Flavia wanting to come to Argentoratum; she won't even visit Cosa. You can keep an eye on them for me, Magnus, and Caenis.'

'And how am I supposed to do that when I'm a thousand miles away?'

Vespasian frowned. 'Where are you going, then?'

'With you of course.'

Vespasian looked at his friend as if he had lost his senses. 'Why in the name of every god that you hold sacred would you want to do that?'

'Well, you've got to have someone with you who knows the way and what to look for, if you take my meaning?'

Vespasian was none the wiser. 'I'm sorry, I don't.'

'Come on, sir, use your brain; I told you back in Thracia that before I was transferred to the Urban Cohorts I served with the Fifth Alaudae.'

'Yes, and?'

'We were stationed on the Rhenus. We were part of Caecina's army when he and Germanicus went back into Germania after Arminius. I've been to the site of the Teutoburg massacre, I saw the remnants of our lads nailed to trees, strung up in the branches and scattered along the forest floor; we buried them, as many as we could find, that is. But more to the point, I was part of the force that found the Eighteenth's Eagle. I've seen how they hide them, so I've got to come.'

PART II

❧ ❧

GERMANIA, SPRING AD 41

CHAPTER V

'NOW I UNDERSTAND why our parents have chosen to stay here,' Vespasian said to Sabinus as the brothers pulled up their horses. They gazed at a newly constructed country villa set on a gentle slope that ran down to the shore of Lake Murten, in the tribal lands of the Helvetii. 'Father's banking business must be doing very well to afford all this.'

'He won't be needing to buy wine again,' Sabinus observed.

Countless neat rows of vines surrounded the villa and trailed up the hill behind it, framing it with pleasing regular stripes. Even the gangs of slaves toiling between the lines seemed to be spaced at even intervals. The orderly agricultural arrangement of the estate contrasted markedly with the distant, irregular peaks of the snow-bound Alps, gleaming white and streaked with blue-grey. The strengthening spring sun had, as yet, had little impact on that soaring realm where winter still held sway; but here, down at the limits of the foothills of Italia's northern shield, spring was advancing. The pasture beneath their mounts' hooves was losing its brown tinge, gained from months beneath a crust of snow, and was now returning to its former lushness; the horses tugged gratefully at it.

Magnus drew up next to them, slipping his mount's reins so that it too could enjoy the grazing. He took a large gulp of the cool air and grinned at Ziri riding beside him, leading two pack-mules. 'I can't imagine anywhere more removed from that parched, flat wasteland that you used to call home.'

Ziri looked around, evidently unimpressed. 'The desert has nothing to constrict you; no barriers.' He pointed to the brick wall running along the front of the estate and then indicated to the high mountains beyond. 'How far can a man ride in a straight line in this land before he's forced out of his way by somebody's property or an impassable obstacle?'

'A lot further than in Rome and it doesn't stink.'

'But still not as far as you can in the desert, master, and that doesn't stink either.' Ziri gave a wide, white-toothed smile that creased the three strange wavy lines carved into his brown cheeks.

Magnus leant over and cuffed his slave good-humouredly around the head. 'Slaves don't win arguments, you curly-haired camel-botherer; in fact, slaves don't argue.'

Vespasian laughed and kicked his horse forward for the last few hundred paces of what had been a long and tedious journey. Having taken a ship to Massalia they had transferred to a river vessel and sailed up the Rhodanus to Lugudunum. Here they had requisitioned horses from the local garrison commander and made the hundred and fifty-mile journey across country to Aventicum in five days. Having found their father's banking business in the forum of the fast-growing town, they had been told by a couple of harassed clerks that he had not been in for the previous four days because of illness. They had consequently travelled the last few miles from the town in a state of some concern, as Titus, their father, was now in his eighties.

They cantered through the estate's gates, set in a tall, brick-built gatehouse, and on up a straight track bordered by freshly dug vegetable patches alternating with small orchards of apple and pear trees, in front of long, low outbuildings. The track ended at a neatly laid-out formal garden, centred on a fishpond and fountain; it was bordered on three sides by their parents' two-storey country villa. A waist-high wooden balustrade ran around the outside of the house enclosing an area of decking, four paces wide; this was sheltered by a slanting, tiled roof jutting out from just below the level of the first floor's uniformly square windows and supported on wooden columns. Climbing plants had been trained up the columns; their first green shoots of the season waved gently in the light breeze. Doors and windows punctuated the two protruding sides of the villa with exact symmetry. As Vespasian and his party dismounted, one of the doors, to their left, opened and a familiar figure stepped out onto the shaded decking.

'Minerva's mangy minge,' Magnus exclaimed, 'Artebudz! What are you doing here?'

Vespasian was as surprised as Magnus to see the ex-hunting slave whose freedom he had procured from the Thracian Queen, Tryphaena, while he had been a military tribune serving in that client kingdom. Vespasian had last seen him ten years previously, when Artebudz had accompanied his parents north out of Italia after the raid on their estate at Aquae Cutillae by agents of Livilla and her lover Sejanus.

Artebudz smiled in recognition. 'Magnus, my friend; Vespasian and Sabinus, it's good to see you, sirs.' He walked around the decking towards the double doors at the front of the house. Leaving their mounts with Ziri and a stable-lad who had come scuttling from an outbuilding, Vespasian, Sabinus and Magnus joined him there.

'I've been here for three years now,' Artebudz told them, taking Magnus' proffered forearm and bowing his head to Vespasian and Sabinus; his curly hair, once jet black, was now streaked with grey. 'After I arrived at Aventicum with your parents I returned to my home province of Noricum; I found my father, Brogduos, still alive but very old. When he died I buried him, with an inscription with both our names on it marking his grave, and then came back here to repay the debt that I owe your family for my freedom.' He looked with concern at the brothers, creasing the Greek sigma branded on his forehead with a frown. 'But you have come in time, sirs; your father's been ill for some while now; he took to his bed a few days ago. The doctors think that he has the wasting disease; he's been steadily getting worse.'

Vespasia Polla's pleasure at seeing her two sons after so long was tempered by her worry about her husband. After no more than a perfunctory embrace in the spacious atrium, whose vaulted, lofty ceiling was fully enclosed in defence against the northern climate, she led them along a corridor and up a set of wooden stairs. Her once proud, slender face was now careworn and she wore her greying hair haphazardly pinned atop her head, taking no pride in her appearance. There was no sparkle in her dark eyes and the thin flesh beneath them hung in slack bags, telling of tears and sleepless nights.

'These doctors here know nothing,' she complained as she led the brothers along a first-floor corridor with views over the vineyards and on to the distant Alps beyond. 'I've tried to persuade Titus to return to Rome since he first started feeling weak a few months ago, but he won't go. He says that whatever the Fates have decreed for him is not going to be altered by changing from Greek quacks in Germania Superior to other Greek quacks who charge twice as much just because they live in Rome.'

Vespasian could see the logic of the argument but refrained from saying so.

Vespasia paused by a plain wooden door. 'He says that the time that Morta chooses to cut the thread of a man's life is determined solely by her whim and has nothing to do with your geographical whereabouts.' With a disparaging scowl she opened the door.

The brothers followed her in and were surprised, but delighted, to see their father sitting up in bed; he raised his eyes from the scroll that he was perusing and a smile cracked his pallid, hollow-cheeked face. 'Well, well, my sons; either the messengers got to Rome and Pannonia in record time and you beat that again travelling here, or I wasted my money writing to you both, four days ago, asking you to come.' He held out both hands and Vespasian and Sabinus took one each. 'But seeing as you're both here and that I'm feeling a little better today, despite the doctors' best endeavours to finish me off, I'll get up for dinner.'

Titus set down his wine cup and looked disbelievingly at Sabinus. He rubbed the puckered, red scar where his left ear had been and then turned to his wife reclining on the couch next to him. 'It seems that we brought up our eldest son to be an idiot with a suicidal sense of honour.' He glanced over to Clementina, reclining next to her husband, and added: 'Although, of course, my dear, the wrong that had been done to you had to be avenged at some point, but not at the expense of your brother and husband.'

Clementina nodded vaguely at Titus, her red eyes rimmed with tears for her brother; she wore a simple stola of yellow wool and her hair hung dishevelled around her shoulders. Since being told, upon returning from a walk with her children an hour earlier, of the part that her menfolk had played in the assassination of Caligula, she had been torn between mourning for Clemens and relief at Sabinus' reprieve. She decided to attend dinner so as not to be parted from her husband for a moment, but had not been the best of dining companions and had eaten nothing. 'My shame was not worth my brother's life; nor my husband's.' She ran a hand up Sabinus' muscular forearm. 'But I thank the gods that one, at least, remains to me.'

Sabinus shifted uneasily and placed his hand over Clementina's. 'Only if we can find the Eagle.'

Vespasian held up his wine cup for a slave to refill. 'And to do that Pallas thinks that we should try to find Arminius' son, Thumelicus, whom he suspects has returned to his tribe's homelands. And how do we do that? We don't even know what he looks like.'

'Exactly like his father, I should expect,' Titus said. 'At least he did as a child.'

The brothers both stared uncomprehendingly at their father.

'You've seen Thumelicus?' Sabinus asked, frowning.

'I only saw him as a small child at Germanicus' triumph; it was the May of the year that your mother and I went to Asia; we sailed from Ostia two days later. I remember remarking on how the boy looked so like his father: long, almost black hair with piercing, bright blue eyes and thin lips. The only difference was a slight cleft in his chin that his mother had passed on to him.'

'But how could you compare them?'

'Because I knew Arminius as a child; I saved his life, as a matter of fact.' Titus gave a rueful smile. 'Looking back, perhaps if I hadn't, things might be different; you see, boys, it's not just men from the great families who can change the course of history.'

'How did that come about?' Sabinus asked.

But Vespasian remembered. 'Of course, you served with the Twentieth Legion.'

The look of pride on Titus' gaunt face as he recalled his martial youth seemed to take twenty years off his age. 'Yes, Vespasian, I did. After we had defeated the Cantabri in Hispania we were sent to Germania. We were part of Drusus' army, Tiberius' elder brother, whilst he pursued Augustus' policy of conquering Germania Magna as far as the Albis River. With him we fought campaigns all over that forest-infested land, against the Frisii and the Chauci along the low-lying coast of the cold Northern Sea and against the Chatti and the Marsi in the dark forests and hills inland. When I was thirty-four and had been a centurion for two years, we fought a battle against the Cherusci, almost on the banks of the Albis. We beat them, and then their King, Segimerus, submitted to Drusus in one of their sacred groves. To seal the pact, his nine-year-old son, Erminatz, was given as a hostage to Rome. As one of the most junior centurions at the time it fell to me and my century to escort the boy back to Rome so I got to know him quite well – and I saved him from being butchered by some Chatti tribesmen who ambushed us on the way back to the Rhenus.'

'Erminatz was Arminius, Father?' Vespasian asked.

'Yes, his name was Latinised to Arminius. He stayed in Rome for seven years and was given equestrian rank before serving as a military tribune in the legions. He eventually returned to Germania Magna as the prefect of a cohort of German auxiliaries. And the rest is history: three years after his return he betrayed Varus and almost twenty-five thousand legionaries and auxiliaries were massacred. Perhaps I should have left him to the Chatti after all.'

Sabinus took a sip of wine, looking less than pleased. 'How does this help us, Father? You saw Thumelicus when he was two and his father when he was nine and you thought that they looked very similar. Both had black hair and blue eyes, just like many thousands of other Germans, but Thumelicus had a cleft chin.'

'Exactly,' Vespasian agreed. 'And wandering around Germania Magna looking underneath the beard of every German we can find is not going to get us any closer to Thumelicus.'

Titus nodded and picked up a wrinkled winter apple. 'So you are going to have to get him to come to you.'

Sabinus almost scoffed but then remembered that it was his father that he was talking to and pulled his face into a more respectful expression. 'And how are we going to do that?'

Titus took his knife from the sheath on his belt and started to peel his apple. 'As I said, I got to know Erminatz or Arminius quite well. It took us nearly two months to get back to Rome; on that journey the lad began to realise just how far he was being taken from home and he began to despair about seeing his parents again, especially his mother. The Germans hold their mothers and wives in very high regard and even take their advice on subjects that we would consider to be male concerns.' Vespasia snorted; Titus carried on without seeming to notice. 'The morning that I handed him over to Drusus' wife, Antonia—'

Vespasian was surprised. 'You met Antonia when you were younger?'

'Hardly, she dismissed me as soon as I walked through her door; I was far too lowly to be noticed. Anyway, before I left him, Arminius gave me something and made me promise to give it to his mother. I promised of course, thinking that I would be rejoining my legion, but what I didn't know was that Drusus had fallen from his horse two days after we'd left and he had died a month later. We met his funeral cortège on our way back and my legion was with it. We were then posted to Illyricum and, with Tiberius, campaigned in Germania Magna again a few years later. This time we came in from the south and never reached the Cherusci lands. Then, four years after that, I was almost gutted by a spear-thrust and was invalided out of the army; so I never returned to the Cherusci lands and I never gave this thing to Arminius' mother. By the time I'd recovered from my wounds and got back to Rome, Arminius was serving with the army far from the city so I couldn't return it to him.'

Sabinus' eyes brightened with hope. 'So you've still got whatever it is?'

'Yes, in fact I still use it,' Titus said, quartering his apple.

'How?'

Titus carved the core out of a quarter. 'Use your eyes.'

The brothers stared at the knife in their father's hand. 'Your knife?' they exclaimed simultaneously.

'Yes, the knife that I use every day. The knife I use for peeling fruit and for sacrifices.' He held up the sleek blade. 'I even used it at both your naming ceremonies.'

Vespasian and Sabinus both got up and went to examine with fresh eyes the blade that they had seen every day when they were younger.

'I don't think that it would be a big enough incentive to get Thumelicus to help you, but I believe if you let it be known that you have Arminius' knife, then he would at least be willing to talk to the sons of the man who saved his father's life in return for a memento of the father he never knew. After that it would be down to you to persuade him.'

'But what would make him believe that it did belong to Arminius?' Vespasian asked, admiring the plainness of the weapon.

'Look at the blade closely.'

'Oh, there are strange letters engraved on the blade, aren't there, Titus?' Vespasia said, frowning with recollection. 'It's the same knife that you gave me to kill myself with on the night that Aquae Cutillae was attacked by Livilla's men. I held it to my chest and stared at my reflection in the blade. I was terrified, thinking that it would be the last time that I saw myself. Then I noticed these lines distorting my image and I tried to calm myself by working out what they were. I meant to ask you about them afterwards but the shock of everything drove it from my mind.'

Vespasian squinted. Along the blade close to the hilt were a series of fine lines and curves recognisable as a sort of writing. 'What are they, Father?'

'Those are runes; they're Germanic letters. Arminius told me that they say "Erminatz".'

*

Five days later the brothers knew that they could delay their departure no longer. Vespasian sat with his parents on the decking at the front of the house watching Sabinus and Clementina walking towards them with their two children, Flavia Sabina and young Sabinus, now eleven and nine respectively. Outside the stable block, to their left, Magnus and Artebudz were supervising Ziri and a couple of lads saddling their horses and loading the provisions onto them for the hundred-mile journey to the II Augusta's camp at Argentoratum.

'I made arrangements yesterday for the banking business to be sold,' Titus announced, shivering slightly. Despite the warm spring sun, he had a blanket wrapped around his shoulders.

Vespasia frowned at her husband. 'Have you finally made up your mind to go back to Italia?'

'No, Vespasia, I shall die here and it will be soon.'

Vespasian remained silent knowing that his father was right: his health would not allow him to see midsummer. This would be their final farewell.

'And what shall I do, Titus?' Vespasia demanded.

'Whatever you like. I shall leave this estate to you; the income from it and the money from the sale of the banking business will keep you very comfortably. You could stay here or go back to our estates in Italia; either Aquae Cutillae, which I shall leave to Vespasian, or Falacrina, which I shall leave to Sabinus.'

'You expect me to live in places where every room will remind me of you? How can you still be so stupid after all these years?'

Titus chuckled, smiling fondly at his wife. 'Because, Vespasia, your wilfulness will not allow me to appear otherwise in your eyes.'

Vespasia looked momentarily confused. 'I can't work out whether that's a compliment or an insult.'

'It's both, my dear.'

Vespasia sniffed in derision. 'Titus, if you're so determined to die on me then the last thing that I shall do is sit around in a place where I shall constantly be reminded of your selfishness. Flavia is going to give birth to Vespasian's second child soon and Clementina will no doubt be taking her children back to Rome, so I can be of some use there. I shall go to my brother Gaius' house.'

Vespasian closed his eyes, imagining his mother and Flavia living in the same house, and shuddered. He wondered how his uncle would react; Gaius would probably find a lot of correspondence to deal with.

'Now why didn't I think of that?' Titus muttered with a slight grin.

Vespasia stared sternly at her husband and then her face relaxed; she put a hand on his knee. 'I'm sure you did, but thought that I would dismiss it as stupid.'

Titus placed a hand on his wife's, squeezed it gently and looked over to the stables where Sabinus had sat his young son on a horse and given him a sword to hold; the boy was waving it above his head and shouting a high-pitched battle cry whilst his sister looked on clapping her hands excitedly. Sabinus put his arm around his wife as they watched their children.

Titus smiled contentedly at the family scene and then turned to Vespasian. 'Do you remember that oath that I got you and your brother to swear to each other before we left for Rome all those years ago?'

'Yes, Father,' Vespasian replied, looking cautiously at his mother.

'You can talk about it freely,' Vespasia assured him. 'Titus has told me about it and why he made you swear it.'

Titus leant forward. 'What was the purpose of the oath?'

'If one of us was unable to aid the other in time of need because they were bound by a previous oath then this oath superseded it, as it was made before all the gods and the spirits of our ancestors.'

'And what do you think that I had in mind when I made you swear this oath?'

Vespasian felt his stomach tense; he had wanted to talk to his father about this for fifteen years but knew that the subject was taboo. 'It was to supersede the oath that Mother had the whole household, including Sabinus, swear after my naming ceremony, nine days after my birth, never to reveal the omens at the sacrifice and what they prophesied. I don't know what they were because no one would tell me.'

'Because of the oath that we all swore.'

'Exactly. But since then I've encountered two other prophecies that have given me cause for thought. The first was at the Oracle of Amphiaraos in Greece; it was vague but seemed to imply that the King of the East would one day gain the West if he followed Alexander's footsteps across the sand with a gift.'

'What does that mean?'

'I'm not sure, but when I was in the Oasis of Siwa, in Cyrenaica, I witnessed the rebirth of the Phoenix.'

Titus and Vespasia looked at their youngest son with a mixture of incredulity and wonder.

'I was taken to the Oracle of Amun and the god spoke to me; he told me that I had come too soon to know what question I should ask and that I should come again with a gift that matches the sword that Alexander had left there.'

'Was that the second prophecy?' Titus asked. 'That you would return?'

'No, it was more of an invitation to come back with a gift and the correct question; it seemed to relate to what Amphiaros had said. The other prophecy was made by Thrasyllus, Tiberius' astrologer; he said that should a senator witness the Phoenix in Egypt then he would found the next dynasty of emperors. But I didn't see the Phoenix in Egypt; Siwa used to be a part of Egypt but it's in Cyrenaica now; so I don't know what to think. You must tell me what the omens of my birth foretold so that I can see my path more clearly.'

'We can't, my son.'

'Only because of the oath you all swore,' Vespasian almost shouted, exasperated.

'I was right to make people swear never to reveal what was predicted for you, Vespasian,' his mother asserted. 'It was done to protect you. However, your father was also right to give Sabinus a way to do so if he deems that you should be told.'

Vespasian, bursting with curiosity, struggled to control himself. 'But when will that be?'

Titus shrugged. 'Who can say? But what I do know is this: should you not recover the Eagle and Sabinus' life is forfeit, then he will tell you what he knows before he dies. I spoke to him yesterday and have convinced him that he won't be breaking the first oath if he does so. You will need his help at some point and this way he can give it from beyond the grave.'

'Let's hope that it doesn't come to that,' Vespasian muttered, although his curiosity was almost forcing him to think the exact opposite.

'Yes, let's hope so,' Titus said, struggling to his feet with Vespasia's help. He looked around the estate and smiled approvingly. 'This has been a good place to live out my last years and the people of Aventicum have provided me with a good income.' Vespasia handed him his walking stick and he began to hobble towards the door. He looked over his shoulder at Vespasian. 'The family should reward this town sometime for all it's done for Vespasia and me. Perhaps one day you'll see to it that it's granted the rights of a *colonia*.'

Vespasian stared at his father's slowly retreating back, wondering if the thought that had been growing in the back of his mind, a ludicrous thought that he had tried to suppress, was true. Could it really be possible? Would he really be in a position one day to grant his father's wish?

CHAPTER VI

'AS FAMILIAR AS your mother's tits,' Magnus announced, staring down at the permanent camp of the II Augusta constructed on flat ground half a mile back from the Rhenus, two miles distant.

Vespasian was forced to agree with his friend's sentiment if not his simile. 'I would say your mother's eyes, but I take your meaning.' He admired the tall, rectangular stone ramparts, punctuated by watchtowers, encompassing the rows of exactly spaced barrack huts, each the regulation distance from the next. Between the huts and the ramparts was a ribbon of open ground more than two hundred paces across – an arrow's flight – in which centuries of legionaries were being drilled. Two wide roads cut through the camp, quartering it. At their junction, just shy of the exact middle, the regulation brick barrack huts were replaced by the more substantial command and administration buildings. Taller and built of stone, rather than brick, they provided a grand focus at the centre of the camp that was otherwise very drab and uniform. It looked like any other legionary camp anywhere.

What did surprise Vespasian, however, was the landscape on the other side of the river. He had expected shadowy, brooding forest untouched by the civilising effect of Roman law; instead the eastern bank was speckled with neat farmsteads surrounded by cultivated fields or pasture upon which grazed herds of cattle. This was not the wild lands of Germania as spun in veterans' tales, where a man could wander for days on end without a glimpse of the sky, although a few miles distant the smooth farmland broke up into dark, conifer-covered hills that fitted far better the stereotypical view of Germania Magna. Trade with the lands outside the Empire was evidently brisk as the river, three hundred paces wide, was busy with craft crossing to and from the east and the substantial town, with a small port in its midst, on the western bank, close to the camp.

'The only thing that ever changes is the size of the settlement that has grown up next to it,' Sabinus observed, urging his horse forward down the hill.

'And the price of the whores living in it,' Magnus commented sagely and then thought for a moment before adding: 'And, of course, the pomposity of the arsehole in command.'

Gnaeus Domitius Corbulo grasped Vespasian's arm. 'So you're here to replace me, Vespasian? I can't say that I'm displeased; Caligula gave me the Second to humiliate me after I told my half-sister that just because she was the Emperor's wife was no reason to shame our family by allowing him to parade her naked at dinner parties. As an ex-consul I should have been given a province not a legion, but this should suit you very well.' He indicated with his other hand the grand interior of the *praetorium*, the legion's headquarters. At the far end, the legion's Eagle stood in its shrine surrounded by flaming sconces and guarded by eight legionaries.

'Thank you, Corbulo,' Vespasian replied, while trying to keep a straight face. 'I consider it an honour.'

'And so you should, so you should,' Corbulo agreed, looking approvingly down his long nose at Vespasian. He studiously ignored Magnus standing next to him and took Sabinus' arm. 'What I don't understand is why they seem to have sent two people to replace me.' He made an extraordinary sound, rather like a ram in pain. Vespasian realised it indicated that he had made a rare but valiant attempt at humour.

'Perhaps they felt that one replacement wouldn't produce a sufficient amount of hot air,' Magnus muttered, not altogether to himself.

Corbulo bristled slightly but could not bring himself to acknowledge that someone as lowly as Magnus was even in the room, let alone had insulted him. 'But no doubt that will become clear soon enough, Sabinus. I'll be inviting all my officers to meet their new legate.'

'That will be an ideal time to discuss it, Corbulo,' Sabinus replied.

'I'm afraid that I have to give you this, Corbulo.' Vespasian proffered the scroll that Narcissus had sent. 'It's your official orders, signed by the Emperor.'

'I see,' Corbulo murmured, looking at the scroll and frowning. He then looked Vespasian in the eye.

Vespasian understood Corbulo's unease. 'No, I don't know what it says.'

Corbulo considered the scroll for a few moments before taking it. 'I wouldn't be the first person to receive a letter ordering them to commit suicide.' He weighed the scroll in his hand as if he could thereby judge its contents. 'I wouldn't blame Claudius; he must think that I will want a blood-price for my slut of a half-sister. Well, he's right, I do, and it's no more than what you could squeeze out of a pin-prick.' He gave another imitation of a distressed ram, which shocked Vespasian as he had never before witnessed Corbulo essay humour twice in one day. Corbulo broke the seal. 'Do you know that I had the legion swear loyalty to Claudius as soon as the news arrived? I'm loyal to him, however ungainly and unstatesmanlike he may look.' He perused the contents and breathed a sigh of relief. 'It seems that I don't have to fall on my sword after all; I just have to return to Rome and remain under house arrest until it's decided whether or not I can continue my career. Minerva's tits, I'll never get a province to govern. Thank the gods that bastard half-sister of mine has gone! Her inability to keep her legs together brought nothing but disgrace to the family and now it's hindering my prospects.'

'I think that your prospects would have been permanently hindered if Narcissus hadn't been in your debt,' Vespasian pointed out. 'Our killing Poppaeus left his patron very well off.'

Corbulo wrinkled his nose as if an unpleasant odour had wafted into the room. 'That's not a deed that I like to be reminded of, Vespasian, but if something good has come out of that shameful murder then so much the better. However, I'll thank you not to speak of it again. Now you may wish to take a bath and change into uniform; I shall have the officers assembled here in an hour to meet you. I believe you will be particularly impressed by my senior tribune, Gaius Licinius Mucianus.'

'Thank you, Corbulo, but I think you had best make that two hours; I need to report to the Governor.'

'This is most irregular,' Servius Sulpicius Galba barked in the parade ground voice that he had used for the entirety of the interview. 'Arriving to take over the legion and then leaving the very next day on some mission, across the river, that you are unable to confide in me about? Most irregular. But then everything these days seems to be most irregular, what? Freedmen and cripples giving orders to men who can trace their families back to the first days of the Republic and beyond; New Men like you with no family to speak of becoming legates and replacing ex-consuls who should be governing provinces. It's time for a return to traditional Roman ways; we're lacking discipline, wouldn't you agree, er ...' He quickly consulted Vespasian's orders. 'Vespasian?'

'Yes, Governor,' Vespasian replied as he adjusted his position on the uncomfortable plain wooden chair.

He looked around the room whilst Galba studied the Emperor's mandate again. It was not what he would have expected for the study of a provincial governor; it was minimally furnished with plain practical furniture that paid no heed to comfort and was completely lacking in ornamentation; even the inkpot on the rough desk was of undecorated fired clay.

Galba rolled up the scrolls and handed one back to Vespasian. 'It's been most awkward having a man of Corbulo's rank placed below me, for both of us; at least your appointment deals with that. Very well, take what you need for this mission. But be warned, the German tribes are a bloodthirsty bunch of undisciplined barbarians. A couple of months ago I was obliged to throw a Chatti war band back across the river when they crossed further downstream whilst it was frozen.'

'Judging from the maps, I'll have to pass through their lands.'

'Then do it quickly.' He waved the Emperor's mandate at Vespasian. 'I'll be at the camp shortly before noon to give you the mandate officially and publicly confirm your appointment with the men, although why they need that defeats me; they should just do as they're told. No discipline, you see, no discipline.'

'The best unit for the job is the First Batavian Cavalry Ala,' Gaius Licinius Mucianus stated without even being asked his opinion. 'You obviously have to take mounted troops but these lads are more than that: their homelands are at the mouth of the Rhenus and they learn to swim almost before they can walk, and they're great boatmen. With all the rivers that you may need to cross those abilities will be essential. What's more, being Germanic they'll be able to communicate with the local tribes and have a good knowledge of the terrain.'

'Where are they based?' Vespasian asked, liking the young thick-stripe military tribune immensely for his correct assessment of the problem and pertinent suggestion so quickly after he, Vespasian, had finished briefing the senior officers of the II Augusta as to what was required of him.

'At Saletio, about thirty miles downriver, north from here.'

'Thank you, Mucianus.' Vespasian looked around the faces of the other officers sitting across the desk from him and Sabinus in the praetorium. The five junior, thin-stripe tribunes, whose names he had not yet managed to remember, were all looking supportive of the idea, but he was less interested in the opinions of the young and inexperienced than he was in those of the primus pilus, Tatius, the senior centurion of the legion, and the camp prefect, Publius Anicius Maximus. The latter two were both nodding their agreement; only Corbulo seemed less than enthusiastic. 'Whose command do they fall under?'

'Yours now,' Corbulo said, 'but I'm not sure that you will like their prefect; he's an arrogant young man of very little ability, who has none of the qualities of his father. I'm afraid that Paetus' untimely death meant that his son grew up without proper paternal guidance.'

'You mean Lucius, son of Publius Junius Caesennius Paetus?' Vespasian exclaimed, remembering his long-dead friend who had been a comrade of his and Corbulo's when they had served together in Thracia. He had been murdered ten years previously by Livilla when, as an urban quaestor, Paetus had tried to arrest her on the Senate's orders after her lover Sejanus' downfall. With his dying breath Paetus had asked Vespasian to keep an eye on Lucius; Vespasian had made the promise but he now felt very keenly just how remiss he had been in keeping it.

Sabinus shifted uneasily in his seat next to Vespasian. 'Is there no other unit available?'

Corbulo shook his head. 'There are two Gallic cavalry alae attached to the legion but they're too ... well, too Gallic. They hate all Germans on principle and would be spoiling for a fight with any that they came across; not conducive to a successful outcome to the mission. And our own legionary cavalry detachment is no match for German cavalry if it should indeed come to a fight. I'm afraid that Mucianus is right; the Batavians are the best men for the job.'

'Then we shall have them; and besides, I owe young Lucius.' Vespasian glanced sidelong at Sabinus who refused to meet his eye. 'As, indeed, does my brother,' he added quietly. 'Mucianus, send a message to Lucius Paetus immediately and tell him to be here tomorrow with six *turmae* of his Batavians; I think that one hundred and eighty men should be enough for security and not so many as to cause alarm. And tell him I want a few who have a good knowledge of the interior of Germania Magna. Maximus, have six transport ships ready to embark them at the port tomorrow afternoon. Dismiss, gentlemen.'

'You haven't paid the hundred thousand denarii that you borrowed off Paetus back to his family, have you?' Vespasian accused Sabinus as soon as they were alone. 'I told you that you should never have borrowed it.'

'Don't lecture me, brother; I borrowed it because Paetus offered and it was the only way that I could get a larger house at the time. Just because you're parsimonious doesn't mean that everybody should live the same way. Saturn's stones, you don't even own your own house.'

'Perhaps; but at least all my money is my own and I sleep better at night knowing I'm not in debt. How do you sleep?'

'In a lot more comfort than you and very well.'

'But how can you? That debt is accruing interest every month. When are you going to pay it back?'

'Soon, all right? I was going to pay it back years ago but when the Aventine burnt down taking my house with it I needed to hang onto the money to rebuild. Then I sort of forgot about it.'

'Lucius won't have.'

'Lucius probably doesn't even know that I still owe it.'

Vespasian stared disapprovingly at his brother. 'Then I shall tell him.'

'You judgemental little shit.'

'Well then, you sort it out with him when he arrives because I don't want this festering between you whilst we're wandering around Germania trying to save your profligate life.' Vespasian turned on his heel and stormed out of the praetorium.

Vespasian's back stiffened with pride as he walked out of the camp's gates with Galba to inspect the II Augusta the following afternoon. Although not at full strength owing to a few centuries being on detachment, manning smaller forts and lookout towers along the Rhenus, it was still an impressive sight: more than four thousand legionaries in neat ranks and files formed up in cohorts on the flat ground between the camp and the river. As he mounted the dais he wished that his father could see him, but he knew that they would probably never meet again. They had said their goodbyes and both had been grateful for the chance to do so; it was more than most people got.

'The Second Augusta,' Primus Pilus Tatius bellowed, 'will come to attention!'

The *bucinator* next to him brought his horn to his lips and blew three ascending notes; as the last one died every centurion simultaneously bawled an order and the entire legion came to a crashing, synchronised attention, thumping the butts of their *pila*, javelins with long iron shanks, onto the ground and slamming their bronze-fronted shields, adorned with a white Pegasus opposite a Capricorn, across their chests. Silence followed, broken only by the fluttering of standards and the cawing of crows high up in a copse of trees to Vespasian's left.

Vespasian surveyed the rows of hardened faces, crowned with burnished-iron helmets reflecting the weak sun, staring straight ahead over shields, for a few moments relishing his feeling of pride.

'Legionaries of the Second Augusta,' Galba thundered in a voice that Vespasian thought barely louder than at his interview the previous evening, 'the Emperor has seen fit to appoint Titus Flavius ...' He quickly looked at a wax tablet in his hand. '... Vespasianus as your new legate. You will obey him in all things.' With a curt nod of his head to the assembled legion he turned and re-presented the Emperor's mandate to Vespasian.

Vespasian stood on the dais and raised the mandate in salute to the men now under his command; the light wind picked at his scarlet legate's cloak and the white horsehair plume on his helmet. With a massive roar the legion hailed him as he displayed his mandate from right to left so that each man could see his symbol of authority as their rightful commander.

With a dramatic sweep he lowered his arm and the men fell silent. He took a deep breath so that his chest swelled against his muscled bronze cuirass and placed his left hand on the purple sash tied about his waist. 'Men of the Second Augusta, I am Titus Flavius Vespasianus and I am charged by the Emperor to command this legion. You will come to know me well, as I will you. I will not make long speeches praising your courage or bravery. If you deserve praise you will get it with a word or two; and if I find you lacking then you will know with a word or two.'

'You should flog them,' Galba growled, sotto voce so that only half the men present could hear.

'I will always make time to hear your grievances; bring them to me and do not take matters into your own hands. We are bound in a mutual bond of discipline and it is that bond that will ensure that we live in harmony and fight in unison; if anyone breaks that bond then that man lets down every man in the legion and he will be punished.

'However, I have no doubt that the words of praise that I will give you will far outweigh the words of reprimand. I know that as citizens of Rome and soldiers in her glorious Second Augusta you will do your duty with honour and diligence; I place my trust in you and I ask in return for your loyalty and obedience. I commend myself to you, legionaries of the Second Augusta!'

Primus Pilus Tatius swept his sword from its sheath and held it aloft. 'The Second Augusta welcomes Legate Vespasian. Hail, Vespasian!'

With a thunderous cheer that sent the crows scattering from their trees, the whole legion waved their pila in the air, following their senior centurion's lead. The cheers quickly turned into a chant of 'Vespasian'; the legionaries punched their weapons above their heads, marking the beat.

Vespasian knew better than to let the chorus continue for too long – many a legate had been removed from his command by nervous emperors jealous of any man gaining too much acclaim; spies were everywhere. Sweeping his outstretched arms across his chest, he again signalled for silence; the effect was immediate. The legion brought their pila thumping back down to the ground, rippling from the front rank to the rear, and awaited their legate's words.

Vespasian paused, wishing again that his father could see him and wondering how to best phrase the last part of what he needed to say. The crows, circling overhead, began to return to their nests now that peace had returned. 'This is a short first meeting as I will be absent for the next month or so on the Emperor's business. I will leave my senior tribune, Mucianus, in command supported by the prefect of the camp, Maximus. You will obey them as if I were in command.'

To Vespasian's left the crows that had barely settled since their last disturbance suddenly rose in a cacophony of cawing into the air. From beneath them came the thunder of massed hoofbeats. Vespasian turned to see a unit of almost two hundred cavalry galloping, in a column, four abreast, towards them. As they got closer he could make out the long beards and trousers favoured by the German tribes. At their head rode a young Roman officer. At fifty paces from the dais the officer let go of his reins and raised both arms in the air then extended them down to point left and right. He took up the reins again and began to slow his mount; the troopers behind him proceeded to fan out to either side, starting from the rearmost and only reducing speed once they had drawn almost level with their officer.

As he brought his horse to a walk, without looking behind the young officer raised his right hand and after a few steps brought it down; his troop halted immediately in two perfect lines of ninety. 'Lucius Junius Caesennius Paetus, prefect of the First Batavian Cavalry Ala, reporting on Legate Vespasian's orders.' Paetus snapped a salute and then looked around before asking innocently with a white-toothed grin: 'I haven't interrupted anything, have I?'

'He's been nothing but disrespectful and impertinent in all the dealings that I've had with him,' Corbulo informed Vespasian as they watched Paetus supervising the Batavians loading their horses up ramps and into the river transports in the pale, late afternoon sun. 'Just because his family can boast over ten Consuls he thinks that he can treat anyone how he pleases. He's even criticised my leadership and questioned my judgement; can you imagine it?'

'Really? That's disgraceful.' Vespasian, however, found himself more than able to imagine it. Although Corbulo's branch of the Dometii had had senatorial rank for a couple of hundred years, Corbulo had been the first to achieve the consulship. Vespasian could quite understand how Paetus, coming from a far older and more noble family, would see someone as stiff and formal as Corbulo as a bit of a jumped-up joke. He refrained from mentioning this.

'Well, good luck with him; I hope he never crosses my path again,' Corbulo muttered as the object of his indignation came up to them.

'Your four horses and the spares will be loaded on last, sir,' Paetus reported, 'just before we go. My chaps' mounts are used to boats so won't mind the wait.'

'Very good, prefect.'

Paetus looked quizzically at Corbulo. 'I don't seem to have a horse for you; are you planning on coming too, *ex*-legate?'

Corbulo snorted in outrage and, with a curt nod of farewell to Vespasian, turned on his heels and stormed away down the quay.

'There will be less flamboyance and more decorum whilst you're serving with me, Paetus,' Vespasian informed him as they watched Corbulo go.

'More decorum, got you, sir,' Paetus replied, giving Vespasian the distinct impression that he had not 'got' him.

Vespasian decided not to pursue the matter for the present as, despite himself, he had taken a liking to his old friend's son. With his open, amiable, round face and humorous blue eyes he was the image of his father when he and Vespasian had first met in Thracia; that, plus the guilt that Vespasian felt at not keeping his promise to take some interest in his upbringing, was enough to make him feel that he owed him some latitude in his behaviour. He could see why Corbulo, with his aristocratic reserve and prejudices, has taken a dislike to him, but he felt that he could not judge him until he had seen how he performed leading his men. Although Paetus was young to be a prefect of auxiliary cavalry it did not surprise Vespasian, as patrician families such as the Junii, with their long line of Consuls, could expect rapid promotion; his father had achieved the same rank at roughly the same age.

'How many more to go, Ansigar?' Paetus shouted at a full-bearded decurion – the Batavians served under their own officers.

'Four, sir,' was the heavily accented reply.

'It looks like your turma is going to win.' Paetus looked up the stone quay at the queues of horses waiting to board the other five ships. 'That'll be as much beer for you and your lads as you can drink when we get back to our camp.'

Ansigar grinned. 'If the Norns who spin our fate have made our life threads long enough, but they're devious bitches.'

Paetus slapped his subordinate on the shoulder. 'That's women for you.'

'No, prefect, that's goddesses for you.'

Paetus gave a loud laugh. 'Female gods! Tricky beasts; nothing worse, eh?'

'No wonder the pompous arsehole doesn't like him,' Magnus observed, walking up to Vespasian with Ziri who handed him an old and battered travelling cloak. 'He can't even bring himself to acknowledge his men let alone join in with a bit of banter.'

'I presume you're talking about Corbulo, the former Consul.'

'The one with a long nose who spouts hot air whom I've just passed in an advanced state of outrage barging people out of the way on the quay? Yeah, that's the one.'

Vespasian shook his head, sighing, and took off his military cloak, giving it to Ziri. He looked up at the sun; it was reddening as it fell towards the western horizon. 'Where's Sabinus?'

Magnus grinned. 'He's got a bull and is waiting for sunset to sacrifice it to Mithras for the success of our mission.'

Vespasian tied the travel cloak over his *lorica hamata*, the chain mail tunic issued to auxiliaries. 'Well, he'd better hurry up; I want to get going as soon as it's dark.'

'Get going where, though?'

'We need to get as far downstream as we can and then cross the farmland on the other side of the river with as few people as possible noticing us and be in those hills before it gets light.'

'Yeah, I know that, sir; what I was asking was: where are we actually going?'

'What do you mean? You said that you knew the way.'

'Did I?' Magnus paused as a look of understanding slowly dawned on his face. 'Oh! I see. You expect me to get us to the Teutoburg Forest.'

'It's the obvious place to start looking.'

'It may be the obvious place to start looking but if you want me to find it then this ain't the obvious place to start from. We were based at Noviomagus up in the north. We started by going east along the coast and then headed south through the lands of the Chauci. We got to the battle site by following a river called the Amisia.'

'Well, that's a start; we'll head northeast until we find that river. Paetus has got men with him who know the country. Once we get there, you can show us the site of Arminius' greatest victory, and we'll send a message to Thumelicus telling him that we have something of interest to him, something of his father's, then he'll come; his curiosity will force him to.'

Magnus looked dubious. 'Won't his first reaction be to suspect a trap?'

'Maybe; but that's why I'm only taking six turmae with us. A man of Thumelicus' standing will be able to muster a lot more than a hundred and eighty men; he'll have nothing to fear from us.'

'But we'll have a lot to fear from him! Fucking great, we're going to go to the site of the biggest massacre in living memory and invite a repeat performance, even if it's on a much smaller scale.'

'Well, you didn't have to come.'

'Of course I did, I always have to because I owe my life to your uncle.'

'You've paid that debt off many times over by now.'

'Perhaps,' Magnus muttered. 'Anyway, do you know where Thumelicus is?'

'No.'

'Then how are we going to get a message to him once we get there?'

Vespasian shrugged.

'You don't know, do you?'

'No,' Vespasian admitted, 'I haven't got that far yet.'

CHAPTER VII

'EASY WITH HIM, lads,' Paetus hissed as one of the Batavians' horses started to shy whilst being led up the ramp from the boat's open hold.

Vespasian's fingers twitched behind his back as he watched two auxiliaries fighting to control the beast, pulling down on its halter, whilst stroking its muzzle and talking soothingly to it in their strange, unmelodic language. The words seemed to calm the animal and it eventually allowed itself to be led up the ramp and then down another, over the side of the vessel and into the shallow water just a few paces from the eastern bank.

Vespasian shivered and pulled the travel cloak tighter around his shoulders. Upriver to him the five other transports were hove to, as close as their shallow hulls could get up the river's bank. In the thin light of a quarter-moon the silhouettes of horses and men could be seen disembarking. Each whinny, muffled shout or splash caused Vespasian to tense and peer east into the gloom; but there was nothing to see.

Once Sabinus had rejoined them, having made his sacrifice, they had sailed downriver for six hours until they had found a stretch of bank devoid of any glimmers of light from farmstead windows; but that did not mean that there were no dwellings nearby. Vespasian was anxious to get his small force ashore without it coming to the attention of the local population; he did not want news of their arrival to precede them on their journey. Although the tribes along the river lived and traded in peace with the Empire, the more inland ones were not beyond butchering even the best-guarded Roman merchants' trains.

'I've sent Ansigar and eight of the lads out to scout around whilst we finish disembarking, sir,' Paetus informed him as another horse plunged up to its chest into the river with a worry-ingly loud snort.

'Good. Can't this be done any quieter?'

'This is quiet; all our mounts have done this before. You'll realise just how noisy it can be in a moment when we try and get your four horses and the spares out; they won't like it.'

Vespasian grimaced. 'Do it as quickly as you can, then; I'm going ashore.'

'Probably best, sir. It won't sound nearly so loud there, you'll be able to relax more.'

Vespasian glared at Paetus but his back was already turned, his attention refocused on the disembarkation.

'Coming round to Corbulo's point of view, eh, sir?' Magnus asked lightly, heaving his kit bag onto Ziri's shoulder.

'Bring mine ashore too, Ziri,' Vespasian snapped a little more tersely than he meant to. Annoyed with himself, he walked up the ramp.

He emerged cold and wet from the river to find Sabinus already on the bank rubbing his thighs vigorously with a cloth. All around the auxiliaries were busy saddling their horses; most were now on land.

'Did you talk to Paetus?' Vespasian demanded; his mood had not been improved by the dunking.

'I did as a matter of fact and very accommodating he was too.' Sabinus handed Vespasian his damp cloth.

'What do you mean?'

'I mean that he was very grateful that I brought the subject up; he didn't know about the debt at all and as a mark of his gratitude has waived all interest apart from the first two years and has told me to repay it as soon as I'm able; assuming that I survive this expedition, of course.'

Vespasian rubbed his arms irritably with the cloth. 'He's let you off thousands; I can't believe it.'

'I knew that you'd share my relief, brother. I'm coming to the conclusion that he's a very generous and decent young man, just as his father was, and what's more he comes from a powerful family and will surely be consul one day – if we don't get him killed first. Just the sort of man I'd find useful as a son-in-law; after all, my Flavia's eleven and I'll be looking for a husband for her in a year or two.'

'You'd marry your daughter to him so you could take advantage of his money?'

'That's what daughters are for, isn't it?'

A pounding of hooves on wood and a shrill equine screech prevented Vespasian from expressing his opinion; he turned to see a horse rearing up at the top of the ramp. It brought its front hooves crashing down with an echoing report and then kicked out with its hind legs, catching an auxiliary's outstretched forearm, snapping it back like a twig so that a jagged shard of bone tore through the flesh. The man screamed as he clutched his shattered limb, adding to the horse's terror; it jumped forward half landing on the descending ramp, buckling a foreleg beneath it at an impossible angle and then rolled, with its three intact legs thrashing, shrieking into the river with a mighty splash.

'Silence that man,' Paetus called over the injured Batavian's agonised groans, 'and get a javelin into that horse and put it out of its misery.'

In the river the horse continued to struggle and bellow as half a dozen auxiliaries lined the side of the boat hefting javelins. After a moment's pause to pick out the stricken beast's shape amidst the turbulence it was creating, they flung their weapons. Another long screech testified to the accuracy of some of the throws; it was cut short by a gurgling and a rasping wheeze as the animal fought, unsuccessfully, to keep its head above the surface. It sank with an explosion of bubbles on the churned, moonlit water.

'Thank the gods for that,' Vespasian muttered as relative peace returned.

'Perhaps I should have also sacrificed to the lares of this river,' Sabinus said, 'then they might not have felt compelled to take one of our horses.'

Vespasian turned and looked at his brother; there was no irony in his expression. 'I thought you worshipped only Mithras.'

Sabinus shrugged. 'We're a long way from my Lord's birth-place; perhaps some help might …' An agonised scream, not far inland, cut him short, and then another, the same voice but higher pitched. Finally a third that turned into a wail, lowering in tone that was then abruptly cut off. Someone, not far off, had just died in great pain.

All work on the shore and the six boats had ceased as the auxil-iaries stared into the darkness, chilled by the sound whose memory seemed to echo still, uncannily, around them. Distant hoofbeats, galloping fast towards them, broke the silence.

Vespasian glanced around; most of the troopers were still in the process of readying their mounts, very few were fully armed and mounted. 'Form up on me in two ranks on foot!' Vespasian bellowed, drawing his sword.

The shouted command galvanised the auxiliaries into action; they unslung their oval shields from their backs and grabbed spears or swept their *spathae*, cavalry swords longer than an infantry gladius, from their scabbards as they ran to obey. Their comrades still aboard the boats followed Paetus' lead, jumping into the river and wading ashore as the hoofbeats pounded closer, out of the night.

Vespasian felt Magnus' shoulder to his right as Sabinus took up position on his left, interlocking their shields. He glanced right, past Magnus, down the line to see a wall of shields solidly formed up with Paetus at the centre and a second rank behind; some stragglers were still running up but otherwise the manoeuvre had been completed in less than a hundred heart-beats.

'These Batavians know their business,' Magnus muttered, 'for cavalry, that is.'

'Paetus! Paetus! Batavian!' bawled a voice over the incoming hoofbeats. Their pace suddenly lessened as the shadowy figures of horsemen materialised out of the gloom; Vespasian counted eight of them.

The riders swerved around the shield wall with Ansigar in the lead. Along the line some auxiliaries began to relax their guard only to be bawled at by their decurions to raise their shields again. Ansigar pulled his horse up and dismounted. Paetus left his position and walked towards him; Vespasian and Sabinus joined them.

'Well, decurion?' Paetus asked.

'I'm not sure, prefect,' Ansigar replied, taking off his helmet and wiping his arm across his forehead. 'One of my lads, Rothaid, suddenly wasn't there any more; none of the boys noticed him go, he just disappeared. Then we heard the screams; they sounded to be about half a mile from where we were but they were over so quickly and we couldn't locate them so we hurried back.'

'Was it Rothaid, though?'

'Screaming? Yes, we're certain of it; but we saw nothing out there.'

'Thank you, decurion; stand the men down and set some sentries whilst you get the rest of the horses on land.'

Ansigar saluted and led his patrol away, barking orders to resume the disembarkation.

Paetus turned to the brothers. 'I'd like to think that we've just been unlucky and run into some bandits or suchlike, but there's something not right about this.'

'I agree,' Sabinus said. 'Why would bandits draw attention to themselves by taking one man from a patrol?'

'It's not so much that,' Vespasian put in, 'it's why would they kill him in such a public way? They wanted us to hear him.'

'Sending us a warning, you mean? But who knows that we're here to warn us off?'

'Precisely; we didn't even know where we were going to land, so that rules out the idea of a traitor. So we must assume that we were either tracked down the river by people who aren't as friendly to Rome as we would hope or—'

'Or we have indeed been unlucky,' Paetus cut in. 'Either way, they didn't challenge us whilst we were landing so we can assume that there aren't enough of them to worry us.'

'Yet,' Vespasian reminded them, letting the word hang.

*

The first pale glow of dawn was touching the sky ahead of them as the column began to climb, leading their horses, up into the wooded hills beyond the flood plain. There had been no more disturbances during the disembarkation, nor had there been any sign of the men who had killed Rothaid as they crossed the plain; his body, however, had been found with his eyes gouged out and his throat cut. What had interested Vespasian about the find was that Rothaid still held a sword in his right hand but, judging by its pristine condition, had made no attempt to defend himself whilst being so terribly mutilated. Having ordered complete silence during the ride he felt unable to break his own command by asking for an explanation.

They climbed higher as the sun rose and soon there was enough light to ride without risk of their mounts stumbling and they were able to put a good few miles between themselves and the river. Paetus had chosen a couple of the auxiliaries who claimed to know the way to the Amisia to lead them, and once they had threaded their way through the range and then down into the undulating forest beyond they steered the column just east of north at the beginning of what they assured their superiors would be a six- to seven-day journey.

The forest was thickly wooded with mainly pines and firs; the undergrowth, however, was surprisingly light. They were able to walk their horses with ease and occasionally break into a trot, something that would have been impossible, Ansigar had informed them, if they had been in the main body of the forest that stretched over two hundred miles to the south of them. As it was they had entered it at its northern tip where the trees, being more spaced out, allowed easier passage and let more light through the canopy, giving the lie to the forest's name, which Ansigar said in his own tongue before explaining that the word meant 'black'.

They pushed on throughout the daylight hours even though they had had no sleep the previous night. Travelling in the dark would have been impossible in these conditions and so Vespasian had decided to press on and camp at nightfall. As they journeyed further into the forest the air grew heavier and the canopy denser, creating a sense of thickening gloom. Vespasian's breathing became laborious and he found himself constantly looking over his shoulder, peering into the massed shadowy ranks of tree-trunks, or up into the weave of boughs that seemed to press down on them with menacing intent. Judging by the muttering and the nervous looks of the Batavians he was not the only one to feel an ever-increasing threat enclosing them from all sides.

'If it's like this at the edge of the forest,' Magnus grumbled, sharing Vespasian's unease, 'I wouldn't like to go into the heart of it; the German gods must be very powerful there.'

'Yes, I'm getting the impression that they're not keen on Romans.'

'I'm getting the impression that they're not keen on anyone.'

Throughout the day Paetus sent out patrols in all directions but they reported back after an hour or two having seen nothing more threatening than a couple of very large wild horses, some deer and a few wild boars, two of which had not been fast enough to evade the spears of the Batavians.

As the sun fell, they stopped and made camp, setting a turma on guard in pairs around the perimeter. With the forest disappearing in an all-encompassing dark, the visual menace lessened to be replaced by eerie night-sounds: owls' hoots, strange animal cries and wind working on groaning trees.

The boars were gutted and roasted on a spit over a couple of fire-pits and provided enough hot flesh for a few mouthfuls each to supplement their army rations. It warmed them but it did not cheer them and conversation was very muted.

The five remaining turmae drew lots for their sentry duty during the night; the lucky ones getting the first or the last slot whilst the rest rolled up in their blankets grumbling, knowing that they would get a broken night's sleep, if sleep would be at all possible with the sense of foreboding weighing down their spirits.

As dawn was breaking, Magnus nudged Vespasian's shoulder. 'Here you go, sir, get that down you.' He offered him a cup of steaming hot watered-wine and a hunk of bread.

Vespasian sat up stiffly, his back aching from a night on the knobbly forest floor, and took his breakfast. 'Thanks, Magnus.'

'Don't thank me, I don't have to get up early to build up the fire and heat the wine. That's Ziri's job and as a slave he don't deserve thanking.'

'Well, thank him anyway.' Vespasian dunked his bread into the cup.

'If I start doing that then the next thing he'll want is paying,' Magnus muttered as he woke Sabinus. All through the camp men were rousing, stretching their stiff bodies and talking quietly in their native tongue as they prepared their breakfasts.

'Good morning, gentlemen,' Paetus said, striding over, looking decidedly cheerful; behind him the last turma on sentry duty was coming in and forming up to be counted off. 'I've just had a word with the two chaps leading us; they reckon that we'll leave the forest around midday and get into more open country.'

'What does that mean?' Sabinus asked, sipping his wine. 'A tree every ten paces instead of every five?'

Paetus laughed. 'That's about the size of it, Sabinus, but different sorts of trees and hardly any undergrowth, so we should be able to go a lot faster and we won't have the feeling of being stalked by hideous Germanic forest spirits. We'll just have to be a little more wary, as the land we'll be going through is far more settled and the locals are not too keen on Rome.'

'What savage is?'

'Prefect!' the decurion of the returning turma shouted.

'What is it, Kuno?'

'We're two men short, sir.'

Paetus frowned. 'Are you sure?' he asked in a manner that questioned Kuno's arithmetical skills.

'Batavians can count, sir.'

Vespasian looked at Sabinus in alarm. 'That doesn't sound good.'

Sabinus started strapping on his sandals. 'We'd better go and look for them.'

*

Kuno led the way with eight of his turma to where the missing men had been posted; there was no sign of them, just a tangle of footprints in the earth where they and previous sentries had been pacing around.

'There's no indication of a struggle,' Vespasian observed, looking at the ground, 'no blood, nothing discarded.'

'Decurion, have your men spread out and search,' Paetus ordered. 'But they're to keep in sight, understood?'

'Yes, sir.'

'Do you think they could've deserted, Paetus?' Sabinus asked as the Batavians started to fan out.

'Unlikely so far from home and especially not here.'

'What's so special about here?'

'The guides tell me that very soon we'll come to a river called the Moenus; they know a ford and once we cross it we enter the homeland of a tribe called the Chatti. They and the Batavians are enemies. They used to be a part of the same people but fell out a couple of hundred years ago, I've no idea what about because no one seems to remember; anyway it's still very serious. The Batavians went north and the Chatti settled here but there is still a blood-feud between them. They'd be mad to go wandering around so close to Chatti land by themselves.'

'Prefect! Look at this,' Kuno shouted, walking towards them whilst brandishing an auxiliary helmet.

Paetus took the helmet, gave it a quick glance and then showed it to the brothers; blood and some matted hair clung to the rim. 'I doubt very much whether we'll be seeing them again.'

News of the sentries' disappearance and probable murder spread throughout the column as it formed up not long after and it was with an increased air of trepidation that they moved out of the camp, keeping just east of north, down a gentle slope.

'So do you think that it could be the Chatti carrying on their blood-feud with the Batavians?' Magnus asked after the brothers had filled him in on the history between the two tribes.

Sabinus shook his head. 'Unlikely. The Chatti's lands start after the Moenus; they don't live near the Rhenus so what would they have been doing there in the first place?'

'Galba told me that he had repulsed a war band raiding across the river earlier this year,' Vespasian informed them, 'so they do stray this far west.'

Sabinus shrugged. 'Well, even if they do, how would they have known that six boatloads of Batavians were going to be landing where we did?'

'Fair point,' Magnus acknowledged, 'but someone did and that someone is following us. I've a nasty suspicion that those sentries ain't going to be the last men to go missing on this trip.'

'I'm afraid that you might be right, Magnus.' Sabinus turned his head and peered into the shadow-ridden forest. 'Even my Lord Mithras' light has trouble piercing that gloom; without his constant protection whoever is trailing us will have a far easier time of it.' He suddenly loosened his sword in its scabbard. A couple of Batavian outriders came into view, flitting through the trees; he let go of the hilt. 'But what's their objective? Are they trying to scare us off?'

'Scare us off from what?' Vespasian questioned. 'How would they know where we're going? I keep on thinking about how they found us when we landed at random in the middle of the night on the eastern side of the river.'

'Yeah well, I think that I can answer that,' Magnus replied. 'They couldn't have been waiting because they wouldn't have known where to wait, so they must have followed us. Now, they couldn't have started on the eastern bank because they wouldn't have seen us come out of the harbour at night; so they had to be either in the port, in which case we would have noticed them, or already on the river slightly upstream, that way they could have tagged along behind us without our seeing.'

Vespasian digested this for a few moments and then nodded as the column broke into a trot. 'Yes, I think you're right. In which case whoever it is knew that we would be sailing from Argentoratum but nobody there knew that until the day before.

More to the point, nobody knew that we would be leaving almost as soon as we arrived.'

'Unless they were told before we arrived.'

'But who else here knew what we were planning to do?'

'No one here, but I can think of three people back in Rome who knew.'

'Claudius' freedmen?'

Magnus nodded.

'But they've got a vested interest in our success. They wouldn't want to jeopardise the mission; it was their idea.'

'Then you tell me who else knows that we're here apart from your family?'

'Just Galba,' Vespasian admitted, flummoxed, 'but I didn't tell him exactly where we were going. And why would he want to help the Chatti? He hates them. Mind you, he hates everyone who can't trace their family back to the founding of the Republic.'

'Halt!' Paetus called from just in front of them.

'What is it?' Vespasian asked, following Paetus' gaze.

Up ahead the trees thinned considerably, letting far more light in through the canopy in thick, golden shafts, dazzling them after so long in the relative gloom.

Paetus pointed in front of them to a couple of saplings no more than six feet tall, directly in their path, twenty paces away. Vespasian squinted; as his eyes got used to the bright light he realised that each tree bore one horrific, round fruit.

'Cut them down,' Paetus ordered the two guides next to him.

The two Batavians edged their horses forward nervously, towards the severed heads suspended within the branches of the small trees. As they approached, one of the horses caught a front hoof on an obstruction hidden beneath the leaf mulch. There was a loud crack, followed by the creaking of swaying rope; two dark shadows swung down from above, flicking through the streaks of sunlight, directly at the troopers. Their mounts shied, whinnying shrilly, hurling them backwards, as the right-hand shape thumped into one horse; the other narrowly missed the second horse, to continue its arc towards the head of the column.

It brushed the forest floor, scattering dead leaves, and then swung upwards, oozing liquid as it did, until its momentum was lost; it hung for a moment in midair and Vespasian looked up at the headless corpse of one of the sentries as he fought to control his spooked mount. Droplets of noisome fluid splashed down from the gaping neck, further unsettling the mounts below, as the body arced back down towards the two riderless horses; they could take no more and bolted.

'This is starting to piss me off,' Magnus complained; behind him the column was in disarray as panic swept through the animals.

Vespasian leapt from his horse, narrowly avoiding the stamping back hooves of Paetus' mount, and ran towards the line of the body's swing as it came creaking back at him. He braced himself on his left leg and stuck out his right so that the sole of his sandal met the corpse's chest as it swung through the perpendicular, forcing his knee to bend on impact and throwing him onto his back. He landed with a jolt and immediately raised his head to see the corpse dangling, rotating slightly, next to the second suspended body; both had their arms bound across their chests and a dagger was secured with a length of twine in each right hand. Before he had time to ponder the weird sight, screams of pain and screeching of wounded horses rose above the shouting and whinnying; he looked back to see arrows spitting out of the trees and into the column. A few men and horses fell to be trampled where they lay writhing as the salvo carried on for no more than ten heartbeats before stopping as abruptly as it had started.

Looking to the direction whence the arrows came, Vespasian caught a glimpse of some shadowy figures fleeing on foot. 'Paetus, we could catch them,' he shouted, jumping to his feet and looking for his horse; it was nowhere to be seen.

'With me!' Paetus bellowed above the din to the steadiest troopers nearest him. He kicked his horse forward; it responded immediately, pleased to be driven from the scene of terror. A dozen Batavians followed their prefect into the shadows; they were soon out of sight.

Vespasian went to grab Sabinus' mount's bridle and helped to calm the beast as Magnus and Ziri both dismounted, gently rubbing their horses' flanks as they began to settle down. Gradually a semblance of calm spread throughout the turmae with just the moans of the wounded and the snorting of unsteady, skittish horses to disturb the air.

Ansigar appeared through the disarray of the column. 'We've lost three dead and five wounded, one badly, and four horses, sir,' he reported. 'Where's the prefect?'

'Chasing our attackers,' Vespasian answered. 'Here, let me show you something.' He led the decurion to the dangling corpses; the two unseated guides were getting painfully to their feet and staring at the macabre sight. 'What do you make of that?' he asked, pointing at the daggers in the corpses' right hands. 'Your man, Rothaid, was found clutching his sword, un-blooded, as if it had been placed there.'

Ansigar smiled without humour, smoothing his long, well-combed beard. 'That's because it *was* placed there.'

'What does it mean?'

'It means that we are fighting honourable men.'

'You call sneaking up on people and murdering them honourable?'

'These men don't condemn their victims to wander the earth as shapeless forms after their death. By placing a weapon in their hands when they die, they guarantee that the All-Father Wotan's shield maidens will find them and take them to Walhalla to feast and fight until the final battle.'

'So it's just a religious thing, then, and has no significance for us to worry about?'

'It has a great significance: it means that whoever is preying upon us is definitely Germanic, but their argument is not with us Batavians. If it was they wouldn't worry about the niceties of caring about our afterlife. Their argument must be with what we represent: Rome.'

Warning shouts came from the forest and Paetus soon appeared leading his men back in.

'Did you get them?' Vespasian asked the prefect as he swung off his horse.

'One of them.'

Behind him the troopers dismounted; they heaved a dead body off the rump of one of the horses and flung it face up on the ground. He was in his mid-twenties; his blond hair was tied in a top knot and the obligatory beard was streaked with blood. He wore only plain brown woollen trousers and leather boots, leaving his swirling-tattooed chest bare and slick with the blood seeping from a spear-thrust to his heart. There was a thick silver arm ring just above his right elbow.

'How many were there?'

'About twenty.' Paetus looked down at the body, shaking his head. 'He turned to fight us to allow the others time to get away, it was suicidal. By the time we killed him the rest had disappeared into the forest as if it just swallowed them up.'

Ansigar knelt down and lifted the flowing beard; under it, around the man's neck, was a metal band almost a hand's breadth wide. He spat in disgust. 'There's only one tribe that wears an iron collar; this man's Chatti.'

CHAPTER VIII

F OR THREE DAYS the column moved on as fast as it could, crossing into the lands of the Chatti, and for three nights their ethereal hunters preyed upon them, taking men seemingly at will during the hours of darkness without ever revealing themselves. Indeed, there had been no sign of them since the ambush, but their brooding presence was confirmed every morning by the slowly dwindling number of auxiliaries at muster and the grisly finds of decapitated bodies in their path later in the day. On the second night, in an attempt to stem the flow of silent death, Paetus had ordered a doubling of the guard so that the sentries patrolled in fours, but to no avail: four men died that night. On the third night he had set no sentries around the perimeter of the camp, keeping them instead patrolling amongst their sleeping comrades; a man had still somehow disappeared.

'Every day they manage to leave the bodies three or four miles along our route,' Vespasian observed as they stood surveying the latest headless auxiliary nailed to the thick trunk of an oak. 'They must know where we're headed for.'

'And that's something that only Pallas, Narcissus and Callistus knew,' Magnus pointed out, swatting away one of the many flies that had been attracted by the stench of death.

Sabinus frowned, mystified. 'It just makes no sense. Why would Narcissus spare me for a task that he's going to try and sabotage?'

'It don't have to be him, it could be either Pallas or Callistus,' Magnus suggested.

'Have him cut down and buried,' Paetus ordered Ansigar as he remounted.

129

Ansigar barked a couple of orders in his harsh tongue and a group of frightened-looking auxiliaries came forward and began their unpleasant task, muttering sullenly amongst themselves.

'The men won't stand for much more of this, Paetus,' Vespasian said, swinging himself up onto his horse next to the prefect. 'How much longer are we going to be in the Chatti's lands?'

'Another day according to the guides. We need to cross the Adrana River and then it's comparatively flat and mostly culti-vated terrain to the Amisia in the Cherusci's lands. So hopefully we'll be able to pick up a bit of speed.'

'And be more exposed.'

Paetus shrugged. 'So will whoever's tracking us.'

Vespasian thought of how their tormentors had managed to stay so elusive in the past days. 'I very much doubt it, Paetus.'

As the sun reached its zenith they finally broke out of the forest onto undulating pasture; there were a few mean dwellings scat-tered around in the middle distance, with pasture fields surrounding them in which cows grazed. After the endless trees of the forest it seemed like a wonderfully spacious, sunlit paradise where one could breathe easily and not have to be constantly peering into the shadows looking for an unseen enemy.

'The Adrana is less than a quarter of an hour's ride north of here, prefect,' one of the guides informed Paetus, pointing to a long hill a mile ahead of them. 'We should be able to see it from the top of that. However, we can't ford this river; we'll have to swim across.'

'I'm well overdue a bath,' Paetus replied cheerily. 'Ansigar, send a four-man patrol ahead of us to find out whether our mysterious friends are holding the river against us.'

As the patrol galloped away, Paetus led the rest of the column off at a canter. Vespasian kicked his horse forward, feeling invig-orated by the space; his fear of being too exposed to unfriendly eyes was for the moment overtaken by the relief at finally being able to travel at some speed. 'I'm looking forward to washing the smell of the forest off my skin.'

Magnus did not look so sure. 'Nothing good ever came out of swimming a river, especially wearing these.' He rubbed his chain mail tunic. 'They ain't designed for buoyancy.'

'Take it off and strap it to your horse, it'll be able to support it.'

Magnus grunted and turned to Ziri who was riding next to him. 'How's your swimming, Ziri?'

'I don't know, master, I've never tried.'

'Fucking great! This is not going to be the time to learn.'

The column pounded over the grassland, climbing steadily until they reached the top of the hill. Paetus reined in his horse; Vespasian slowed next to him and shaded his eyes against the glare. Below them, a couple of miles away, a river meandered through verdant countryside irregularly divided up into fields. Its banks were mainly lined with a thick layer of trees but here and there they were open, revealing a slow-running, sediment-tainted body of water. The four-man patrol was already a third of the way to it. Beyond it were fields and copses for as far as the eye could see; a fat land brimming with agriculture.

'That doesn't look to be more than thirty to forty paces across,' Paetus said confidently. 'That won't delay us for too long.' He raised his arm in the air and turned in the saddle to order his men on; his face fell. 'Shit!'

Vespasian spun round to see a dark shadow emerging from the forest; horsemen, scores of them, at least a hundred, he estimated.

'This is not going to be fun,' Paetus muttered almost to himself before throwing his arm forward and urging his horse as fast as possible into a gallop. The column followed immediately.

One mile behind them so did the Chatti.

Vespasian leant forward in the saddle pushing his horse on downhill, his cloak flapping noisily behind him as all around him the Batavians kicked their mounts into greater speed, yelling over the thunder of hoofbeats. Very quickly they covered half the distance, gaining on the patrol ahead; Vespasian looked over his shoulder to see the first of the Chatti breasting the hill and, with a quick mental calculation, he accepted the inevitable and shouted at Paetus: 'They'll pick us off whilst we're in the river.

We need to turn and face them; we must outnumber them by at least fifty.'

'My lads are fast swimmers, sir,' Paetus yelled back over the deep rumble of the gallop. 'We'll lose fewer in the river than we would in a fight; it's our best chance to make it home again.'

Vespasian could see the logic: the more men they lost now the more vulnerable they would be when and if they got to the Teutoburg Forest. He looked up towards the river, it was just over half a mile away; the patrol was just arriving. He glanced back; the Chatti were not gaining on them, perhaps there was still a chance. As he steeled himself with this faint new hope, one of the patrol's horses stumbled, falling to the ground and trapping its rider beneath it. Within an instant two more riders were punched from their saddles; the fourth turned his horse and began to bolt back up the hill. Behind him, on the far bank, there was movement; within moments the river was lined with a hundred and more warriors.

They were trapped.

'Halt!' Paetus screamed, raising an arm into the air, 'And about face.' Most of the Batavians had seen the new threat to the north of the river and did not need to be told twice; with prodigious skill they pulled up their frothing, wild-eyed mounts and turned, forming up two deep in their turmae. As they did, the Chatti slowed, coming to a trot, and formed an arrowheaded wedge, advancing steadily; one man was to their front with the rest of the warriors echeloned back at an angle on both sides.

Paetus took one look at the enemy formation and turned to Ansigar next to him. 'The two outer turmae form up in column to our rear, we'll release javelins then do a split before contact.'

The decurion nodded and barked a couple of orders that were echoed by his five other colleagues. The turmae on the extreme left and right retreated behind the central four in a precise, brisk manoeuvre and formed into columns, two abreast.

'Batavians! Prepare to advance!' Paetus called, his voice rising an octave on the last word.

Throughout the turmae the troopers grabbed javelins from the leather carry-cases attached to their saddles and slipped their forefingers through the thongs knotted around the centre of the shaft. Their horses stamped and snorted, heads tossing, their powerful chests expanding and contracting as they breathed deeply.

'We're going to try a rather tricky manoeuvre,' Paetus informed the brothers, 'it would be best if you and your two chaps get behind Ansigar and me and follow our lead.'

Sabinus bristled, not liking being told to fight in the rear rank, but Vespasian reached out and put a hand on his shoulder. 'I've seen how he manoeuvres his cavalry; I think it's probably best to do as he suggests.'

'I ain't ever fought mounted before,' Magnus grumbled as they took their places behind Ansigar's turma in the centre of the line, 'it ain't natural.'

'What about in Cyrenaica, against Ziri's people?' Vespasian asked, adjusting the arm strap on his shield.

'I just tagged along behind you in the charge and then got to my feet as soon as possible.'

'Then do the same this time; you and Ziri cover mine and Sabinus' backs.'

'I will; and I'll also keep an eye on you, making sure you don't get too carried away, if you take my meaning?'

Vespasian grunted but knew his friend was right: he had often endangered himself in the past by losing control and fighting in a frenzy, heedless to what was going on around him. He would not allow himself to do that today.

A quarter of a mile in front of them the Chatti leader raised his right arm in the air; the hand was missing. The Chatti halted but their leader walked his horse on until he was just fifty paces away; he paused and stroked his blond beard that bushed out from between his cheek-guards whilst he surveyed the Batavians.

The Batavians watched him in silence.

Vespasian looked over his shoulder; the warriors remained on the far bank. He called to Paetus: 'We'll hear what he has to say, prefect.'

'Romans and Batavians in the pay of Rome,' the Chatti leader shouted in surprisingly good Latin. 'You outnumber us but we have the advantage of charging downhill. Perhaps you could kill us all but not before you'd lose so many of your number that the survivors wouldn't stand a chance of getting back to the Empire alive.' He took off his helmet and wiped the sweat from his bald head with the stump of his right arm.

Vespasian had a jolt of recognition and turned to Sabinus but the man carried on before he could say anything.

'I offer you this, Batavians: hand over your Roman officers and your weapons and we will escort you back to the Rhenus; you will then be free to go.'

Ansigar spat. 'Surrender our swords to Chatti! And so few of them? Never!'

All along the Batavian line there was much spitting and growling in agreement.

Ansigar turned to Vespasian. 'The Chatti fight mainly on foot, these aren't cavalry, they're just mounted infantry; they're no match for us.'

Vespasian nodded. 'Thank you, decurion. I think we've heard enough, prefect, let's get this over with.'

'I couldn't agree more, sir.' Paetus waved a hand dismissively at the Chatti leader. 'Get back to your men, the parley is over.'

'So be it.' He replaced his helmet and rode quickly back to the wedge of cavalry. A rider met him and gave him a shield that he slipped on his maimed right arm and then drew his sword with his left.

'Decurions, watch for my signal to release, then split,' Paetus shouted. 'Batavians, at a trot, advance!'

With a jingling of harnesses and a stamping of hooves the six turmae moved forward. From up the hill came a roar and the Chatti began to descend towards them.

'Canter!' Paetus yelled when the two forces were four hundred paces apart.

The effect was instantaneous and Vespasian found himself lagging behind as he failed to respond to the order with the alacrity of Paetus' well-trained men.

With the hill in their favour, the Chatti were now hell-for-leather, keeping roughly to their wedge shape, screaming their war cries through spittle-flecked beards whilst brandishing spears or javelins or swords over their heads.

'Batavians, charge!' Paetus screamed at two hundred paces and the troopers surged forward; a wall of horseflesh, shields and chain mail.

Vespasian felt the thrill of the charge as he let his horse extend itself into a full gallop; his mouth had dried and blood pumped fiercely around his body, heightening his senses, as the pounding of hundreds of hooves and the cries of man and beast filled his ears. Two ranks ahead of him, Paetus raised his sword over his head, his red horsehair plume streaming from his burnished iron helmet, as the gap narrowed inexorably with terrifying speed. The four front rank decurions followed their prefect's lead and raised their weapons; their men pulled their right arms back, keeping a firm grip on their javelins. At fifty paces to impact Paetus' sword flashed down, immediately followed by those of his subordinates. As the Chatti released their throwing weapons one hundred and twenty javelins hurtled into the air towards the oncoming wedge. The two sets of missiles flashed by each other in midair as, without a shouted command, Ansigar's turma veered to the right at forty-five degrees taking the turma outside it with it, sweeping their swords from their scabbards as they went. Vespasian pulled his horse to follow; the two turmae to his left swerved away in the opposite direction splitting the formation down the middle.

The first of the missile-hail landed amongst the Batavians, felling two troopers in front of him in a screaming flurry of animal and human limbs; unbidden by him, Vespasian's mount leapt the thrashing obstacle as the screeches of the wounded cut through the thunder of the charge. Landing with a spine-jarring jolt, Vespasian looked up; the one-handed man at the apex of the arrowhead was now level with him but had no one to face as he ploughed through the thirty-foot gap. Although now disorganised by felled horses within it, the momentum of the warriors behind him drove the wedge forward as Ansigar's turma sped on at their angle directly at the rear third of the Chatti formation. In the time it took Vespasian to blink the dust from his eyes the two sides' mounts shied as they closed, unwilling to charge home into fellow beasts; however, the momentum carried them on to a shattering impact of metal upon metal, beast upon screeching beast in a maelstrom of terror, battle-joy and blood-lust. The shock of impact, mirrored on the far side of the wedge, split it in two; as the back third was brought to a bone-breaking halt the rest flew through the gap. Vespasian chanced a quick look round, worried that they might turn and fall on the Batavians' rear. His concern was groundless; the troopers in the rear two turmae had turned at ninety degrees from a column into two lines and had charged; Vespasian turned back to the melee before him as they simultaneously hit either flank of the wedge's severed head.

The troopers in front of him lost cohesion as the two formations melded into a chaotic hand-to-hand struggle; iron clashed on iron, shields resounded to mighty blows, horses screeched, men screamed and gobbets of blood slopped through the air. A flashing blur of motion to his left caused Vespasian to raise his shield above his head; he blocked the downward swipe of a razor-sharp sword, jolting it to a halt, embedded in his shield boss. His left arm juddered at the impact but he forced it up as he twisted his torso round to bring his sword punching into the exposed, naked chest of his adversary. The man's eyes, already wide with the thrill of carnage, bulged in agony and he shrieked a blood-misted cry as Vespasian twisted his blade, grinding ribs and forcing it further through the lung to jolt to a halt on the spinal column, pushing the dying man back. With a monumental effort and gripping his mount fiercely with his thighs, Vespasian ripped his sword clear, to avoid being dragged to the ground, as the dead man's horse sank its bared teeth into the rump of his own; it reared up in pain, thrashing its forelegs. Vespasian lurched forward, pushing his head into the beast's mane and wrapping his shield arm around its neck to steady himself. Behind him, Magnus thrust the point of his sword into the eye of his mount's tormentor and on into its brain.

'It ain't fucking natural!' Magnus bellowed as horse blood sprayed up his arm. His victim dropped its head, unbalancing

Magnus, then all four legs buckled simultaneously; it collapsed, hauling Magnus with it.

Vespasian's mount, released from the searing pain of ripping flesh, crashed back down, cracking a hoof on the mucus-streaming nose of a Chatti horse as it did so; Vespasian managed to cling onto its neck as it regained its balance. Out of the corner of his eye, to his right, he saw a mounted warrior had pushed Sabinus, next to him, back and was hammering blows down on his shield. He exploded up, flinging his right arm round to swipe the honed edge of his sword across the shoulder blades of his brother's opponent. The man arched back as the blade tore sinew and split bone and Vespasian turned quickly back to his left, leaving Sabinus to fend for himself, just in time to see Magnus get to his feet, unarmed, in the path of a warrior forcing his spear, underarm, towards him. Vespasian punched his shield out, deflecting the thrust; Magnus reached forward grabbing the shaft and yanked it brutally, hauling the man out of his saddle.

'Come down here, you hairy cunt!' Magnus roared as the warrior toppled towards him. He ripped the spear free and slammed it down onto the back of the unhorsed man's head as he hit the ground; he did not get up. Ziri jumped from his horse to stand at his master's side, deflecting a slashing downward stroke with his shield from the left. Magnus spun the spear and jabbed forward into the chest of an oncoming horse as Vespasian flicked his concentration back ahead of him.

Paetus' red plume could be seen deep in the chaos with Batavians to either side; their swords, streaked with crimson, flashed around him as they carved their way forward through the tangle of Chatti now so compact that all they could do was fight where their horses stood. An instant later a mighty crash ripped through the screams and clash of weapons: the two outermost turmae had rounded the wedge's flanks and charged its unprotected rear. The Batavians, sensing victory, roared in triumph and worked their blades harder, pressing forward onto an enemy that had no place to go but down. And down they went beneath the hissing edges of the auxiliaries' swords, pushed from all sides, as the remnants of the wedge's severed head were forced back by the two rear turmae. The Chatti were penned in.

Vespasian's heart pounded as he felt a surge of joy well up inside him and knew he had to control himself. He desired nothing more than to kill; and kill he did but not in a mad frenzy but with measured determination. For how long the killing lasted, he did not know; it felt like an age as time was slowed by his heightened senses but in reality it was no more than the length of a chariot race, seven rounds of the track.

And then suddenly it was over.

The brutal cacophony of combat had given way to a dissonant mixture of pitiful cries and whimpers of wounded men and beasts; the Batavians found themselves without opponents. Not all had died, however; more than a score of the warriors from the tip of the wedge had broken out and were now fleeing towards the river. Here and there around the hillside, either singly or in pairs, a few others, who had been as fortunate, rode to join them but most now lay beneath the hooves of the Batavian's mounts; almost thirty Batavians lay with them. Magnus, Ziri and a couple of unhorsed troopers stalked around, finishing off the Chatti wounded and those Batavians too cut up to ride.

Vespasian surveyed the carnage, gasping for breath and then looked down at his blood-splattered arms and legs in sheer wonder that they were still there. Having satisfied himself that he was indeed in one piece a sense of urgency came over him. 'Magnus, keep a couple alive and that one-handed bastard if you find him.' He dismounted and began looking at the Chatti dead.

Sabinus rode over; blood oozed from a cut on his forehead. 'Thanks for your help, brother; I just managed the bastard in the end, but just is good enough.'

'You can thank me by helping to look for that one-handed man.'

'What was it about him?' Sabinus asked, swinging off his horse. 'You were about to tell me something.'

Vespasian turned a corpse over with his foot. 'I recognised him from Rome.'

'Where've you seen him?'

'On the day of Caligula's assassination, Uncle Gaius and I were in the theatre as you know. We managed to get out and then slipped down an alley to get away from the crush. We passed a dead German Bodyguard, and then at the end of the alley there was another one, leaning up against the wall, wounded; he was bald with a blond beard and you had just cut off his right hand.'

'Me?'

'Yes, you. I came out of the alley and saw a man in a cloak limping away with a wounded right thigh; that was you, wasn't it?'

Sabinus thought for a moment and then nodded his head. 'Yes, I suppose it was; two of the surviving Bodyguards followed me from the palace. I know that I killed one but whatever I did to the other I don't know because he wounded me at the same time; but he went down screaming and I stayed standing and managed to escape. So you think that this is all about vengeance for me depriving him of his drinking hand?'

'No, it's more than that. If we assume that Magnus is right and only Claudius' freedmen know where we're going then it has to be one of them who is trying to stop us. It was Pallas' idea, so why would he try and sabotage it? It also doesn't make sense, as you said, for Narcissus to spare you and then try and kill you here. So that leaves Callistus; I'm sure that he's behind it.'

'Why?'

'It's something that Pallas said when he told me how he knew that you were wounded and therefore must be still in the city. He said that Callistus had questioned the wounded Bodyguard.'

Sabinus wiped a drop of blood from his eye and looked thoughtfully at it. 'Fair enough; that connects the one-handed bastard with Callistus but it doesn't explain what Callistus has to gain by stopping us from finding the Eagle. He needs Claudius to gain favour with the army as much as Pallas and Narcissus do.'

'Yes, but he's also in a power struggle with them. Pallas told me that Narcissus is the most powerful of the three and he and Callistus are secondary. I watched them leave the dais on the night that the Senate went to see Claudius outside the Praetorian camp. Narcissus had the place of honour, helping Claudius down; then Pallas and Callistus both tried to patronise one another by offering the other the second place. Neither would accept the other's condescension and they ended up going down together. Now if Pallas' idea works and we come back with the Eagle then Claudius will favour him greatly and Callistus will feel that he's relegated to third place.'

'But if we fail then Pallas will take the blame.'

'Exactly, Sabinus; and Callistus will feel he's won this round.'

'Even though he's jeopardised the grander strategy of gaining Claudius a victory in Britannia?'

'Not if at the same time he has his own scheme for gaining Claudius popularity with the army.'

'How?'

Vespasian sucked on his lip and shook his head. 'I don't know; but Callistus isn't stupid so he'll have one.'

'We've got two who are alive enough to answer some questions,' Magnus said, walking up to the brothers, 'but no sign of old one-handed matey-boy. He must have made it out and is across the river by now; but I reckon we'll see him again.'

Vespasian turned and looked north; on the far bank two hundred or so warriors stood holding the river against them. 'We won't be able to cross here but we'll worry about that once we've found out what the prisoners know.'

'Take another one, Ansigar,' Vespasian ordered, 'and then ask him again.'

Ansigar pushed his weight down on his knife; after a moment's pressure it cut through the bone and, with a spurt of blood, the ring finger was severed, falling to the ground to land next to its smaller, erstwhile neighbour. Ansigar growled again in German but his victim, an older Chatti warrior held down on his back by two auxiliaries, just screwed up his face against the pain and said nothing; his chest heaved unevenly, glistening with sweat. He had a deep stab wound in his left shoulder, just below his iron collar.

Vespasian looked down at the wreckage of the man's left hand on the blood-drenched stone that was the chopping board; it was limp and extended at a strange angle from his forearm, which had been brutally broken after his first refusal to say why the Chatti had attacked them. 'Take the third,' he hissed, 'although I've a feeling that it's going to be a waste of time with this one. But it may encourage our other friend to talk.' He glanced over at the second prisoner, a younger man, kneeling with his hands bound behind him, staring with terrified eyes at his tormented comrade; he tried to tear himself loose from the two Batavians holding him as the third finger dropped to the ground.

The older man still refused to talk.

'Shall I take off his hand, sir?' Ansigar asked.

'Yes.'

Ansigar drew his sword and laid it on the wrist; the warrior tensed at the touch. The young man let out a sob.

'Wait!' Vespasian shouted as Ansigar raised the blade. 'Take his friend's right hand.'

The maimed warrior was dragged away and the younger man's bonds were cut. He started to scream and writhe like a landed eel as his two guards hauled him towards the stone. They forced him down onto his back and pulled out his right arm. Ansigar showed him the sword; a stream of German poured from the terrified man's mouth.

'He says that the one-handed man came half a moon ago and spoke with their King, Adgandestrius,' Ansigar translated. 'He doesn't know what was said but when the man left, the King ordered a hundred warriors to go with him and to obey him in all commands. He led them to the Rhenus, opposite Argentoratum, and told them to wait on the east bank whilst he took two fishing boats with three men in each over to the west.' Ansigar looked at the man who spoke some more and then carried on the translation: 'They waited for seven days then one of the boats came back at night with orders to ride north along the river until they met up with the one-handed man.'

'What's his name?' Vespasian asked.

Ansigar asked the question.

'Gisbert,' came the reply followed by another stream of the harsh language.

'When they found Gisbert,' Ansigar continued, 'he told them that he had followed a Roman raiding party; what's more, they were

141

Batavians, who are their enemies, and he proved it by showing them the body of one that he had killed. He said that they should track them and kill one or two every night but to always allow them to be holding a weapon when they died.' Ansigar paused as the young man carried on his tale and then repeated it: 'He said you would always be heading just east of north and they were to put the corpses ahead of you every day. They didn't understand why but they obeyed him as they would their King. Yesterday Gisbert sent a message to Adgandestrius, in Mattium ...'

'What's Mattium?' Vespasian asked.

Ansigar asked the question and the young man looked at Vespasian, frowning quizzically before answering.

'It's the chief settlement of the Chatti, to the east of here,' Ansigar translated. 'The message was for two hundred men to wait on the northern bank of the river and kill you as you tried to swim it but they stupidly gave away their position by shooting at the patrol. Gisbert then told them that we'd come to kill their King in vengeance for the raid across the Rhenus.'

'Kill their King? Are you sure?'

Ansigar questioned the man again; he answered, nodding, but with a look of puzzlement still on his face.

'That's what he said. He ordered them to charge us; they knew that they wouldn't win because they normally fight as infantry and dislike fighting mounted, but the King had told them to obey so they had no choice.'

'Ask him what he thought Gisbert was trying to achieve by sacrificing so many of them.'

'He can only assume that he wanted to kill as many of us as possible,' Ansigar said after listening to the answer, 'so we'd have no chance of crossing the river against the two hundred men on the other side.'

'He's done a reasonable job of that,' Paetus observed. 'We're down to just over a hundred and thirty troopers now; we won't be able to force a crossing against those odds.'

'Then we'll follow the river until we find another place to cross,' Sabinus suggested.

Vespasian looked at the force holding the north bank. 'They'll just keep pace with us. Ansigar, ask him if there's a bridge anywhere.'

'He says that there's one at Mattium,' Ansigar said after a brief conversation in German. 'But it is very well guarded.'

'I'm sure it is. Well, gentlemen, it looks as if we're fucked; any suggestions?'

'It seems to me that we either follow the river east and try and sneak across at night, or we storm the bridge, or we turn back.'

Vespasian and Sabinus looked at each other; they both knew what turning back would mean for Sabinus.

'We'll build a pyre for the dead,' Vespasian said, 'and then go east and see what Fortuna presents us with.' He looked down at the Chatti captives. 'Finish them, Ansigar.'

Ansigar took his sword and placed it on the young man's throat; his eyes widened in terror and he began speaking with urgency. Ansigar lowered his weapon and the captive looked up at Vespasian, nodding furiously.

'He says that he can help us cross the river,' Ansigar informed them.

'Oh really?' Vespasian was unimpressed. 'And just how does he think he can do that? Fly us across?'

'No, he says that the men on the other side will shadow us wherever we go but they won't cross because they'll lose too much time in doing so. He says that the river does a large loop to the north and then curves back, about ten miles east of here; if we follow it until the point that it changes direction and then leave its course and head due east we'll rejoin it again after three miles across country. The men on the other side will have to travel eight miles following the course, but we'll have time to cross and be away before they catch up with us.'

Vespasian looked at the young man's terrified eyes. 'Do you trust him, Ansigar?'

'There's only one way to find out, sir.'

CHAPTER VIIII

THE THICK SMOKE of the funeral pyre climbing high into the air was still visible, four miles behind the Batavian column, as they trotted east towards the curve in the river. They kept to a slow pace, saving their horses for the gallop across country that would put sufficient distance between them and the Chatti for a river crossing to be possible. As predicted, the Chatti were shadowing their movement on the northern bank; their silhouettes could be occasionally glimpsed through the trees that lined both sides of the river, just over an arrow's flight away.

The landscape had become gradually more agricultural; small, enclosed, family settlements of a few huts surrounding a longhouse were dotted around the gently undulating terrain; wood smoke from their cooking fires wafted skywards, occasionally adding a sweet tang to the air. Older men, boys and some women worked the fields, taking little notice of the column unless it came within a mile or so of them, then they would scuttle away to the relative safety of their settlements.

After a couple of hours' steady progress they came to the top of a grassy hillock; half a mile before them the river swept north to begin its ponderous loop. Its tree-lined course wove a lazy pattern into the distance before disappearing behind a line of small hills that had forced its diversion.

The Chatti captive gabbled excitedly to Ansigar who then turned to Vespasian, Sabinus and Paetus riding behind him. 'He says this is it. If we keep going straight we can't miss the river as it loops back round.'

Vespasian glanced over to the north bank; the trees were too thick to see through but he knew that the Chatti were there. 'We'd better make this quick, then; if they thrash their horses all the way they can still be at the crossing point a quarter of an hour after us.'

'Their horses will be blown, though,' Paetus pointed out.

'Yeah, but their spears won't be,' Magnus grumbled from behind him.

Vespasian ignored the gloomy comment and kicked his horse forward. 'Let's get this done.'

The column surged down the gentle slope behind him, hooves thundering and bridles jingling, accelerating along the last half-mile of east–west-flowing river. To their north the occasional flitting shape beyond the trees testified to their shadows keeping pace with them. As the river curved away, Vespasian led the column straight on. He was vaguely aware of some faint shouts from their pursuers as they were forced north away from their quarry; he did not look back but, instead, concentrated on keeping his horse at a gallop that it could sustain for three miles and still be able to swim a river.

The countryside rolled out ahead of them and they began to rise steadily, their mounts forcing their muscles to work harder against gravity as each downward slope led to a longer ascent until they were at the summit of the line of small hills. The great oxbow of the river could be seen in its entirety and Vespasian felt a surge of relief as, directly ahead of him, he saw it return to its original course; the captive had not lied. Then a pall of smoke hovering over a hill on the other side of the river, a mile beyond the curve, made him realise with a jolt that he had also not been completely truthful. The smoke partially concealed a large stockade hilltop town.

'Ask him what that is,' Vespasian shouted at Ansigar, knowing in his heart the answer and not liking it one bit.

Before Ansigar could frame the question the captive pulled his horse away to the south, kicking it for all he was worth, urging it into yet more speed; Ansigar made to follow.

'Let him go!' Vespasian shouted. 'We haven't got time to waste chasing him.'

'I've been here before,' Magnus told Vespasian as Ansigar pulled his horse back into the column. 'We sacked that place twenty-five years ago; they've evidently rebuilt it. That's Mattium, the Chatti's chief settlement.'

'I should have guessed; he said it was east along the river and he's led us right to it.'

'We could always turn back.'

'No, if I were the Chatti I would have left enough men to hold the river against us in case that was our plan. At least here we can cross unopposed.'

'Unopposed apart from by the rest of the Chatti tribe, that is.'

Vespasian was not about to argue with his friend and prayed that they could get across and away before their presence was noted by sharp eyes in the watchtowers of Mattium.

As they drew closer to the river the troopers began to unsling their water-skins and empty them. Vespasian looked over at Paetus who was doing the same. 'Why are you doing that?'

'Buoyancy, sir; you'd do well to do the same, we won't have a moment to lose; we'll fill them up again once we're across.' Paetus began blowing into the skin, inflating it, concentrating on keeping level in the saddle at the same time.

'Better do as he suggests,' Magnus said, reaching for his skin. 'And you too, Ziri.'

The little Marmarides looked in horror at his master as he emptied the contents of his water-skin. 'No, master! Man must not waste water; it brings bad luck.'

'In the desert it might, but here? Bollocks. Get on with it.'

Vespasian finished inflating his skin as they slowed, reaching the first trees of the riverbank. Paetus jumped from his horse and laid his shield on the ground. 'Tie the skin to the central grip of your shields,' he told the brothers and Magnus as they too dismounted, 'and make sure that the neck is tightly knotted so the air doesn't leak out.'

'Prefect!' Ansigar shouted, pointing back.

'Shit! They crossed!' Paetus exclaimed. 'Get in the river, now!'

Vespasian looked back up the hill; just over a mile away a line of cavalry thundered towards them, about one hundred in total. The Chatti had split their force.

Vespasian fumbled with his inflated water-skin's leather

thong, twisting it around the neck and tying it to the shield grip; around him troopers, well practised at this novel drill, were already leading their horses to the river, urging them to swim the fifty paces across. They placed their shields, with the improvised buoyancy bag underneath, on the surface and lay flat on them; the wooden shields with the added bag of air supported their weight, even with the heavy chain mail. Kicking with their feet and holding the horns of their mounts' saddles as they swam, the Batavians began the crossing.

The Chatti had covered almost half the distance and their shouts could be plainly heard.

Vespasian finally managed to secure the airbag and hurriedly followed Sabinus down to the water's edge.

'Fucking hurry up, Ziri,' Magnus growled, picking up his prepared shield; most of the troopers were already in the water. He looked over to where Ziri was struggling to tie off a knot around his skin's neck. 'You stupid brown desert-dweller! You haven't emptied the water; how the fuck is that going to float?'

'I won't throw water away, master, it's not natural.'

'Fighting on horseback ain't natural, wasting water is, now empty it.'

'No, master.'

Magnus glanced back up the hill; the Chatti were less than half a mile away. 'Fuck it, we ain't got the time; you'll just have to pray that the shield supports your scrawny little brown body by itself. Now get a move on before your arse starts entertaining a Chatti spear.' He hurried his horse into the river; Ziri followed. The lead troopers were already pulling themselves out on the far bank as Magnus lay on his shield and his horse began to pull him across.

Vespasian looked back from halfway to check his friend was following; the Chatti were little more than four hundred paces from the bank. 'Hurry, Magnus!'

'Shout at the horse, not me,' Magnus retorted, striving to keep balanced on his improvised raft as his mount towed him across. Behind him Ziri was the last man in the river and having very little success in staying on his un-buoyed shield; his struggles were spooking his horse.

Vespasian neared the far bank; most of the troopers were already out and hastily refilling their water-skins before mounting up. His horse pricked back its ears as it worked its powerful limbs against the water for the last few strokes; then its hooves hit the river bed and it surged up the bank, churning the brown-green water and splashing it into Vespasian's eyes. Releasing the saddle and grabbing his shield, Vespasian found his footing and pushed himself forward, struggling to find purchase on the slimy bed. Sabinus stretched out a hand to him; he clasped it and was hauled clear. 'Thanks, brother,' he gasped, panting from the exertion. He immediately turned to check on Magnus and Ziri's progress as the last couple of troopers made it out of the water; Ansigar and his fellow decurions were urging their men to mount up. Magnus was ten paces out but Ziri was still mid-stream; he had lost his shield and was floundering, clinging desperately to his horse's saddle. The beast snorted and shook its head in protest as it powered itself across.

The Chatti were approaching the trees lining the south bank, hollering and brandishing javelins.

'Hold on, Ziri, and kick with your feet,' Vespasian yelled, swinging up into the saddle as the first javelins hissed into the water around the struggling Marmarides.

'We move out now,' Paetus shouted, 'there's no time to wait for him.'

Magnus stumbled out of the water. 'You go, I'll wait for him.'

'They'll catch you. We can put a mile between us and the river whilst they cross.'

Magnus' face was set firm. 'I said I'll wait for him!'

Paetus turned his mount and urged it on through the trees, following his men.

Vespasian looked at Sabinus. 'You get on, Sabinus, I'll bring him.'

Out in the river, Ziri's horse let out a bestial screech as a javelin embedded itself in its rump; its back legs thrashed. A moment later another skewered into its neck, forcing an even shriller cry from the stricken animal; it bucked savagely, churning the bloody water around it and dislodging its floundering passenger.

'Master!' Ziri cried, splashing his arms in an attempt to keep his head above water.

'There's nothing you can do for him,' Vespasian urged Magnus, who was watching open-mouthed, clenching and re-clenching his fists impotently, 'unless you want to keep him company.'

Ziri's head dipped below the surface as his horse wallowed weakly next to him. His arms lashed at the water with enough force to bring his face back out. With his head tilted back he stared with wild eyes down his nose at Magnus. 'Master! Mas—' He juddered as a javelin slammed into the crown of his head and exploded through his palate; it punched out his front teeth as it wedged itself in his lower jaw, its bloodied point protruding like a reverse dimple from the middle of his chin.

Magnus let out a bellow of grief-stricken rage as Ziri sank, his arms trailing above his head as it slipped beneath the surface. His fingers disappeared, leaving only the shaft of the javelin poking out of the water to mark his position in the element so alien to his parched homeland.

'The stupid little brown sod,' Magnus hissed through gritted teeth as he jumped up onto his horse. 'I told him to empty the water from his skin but the idiot thought it would bring him bad luck to waste it.' He kicked his horse up the bank.

Vespasian followed as the first of the Chatti made it into the river. 'Now he's going to be drinking water for eternity just because he wouldn't throw a few drops away.'

'That's what I call a fucking irony.'

Vespasian and Magnus drove their mounts as fast as they would go as they strove to catch the Batavians now a quarter of a mile ahead of them. With the looming, smoke-oozing, fortified hilltop settlement of Mattium blocking their way east and the knowledge that the other half of the Chatti cavalry were in front of them following the river to the north, they were heading in the only viable direction: northeast.

So close to the Chatti's major settlement the farmland was well cultivated and they were forced to hurdle low stone walls and hedgerows.

'My horse ain't going to last much longer,' Magnus called over to Vespasian as he landed ungracefully after another leap.

Vespasian did not reply, he knew that his own mount was gradually fading, although not as quickly as some of the Batavians in front of them. In an effort to stay together the column was travelling at the speed of their slowest animal and they were now less than one hundred paces ahead; Vespasian and Magnus were gaining all the time. Glancing behind, Vespasian saw the chasing Chatti starting to swarm through the trees on the north bank, just over a mile away.

'Shit, I don't like the look of that!' Magnus exclaimed, pointing up to Mattium.

The gates had opened and horsemen were making their way along the winding track leading down to the plain.

Paetus too had obviously seen them because the column veered slightly more to the north; then after a few moments on the new course it changed back to its original direction. Vespasian knew immediately what that meant without having to look: the Chatti who had followed the river had left its course and were heading across country to cut them off. They were surrounded.

Paetus brought the column to a halt and Vespasian and Magnus finally caught up. 'We've got no choices but to fight or surrender,' he said to the brothers as they halted next to him.

'Then I'd say that we have no choice,' Vespasian replied. 'If we fight we'll all die. Gisbert offered to escort our men back to the Rhenus if we surrender, at least that way they'll survive.'

'Batavians do not surrender,' Ansigar spat, 'and especially not to Chatti; we would never be able to return home again if we did, such would be the shame.'

Paetus smiled without mirth. 'Well, gentlemen, it looks like a bloody death in the middle of Germania Magna for us, however you look at it. I have to say that I'd much rather go down fighting than be executed by some barbarian who calls himself king just because his great-grandfather came down from the hills and chopped everybody else's head off. Ansigar, form the men up to the north, we'll try to break through that way.'

The decurion saluted and rode away growling orders; the turmae started to form line with the Chatti no more than five hundred paces away on three sides.

'I'm sorry, Vespasian,' Sabinus said with a surprising dose of sincerity in his tone, 'it was my fault that got you into this.'

Vespasian smiled at his brother. 'No, it was Claudius' freedmen playing politics with each other.'

'Bastards.'

'So it looks like the prophecy made at my birth was false; unless of course it said that I was to die at the age of thirty-one butchered by Germans?'

'What? Oh yes, I see what you mean. No, it didn't predict that so it was all bollocks; I never believed it anyway, but Mother insisted that that was what the marks on each of the three livers meant.'

'Meant what?'

Sabinus shrugged, looking around at the three oncoming Chatti units, which had slowed and also formed a line.

'Come on, Sabinus, you might as well tell me now seeing as it was rubbish.'

Sabinus looked at his brother appraisingly. 'Very well. Father sacrificed the normal ox, pig and ram at your naming ceremony. When he took out the livers for examination they all had blemishes on. I can remember being very excited about that because I was sure that meant that Mars was not going to accept you; I hated you, you see?'

'Why? What had I done?'

'I'd heard Father promise Mars to nurture you well, to take great care of you, even over me; I was seethingly jealous of you. But the blemishes did not mean that Mars was rejecting you, far from it. Each liver had a different mark, they were all recognisable, uncannily so, but now what seemed like a blatant pictorial message turns out to be no more than—'

'Romans!'

The brothers looked behind them; the Chatti who had come from Mattium had stopped fifty paces away. One man came forward.

'Shit! That's the bastard that led us here,' Vespasian exclaimed, recognising their erstwhile guide instantly. 'He must have crossed the bridge.'

He shouted a couple of sentences in German.

'Perhaps this is not the end, brother,' Sabinus mused. 'Thank my Lord Mithras I didn't break my oath.'

Vespasian looked at Sabinus, enraged, as Ansigar rode over to them and translated. 'They do not ask for our surrender but they do ask that we come with them to avoid any more bloodshed. We may keep our weapons and our honour. It's a fair deal.'

'What do they want from us?' Sabinus asked, ignoring his brother's frustration.

'Their King wants to talk with the officers; you are invited to the hall of Adgandestrius.'

The gates of Mattium swung open to reveal a mass of rectangular wooden huts of varying sizes, jumbled together without any thought of civic planning. Constructed with thick poles hammered into the earth, there were no windows in the walls, and the doors were no more than sheets of leather; smoke spiralled out of holes in the centre of each hut's thatched roof.

The guide led the column along the main street of compacted earth that twisted and turned as it climbed higher. Narrow alleys ran off into smoky gloom on either side; the tang of wood smoke and reek of human waste filled Vespasian's nostrils. Women and old men peered curiously from doorways at the strangers as they passed and flaxen-haired children stopped their play and scuttled out of the road, away from the horses' hooves.

'Uncle Gaius would like it here,' Vespasian mused, looking at a couple of particularly beautiful, if rather grubby, young boys.

Sabinus laughed. 'Perhaps we should see if we can buy a couple to take home for him.'

'We should. He's always saying that it's so hard to find fresh ones in the slave markets; he enjoys breaking them in.'

'Well, they don't come much fresher than these. Sluice off the dirt and they're ready to be broken into.'

As the brothers laughed, Vespasian glanced at Magnus who sat glumly in the saddle, clearly still in no mood for jokes.

Eventually the road opened out into a clear area with a few market stalls around its circumference; on the far side was a large longhouse, at least twenty feet tall with a sloping thatched roof streaked with green moss.

The guide dismounted and spoke to Ansigar.

'We're to stay here,' the decurion translated, 'where we will be fed. You three are to meet the King in his hall.'

'Do you want to come?' Vespasian asked Magnus as they slipped from their horses.

'Better not, I might spoil the meeting by exacting some vengeance for Ziri.'

'As you wish.' Vespasian patted his friend's shoulder and then, with Sabinus and Paetus, followed the guide into the longhouse.

Stepping through the entrance, Vespasian's eyes took a few moments to adjust to the dim light. Four rows of long tables, with tallow candles placed at intervals down them, filled the first half of the hall up to a blazing, circular log fire whose smoke partially obscured the high vaulted ceiling as it struggled to get out through the round hole in its centre. Antlers, boar tusks and horns lined the wall interspersed with shields, swords and other accoutrements of war. Beyond the fire the hall was empty apart from four huge warriors standing at each corner of a dais upon which, on a high-backed chair, sat an old man with a long, grey beard and silver hair tied in a top knot. A band of gold was placed upon his head. 'I am Adgandestrius, King of the Chatti,' he said in unaccented Latin. 'Come forward.'

The guide led them up the central channel between the tables; their feet crushed the rushes strewn over the floor. Halfway between the fire and the King he stopped and bowed; he was dismissed with the wave of a gnarled hand and went to stand to one side, in front of a red curtain made up of two-foot-square pieces of material stitched together.

Adgandestrius surveyed the Romans for a few moments before his eyes fell on Vespasian. 'So, you are the Romans whom Gisbert told me that Galba had sent to kill me?'

'He lied,' Vespasian replied.

'I know that – now.' Adgandestrius pointed to the guide. 'You were lucky you let this young man live otherwise you would now be lying dead on the plain. He realised that Gisbert had lied when you asked what Mattium was; how could you be coming to kill me when you didn't even know the name of the place where you could find me? We Chatti are honourable men; we speak the truth and despise those who try to deceive us with falsehoods and half-truths. I will not be demanding blood-money from you for the many of my men that you've killed because you were defending yourselves against a lie that I am at fault for believing; I will pay the blood-money and I will spare your lives.'

'You are just, Adgandestrius.'

'I am a king; I have to be just, otherwise someone else would take my place. But I grow old and my judgement fails, that is why I believed Gisbert. Although I found it strange that Rome would send men to kill me just because of an insubstantial raid. I once offered Tiberius to poison Arminius for him but he refused, saying that Rome had no need to assassinate its enemies; Rome would deal with them in battle. So why would Rome resort to assassination now? Then I heard the news that you have a new emperor who is a fool and drools and I thought that the fool must have less honour than his predecessors; so I swallowed the lie. But now I want the truth; why are you here?'

Vespasian knew that to try to deceive Adgandestrius would be dishonourable after the clemency that he had shown them so he opted for honesty. 'We have come to find the Eagle of the Seventeenth Legion lost at the battle of the Teutoburg Forest.'

'Why now after all these years?'

Having embarked on the truth he felt that he had no option but to continue and so told the King of Claudius' freedmen's plan to secure his Principate.

'Britannia, eh?' Adgandestrius mused once he had finished. 'Does Rome never tire of conquests?' The question was rhetorical; everyone in the hall knew the answer. 'So why was Gisbert trying to stop you?'

'We're not sure but we suspect that it's political.'

'We shall ask him, then.' The King spoke in German briefly and two of his guards left the hall. They returned moments later with Gisbert; a strong rope wound around his chest bound him. The guards threw him onto the rushes before the dais; Adgandestrius looked down on him in disgust. 'Liar!'

Gisbert struggled to his knees and bowed his head. 'I had no choice; you would not have helped me if I told you the truth.'

'No, I wouldn't have. I know better than to interfere with Rome. Her legions lie just across the Rhenus and I have no wish to provoke them into a full-scale crossing again. Who made you do this? Who is it in Rome that doesn't want her Eagle found and seeks to make me responsible?'

Gisbert shook his head. 'I can't say.'

A guard went to slap him but Adgandestrius held up a hand. 'If you don't answer, your death will be long and painful and I will not grant the mercy of a sword – you will never reach Walhalla. If you do then you will die swiftly, with a weapon in your hand.'

Gisbert raised his eyes to the King. 'I have your word on that?'

'It takes a liar to doubt the word of an honourable man.'

'Very well; it was Claudius' freedman, Callistus.'

'Why?' Vespasian asked, pleased to have his theory proven correct.

'He wants to claim the glory of finding the Eagle from the Emperor. You see, he knows where it is and he was afraid that you might beat him to it.'

'Where is it?'

'That I don't know, but I do know that he has sent men after it. My task was to kill you and Sabinus, which would have been a pleasure because Sabinus took my hand. But you made that difficult by bringing so many men with you; I had only expected a few, thinking that you would try and pass unnoticed. So I tried to frighten your men away by picking off a couple of them at a time until we got closer to here and I could get reinforcements enough to threaten you.'

'But you didn't bring them over the river? You could have crushed us between the two forces had you done so.'

'I only wanted to kill you two, not the Batavians.'

'You murdered enough of them every night on the way here.'

'Yes, but I always made sure that they had a weapon in their hand and I had no wish to kill more than necessary. You see, the German Imperial Bodyguard is drawn from two of the tribes settled on the west bank of the Rhenus, the Ubii and the Batavii, and I'm Batavian; I try not to kill my own people.'

Suddenly it all made sense to Vespasian and he made a mental note of the debt that he owed his tribune, Mucianus, for suggesting that he take the Batavian auxiliaries: it had saved his life.

Adgandestrius stroked his beard in thought. 'He speaks the truth this time. Is there anything else that you wish to ask him?'

'Just one thing: how did Callistus find out where the Eagle was hidden?'

'I don't know exactly but it has something to do with ships.'

'Ships?'

'Yes; when he summoned me to give me my orders he said that he'd just got a message from someone up in the north who is in charge of getting ships, what for I don't know, but he had heard where the Eagle was.'

Vespasian looked at Sabinus. 'Callistus said that the general on the northern coast would be addressing the shortage of ships stationed up there for the invasion. He mentioned his name, can you remember it?'

Sabinus thought for a moment and shook his head. 'I'm sorry but at the time I had more pressing things on my mind.'

'That's easy,' Paetus said, 'everyone along the Rhenus knows that because he's been requisitioning ships up and down the river since February: Publius Gabinius.'

'That's him. Does that name sound familiar, Gisbert?'

'No, Callistus never gave me details.'

Vespasian inclined his head to Adgandestrius to indicate that he was finished. The King beckoned one of his warriors and spoke in German. The man stepped forward and cut Gisbert's bonds with a dagger. Gisbert remained kneeling, looking up at his executioner's face. The warrior drew his sword and handed it to him, hilt first. As Gisbert clasped it with his one remaining hand, the warrior plunged his dagger into the base of his neck and on down into his heart. Blood pulsed from the deep wound as the weapon was withdrawn. Gisbert carried on staring at his executioner, his chest heaving in an effort to breathe, the light in his eyes slowly fading; a moment before they closed a trace of a smile twitched his lips. He fell forward onto the crimson rushes and lay motionless, his hand still gripping the sword.

The body was hauled away and the King turned his attention back to Vespasian and his companions. 'I don't know who has this Eagle, I never did.' He motioned to the guide standing before the red curtain. The guide pulled it from the middle, it parted and he swung each side open on hinged poles attached to the wall.

The three Romans sucked in their breath through their teeth as the Capricorn emblem of a legion and five cohort standards topped by a raised hand, palm out, were revealed. The curtains themselves were made of the flags that hung from the crossbar of a century's standard, each one representing eighty long-dead men.

'Arminius shared out the trophies in secret, drawing lots for them so that there would be no jealousies between the tribes; each King swore never to reveal what he had received to the others. I received the silver Capricorn legion emblem of the Nineteenth and five cohort standards plus all those century flags. As to the rest, only Arminius knew, and he's dead.'

'But his son is still alive.'

Adgandestrius frowned. 'Yes, he is and I suppose it's possible that he knows. Is that what you planned to do, ask Thumelicus?'

'I thought that if we went to the Teutoburg Forest we could find a way of sending him a message; I have something of his father's that would interest him.' Vespasian took Arminius' knife from his belt and gave it to the King.

Adgandestrius drew it from its scabbard and examined the blade, looking closely at the runic engraving and then handed it back. 'Yes, that would be of great interest to him and may be enough to persuade him to meet with you. I know where he is and will send a message to him that you will be at Kalkriese Hill in the Teutoburg Forest at the next full moon in five days' time.

If he so wishes he can meet you there.' With some difficulty he pulled himself up from his chair and walked over to the standards; he pulled out the Nineteenth's Capricorn from its holder. 'I will give you an escort of my men to see you there safely and when you leave here you will go with the Nineteenth's emblem as my gift.'

The look of astonishment on the Romans' faces as he handed the emblem to Sabinus caused the old King to chuckle. 'You wonder why I help you? It is for the same reason that I will beg Thumelicus to help you; not just for his father's knife but for a far greater prize: if the fool in Rome gets his Eagle back and also the Nineteenth's emblem then it will surely secure his position with the army so he can have his invasion and victory in Britannia. However, the legions will be drawn from the garrisons on the Rhenus and Danubius; at least four legions plus their auxiliaries less to face us. The Celtic tribes of Britannia's loss will be our gain. If Rome goes north to that island then it will not have the power to threaten us again. I'll help you, as, I pray, will Thumelicus, because in doing so we will guarantee that Germania will remain free, for generations; perhaps even forever.'

CHAPTER X

'THIS IS IT!' Magnus exclaimed as the column, led by twenty of Adgandestrius' warriors, slowed owing to the path narrowing, hemmed in by a marsh on the north side and a hill on the south. 'I remember this, it's where Arminius trapped the remnants of our lads after four days of running battles; there were only seven or eight thousand or so left out of almost twenty-five thousand. Varus had been driving them steadily northwest through the pissing rain trying to outrun the Germans but they managed to get ahead of them by taking a short cut across the hills and were waiting in the trees above an area of open ground. Our lads never saw them until five thousand of the hairy bastards started flinging javelins at them. Fifty thousand missiles in under a hundred heartbeats, can you imagine it?'

Vespasian could; he shuddered at the thought. 'That would bring a column to a halt.'

'It did. They couldn't go into the marsh because it had been raining constantly for days, those who tried just sank; they couldn't go forward or back because another five thousand had blocked off their retreat and the path ahead had been dug up and obstacles placed over it.'

'So they had no choice but to fight?'

'No. Soon we'll see a long earth wall that they threw up as a last defence; it goes on for about a quarter of a mile. The survivors managed to hold the savages off for a while but then the rest of the tribes who had been watching decided to join in. Varus saw the futility of the situation and did the decent thing and after that most of our lads were dead within the hour. Only a few escaped and some of them joined us as guides when we went back; I got to know a couple of them quite well.'

'What happened at the beginning?' Sabinus asked.

'Well, Varus was taking his men back from the summer camp on the Visurgis River to winter quarters on the Rhenus; three legions, six auxiliary cohorts and three cavalry alae, over twenty thousand men, minus a few cohorts that had been left at the German tribes' request to preserve Rome's peace. Sneaky bastards did that to lull Varus into complacency, which worked; he'd even sent the legates and some of the tribunes back home to Rome for the winter. He thought everything was fine as he set out west along the military road that followed the River Lupia; it was called the Long Bridges on account of how many bridges it has. Nasty place; we nearly shared Varus' fate when we tried to go home that way a few years later.'

'We crossed what's left of that fifty miles south of here,' Paetus remarked. 'How did they stray so far from their path?'

'Arminius sent a false message saying that there was a rebellion up north of here. Varus trusted and liked him and therefore believed him – even though he had been warned that he was plotting against him – so he decided not to split his column and took everybody north, even the camp followers and slow baggage train, into this terrain of hills thick with trees and cut by deep ravines; fucking idiot! Varus allowed his lumbering, six- or seven-mile-long column to be led by German guides into a valley a few miles back, southeast of here, that was heaving with tribesmen hiding in the trees.'

'Didn't they have scouts out on the flanks?' Vespasian asked, looking up the hill to his left through the oak, beech and birch trees and imagining how easy it would be to hide an army from view.

'Yeah, according to the few lads who survived, they had lots of scouts; trouble was they were Arminius' men and they accidentally missed seeing five thousand or so warriors on either side of the hills above them plus another ten thousand who had decided to come along and watch on the understanding that they would join in if it went well for Arminius. Anyway, Varus thought that it was natural to use Cherusci and Chatti auxiliaries as scouts; the tribes were loyal after all and it meant that he could have all his legionaries marching in nice neat ranks and files, eight abreast, all very lovely and military fashion, just how generals like it.'

'But very slow.'

'Exactly; and they kept on having to fell trees so that the formation wouldn't break up. Also, it was pouring with rain and there was a howling wind blowing in from the west with a force that I've only ever seen in Germania; none of our lads could see or hear the savages until they felt their spears and slingshots crash into the centre of the column. The boys still had their pila tied to their pack-yokes; it was a fucking shambles from all accounts. Then the savages and our own auxiliaries came whooping and hollering down the hill and it all got very personal, if you take my meaning, and before long the column was cut in two.'

'How did they make it here to die along this path?' Sabinus asked, looking at the Nineteenth's emblem and wondering where it had fallen.

'Eventually they regained some semblance of order and Varus got half the lads to build a camp whilst the rest held the bastards off; they finally withdrew at nightfall and Varus allowed a few hours' wet sleep before destroying all the carts and sneaking out of the camp a couple of hours before dawn. The Germans woke up to find the camp empty of legionaries but full of abandoned supplies; well, as you can imagine, they were in no mood to chase our boys until they'd had a good rummage through it all. Meanwhile Varus kept on trying to go northwest to come to Arminius' aid, thinking that the attack was an attempt to stop him from getting to the source of the rebellion rather than Arminius himself; pompous idiot! The army's never been in short supply of them.'

'I'd say he was acting honourably,' Vespasian observed. 'After all, he didn't know the message was false so he was trying to do his duty to Rome and to his friend by going to Arminius' aid.'

Magnus grunted and looked dubiously at Vespasian. 'Anyway, they pressed on all day with a few minor skirmishes and made another camp. The following day the main body of the Germans had caught up and that night our lads fought almost without reprieve to keep the savages out of the camp; then in the morning of the fourth day the Germans withdrew and the remnants of the column moved on. But the Germans harried them all the time, making sure that they always travelled in this direction and eventually they ended up here. And that was that, they were surrounded; nowhere to run to. The surviving cavalry tried to make a break but were ridden down. Varus fell on his sword and the lads had a choice between going down fighting, suicide or surrender to either be sacrificed or to endure a life of slavery. Only a very few managed to slip away; under fifty, out of all those lads.' Magnus pulled up his horse suddenly. 'Shit! We took all those down.'

Ahead of them on either side of the path skulls had been nailed to trees by long spikes through the eyes.

'Looks like the Germans put them back up,' Sabinus observed.

Magnus spat in disgust and clenched his right thumb in protection from the evil-eye. Past the skulls, the path opened up into a wide sandy area, two hundred paces across and half a mile in length; strewn all around it were thousands of human bones of all shapes and sizes, weathered and tinged with lichen. 'They've done more than that; they've dug a lot of the lads back up.'

The column crunched along through the clearing; the last desperate earthwork of Varus' legions to their left was broken down in places as if trampled upon by hundreds of feet; the rotted hoof of a dead mule protruded from one section. The reek of stagnant water wafted across from the extensive bog to their right and ahead the trees closed in again making it a perfect killing ground. Although birds were singing in the boughs of trees laden with spring-green leaves, Vespasian found the atmosphere oppressive, as if thousands of eyes were watching them. He tried not to look down at the bones of the long-dead legionaries but his morbid curiosity got the better of him. Leg bones, arm bones, vertebrae, ribs, skulls and pelvises were all scattered haphazardly; some were whole, others had been cut or hacked into and more than a few showed signs of being gnawed at by wild animals. Here and there they passed crude altars fashioned out of stone; on them more bones lay but these were blackened by fire. 'How long ago were you here, Magnus?'

'Must be twenty-five years now.'

'What's so strange is that they haven't been buried over that time by nature. It's as if someone looks after them.'

'Them, perhaps?' Magnus suggested as a group of five horsemen rode out of the trees and blocked their path a hundred paces ahead of them.

The Chatti warriors leading the column raised their hands to signal a halt. Two of them rode forward to talk briefly with the new arrivals before returning and speaking to Ansigar.

The decurion nodded and turned to the Roman officers. 'They are Cherusci; Thumelicus is waiting for us at the summit of this hill.'

The hill was not high, no more than three hundred and fifty feet, and they mounted it swiftly, even though it was thick with trees; Vespasian could well imagine how so many warriors could have concealed themselves on its slopes. Towards the summit they took a detour around a clearing with a grove of beech trees at its centre in which a tethered white horse grazed peacefully next to an altar. Three heads, one of them fresh but the rest in various states of decomposition, hung by their long hair from branches around its edge; skulls with scraps of flesh and hair still clinging to them lay on the ground beneath them as testament to the ripening of this ghastly fruit. Blood dripped from the altar.

As the slope petered out so did the wood; they reached the summit, which had been cleared of trees to leave an incongruous meadow, alive with spring flowers, but dominated by the most unlikely of sights: a ten-foot-high, fifty-foot-square, red leather tent next to a solitary, ancient oak.

Vespasian took one look at it and knew what he was staring at.

'Mercury's sweet arse,' Magnus exclaimed, 'that must be Varus' command tent, captured amongst the abandoned baggage all those years ago.'

Sabinus was equally awed. 'I suppose they got everything that the column was carrying; they couldn't have burnt it because it would've been too wet.'

The five Cherusci riders dismounted at the tent's entrance and signalled for the column to do the same; their leader, an older man in his sixties, went inside. After a few moments he reappeared and spoke to Ansigar.

'You may go in,' the decurion informed Vespasian, Sabinus and Paetus. 'We'll graze the horses whilst you're gone.'

'Coming this time?' Vespasian asked Magnus, heading for the entrance.

'Does the Emperor stutter?'

Vespasian pushed the leather flaps aside and found himself in a short, leather-walled corridor, just like the praetorium tent in Poppaeus' camp back in Thracia, although this one did not have a transportable marble floor and made do only with waxed bare boards. He walked a few steps down the corridor and through a door into the main part of the tent. Tallow candles flickered all about, illuminating a room elegantly furnished with well-upholstered couches, finely carved chairs and tables and decorated with small bronze statues in amongst ceramic or glass bowls and vessels. At the far end was a sturdy oaken desk with rolled-up scrolls arranged on it; next to it, on a curule chair, sat a Roman Governor in full military uniform. And yet it could not be, for he was too young to be a governor and he wore a full black beard.

'Welcome, Romans,' the Governor said, 'I am Thumelicus, son of Erminatz.'

Vespasian opened his mouth to greet Thumelicus but was halted by the raising of a hand.

'Do not tell me your names,' Thumelicus insisted, staring at him from beneath a firm brow with penetrating, blue eyes, devoid of feeling. 'I have no wish to know them; after I escaped from your Empire I swore to Donar the Thunderer to strike me down with a lightning bolt from above if I ever have anything to do with Rome again. However, at the behest of my old enemy, Adgandestrius, I have asked the god to make an exception this one time for the sake of my tribe and Germania.' He indicated to the couches around the room. 'Sit down.'

Vespasian and his companions accepted the invitation, making themselves as comfortable as was possible whilst under the glare of Thumelicus' intense gaze. His nose was pronounced but slender, showing signs of many breakages. His cheekbones were high and his luxuriant, well-combed black beard climbed almost up to them. The long hair of his moustache partially obscured thin, pale lips. Vespasian concentrated on his chin and was able to make out its outline beneath the beard; there was a cleft, this was definitely the man.

'Adgandestrius tells me that you wish for my help in finding the one remaining Eagle lost by your legions at my father's victory here in the Teutoburg Wald.'

'He is correct.'

'And why do you think that I would help you?'

'It would be in your interests to do so.'

Thumelicus scoffed and leant forward, pointing his finger at Vespasian's face. 'Roman, at the age of two I was paraded, with my mother, Thusnelda, in Germanicus' triumph; a humiliation for my father. Then in another humiliation to him we were sent to Ravenna to live with his brother Flavus' wife; Flavus, who always fought for Rome even against his own people. Then in a third humiliation I was taken at the age of eight and trained to be a gladiator; the son of the liberator of Germania fighting on the arena sand for the gratification of the mob of some provincial town. I fought my first bout when I was sixteen and I won my wooden sword of freedom fifty-two fights later, four years ago, at the age of twenty. The first thing that I did once I was free was settle my score with my uncle Flavus and his wife, and then, with my mother, I came back here to my tribe. With all that Rome has done to me, how could my own interests and yours ever coincide?'

Vespasian told him of the planned invasion of Britannia and Adgandestrius' strategic view of its consequences.

'And you can guarantee that Rome won't just raise three or four more legions and replace the ones in Britannia?' Thumelicus asked. 'Of course not; Rome has the manpower for many more legions and that old man should realise that. Unless the Empire is hit by a terrible plague it will continue to grow in population. Citizenship is being awarded to more and more communities in every province. All the time, slaves are being freed and receiving citizenship; they aren't eligible to join the legions but their sons are. But I agree with Adgandestrius in the short term: an invasion of Britannia will very likely keep us safe for a generation or so.' Thumelicus removed the crested helmet and placed it on the desk; his hair fell to his shoulders. He looked at the Romans and laughed low and mirthlessly. 'If it had not been for my father then there would still be a Roman wearing this uniform even now in Germania; but because of him I can wear it now as I deal with the successors of the man to whom it belonged. I can also entertain them in his tent and serve them refreshments on his plate.'

At a sharp double clap of Thumelicus' hands, the entrance behind him opened; two bearded slaves in their fifties shuffled in with trays covered with silver cups, jugs of beer and plates of food. As they padded around the room placing food and drink on tables near their master's guests Vespasian noticed with a shock that their hair was cut short, Roman style.

'Yes, Aius and Tiburtius were both captured in this place, thirty-two years ago,' Thumelicus confirmed, reading the look on Vespasian's face. 'They have been slaves here ever since. They have not tried to run away; have you, Aius?'

The slave serving Vespasian turned and bowed his head to Thumelicus. 'No, master.'

'Tell them why, Aius.'

'I cannot return to Rome.'

'Why not?'

'Shame, master.'

'Shame of what, Aius?'

Aius looked nervously at Vespasian and then back to his master.

'You can tell them, Aius; they haven't come to take you back.'

'Shame of losing the Eagle, master.'

'Losing the Eagle?' Thumelicus ruminated, turning his blue eyes onto the old soldier.

The years of servitude and shame came to tell in Aius and he hung his head, and his chest heaved a couple of times with repressed sobs.

'And you, Tiburtius?' Thumelicus asked, giving the second man, slightly older and with almost silver hair, the full force of his stare. 'Do you still feel shame?'

Tiburtius just nodded dumbly and placed his last jar on the desk next to Thumelicus.

Vespasian's shock turned into anger as he looked at two Roman citizens so beaten down by years of disgrace and slavery. 'Why haven't you done the honourable thing and killed yourselves?' he asked, barely concealing his disgust.

A smile played at the corners of Thumelicus' mouth. 'You may answer him, Aius.'

'Arminius gave us the choice of being sacrificed by burning in one of their wicker cages or swearing upon all our gods to stay alive for the task that he wanted us to perform. No one who has seen and heard a wicker sacrifice will face the fire; we chose what every man would.'

'I wouldn't argue with that, mate,' Magnus chipped in, getting a look of distant recognition from Aius at the use of such a familiar term. 'The idea of my balls roasting over the fire would be enough to make me swear to anything.'

'But they wouldn't have roasted,' Thumelicus informed him, taking the lid off the jar, 'we always take care to remove the testicles first.'

'That's very considerate of you, I'm sure.'

Thumelicus dipped his fingers into the jar. 'I can assure you that it's not out of consideration for the victim that we do this.' He pulled out a small, off-white, egg-shaped object and bit it in half. 'We believe that eating our enemies' testicles brings us strength and vigour.'

Vespasian and his companions looked on in horror as Thumelicus chewed loudly on it, savouring its taste. He popped the other half into his mouth and, with equal relish, ate that as the two slaves, surprisingly, took a seat each on the far side of the desk.

Thumelicus washed down his snack with a swig of beer. 'After the battle here and all the battles and actions that my father fought in our struggle for freedom we had almost sixty thousand testicles pickled; my father shared them out amongst the tribes. This is the last jar left to the Cherusci; I keep it for special occasions. Perhaps we should think about refilling our jars again soon?'

'You'd be mad to try,' Sabinus said, 'you could never cross the Rhenus.'

Thumelicus inclined his head in agreement. 'Not if we stay as disunited as we are now, and even if we could you would use the resources of your Empire to beat us back in time. But you still have the strength to cross the other way and that is why I am here talking to you against all my principles. One of you has something to show me, I believe.'

Vespasian got out his father's knife and passed it to Thumelicus.

'How did you come to be in possession of this?' he asked, examining the blade.

Vespasian explained the knife's history whilst Thumelicus traced the runes with a finger.

When he had finished, the German thought for a moment and then nodded. 'You speak the truth; it is exactly how my father set it down in his memoirs.'

'He wrote his memoirs!' Vespasian exclaimed, unable to keep the incredulity out of his voice.

'You forget he was brought up in Rome from the age of nine. He learnt to read and write, although not that well as it had to be beaten into him; we do not consider them to be manly practices. However, he had a better idea: he would dictate his memoirs to his crushed enemies and he would keep them alive so that they could read them out whenever it was necessary, and today it may be necessary. Mother, would you join us?'

The curtain opened and a tall, proud, greying woman with the deepest blue eyes that Vespasian had ever seen entered. Her skin was lined and her breasts fell low but she had evidently been a beauty in her youth.

'Mother, is it necessary to tell Father's story to these Romans? What do the bones say?'

Thusnelda pulled from a leather bag at her waist five straight, carved, thin bones covered on all four sides in what Vespasian now knew to be runes. She breathed on them and muttered some half-heard incantations over them before casting them to the ground.

Stooping, she examined their fall for a few moments, pawing at them. 'My husband would wish his story told to these men; to understand you they must understand where you come from, my son.'

Thumelicus nodded. 'Then so be it, Mother, we shall begin.'

Vespasian indicated to the two slaves now sorting out scrolls and putting them in order on the desk. 'So he spared these two to write down his life and read it out?'

'Yes, who better to tell of the life of Arminius than the *aquiliferi*, the Eagle-bearers, of the Seventeenth and Nineteenth Legions?'

The sun was long set by the time the two old slaves, once proud bearers of their legions' most sacred objects, finished the tale of Arminius' life with their verbal account of how he was murdered by a kinsman. It had not just been a simple reading; Thusnelda had contributed parts from her recollection and Thumelicus had encouraged Vespasian and his friends to question Aius and Tiburtius about their memories of the battle at Teutoburg; he also ordered the old men to write their answers down. Magnus, who, whilst serving in the V Alaudae, had been present at the battle of the Long Bridges and the following year at the battles of the Angrivarii Ridge and Idistavisus, Arminius' first defeat, had shared his memories of Germanicus' two campaigns, six and seven years respectively after the massacre – before he had been recalled by Tiberius, jealous of, and frightened by, his success. Thumelicus had seemed genuinely pleased at hearing this new point of view and had told his slaves to make notes, which they duly did with misty looks of longing in their eyes as they heard the legions spoken of in plain, legionary-mule terms; their ageing faces registered the depth of their shame in not only losing their legions' Eagles but also in being unable to face the fires afterwards and so being condemned to live without hope of redemption. Apart from the occasional question, Vespasian,

Sabinus and Paetus had nothing to contribute and sat listening as the tale unfolded, sipping their beer and nibbling at the food arrayed around in bowls; on numerous occasions they politely declined the offer of a treat from Thumelicus' jar.

No one spoke as the two old men finished and began rolling up the scrolls and replacing them in their cases, their eyes never leaving the work on the desk in front of them.

Thumelicus looked thoughtfully into his beer cup. 'My father was a great man and it is my loss that I never met him.' His eyes flicked up and bored into Vespasian. 'But I've not had you sit here with me and listen to his story just so that I can wallow in a bit of self-pity afterwards. I wanted you to hear it so that you can understand my motives in what I shall do next; I intend to go against everything that my father stood for.'

Sabinus leant forward. 'Does that mean you can tell us where the Eagle is hidden?'

'I can tell you which tribe it is with, that is easy; the Chauci, on the coast to the north of here, have it. But I'll do more than that; I will actively help you find it.'

'Why would you do that?' Vespasian asked.

'My father tried to make himself king of a Greater Germania, uniting all the tribes under one leader. Imagine the power he would've had if he'd succeeded. He would have had the strength to take Gaul; but would he have had the strength to hold it? I don't think so; not yet, whilst Rome is so strong. But that was *his* dream, it's not mine. I look far into the future to a time when Rome starts her inevitable decline as all empires have done before. For the present I see the idea of a Greater Germania as a threat to all the constituent tribes. It is the potential cause for a hundred years of war with Rome; a war for the next few generations that we don't yet have the manpower to win.

'So I do not desire to be the leader of a united Germanic people but there are many of my countrymen who suspect that I do. Some actively encourage me by sending messages of support but others are jealous of me and would see my death as furthering their own ambitions. But I just want to be left in peace to live, in the manner that was denied me all my youth, to live as a Cherusci in a free Germania. I want nothing of Rome, neither vengeance nor justice. We've freed ourselves from her once; it would be foolish to put ourselves in the position where we have to fight for our freedom again.

'However, Rome will always want her Eagle back and whilst it's on our soil she will come looking for it. The Chauci will not give it up and why should they; but their keeping it puts us all at risk. I want you to have it, Romans; take it and use it for your invasion and leave us in peace. So I'll help you steal it and the tribes will learn that I helped Rome and they will no longer want me to become – or fear me becoming – an image of my father.'

'Won't the Chauci see that as a declaration of war against them?' Vespasian asked.

'They would if there weren't other circumstances involved. I know that Rome collects tribute from many of the tribes in Germania and I also know that recently she has been demanding ships from the coastal tribes instead of gold. Now, the Chauci's neighbours the Frisii are very fond of their ships and I heard that to avoid handing too many of them over they sold the secret of where the lost Eagle is to—'

'Publius Gabinius!'

'Exactly. So the Chauci are going to lose their Eagle soon, but if we can get it before Publius Gabinius arrives with a Roman army then many Chauci lives might be saved.'

'How far is it?'

'Thirty miles east of here is the Visurgis River; that takes us all the way to the Chauci's lands on the northern coast. We'll be there the day after tomorrow if we go by boat.'

CHAPTER XI

A T MID-MORNING the following day the column rode into the dilapidated remains of a small, Roman military river-port, uncared for since the final withdrawal of the legions back across the Rhenus twenty-five years previously. Although the roofs of most of the single-storey barrack buildings and ware-houses were still reasonably intact, their brick walls were being eaten into by dense, dark ivy and other climbing plants. Barn swallows swooped in and out of open windows, whose shutters had long since rotted away, constructing their mud nests in the eaves of the deserted buildings. A pack of wild dogs, which seemed to be the only other inhabitants, trailed the column as they made their way along a grass-tufted, paved street down to the river.

'My people didn't burn this port because my father felt that it was of some strategic use,' Thumelicus explained; he had divested himself of Varus' uniform and wore a simple tunic and trousers, in the manner of his people. 'He made it a supply depot from where he could provision his forces quickly using the river, but after his murder it was abandoned to rot.'

'Why?' Vespasian asked. 'It could still be extremely useful to you.'

'Yeah, you would have thought so; but the problem would be: who would stock it and who would guard it?' Magnus pointed out. 'I imagine there would be a lot of competition for the latter but very few volunteers for the former.'

Thumelicus laughed. 'I'm afraid that you have understood my countrymen all too well. No clan chief is going to give up his grain and salted meat to be guarded by men from another clan, even though they are all Cherusci. My father had the strength to make them do it but since he's gone they've returned to the old ways of bickering amongst themselves and only ever uniting in the face of an external threat from another tribe.'

'It makes you realise just how close we were to subduing the whole province,' Paetus said as they passed a crumbling brick-built temple. 'To have built all this so deep into Germania shows that we must have been pretty confident of remaining here.'

'It was confidence or rather overconfidence that was Varus' problem.'

Magnus scowled. 'Arrogance more like; yet another pompous arsehole.'

Vespasian opened his mouth to defend the long-dead general again but the pointless argument was driven from his mind as they passed between a line of storehouses and onto the riverside quay. Before them, each tied to a wooden jetty, were four sleek boats; long with fat bellies and high prows and sterns with a single mast amidships and benches for fifteen rowers on each side.

'We live in longhouses and we sail in longboats,' Thumelicus quipped. 'We Germans think that it's quite a good joke.' When no one laughed he frowned and looked around at Vespasian and his companions; their expressions were all similar: confusion. 'What's the matter?'

Paetus turned to him. 'Horses, Thumelicus, that's what the matter is. How do we take our horses with us?'

'You don't. The horses are the price for the boats.'

'Then how do we get back across the Rhenus?'

'You'll get home by sailing on out to the sea and then follow the coast west. Your Batavians can handle this sort of boat, they're good seamen.'

'But good seamanship won't protect us against storms,' Magnus muttered. 'Last time Germanicus sailed back to Gaul he lost half his fleet in the Northern Sea. Some of the poor buggers were even driven ashore in Britannia.'

'Then you'll be there, ready and waiting, when the invasion fleet finally arrives.'

Sabinus looked sourly at Thumelicus. 'Is that another German joke because I didn't find that one particularly funny either?' His sense of humour was not helped by contemplating a sea voyage; he was not the best of sailors.

'No, merely an observation. But that's the deal: horses for boats and you'll be in the Chauci's lands tomorrow.'

Vespasian pulled Sabinus and Magnus aside. 'We've got no choice but to take it; if Gabinius beats us to that Eagle then Callistus will take the credit and Narcissus could easily say that Sabinus didn't keep his end of the bargain and his life is still forfeit. Besides, it will be a lot easier trying to get back by sea rather than overland with Chauci cavalry chasing us all the way.'

'But at the least the contents of my stomach will be staying where they belong.'

'Not if you get gutted by a Chauci spear,' Vespasian observed.

Sabinus paused to reflect upon this detail. 'Well, brother, I suppose you've got a point. Boats it is, then.'

Vespasian looked at Thumelicus. 'It's a deal.'

'But what about my horses?' Paetus asked through clenched teeth. 'It takes months to train them and—'

'And you'll do as you're told, prefect,' Vespasian snapped before turning back to Thumelicus again. 'But we keep the saddles and bridles.'

'Agreed.'

Paetus relaxed somewhat but still did not look happy. 'I'll get the men dismounted and start the embarkation.'

'I think that's a very good idea, prefect,' Vespasian said, slipping off his horse.

'I think it's a shit idea,' Magnus mumbled, staying put on his.

'Oh, so you like being a cavalry trooper now all of a sudden, do you?'

'It's better than having to swim home.'

The Batavians sang low and melancholically, with a slow beat to match the rhythm of the stroke, as they rowed the longboats downstream; their shields were slung over the sides next to them to afford some protection against a surprise arrow attack. Birds flitted in the still air, replaying spring mating rituals over the smooth surface of the river and in amongst the trees, fresh with new leaves, overhanging its banks. The sweet smells of the new season occasionally broke through the musky tang of the Batavians as they sweated at the oars, stripped to the waist, their arm, chest and stomach muscles toned, squinting into the midday sun as they glided northwards through mainly flat lands towards the sea.

Vespasian and Magnus stood at the stern of the second ship, on a small fighting platform, next to Ansigar at the steering oar who kept a course directly down the middle of the hundred-paces-wide river; ahead of them Thumelicus commanded the lead vessel with one of his men as the steersman.

The current was sluggish and their pace was not quick, despite the crews' exertions; Vespasian was growing impatient. He glanced at Magnus, next to him, who had not said a word since reluctantly getting off his horse and coming aboard once it had become apparent that he had no choice other than to be left behind. 'You said that you knew how the Germans hid the Eagles.'

Magnus looked glumly ahead as if he had not heard.

'Oh, come on, Magnus, this boat isn't that bad.'

Magnus roused himself from his gloom. 'It ain't that, sir. It's just that Germania seems to bring nothing but bad luck. When you look at all those Roman bones just lying there it makes you think that there's some sort of curse against us in this land. Somewhere around here we fought Arminius' army at a place called Idistavisus; the Germans withdrew with heavy casualties and Germanicus claimed a victory, but it weren't so straight forward. I lost a good few mates that day.' He looked to the east bank. 'They're lying out there somewhere, just like Ziri is lying at the bottom of a river; all of them dead in a land with different gods.'

'Surely your gods follow you wherever you go if you believe in them and worship them.'

'Perhaps they do, but their power gets weaker the further they get from their homeland. Here in Germania the power of Wotan and Donar and whatever other gods they have is strong, you can tell. You saw that grove on the way to Thumelicus' tent; those heads didn't just grow on the trees, they were put there after being sacrificed. We ain't had nothing but trouble since we crossed the Rhenus and now we're sailing into a whole lot more; even if we sacrifice a whole herd of white bulls to Neptune to keep us safe on the Northern Sea how's he going to hear us and help us if the local gods are getting human victims?'

'Human sacrifice is abominable.'

'You tell that to the German gods; I don't think that they'll agree with you judging by how well they look after their people. I don't like the idea of stealing back the Eagle and then going to sea with it with the wrath of the German gods following us.'

'Why should they be angry with us? We won't be taking it from them, we'll be taking it from the tribe.'

Magnus looked at his friend with an expression of incredulous amazement. 'Of course we'll be stealing it from the gods; I told you that I've seen how the Germans hide an Eagle. It'll be in one of their sacred groves dedicated to whichever one of their blood-thirsty gods they think can best protect it and they won't be too pleased with us when we take it; *if* we take it, for that matter, because it ain't as simple as walking through the trees into the clearing and pulling the Eagle's pole out of the ground. Oh no, they make traps.'

'What sort of traps?'

'Nasty fucking traps.'

'How nasty?'

'Put it this way; when we found the Nineteenth's Eagle in the Marsi's territory the young tribune who tried to lift from the altar that it was laid upon ended up in a pit ten foot below the ground, with a stake so far up his arse that his last sensation was the taste of his own shit.'

'That *is* nasty.'

'Yeah, tell me about it. Then the lads that went to try and help him got smashed to a pulp by two swinging boulders that came out of the trees. You saw how the Chatti got those corpses to swing down on us; they're good at that sort of thing here.'

'Then we'll just have to be very careful. Anyway, they got the Eagle in the end.'

'But that's just my point, they did get the Eagle but they took it straight back across the Rhenus; if we find this Eagle then we're going to take it back by sea. When Germanicus took us back by that route after his victories here the German gods sent the storm after us in vengeance and you know the rest. And we're about to do the very same thing.'

'Then we shall make sure that we sacrifice to the right gods. The Batavians worship them after all.' Vespasian turned to Ansigar who looked concerned; he had evidently been listening to the conversation. 'Who is your god of the sea, Ansigar?'

'There's a few who could help but I think we should be specific in this case and sacrifice to Nehalennia, the goddess of the Northern Sea. We always call on her before a voyage; if anyone can help us she can.'

'What does she require?'

The decurion scratched his beard. 'The more that we can give her the more she'll help us.'

A pale mist had settled as dawn broke the following morning and a thin layer of snow lay on the ground, making the flat countryside seem monochrome; trees and other natural features in the distance were just two-dimensional, slightly darker shades of grey. As Vespasian sat up blinking his eyes, the troopers were rousing themselves from their damp blankets, their breath steaming in the cold air, complaining about their stiff and aching limbs. Apart from a couple of hours in the late afternoon when there had been enough of a breeze to warrant the hoisting of the sails – emblazoned with the boar's head emblem of the Cherusci – they had rowed constantly until nearly midnight with the almost full, waning moon, sparkling on the river's surface, guiding them; their arms and legs were now suffering after a chill few hours sleeping on hard ground, dusted white.

'The Ice Gods,' Ansigar informed Vespasian as he brushed the snow from his blanket.

'What?'

'Every May the Ice Gods walk through Germania for three days, surveying the country before they return to their realms until it is time to bring winter back to the land. Only once they've completed their journey do the spirits of spring feel it safe to emerge.'

'You see,' Magnus said, clutching his thumb again, 'they do have weird gods.'

Within half an hour, after a decent breakfast of bread and pickled cabbage that had been stowed in the boats, they pushed off from the riverbank and continued downstream. The shroud of mist that obscured both banks, as well as the disembodied, muffled calls of birds, gave the river a foreboding air. The rhythmical dipping of the oars, breaking the water with soft splashes, and the creaking of the wooden vessels seemed loud compared to the deadened sounds around them, and the Batavians started looking nervously over their shoulders as they rowed, now that they were, as Thumelicus had informed them upon departure, in the lands of the Chauci.

They rowed on through the early morning and, although it cleared somewhat as the sun rose higher and fought off the effects of the Ice Gods, the mist remained.

'What sort of people are the Chauci?' Vespasian asked Ansigar in order to take his mind off the unease that had been growing within him.

'Like their neighbours, the Frisii, they divide into two. On the coast where the land is low, wet and unproductive they're seafaring – fishing and raiding up and down the coastline in boats like these. But here, further inland, they have cattle and horses and good land for cultivation. They have treaties with Rome to provide men for the auxiliaries, which they fulfil, as well as paying a nominal tax. Like most of the tribes, they want to stay on good terms with Rome so that they can concentrate on fighting their neighbours and the tribes further east who would dearly love to have our lands. They, along with the Langobardi, hold the wilder tribes at bay on the eastern side of the Albis.'

'What tribes are out there?'

'We hear rumours of many names but we only know a few: Saxones and Anglii along the coast and Suebi along the Albis and then further east the Gothones, Burgundiones and Vandilii;

they're all Germanic. We have no contact with most of them, although occasionally a Saxon or Angle trading or raiding party comes south and we have to deal with them; sometimes with force.' Ansigar suddenly pushed on the steering oar and the boat veered around sharply. Vespasian looked back towards the lead boat; it was doing the same. Beyond it he could see the cause for the sudden manoeuvre: as the mist rose, faint silhouettes were turning into sharper outlines; a Roman fleet was drawn up on the bank and was disembarking thousands of legionaries.

Publius Gabinius had beaten them.

'That's the Chauci's main township,' Thumelicus whispered, pointing to a large settlement about a mile away, built along a low ridge; the only high land in an otherwise flat and dismal snow-dusted landscape still swathed in a light mist. 'Their sacred groves are in the woods to the east; the Eagle will be in one of those.'

But Vespasian was not interested in the Chauci's town or the woodland as he peered out from the cover of a copse. His eyes were fixed on the six cohorts of auxiliary infantry formed up, to the northwest of it, in a line across frosted farmland, shielding a legion deploying from column to battle order behind it. Before the Roman force was a massed formation of Chauci, growing all the time as men rushed in from the surrounding areas, answering the booming, warning calls of horns that echoed all around and off into the distance.

'This could be a welcome diversion for us,' Vespasian suggested, his breath steaming.

'First bit of luck we've had,' Magnus agreed with a grin. 'It looks like they're all going to have plenty to keep them occupied for a while.'

Sabinus looked equally pleased. 'We should get going before we freeze our bollocks off; if we skirt around to the south the mist will obscure us and we should be able to reach that woodland undetected.'

Thumelicus did not look so sure. 'It's not ideal; the Chauci will know why they've come and will either be moving the Eagle or sending a large force to defend it.'

'Then we should do this as fast as possible,' Vespasian said, blowing into his chilled hands. 'It's a mile back to the boats and a mile and a half to that woodland; with luck we could be on the river with the Eagle within an hour.' As he spoke a group of mounted warriors emerged from the Chauci ranks and rode slowly towards the Roman line; one held a branch in full leaf in the air.

Thumelicus smiled. 'They're going to parley; that may give us more time. Let's get moving.'

They made their way back through the copse to where Ansigar and five turmae of the Batavians crouched, waiting; the sixth had been left guarding the boats pulled up on the bank out of view from the Roman fleet.

'Leave a turma here to cover our escape,' Paetus ordered, 'and bring the rest with us, they need to keep low and move fast.'

Thumelicus and his men led them at a fast jog across the flat terrain; to the north the two armies were mainly obscured by the freezing mist but it was thinning all the time as the sun climbed higher. Every now and then it lifted slightly and figures could be seen; but they were still stationary.

A huge shout rose up after they had covered nearly a mile, followed by a roar and then the rhythmical hammering of weapons against shields as the Chauci began to work themselves up into battle fever.

'Sounds like they've decided not to become friends,' Magnus puffed, his chest heaving with the exertion. 'Let's hope they're evenly matched and they slog it out for a while.'

They broke into a run, splashing through an icy stream, brown with the filth discharged from the Chauci's settlement, and pressed on, keeping well to the south of the ridge.

Cornua started their low, rumbling calls, signalling orders throughout the cohorts; these were countered by the blaring of Chauci horns used more to intimidate the enemy than to inform comrades.

More bellows and war cries filled the air until there came the unmistakeable yells and ululations of a barbarian charge. As Thumelicus led them into the wood the first clashes of iron against iron and the dull thumps of shields taking blows resonated in the air; they were soon followed by the shrieks of the wounded and the dying.

'The first grove is due east, about four hundred paces away,' Thumelicus said, increasing his speed.

They ran on, following a weaving snow-patched path deeper into the wood, occasionally having to hurdle the fallen branch of an oak or beech. Behind them the decurions were struggling to keep their turmae in some sort of semblance of a two-abreast column but were losing the fight, their men being unused to acting as infantry.

Vespasian's heart was pounding as he worked his legs hard to push himself forward with the added weight of the cavalry chain mail tunic; he sighed with relief as Thumelicus started to slow. Paetus turned and signalled to Ansigar who, with a couple of movements of his hand above his head, ordered the columns to fan out into line, just as they would have done had they been mounted. They carried on, crouching low, taking care with their steps, easing forward through the trees, javelins at the ready.

'It's straight ahead,' Thumelicus whispered as he signalled a halt.

Vespasian peered through the light haze of the wood shaded from sunlight by the thick canopy; up ahead the atmosphere was brighter where the sun shone down directly onto the thinning mist. The faint sounds of the battle could be heard far off, but nearer at hand the only sound to disturb the peace was birdsong. 'Keep your men here,' he told Paetus. 'Sabinus, Magnus and I will go forward with Thumelicus and his men to have a look.'

Paetus nodded and whispered a few words to Ansigar as Thumelicus led them off at a crouch. As they came closer to the grove the mist became more translucent and Vespasian could see how the trees thinned leaving a clearing that had four ancient oaks at its heart; in the middle of these, resting on two large flattened stones, was a slab of grey granite next to which was piled a mound of wood. Above it dangled a cage, swinging gently, made of thick wicker, the exact shape of, but slightly larger than, a crucified man.

Magnus spat and clenched his right thumb in his fingers. 'It looks like they were planning one of their wicker sacrifices that they seem to be so fond of.'

'There's no one in it,' Vespasian said, edging forward, 'I can see light coming through the gaps. Thumelicus, what do you think?'

'There doesn't seem to be anyone around; if the Eagle's here it'll be close to the altar, but the lack of guards makes it seem unlikely.' He walked out into the clearing, his men either side of him; Vespasian, Sabinus and Magnus followed nervously, poking the ground with their javelins, fearful of stakes concealed in hidden pits.

A search of the altar and the surrounding area proved fruitless. They searched the wood pile and checked for crevices in the trees, all the time aware that capture could mean a ghastly fate burning in the wicker man above them.

'It's not here,' Thumelicus concluded eventually, 'we should move on to the next one about half a mile north of here.'

Vespasian signalled back to Paetus waiting on the edge of the clearing to move his men out as they began to head north.

This time they proceeded with even more caution, a turma, split up into pairs, scouting ahead with Thumelicus and his men, just visible in the ever-thinning mist. The ringing cacophony of battle had escalated but had drawn no closer as they moved onwards. The fresh scents of damp vegetation, musty leaf mulch and clean bracing air made Vespasian wish he was taking a morning stroll in the woods on his estate at Cosa, so far away from this strange land full of danger and alien practices. With a quick, silent prayer to Mars, his guardian god, he asked never to have to return to Germania Magna should he escape this time. An answer seemed to form in his heart; it was not that: all would be well; it was one word: Britannia. He shivered as he imagined the terrors that awaited the Roman legions on that fog-bound island almost completely untouched by Roman civilisation, and for the first time it occurred to him that he and the II Augusta might be a part of the invasion force.

He pushed the unsettling thought from his mind and stalked on, glad of Magnus' and Sabinus' comforting presence either side of him; ahead, Thumelicus raised a hand and went down on one knee. Vespasian and his companions padded forward to join him.

'Sacred horses,' Thumelicus whispered.

The second clearing was larger than the first and this time had a small grove of elm trees in its midst. Surrounding these was a henge of rough wooden columns, ten feet high and a pace apart; each had a skull placed upon its top. Four tethered white horses grazed on hay spread out for them on the patchy snow around the circle, reminiscent of what they had seen on their way to meet Thumelicus; and, in an echo of that scene, three heads, one fresh and the other two decomposing, hung from the branches of the grove above a wooden altar.

After waiting for a few heartbeats it became apparent that, again, there was no one else around. The horses looked up at them curiously as they moved towards the grove and then resumed their meal, satisfied that the intruders neither posed a threat nor possessed any equine treats.

Vespasian passed between two of the wooden columns and into the grove; scattered around on the ground were more heads in various stages of decomposition. Clumps of hair tied to branches above showed where they had hung until decay had eaten away the scalp and they had fallen free. 'Who were these men, Thumelicus?'

'Slaves probably; or sometimes a warrior from another tribe captured in a skirmish; any man who is taken prisoner will know what he can expect.' Thumelicus swept the dusting of snow from the altar; the wood was ingrained with dried blood.

'Lovely,' Magnus muttered, prodding the ground with a javelin and looking for signs of something being recently buried. 'I suppose your gods lap it up.'

'Our gods have kept us free so, yes, they must appreciate human sacrifice.'

'Free to fight each other,' Sabinus pointed out, checking the underside of the altar for anything attached beneath it.

'That is the way of all men: your biggest enemy is closest at hand until foreign invasion makes that enemy your most valuable ally. But come, it's not here; there's one more grove to try to the east, if I remember rightly.'

They made their way deeper into the forest; here the mist remained in patches, clinging to ferns and low branches. Although they were travelling away from the battle the noise of it seemed to be growing.

'It sounds like our lads are pushing them back,' Magnus observed after a while. 'For once I'd say that ain't a good thing.'

Sabinus shrugged. 'There's nothing we can do about it other than hurry up. I don't fancy being caught by Gabinius with the very thing that he's after; that would make for an interesting exchange of views.'

'Let's hope that it doesn't come to that,' Vespasian said as Thumelicus signalled for silence and crouched down.

'What is it?' Vespasian whispered, squatting down next to him.

Thumelicus cocked his ear and pointed ahead. Faintly through the mist, voices could be heard, talking quietly. 'They're no more than a hundred paces away, which means that they must be guarding the grove; I think we're in luck.'

Vespasian beckoned Paetus to join him. 'Send a man forward to find out how many there are.'

The prefect nodded and slipped back to his men; moments later a Batavian crept forward into the mist and Paetus returned.

'They'll be expecting an attack from either the north or west,' Vespasian said softly, 'so we'll split up. You take two turmae around to the north and I'll take the other two to the south where, hopefully, they won't be anticipating a threat. Wait until you hear us charge and make contact, then take them in the rear.'

'I'll give you Ansigar's and Kuno's turmae.'

Vespasian nodded his thanks and then peered forward. Not long later the scout reappeared. 'Fifty, maybe sixty,' he said in a heavy accent.

Vespasian looked relieved. 'Thank you, trooper.' He turned back to Paetus. 'Nothing we can't manage. Get going, we'll give you a count of five hundred to circle around them.'

'These men will give no quarter,' Thumelicus warned the prefect as he left. 'They've sworn to protect the Eagle with their lives.'

'If it's there,' Magnus pointed out.

'Oh it's there all right; why else would they be guarding this grove and not the other two?'

Magnus checked his sword was loose in its scabbard. 'Fair point.'

Sabinus got to his feet. 'Come on then, up and at them.'

The clearing came in and out of view as a light breeze got up and started playing with the mist. The Chauci warriors could be occasionally seen standing to the northeast of the grove of twenty or so trees of mixed species.

'Donar, sharpen our swords and give us victory,' Thumelicus mumbled, clutching a hammer amulet that hung on a leather thong around his neck. 'With this Eagle we shall rid our Fatherland of Rome forever.'

'And you're welcome to it,' Magnus added.

All along the line, men were going through their pre-combat rituals, checking weapons, tightening straps and muttering prayers to their guardian gods.

'Right, let's get this done,' Vespasian said, having made another entreaty to Mars Victorious to help him control himself in the heat of the fight; he had managed it against the Chatti, he could do it again. He signalled to Ansigar to his left and Kuno on his right to move out.

Almost sixty men, in two lines, crept forward towards the edge of the clearing; ahead of them the Chauci talked amongst themselves, sharpening their swords and spear points on stones or flexing their muscles, suspecting nothing as the noise of the battle still raged.

Vespasian raised his arm, took a deep breath, looking left then right to check the decurions were watching, and then flung it forward. As one, the Batavians screamed their battle cry and then pelted out of the trees towards their enemy, shield to shield with javelins at the ready.

Taken completely by surprise the Chauci struggled to form up into two lines, their captains bellowing at them and shoving them into position as the low-trajectory javelin volley hit hard, tearing through the gaps in the incomplete shield wall. Screams filled the clearing as a dozen and more warriors were punched off their feet with the slender, bloodied tips of javelins protruding from their backs. Vespasian watched his missile slam into the throat of a huge blond man, throwing him backwards in a spray of gore with his blood-soaked beard resting on the shaft; he charged across the clearing, whipping his sword from its scabbard.

Keeping in good formation, the two turmae hit the disorganised Germans in unison, cracking their shield bosses, with explosive force, up into faces whilst thrusting low with their long cavalry spathae at fleshy groins and bellies, harvesting the slimy grey contents within. In a couple of places a wall had been formed and these warriors fought back with the ferocity of desperate men, jabbing their long spears over the shield rims at their onrushing foe with such strength that, with the momentum of the charge, their tips cracked through the chain mail, to lodge half a thumb's length in a few screaming Batavians' chests; not deep enough to kill outright but painful enough to incapacitate whilst a killing blow was administered.

Vespasian pressed his left leg forward onto the back of his shield giving it further support; he rammed it against the flat wooden shield of a young warrior snarling at him with bared teeth as he slashed downwards with his long sword. Magnus, on Vespasian's right shoulder, punched his shield up taking the blow on the iron rim with a cloud of sparks. Vespasian ducked involuntarily and in doing so saw his opponent's left foot exposed; with a fleet, brutal motion he sent the tip of his spatha crunching through the unprotected bones and on into the earth beneath. With a high, piercing scream the young Chaucian staggered back pulling his skewered foot away; Vespasian heaved his shoulder into his shield with enough force to send his unbalanced opponent tumbling onto his back. Taking a quick pace forward, he kicked the grounded man's shield away to reveal his groin and slid his blood-slick sword between the legs; he held his wrist firm as the German juddered violently in agony and then ground it left then right as the warrior's shrieks intensified. With a spray of crimson he yanked his weapon back out and moved forward on to the next man as the Batavian behind him punched his sword down into the writhing warrior's throat, stilling his cries and severing the cord of his life.

Vespasian cracked his sword against a shield ahead as Magnus and Sabinus, one to either side, drew forward to stand shoulder to shoulder with him, sweating and blood-spattered, roaring their defiance with inarticulate bellows. Suddenly a shockwave rippled through the whole melee; Paetus' turmae had struck the Germans in the rear. It was now just a matter of time. The Batavians pressed their advantage as the dwindling Chauci retaliated with ever-diminishing force until the last one slid to the churned ground with brains spilling out of what was left of his skull.

'Halt and re-form!' Paetus cried as the two opposing Batavian forces met either side of a ridge of mainly German dead and moaning wounded. The decurions bawled their wide-eyed, panting men back and into lines before they could do their own comrades any harm whilst under the influence of the rush of combat.

Vespasian sucked in cool air as he tried to steady his heartbeat and calm himself after the short but ferocious clash, feeling relief at having not lapsed into the mindless battle-frenzy. 'We should get searching,' he puffed to Thumelicus whose sword arm was streaked with blood.

The German nodded and barked at his five men to follow him as he turned towards the grove.

'Have the men ready to move out as soon as we come back,' Vespasian ordered Paetus as he, Sabinus and Magnus followed.

The grove consisted of about two dozen trees of such a variety of types that Vespasian realised that it must have been planted by man many years ago. He found Thumelicus by the stone altar at its dark centre between an ancient holly and a venerable yew.

'There's no sign of the Eagle here,' the German said, puzzled. He kicked at the mossy, frozen ground but it was solid and showed no signs of recent disturbance.

'What about in the surrounding trees?' Sabinus asked.

After a futile search Thumelicus shook his head. 'It's not here.'

'But you said it would be,' Vespasian almost shouted in his frustration.

'That doesn't mean it has to be; perhaps they moved it deeper into their lands.'

'Then why were they guarding this grove?'

'I don't know.'

'Perhaps they just wanted us to think it was here,' Magnus suggested. 'After all, fifty or so men aren't going to stop determined people getting the Eagle, but it would be enough to convince people to look in the wrong place.'

Vespasian frowned. 'So where could they have hidden it?'

'I don't know, perhaps we should ask one of their wounded.'

'They won't talk no matter what you threaten them with,' Thumelicus stated.

'What about the prospect of a nasty time in that wicker man back at the first clearing? That might—'

'Of course!' Vespasian exclaimed, turning to Magnus. 'You're right. They were trying to draw attention away from where they had hidden it by guarding the wrong grove. It's in the first grove; we checked everywhere but we didn't look inside the wicker man – gods, who'd go near such an unnerving thing? And it seemed to be empty because light was shining through it. But how come it was swinging when there was no wind? Because they had just finished hanging it up when we arrived! We must have just missed them. It's in there.'

Sabinus smacked himself on the back of the head. 'Of course, how stupid. I almost said that would be a good place to hide it as a joke.'

'Would that have been funny?' Thumelicus asked.

'Not really.'

'I thought not. We should go.'

'We're looking in the wrong place,' Vespasian called to Paetus as he followed Thumelicus out of the grove. 'We need to hurry.'

'What about my wounded?'

Vespasian did not reply; he knew that Paetus would know what to do with those too severely hurt to be carried fast.

Thumelicus led them southwest along the side of the triangle they had not yet travelled. Despite the exertion of the previous hour Vespasian did not feel weary but, rather, invigorated by the prospect of finding the Eagle. The raucous sounds of battle growing ever closer, away to his right, gave even more urgency to the final sprint; he knew that as soon as the Romans broke the Germans the wood would be filled with not only defeated fugitives but also with Gabinius' troops hunting the same trophy.

After a lung-tearing run of almost a mile they entered the first clearing from the opposite side. The wicker man was still visible hanging over the altar at the centre of the four oaks that made up the small grove. Thumelicus ran over to it and stopped, looking up at the chilling artefact.

'Can you see it?' Vespasian asked, stopping next to him.

'No, I can't make out anything inside it; we need to get it down.'

'We should be very careful.'

Thumelicus looked at Vespasian with a pained expression. 'Do you really think that I don't know what sort of traps could be protecting this?' He turned to his five men and spoke to them in German; they immediately began to hoist the lightest of their number up on to the lowest branch in the grove using their clasped hands as steps. 'Move away from the altar,' Thumelicus advised Vespasian, Sabinus and Magnus.

They stepped back, looking up nervously as the leaves above them started to rustle and the wicker man began to twist and sway as the man ascended higher. Thumelicus glanced at the swinging man and shouted what sounded to be a warning; the pace of the climb slowed and the wicker man's movement lessened.

A cry of alarm followed by the creaking of straining ropes caused Thumelicus to jump back. 'Get down!'

Vespasian threw himself to the ground as the strained creaking grew; two huge logs, sharpened to points at either end, swung down from the treetops, lengthways, arcing through the clearing so that at their lowest point they were chest high, passing just either side of the altar. The creaking rose in tone and volume as the logs swung through to their zenith, straining at the hemp ropes, pausing for a heartbeat at the extreme of their pendulum, before reversing direction.

As they flashed back through the clearing Vespasian saw that they were not independent but, rather, joined by a thin iron blade at their centre that passed between the top of the altar and the feet of the wicker man. 'That was designed to slice in half anyone who tried to take the man down.'

'Nice lot, these Germans,' Magnus growled as the logs swung back through with lessening force.

'And you think you Romans are nicer because you crucify people or throw them to the wild beasts?' Thumelicus asked, getting to his feet.

'Another fair point.'

As the swinging slowed, Thumelicus ordered his men to still the logs and then sever the ropes; they did so cautiously, stepping back quickly as they cut each one and looking nervously up at the trees, but no more traps sprang from the heights.

Thumelicus shouted to his man above, who replied briefly. 'He can't see any more ropes up there other than the one supporting the wicker man,' Thumelicus informed Vespasian, 'we should be safe to approach it.' He climbed onto the altar and stood up so that his head was knee-height to the wicker man. 'They're made so that they can open, for obvious reasons,' he said examining the thick wickerwork. 'This one opens along either side; we'll have to get it down.' He drew his sword and stood on tiptoe; the end of the blade just reached the rope. He started to saw; two of his men came to stand either side of the altar to catch the wicker man as it fell. The rope thrummed as the sharp edge worked its way through it. Vespasian glanced up to see what it was attached to that made it hang dead centre between all four trees but they were too tall and a thin mist still clung to their dark, upper reaches.

Thumelicus sawed harder as the strands of the rope sprang back, one by one, until there were only a couple left. He looked down at his men, checking that they were ready to catch and then worked his blade for the final cut. The rope parted; the loose end flew up into the trees and the wicker man fell, its feet landing with a crunch on the altar. The two Cherusci grabbed the legs, preventing it from toppling in any direction as a faint metallic ring sounded from above. Vespasian saw Thumelicus freeze for an instant and then turn his head up towards the noise; his eyes and mouth opened in alarm as the sun broke through the mist and two flashes of burnished iron blazed like lightning down from the canopy. 'Donar!' he shouted at the sky.

With a crack a sword hit the altar, bending slightly before springing back up, vibrating with a thunderous roll and falling to the ground; a thin twine was knotted around its handle, leading up into the heights. Vespasian looked for the other only to see Thumelicus' legs start to buckle. He raised his gaze; Thumelicus' head was tipped back and protruding from his mouth, like some cross perched upon a hill of execution, was the hilt of the second sword. Blood flowed freely around it, trickling into Thumelicus' beard; the blade had entered his throat at an exact perpendicular, slicing its way down through the internal organs until it came to a jarring halt on the base of the pelvis. Thumelicus' eyes focused in disbelief at the hilt just before them, unable to comprehend how it got there. A grating gargling sound exploded from his throat and blood slopped onto the pommel and the twine attached to it; he fell against the wicker man, pushing it back off the altar. Leaving an arced trail of blood globules marking his descent, Thumelicus fell with it, crashing onto its chest as they hit the ground and then bouncing up slightly, owing to the springiness of the branches woven together. As Thumelicus thumped back down a second time the wicker man broke open; a bundle wrapped in soft leather rolled out.

Vespasian stooped down and picked it up; it was heavy. He glanced down at Thumelicus; the light faded from his eyes but Vespasian felt that he detected a glimmer of triumph. Sabinus looked at his brother with disbelief. Vespasian raised his eyebrows and hefted the bundle over to him.

Sabinus placed it down on the ground and pulled back the leather. 'We've got it,' he whispered as the last flap fell free to reveal a golden eagle, wings spread, neck arched, ready for the kill and holding Jupiter's thunderbolts in its talons; the Eagle given by Augustus, more than fifty years before, to his XVII Legion.

Sabinus looked at Vespasian and for the first time ever there was genuine fraternal emotion in his eyes. 'Thank you, brother. I owe you my life.'

CHAPTER XII

Flames raged on thatched roofs and smoke billowed up from the township, melting away the last of the haze and replacing it with a bitter-smelling pall. Remnants of the Chauci poured from the field of battle, heading for the relative safety of the woods, pursued, in good order, by six cohorts whilst the remainder sacked the town. The screams of the women within were plainly audible as outrage after outrage was committed.

Vespasian pushed himself onwards, next to Paetus at the head of the lead turma, with Magnus and Sabinus puffing behind as they retraced their steps to the rearguard at the copse. Thumelicus' men bore their leader on their shoulders, the sword still embedded in his stiffening body; they had been unwilling to remove it without a priest, fearing that it may be cursed. Vespasian could well believe it as he remembered Thumelicus' words: 'I swore to Donar the Thunderer to strike me down with a lightning bolt from above if I ever have anything to do with Rome again.'

Splashing through the rank, contaminated stream, Vespasian glanced away to his right and then looked back in alarm at Paetus. 'Look, they're coming around this side now, they're bound to see us.'

Paetus looked up without breaking his step to see the best part of an ala of auxiliary cavalry swooping around the west side of the township in pursuit of fifty or so Chauci horsemen. 'With luck they're too busy to worry about us; we are Roman after all.'

'We may be,' Magnus agreed, 'but we're Romans running in the wrong direction.'

'In that case let's stop running,' Vespasian suggested.

'Not a bad idea, brother,' Sabinus wheezed, immediately slowing his pace.

There were no objections to the suggestion from the exhausted Batavians who at a signal from Paetus and barked orders from the decurions slowed into a quick march, dressing their ranks into some semblance of military order.

'Get Ansigar to take Thumelicus' men's weapons from them,' Vespasian ordered Paetus, 'and have a turma surround them. Explain to them it's just for appearances' sake until we get back to the river.'

Paetus grinned and dropped back to find his senior decurion.

Sabinus swapped his weighty trophy from under one arm to the other. 'Why did you ask for that?'

'You'll see very soon,' Vespasian replied, watching three turmae peel off from the ala and head in their direction.

Paetus caught up with him. 'They understood; it wasn't a problem. I'll deal with those chaps if that's all right, sir; I think that I know what to say.'

They did not have long to wait; by the time they had covered another couple of hundred paces the cavalry had cut them off and were formed up across their path. Paetus brought the Batavians to a halt and walked forward with a look of righteous indignation on his patrician face. 'Just what do you think you are up to, decurion?' he roared at the leading officer in the central turma. 'How dare you block my unit's path as if we were part of the rabble that we've just defeated? We did the hard work whilst you were pissing about on your horses pretending that it's dangerous on the extreme right flank.'

The decurion, clean-shaven and in his late twenties, looked nervously down at Paetus from under the thin rim of his cavalry helmet. 'I'm sorry, prefect, my commander wanted me to find out what you were doing.'

'None of his fucking business is what we're doing; I suggest that he carries on occupying himself with chasing small contingents of beaten Germans around the countryside whilst proper soldiers take the body of a chieftain, whom they've just despatched to German Hades, back to the fleet so that we can dispose of his body a long way from here. Now move out of the way, soldier.'

The decurion looked behind Paetus to where Thumelicus' men stood with his body in the midst of Ansigar's turma. 'But you're cavalry, sir.'

Paetus went puce. 'Of course we're fucking cavalry, you idiot, but when cavalry lose their horses because the cock-hungry sailors of the transports failed to keep up with the rest of the fleet, what happens then? They become sodding infantry, decurion, that's what happens; now fuck off before I get cross.'

The decurion saluted briskly. 'My apologies, sir.' With a quick hand signal the turmae parted to let them through. Paetus gave a bad-tempered growl; Ansigar bellowed an order and the Batavians moved forward, jeering at the mounted auxiliaries until a huge roar from Ansigar made them decide to keep their opinions to themselves.

Vespasian breathed deeply again as he passed by the rear ranks of troopers, keeping his eyes fixed on the copse, now only half a mile distant. 'You reminded me of your father when he was making his report to Poppaeus, our commanding officer in Thracia, Paetus.'

Paetus smiled ruefully. 'He used to do his centurion voice for me when I was small, it always made me laugh.'

Vespasian patted Paetus' shoulder, remembering with affection his long-dead friend. After they had gone a couple of hundred paces he looked over his right shoulder; the turmae were galloping east to catch up with the rest of their ala. 'Time to run, Paetus.' He broke into a jog and then slowly increased his pace so that the men behind him would not lose their formation. To the front of the township was a mass of bodies splayed out over the plain; walking wounded and surgeons' stretcher parties picked their way through it back to the hospital tents by the fleet.

They soon passed into the copse, leaving the burning township and the desolation behind, and pressed on towards the river with the rearguard falling in behind them.

Vespasian eased the pace off, well aware that the men were exhausted and there was a long, fast row ahead of them to slip past the Roman fleet. 'We'd do best to abandon a couple of the boats, Paetus, and fill the other two so we can row in shifts and have men to fight off an attack if we're unlucky enough to be followed.'

Paetus did a quick mental calculation and then called back to Ansigar: 'Can the boats take almost seventy men each?'

'Yes, but they'll be lower in the water and slower.'

'We'll take three, then,' Vespasian decided as the river came in sight.

The turma guarding the boats started pushing them off the bank, floating them ready, as they pounded down the gentle grassy slope to the river's edge.

Ansigar shouted orders to his fellow decurions and somehow the turmae sorted themselves out, two to a boat.

'What are Thumelicus' men going to do?' Vespasian asked the decurion once he had finished terrorising his men.

After a brief conversation with the Cherusci Ansigar came back. 'They'll take the last boat south to return Thumelicus' body to his mother, sir.'

'Just five of them to row that?'

Ansigar shrugged. 'They say they can manage if they keep close to the bank away from the main current.' He stuck his finger in his mouth, wetted it and then held it in the air. 'They think that this slight northerly breeze will grow and they'll be able to hoist the sail soon.'

Vespasian looked at Ansigar's finger and then wetted his own and held it up. The side facing north felt slightly colder. 'That'll mean it will be blowing against us. Well, wish them luck and thank them for me.' He turned back to the Batavian boats that were now almost fully loaded and waded out and climbed aboard using a rope ladder slung over the stern.

Magnus hauled him over the rail. 'Time to go, wouldn't you say, sir?'

'Long overdue, Magnus,' Vespasian replied as Ansigar clambered up the ladder after him. He took the steering oar and shouted what Vespasian took to be a series of numbers, then as one the Batavians dipped their oars in the water and heaved back; the boats slid forward into the gently flowing river.

*

Vespasian ordered Ansigar to steer a direct course for the opposite bank to keep as far away as possible from the Roman fleet;
the current pushed them downstream as they crossed and by the
time they had reached the far side they were almost level with the
fleet, plainly visible now that the mist had lifted, five hundred
paces to the east. A couple of miles ahead the river curved away
to the west.

'Increase the stroke rate, Ansigar,' Vespasian commanded as
the decurion eased the steering oar away from him, turning the
longboat north. 'If we can get round that bend before they notice
us we'll be away.' He kept his eyes firmly fixed on the Roman
ships, mainly biremes, hauled up along a half-mile stretch of
riverbank. The shouts of their crews drifted across the flat water,
which shone like a mirror, reflecting the noonday sun.

'We'll be lucky to escape their notice,' Sabinus said, hugging
the Eagle in its leather wrapping to his chest. 'I should imagine
that right about now Gabinius is discovering that we got there
before him, thanks to Thumelicus.'

'That's another fucking irony, isn't it? This country's full of
them,' Magnus declared. 'The son of Arminius tried to steal a
Roman Eagle that his father captured, so that he could return it
to Rome, thus breaking an oath to Donar who struck him down
from above with a German trap. And all because three ex-slaves
want to keep their master and themselves in power, but at the
same time they fight each other for the privilege of being considered the most useful by a drooling fool.'

Vespasian's brow creased into a frown. 'It does make you
wonder what sort of government we're going to have under
Claudius.'

'The same as always, I suppose.'

'No, it's been different with each Emperor. Augustus managed
to rule with the Senate without making it seem that he was ultimately in charge although everybody knew he was. Tiberius wasn't
subtle enough to play that game so the relationship broke down
because neither could understand what the other wanted. Caligula

then drew all power into his own hands, ruling with the approval of the mob whilst the Senate cowered, scared of arbitrary execution every time the Emperor ran out of money. And now we've got a figurehead emperor who distrusts the Senate because it didn't support him and who's manipulated by three Greek freedmen that no one can trust – even though I would call one a friend – who seem to be running the Empire for their own benefit.'

'That's why I keep out of politics,' Magnus commented. 'I couldn't give a fuck how we're ruled or by whom, so long as they leave me alone in my little corner of Rome, which they do because I don't give a shit about them. If you had the same attitude *I'd* have a much quieter life, if you take my meaning?'

Sabinus scoffed. 'That attitude's fine for your class but how can a senator avoid getting caught up in politics?'

'By stopping being a senator or, if his dignitas won't allow him to resign his place, then at least stopping attending the Senate and stopping trying to get the next prestigious appointment.'

'Then how can a man rise and gain influence?'

'I have a lot of influence in my area.'

'That's because you're the *patronus* of a Crossroads Brotherhood.'

'Exactly, I am at the top of my, er ... trade or sphere, as it were, and I aspire to no more than that. You gentlemen on the other hand run around playing politics in a sphere that you already know you can't get to the top in because you come from the wrong family, so what's the point?'

'I suppose the point is to become consul,' Vespasian said, 'which would be a great honour for our family.'

'It would have been two hundred years ago, but what does it mean now? Nothing apart from being preceded by twelve lictors and having the chance to go and govern a province afterwards, in the arsehole of the Empire, far away from the pleasures of Rome. Face it, sirs, things ain't what they were in the old Republic and you're just helping them to get worse.'

'It's better than sitting on a farm where the only thing to look forward to is seeing whether this year's wine is better than the last,' Sabinus said.

Vespasian did not look so sure. 'I don't know, Sabinus, that's what I wanted to do when I was young and sometimes I wonder now whether it wouldn't be a good idea to return to it.'

'Bollocks, you'd be bored.'

'Would I? I don't know any more,' Vespasian said, looking back out to the Roman fleet. Movement on the bank caught his eye; a large party of horsemen were drawing up. At their head was a man in a general's uniform, his bronze cuirass and helmet glinting in the sun and his red cloak billowing behind him. 'Shit! That has to be Gabinius, and they look to be the auxiliaries who questioned us. I think that he's just worked out that he didn't have any dismounted cavalry in his line.' As he spoke he could see the general shading his eyes and staring towards them; and then he heard him shout. Instantly the sailors on the biremes nearest to him sprang into action; the ships were being made ready for the chase. 'Can we go any faster, Ansigar?'

'Not without risking fouling our oars.'

'Risk it then, they'll certainly catch us if we don't.'

With a shout from Ansigar the Batavians increased their pace and Vespasian felt the ship accelerate slightly but at the same time he noticed the river surface was no longer mirror-flat; the Cherusci had been right, the north wind was freshening. He cast it from his mind, knowing that it would hinder the chasing biremes as much as it would the longboats.

'That's one they've managed to launch,' Magnus said through gritted teeth as a bireme slid back into the water pushed by many men. 'How come we always seem to fall foul of our own navy? I seem to remember being shot at by them in Moesia.'

'Fucking low-life,' Sabinus muttered; as with any man who had served under the Eagles, he had a very low opinion of the navy.

Vespasian watched anxiously as five more vessels, whose prows had been grounded on the bank, were pushed back, each spreading its oars as they floated, like geese warning off rivals.

By the time the longboats approached the bend in the river all six biremes were following less than a mile behind.

Ansigar shouted at his men and the fifteen who had not yet rowed relieved some of their comrades. Vespasian did not feel any increase in speed but knew that a constant recycling of the rowers was their only hope of maintaining their speed and perhaps outpacing the biremes, which would not have such a luxury. For the third time that day he offered up a prayer to Mars to hold his hands over them and prevent what they had struggled so hard to get from being stolen at the last.

The bend neared as the Batavians strained at their oars, sweat pouring off them; they had not had time to remove their chain mail tunics in their rush to escape. Ansigar roared encouragement at them, spittle flecked his beard and his blue eyes burned into his men, willing them on. Just a length behind them the other two longboats were keeping up with the, quite literally, blistering pace.

The river started to ease away to the northwest and Vespasian felt a glimmer of hope as he looked back at the biremes; they seemed to be slightly further behind, perhaps they could win this race. A shout from Ansigar as they rounded the bend, blocking their pursuers from view, made him turn suddenly.

'Juno's gaping arse!' Magnus exclaimed. 'What the fuck are those?'

Vespasian's mouth fell open. Less than half a mile downriver were ten square sails each bearing the image of a wolf; beneath the sails were the high, carved prows and sleek bellies of longboats. They were crammed with men. Vespasian looked at Ansigar; he did not need to ask the question.

The decurion bit his lip. 'The Chauci wolf. The Chauci coastal clans have come to the aid of their inland cousins.'

'Will they let us pass?' Sabinus asked with more than a hint of desperation in his voice.

'I doubt it and we can't outmanoeuvre them because the wind's in their favour; they will stop us and when they hear from our accents that we're Batavians they'll assume that we are part of Gabinius' army taking prizes back to the Empire and then ...' Ansigar did not need to finish the sentence; they all knew what would happen then.

'But surely they'll turn and run when they see the biremes,' Vespasian said, looking back, 'they don't stand a chance against them.'

Ansigar shook his head. 'Each one of those boats is commanded by a clan chief; if one of them turns without making an honourable contact with the enemy then he wouldn't be clan chief by the time he got home; if he got home at all.'

'Then we've only got one option, we wait for those biremes. They'll engage the Chauci and we may have a chance of fighting our way through in the chaos.' Vespasian turned back to his companions; no one had any better ideas. 'Back water then, Ansigar.'

As one, the Batavians dipped their oars in the water on Ansigar's command, slowing the longboat as five of the Chauci fleet peeled off and headed towards them. Paetus' boat came alongside; Vespasian quickly told him what he planned to do. By the time he had spoken to Kuno in the third boat the stroke had been reversed and the three vessels began moving backwards – and the first of the biremes appeared around the bend.

'That's given them a shock,' Magnus chuckled as warning shouts floated across the water from the Chauci's boats. The five longboats still out in midstream altered course to join up with those that were heading towards the Batavians.

The Roman flotilla was now level with them, just a hundred paces away, fanning out into battle order; the shrill pipes of the stroke-masters increased in pace as the artillery crews loaded the small ballistae mounted in each of their prows.

Vespasian watched them bear down on the Chauci. 'They seem to have forgotten about us for the time being. Ansigar, time to go; we'll fight alongside them.'

The three longboats surged forward at an angle edging closer to their erstwhile pursuers; Vespasian, Sabinus and Magnus grabbed their shields and made their way up to the fighting platform in the bow, pausing to take some javelins from the weapons box beneath the mast, into which Sabinus stowed the Eagle next to the Capricorn. The Batavians recently relieved from rowing joined them, sweating and grim, flexing their muscles and testing the weight of their weapons.

A series of loud cracks from their right announced the opening shots of artillery at extreme range of four hundred paces, and six plumes of water spurted skywards just behind the Chauci line.

'Get it right, arseholes!' Sabinus shouted pointlessly at the crews as they reloaded; the groans of exertion from a hundred and twenty rowers on each bireme, the shouts of the marine officers and the pipes of the stroke-masters drowned out his voice.

The two lines were fewer than three hundred paces apart; the Chauci had spread their oars and started rowing to gain some extra momentum. Vespasian could see them clearly now, even with a full complement rowing there were still at least twenty warriors ready to fight; they cheered on the comrades toiling on the oars, urging them to greater speed.

Six more twanging cracks sounded, and as Vespasian watched a Chaucian boat approach, a hole appeared in its sail and the heads of three of the men standing on the fighting platform just disappeared. Those around them turned red with the blood pumping from the gaping necks as the bodies stayed upright, such was the crush of warriors eager to get to grips with the hated invaders. Towards the middle of the Chaucian line one of their longboats started listing; men baled furiously with buckets and shields as water rushed in through the holed hull. Undeterred, its oarsmen rowed on.

At a hundred paces apart the ballistae shot for the last time; ten feet higher on the prows of the biremes than their targets, they had tilted down to aim their heavy stones into the bellies of the longboats. Half a dozen oars from one heaved up at odd angles as a shot carved its way down a line of oarsmen, decapitating and maiming in a spray of gore. Bodies were punched forwards into their fellows causing them to miss their stroke; the dead men's oars fell back into the water and the longboat skewed around them and into the path of its neighbour, striking it amidships and raking it. Rowers were catapulted back as their oars were slammed into them by the solid wooden prow, screams of agony rose above the cheering of the Roman marines as ribs were smashed and arms snapped by the momentous pressure. But the other eight longboats came on.

Archers now took their place on the biremes' decks sending a constant stream of arrows towards the oncoming vessels but the warriors raised their shields, protecting themselves and their comrades at the oars from sudden death.

Vespasian loosened his spatha in its scabbard, his belly tightened and he found himself wishing that he had the shorter infantry gladius for this close-quarters work. Ahead of him, two longboats were aiming straight towards the three Batavian vessels; they were close enough to make out the features of the frenzied men in their bows. To his right the nearest bireme was no more than five oar-lengths away, its bronze-headed ram foaming the water before it.

'Release!' Vespasian shouted, slinging his javelin once he could see the whites of his opponents' eyes. The Batavians, with their shields in front of them, hurled their first volley as Ansigar bellowed an order; the rowers hauled in their oars, grabbed shields and javelins and lined the sides of the longboat that ploughed on under its own momentum. Ansigar steered it directly towards the gap between the two oncoming Chauci; they too hauled in their oars. The first return missiles hit with a heavy, staccato thumping on their shields and the bow as Vespasian prepared his second javelin; but the Batavians' discipline held, as did their shield wall, and there were no agonised cries. To Vespasian's left Paetus and Kuno's men let fly their javelins with a roar; a couple of enemy warriors toppled into the water and sank immediately, leaving crimson stains to mark their passing.

'Release!' Vespasian again screamed at ten paces apart. The second volley slammed into the Chauci taking more down into the river; they readied their long thrusting spears for close combat. A massive cracking of wood to the right caused Vespasian to glance across to see a longboat being pushed back, impaled on the ram of the bireme next to him; Chauci warriors were jumping into the water and grabbing at the bireme's oars, thrusting their spears through the oar-ports into the rowers within and trying to scale the ship's sides; archers leant over the rail picking them off with easy shots.

Ansigar kept his course steady, hoping to pass between the two longboats, but the Chauci steersmen knew their business; at the last moment both boats veered to the starboard heading straight for Vespasian's and Paetus' vessels, leaving Kuno's free to pass by.

'Brace!' Vespasian screamed as a collision became inevitable.

'Fuck me!' Magnus muttered next to him as he gripped the rail. 'First horses and now longboats, don't they do anything natural here?'

A shuddering blow, just to the starboard side of the prow, jolted through the whole boat, throwing a few of the less well-braced Batavians to their knees. Spears jammed forward with determined force into the shields of the Batavians as the boat started to slew round. Vespasian hacked at a shaft embedded in Magnus' shield as, behind him, Ansigar roared for some men to take up oars to steady the vessel. An auxiliary shrieked and fell back, ripping a bloodied leaf-shaped spearhead from his jaw; before the gap could be closed two Chauci warriors had jumped across, spears jabbing down from over their shoulders, whilst their comrades hammered theirs on the Batavians' shields; gradually they gave ground. More Chauci swarmed over, bellowing with battle-joy, pushing the defenders ever back, off the fighting platform and in amongst the rowing benches. The Chauci followed, battering at the shield wall.

Vespasian stood between Sabinus to his right and Magnus to his left, punching his shield forward and up, trying to deflect the long-reaching weapons so that he could get under and close in on his foes; but to no avail. Sabinus raised his shield to a brutal overarm stab, taking the point just above the boss, embedding it with a deadened thump; twisting away from his brother he hauled the spear forward to drag its owner out of the line. Vespasian dipped to his right and swept his sword low below the man's shield; his arm juddered but he kept his grip as it sliced into a shin with the hard, wet sound of a butcher's cleaver thwacking into a side of pork. With an ear-splitting howl the warrior stepped forward to balance himself only to find the bottom part of his leg missing; he tumbled to the deck spraying blood from his newly carved stump over the feet of his comrades.

Vespasian pressed forward his advantage, taking his neighbours with him into the gap, his sword flashing red over his shield and into the face of the next warrior, crunching through the bridge of his nose as the man stared in cross-eyed disbelief at the blade. The Chauci line momentarily faltered. Magnus exploded forward, bellowing curses above the screaming, taking the Batavians to his left with him, and hacked away a spear shaft before him; the warrior slipped on the slick blood-drenched deck lowering his shield for a brief instant. Magnus' sword found its mark.

Now they were past the spears and toe to toe with the boarders; the second rank of Batavians closed up, holding their shields over the first ranks' heads to protect them from the downward spear-thrusts of the Chauci still up on the fighting platform. Vespasian felt the pressure on his back as the man behind him pushed him forward. He stabbed repeatedly with his spatha until he felt it connect with flesh and then he twisted and was rewarded with a scream. To both sides of him the Batavians were making ground and only a few Chauci were left in front of the fighting platform, trapped, unable to get back up. They died swiftly. The warriors on the platform pulled back out of range of a disabling sword swipe to their ankles. They were at stalemate.

Vespasian stepped back, letting the man behind him replace him in the front rank. Ansigar, with five oarsmen on each side rowing constantly, was keeping the longboat at an angle to the Chaucian vessel preventing it from coming alongside and disgorging even more warriors. To his left Paetus' crew were having a hard fight of it, they were almost pushed back to the mast. But of Kuno's boat there was no sign. To the right, the river was littered with flotsam and jetsam; one bireme had flames issuing out of its oar-ports and warriors swarming up its sides from a longboat attached to its bow with grappling hooks. The remaining biremes clustered around the last three longboats afloat, pumping arrows into the shields of their crews who could do nothing but cower.

With a sudden lurch the longboat rocked as a massed cry broke through the cacophony of the river battle. A warrior tumbled from the fighting platform into the water whilst the remainder up there had to grab the sides to steady themselves. In an instant Magnus and Sabinus led the Batavians leaping up, taking full advantage of the enemies' lack of balance; as they did Vespasian looked beyond them to see the cause of the shock: Kuno's boat had circled around and had rammed the Chauci in the rear. Kuno's men leapt onto the surprised vessel, slicing into the crew whose attention had been focused on Vespasian's longboat.

As the last warrior fell from the fighting platform Sabinus and Magnus pushed the Chaucian vessel away, leaving Kuno's men to finish the job.

'Ansigar!' Vespasian shouted, pointing at Paetus' boat where now more than thirty Chauci had pushed Paetus' men beyond the mast.

The decurion understood and pulled on his steering oar, guiding the longboat towards the hard-pressed crew on the boat next to them. With a few pulls at the oars they were almost along-side. Armed with the remainder of their javelins, the Batavians sent two savage, close-range volleys into the Chauci's flank. More than a dozen fell, skewered from the side; a shudder went through the rest and a few paused to look towards the new threat. This was enough for Paetus and his men; they surged forward with renewed vigour, getting between the long spears of their opponents and working their swords through the gaps in their shield wall. As Vespasian's boat drew closer the Chauci nearest the rail turned and fled knowing that they would soon be outnumbered, leaving their three comrades already engaged to the front to succumb to the stabbing swords of the Batavians. Ansigar shouted in German and the defenders swarmed all over them using their shield bosses and fists rather than their blades. As the last one went down, disarmed and unconscious, the Chaucian longboat pushed away, backing oars whilst warriors helped survivors from the other boat out of the water.

'Let them go!' Vespasian shouted. 'Take up the oars and let's get away from here.'

'I don't think that would be a wise thing to do, legate,' a voice called from behind him. 'You've seen how accurate our ballistae crews are.'

Vespasian spun round to see a bireme just twenty paces away; leaning on the rail, resplendent in his red crested helmet, bronze muscled cuirass and flowing red cloak was Publius Gabinius. He smiled without mirth. 'If I were you I would take my generous invitation to come aboard my ship. Oh, and you'll bring that trinket that you found, won't you?'

Vespasian looked down from the bireme's rail at the three streams of blood splashing into the river. Ansigar recited a prayer in German as the lifeblood of the three captives was emptied into the water in honour of Nehalennia, the goddess of the Northern Sea.

'Was that strictly necessary?' Gabinius asked.

Vespasian shrugged as the sacrifices were dumped overboard from Ansigar's longboat. 'I'm not really sure.'

'Well, I am,' Magnus asserted. 'And I have to say that I feel a lot better knowing that we've got a German goddess on our side for the trip home.'

'There can't be any harm in that, I suppose.' Gabinius' attention turned to the bundle; he unwrapped the leather and held the Eagle in his hands, looking at it with admiration. 'Of course I shall be claiming the glory of retrieving this.'

Sabinus looked more than resentful. 'And Callistus will be boasting to the Emperor that it was his plan?'

Gabinius looked up, surprise showing on his thin, long face. 'How did you know that?'

'The man whom Callistus sent to stop us told us in exchange for a weapon in his hand as he died.'

Gabinius sniffed. 'They're very particular about that here; mind you, I suppose we like to have a coin put in our mouth for the ferryman, same sort of thing really. Anyway, he was right; Callistus will be enjoying his perceived victory, but I'll be remembered in the history books as the man who found the Eagle of the Seventeenth.'

Vespasian looked up at the eastern bank of the river moving slowly by as they sailed north towards the sea and back to the Empire. Behind them the rest of the fleet had embarked and were following. 'You know that your theft of this will cost my brother his life, Gabinius?'

'Theft is a very strong word. You could argue that you would have failed had it not been for my attack on the Chauci. But no matter, it's in my possession now and that's what counts. As to Sabinus losing his life because of me, I doubt that will happen.'

'What makes you so sure?'

'Because Narcissus told me so.'

Vespasian was outraged. 'Narcissus knew that you were coming after the Eagle even though he sent us?'

'Of course he knew; he doesn't give a shit who finds the Eagle as long as it's found. The end result is all the same to him and he considers it good politics to have his underlings squabbling amongst themselves.'

Magnus spat on the deck. 'Fucking Greek freedmen.'

Gabinius smirked and gazed proudly at his prize. 'Yes, I'm afraid they're not to be trusted.'

'What about Pallas, did he know too?' Vespasian asked. 'And did he know that Callistus sent someone to kill us?'

'I don't know if he knew of Callistus' plan but I'm sure that he didn't know Callistus had sent an assassin; he would have told Narcissus if he had. Narcissus made no mention of Callistus' assassin, in fact quite the opposite; he was very specific in his letter to me that you were not to be killed if I came across you, so he would have in no way condoned Callistus' little bit of cheating.'

Sabinus looked relieved. 'Well, that's something, I suppose: if he doesn't want us dead I should be free to return to Rome; and I can expose Callistus as a murderous little Greek cunt to Narcissus.'

Vespasian sighed, exhausted by the day and the machinations of Claudius' freedmen. 'I wouldn't bother; what proof do we have other than our word? Callistus will just deny everything and all you'd do is make him even more of an enemy. Besides, Narcissus won't care one way or the other; he sees the bigger picture and as far as he's concerned he has his Eagle for his master and it's time to move on.'

'I think that you're right there, Vespasian,' Gabinius agreed. 'And anyway, Sabinus, you're not free to return to Rome. Narcissus gave me orders for you two in his letter should the Eagle have been found; assuming that you have survived of course. Vespasian, you are to return to the Second Augusta, and Sabinus, Narcissus, or rather, the Emperor, has appointed you legate of the Fourteenth Gemina based at Mogontiacum on the Rhenus.'

Sabinus was shocked. 'The Fourteenth? Why?'

Gabinius shrugged. 'I don't know; imperial politics seem to get more and more unreadable and seemingly random but I'm sure there's a good reason for it.'

'I'm sure there is and it'll be more to do with Narcissus' ambitions than my deserving it.'

'I expect you're right; it's a strange world that we live in when our class is forced to take orders from freedmen. Anyway, you can't have your old legion back, the Ninth Hispana has been given to the Empress' brother, Corvinus.'

'Yes, I know; the only good thing about that is that'll keep him out of our way in Pannonia for a while.'

'Only for a year.'

'What?'

'At the end of the campaigning season next year Aulus Plautius, who was made Governor of Pannonia in thanks for his support of Claudius, is moving to Gesoriacum on the north coast of Gallia Belgae, and he'll be bringing the Ninth with him. The Twentieth will also be going there as well as your two legions and your attached auxiliary cohorts. You, gentlemen, have the honour to be part of Aulus Plautius' invasion force for the conquest of Britannia.'

Vespasian felt a chill as he envisioned more fog-wreathed forests and strange gods; he looked at his brother. 'I had a feeling that "honour" was coming and I've been dreading it.'

Sabinus was astounded. 'It seems that Narcissus is determined to kill us one way or the other.'

Only Paetus looked pleased.

Magnus spat again on the deck. 'Fucking great way to end the day.'

PART III

THE INVASION OF BRITANNIA,
SPRING AD 43

CHAPTER XIII

'BRACE YOURSELVES, MY lovelies!' Primus Pilus Tatius roared at his double-strength century of a hundred and sixty men kneeling on one knee on the wet deck of a trireme hurtling towards the shore. The men immediately leant forward, thumping their right hands and the bases of their shields down onto the planking, their pila clasped in their left along with their shield grips. 'That's my boys; this won't hurt – too much.'

Vespasian nodded to himself in satisfaction at the discipline of the first century of the first cohort of the II Augusta as he watched the oncoming beach, less than a hundred paces away, blinking his eyes against the sheeting rain. Next to him, in the bow of the ship, the aquilifer of the II Augusta held its Eagle aloft; beyond him, a line of ships with no sails set but each with oars dipping in unison as their stroke-masters piped out the same beat disappeared into the downpour. Vespasian cursed the weather in these northern climes and took a firm hold of the rail as two sailors ran forward to man the ropes holding upright the two twenty-foot-long, eight-foot-wide *corvi*, the ramps by which they would disembark.

'Oars in,' the *trierarchus*, who captained the trireme, called through a speaking trumpet at the stern.

A shrill, long call on the stroke-master's pipe heralded the mass rasping of wood on wood as a hundred and twenty oars were drawn in through their ports; the beach was now less than fifty paces away. Again Vespasian nodded to himself in satisfaction: that was the prescribed distance to cease rowing so that the ship would be grounded but not beached. He checked his sword was loose in its scabbard and cast a glance along the line of triremes; only one still had its oars out. 'Who the fuck's that, Tatius?'

The primus pilus quickly counted off the ships. 'Third and fourth centuries, second cohort, sir!'

Vespasian grunted and braced himself solidly against the ship's side whilst Tatius did the same with one hand and with the other took a firm grip of the aquilifer's shoulder so that the Eagle would not fall. With a slight upwards jolt and a grating of churning shingle the hull hit the sea bed; deceleration was immediate and swift, forcing Vespasian to tense his arm and leg muscles as he was propelled forward. The grating transformed into a tooth-aching screech as the speed of the vessel was checked until, with a groan of straining timber and a sudden lurch, the trireme came to a halt, resting – but not embedded – on the beach.

'Up!' Tatius cried.

As one the first century got to their feet, transferring their pila into their right hands; the corvi were released to fall with a descending creak to slam into the shingle.

'The first century will disembark at double time,' Tatius roared as he and the aquilifer stepped on to the ramp. Vespasian leapt onto the second ramp and jogged down, feeling the wood bounce slightly beneath his feet until he hit the shingle; the men raced down to the beach in groups of four behind him.

Bawled at by Tatius and his optio, they had formed up into four lines of forty by the time the last men had disembarked.

'Advance quick time one hundred paces!' Tatius bellowed once he was satisfied that the lines were straight.

Pounding over the shingle, the first century doubled up the sloping beach. Behind them the fifth century moved into place from their landing point to the right and from the left the rest of the first cohort came smartly up to form up next to them.

'Halt!' Tatius ordered from his place just in front of the aquilifer.

The first cohort came to a crunching stop.

Vespasian looked along the beach to see the other nine cohorts of the II Augusta dressed perfectly in two lines along the strand; it had taken little more than two hundred heartbeats. The ships that had disgorged them bobbed on the shallow water afloat once more now that their weight had been drastically reduced; except one: the third and forth centuries of the second cohort.

As Vespasian marched forward to his primus pilus a lone horseman appeared over the scraggy mounds at the top of the beach leading a spare horse; he squinted his eyes against the rain at the oncoming man.

'Sir!' Magnus shouted as he drove his horse down the beach.

Vespasian frowned in surprise to see his friend coming out of the rain.

'What is it, Magnus?'

'Aulus Plautius has called a meeting of all legates and auxiliary prefects, so I thought I'd bring you a horse. Narcissus has just arrived and my guess is something's going on. I don't think he's come all this way for a cup of hot wine and a nice fireside chat, if you take my meaning?'

'Can't he ever stop meddling? All right, I'll be there in a moment.' Vespasian turned to Tatius. 'Very good, primus pilus, apart from that arsehole trierarchus who doesn't know when to stop rowing; go and shout at him for a while, would you?'

'Sir!'

'Get the men and ships back to Gesoriacum, give them something to eat and then do the whole thing again this afternoon with the tide out; and this time I want no mistakes. I'll join you if I can.'

'Sir!' Tatius bellowed, snapping to attention.

Vespasian nodded, mounting the spare horse that Magnus had brought. 'Right, let's go and see what plans that oily Greek's got to make our lives even harder.'

The rain whipped in relentlessly as Vespasian and Magnus made their way the ten miles to Aulus Plautius' headquarters; these were based in the villa that Caligula had had constructed for himself on the coast just outside the walls of the port of Gesoriacum when he had come north to attempt the conquest of Britannia four years earlier. All the land around the port on the Gallic Straits, opposite the island of Britannia, had been either ploughed and sown with wheat or barley or had been fenced off into fields containing more pigs and mules than Vespasian had ever seen. They were riding through what was essentially a huge farm stretching, even on a clear day, as far as the eye could see and then further; much further.

The business of supplying the invasion force of four legions and a similar number of auxiliaries, a total of almost forty thousand men in all, plus all the ancillary personnel – cart drivers, muleteers, slaves and sailors crewing the thousand-strong fleet – had not shocked Vespasian with its magnitude when he had first approached Gesoriacum at the head of the II Augusta six months before; it had, rather, inspired him. The idea that every stomach, whether human or animal, had to be filled every day was a logistical problem of such vast mathematical proportions that it made his head spin just to think of the amount of fodder required to feed enough pigs to provide the entire force with a meat ration for one day, or of how many square miles of pasture the army's five thousand mules would get through in a month. It made his problems of supply for the II Augusta seem trivial and petty in comparison, but they had been problems that he had thoroughly enjoyed tackling once he had returned to Argentoratum.

He and Sabinus had returned to the Empire with Gabinius' fleet – much to Sabinus' discomfort over the two-day voyage – and then made their way down the Rhenus back to their new legions; Paetus and his Batavians had accompanied them on their journey south. The voyage had been on calm seas, thanks, as Magnus had often commented, to Ansigar's timely sacrifice to Nehalennia, the goddess of the Northern Sea.

Upon their arrival at Mogontiacum, news had reached them of their father's death, but this was tempered by the news of the birth of Vespasian's daughter, Domitilla. Flavia had written herself and it was with both relief and joy that he had read the letter; a mother and child's chances of survival in childbirth were about the same as a soldier's on the battlefield.

Having left his brother to his new command and arriving back with his own legion in mid-June, Vespasian had spent the rest of the year and all of the following training the II Augusta in embarking on and disembarking from ships until they could do it as efficiently as he thought possible; this had proved a long task as he only had one trireme available to him, the rest having been commandeered – rather short-sightedly, he thought – for the invasion fleet. Whilst the centuries had been taking it in turns to run on and off the only ship, Vespasian had got to grips with the minutiae of commanding a legion and keeping it supplied with equipment, clothing, rations and livestock. He had revelled in it as now it seemed to him that he had the best of both worlds: he was managing a very large estate and at the same time serving Rome under one of her Eagles.

What Publius Gabinius had done with the Eagle of the Seventeenth, however, Vespasian and Sabinus neither knew nor cared. It had seemed simply to disappear – certainly no official mention had been made of it. However, they were just pleased to have survived and returned to evident favour. Sabinus had kept the Nineteenth Legion's Capricorn from Gabinius and had sent it on to Pallas in Rome in the hope that it would help him in his power struggle with Callistus and also in recognition of his appointment as legate of the XIIII Gemina, the reason for which still mystified the two brothers. Sabinus had written to tell Vespasian that he had received no acknowledgement of the gift but neither had he received any indication that his life was still in danger, so he felt that he could assume now that his part in the assassination of Caligula had been forgotten by the very few people who knew about it. Vespasian, for his part, had been pleased that his family now seemed to be on even terms with Claudius' three freedmen, on a personal level at least. Fom a professional point of view, however, the freedmen's constant in-fighting had meant that the preparations for the invasion had not been straightforward. Each used his own sphere of influence to affect the planning in a way that would reflect well on themselves and badly on their two colleagues. Orders of artillery pieces had been doubled and then abruptly cancelled, before being reordered but at only half the original amount of engines. Gold and silver coin had been despatched from the mint at Lugdunum in the south of the province only for it to have been recalled after travelling almost half the distance north. Ships had disappeared and then reappeared a few days later but with half the complement of crewmen. But most disruptively, conflicting orders as to the timing, speed and objectives of the invasion had come on a regular basis sending Aulus Plautius into fits of rage at the civilian interference in what was, quite obviously, an exclusively military endeavour.

'Perhaps Narcissus' arrival might be a good thing after all,' Vespasian mused as they rode past the first of the four vast legionary and auxiliary camps surrounding Gesoriacum.

Magnus wiped his eyes; despite his sporting of a wide-rimmed, leather hat, the rain still streamed down his face. 'In that now he's here he can change his mind as many times a day as he likes, rather than just when the courier leaves?'

'I mean that perhaps if he's here to see for himself the massive exercise in logistics that's being undertaken then he might refrain from interfering.'

'And the Emperor will no doubt start going through the day without drooling.'

'Thank you, prefect. I'm attaching you to the Second Augusta, you will report to Legate Vespasian after this briefing,' Aulus Plautius said as the prefect of I Cohort Hamiorum sat back down having given his report on the state of readiness of his newly arrived eastern archers. 'That concludes all your reports, gentlemen.' He cast his eyes around the four legates and thirty-three auxiliary prefects sitting on folding stools in the large chamber that he used as a briefing room in his headquarters; the walls had been whitewashed, covering, Vespasian assumed, some very unmilitary frescoes. Through the two open windows the rain beat down mercilessly onto the grey, unsettled sea. 'I think, as we can all see, there is still a great deal more work to be done in terms of filling all the quartermasters' stores. We have enough boots, for example, for every man on the force to land in Britannia decently shod; but what happens after a month of tough campaigning in that damp climate? I will not lose infantry because of a shortage of footwear nor will I lose cavalry because of a shortage of remounts. I've no doubt that you have all got your quartermasters doing everything possible to redress the shortages of reserves but I feel that this is a problem that will benefit from an overall perspective.' Plautius indicated to the almost obese man sitting next to him in a ludicrously extravagant military uniform. 'As you know, Gnaeus Sentius Saturninus will be administering the conquered tribes and keeping an eye on the client kings as the army moves forward; it therefore makes sense if I appoint him in overall command of re-provisioning as all the supply routes will naturally run through territory administered by him.'

Sentius smiled the smile of a man who had just smelt profit.

'That's made it very unlikely that I shall see my entire consignment of reserve tents before we go,' Vespasian whispered to Sabinus next to him as Plautius praised his second-in-command's administrative abilities and integrity.

Sabinus suppressed a grin. 'And I'll give up looking forward to my delivery of shovels, cooking pots and grain mills arriving on time and being complete.'

'I still don't understand how he managed to wheedle his way into this command after suggesting a return to the Republic when Claudius became emperor.'

Sabinus shrugged. 'Why am I legate of the Fourteenth?'

' ... and therefore, if we are to be ready by mid-June,' Plautius was continuing, 'so as to take advantage of the forthcoming harvest in Britannia, I expect every one of you to take your provisioning requests to Sentius.' There was a mumble from the officers present that could have either been construed as consent to a very workable plan or resignation as to the way that resupplying the army worked; Plautius chose to believe the former. 'Good. Tomorrow is the calends of April, which means we have seventy-five days left. Prefects, you are dismissed; legates, you will come with me to report to the imperial secretary.'

Narcissus had taken up residence on the first floor of Caligula's villa and Vespasian was not surprised by the gaudy artwork and statuary that littered the staircase and corridors on the way to his quarters, vestiges of the brash young Emperor's taste in interior decoration. What did surprise him, though, was the presence of Praetorian Guards on duty outside Narcissus' suite of rooms. 'Claudius' freedman is taking on all the trappings of an emperor, it would seem,' he muttered to Sabinus as a centurion left a visibly insulted Aulus Plautius standing outside the door whilst he went to enquire of the ex-slave whether he was ready to receive the general of the invasion army.

'Perhaps the Saturnalia has been extended for the whole year but no one bothered to tell us,' Sabinus suggested.

Vespasian glanced at the other two legates, Corvinus and the recently arrived Gnaeus Hosidius Geta, who had been given the XX in recognition of his part in the annexation of Mauretania the previous year; neither looked pleased at being made to wait upon a freedman, however powerful.

'The imperial secretary will see you now, general,' the centurion informed them as he opened the door.

Plautius bristled. 'That is most gracious of him.'

Vespasian detected a look of sympathy with Plautius' sarcasm in the centurion's eyes as he passed into a high-ceilinged reception room, at the far end of which sat Narcissus behind a large desk; he did not get up. Any thoughts Vespasian might have had about the presumption of the freedman were abruptly curtailed as he saw, sitting by a table to the left of Narcissus, with writing materials at the ready, Caenis.

His heart jumped and he almost stumbled; she smiled at him discreetly with only her eyes.

'General Plautius,' Narcissus crooned, bringing Vespasian back to the matter in hand, 'and Legates Corvinus, Vespasian, Sabinus and Geta, I'm pleased to see you all looking so well in this bracing northern climate. Be seated.' He indicated to Caenis who took up a stylus and began to write. 'This is a formal meeting so my secretary will be minuting it. The Emperor sends his greetings and instructs me to tell you that I speak for him.'

'That is impossible!' Plautius exploded as Narcissus finished speaking.

Narcissus remained unmoved. 'No, general, it's not impossible, it's necessary.'

'We are going mid-June so that we only have to take a month's supply of grain with us to see us through until the harvest is ready.'

'Then you'll just have to take more with you.'

'Have you any idea how much more we'll need if we go next month?'

Narcissus shrugged his shoulders, half closing his eyes and held out his hands, palms up, as if the question was completely irrelevant to him.

'Three pounds a day, times forty thousand men, times sixty days until the earliest harvest is ready, that's … that's …' Plautius looked around at his legates for help with the arithmetic.

'That's one hundred and twenty thousand pounds a day making a total of seven million, two hundred thousand pounds, general,' Vespasian offered helpfully.

'Exactly! And that's just to feed the troops; I'll need a quarter as much again to feed all the ancillary people and then there's the barley for the cavalry mounts and beasts of burden. And it will all have to be transported by pack-mules taking a maximum load of one hundred and sixty pounds each, until we can get a decent road built.'

'Then I suggest making road building one of your priorities, general, because this is how it's going to be.' Narcissus laid a hand on the desk in front of him in a gesture that was at the same time gentle and resolute; his eyes hardened. 'I calculate that it will take one hundred days between the sending of your message and Claudius arriving with you. So if he's to be back over in Gaul before the autumn equinox and the real threat of gales in mid-September you need to have crossed the Tamesis by the beginning of June when you send your message to Claudius.'

Plautius stared at Narcissus with loathing. 'And what should this message say?'

'Oh, that's very simple, general. You should tell your Emperor that you have met with fierce resistance and that you need reinforcements and, if at all possible, his presence, in order that he can take over the reins of command that are proving so weighty.

I will then have it read out to the Senate who will beg him to personally come and save Rome's beleaguered legions, and, dropping everything, he will rush to your aid and bring those much-needed reinforcements.'

'Which will be there ready and waiting outside the city?'

'Wrong, general, they will be *here*, ready and waiting; you'll be able to inspect them in a few days' time, if you like.'

'You've brought them with you?'

'Of course, Decimus Valerius Asiaticus commands them until the emperor arrives.'

'You're just setting me up to look like a fool.'

'No, general, I'm setting Claudius up to look like a hero; how you appear is completely irrelevant.'

'Do you think that the Senate will believe it?'

'Not for one moment; but the people will and when he comes back laden with booty and captives to celebrate his triumph they will see the hard evidence of it.'

'My triumph.'

'No, general, the Emperor's triumph, the triumph that will make the people love him. What use have you for the love of the people? What would you do with it?' Narcissus paused to let the implied threat sink in. 'Now, you can either go along with this in the knowledge that you will be rewarded or I can find someone else who is willing to help my master to win the people's love. Which is it to be?'

Plautius pursed his lips and breathed deeply. 'We go in seventeen days, four days after the ides of April.'

'An excellent day, general, my master will approve; I'm sure the auguries will find it most auspicious once they hear that it is the Emperor's preferred date. Let me not detain you, you all must have much to do.' With an airy wave of a pudgy hand he dismissed his social betters, none of whom saluted him.

Aulus Plautius got to his feet, puce with rage, spun on his heel and almost barged his way through his legates as they too stood. As Vespasian turned and followed he saw Corvinus and Geta exchange a worried glance, echoing how he felt about this new development that threatened the success of the enterprise;

Magnus had not been wrong, he thought, as he fell in beside Sabinus who was looking equally concerned.

'Legates Sabinus and Vespasian,' Narcissus crooned just as they reached the door, stopping them, 'a brief, private word with you both, if you please.'

Corvinus gave the brothers a quizzical look. They turned as Narcissus dismissed Caenis; she left the room passing closer than necessary to Vespasian so that he smelt her scent.

'You may wonder why you both remain in favour,' Narcissus mused as the door closed, 'especially you, Sabinus, seeing as you did not complete your half of our bargain.'

'We found the Eagle,' Sabinus protested, sitting back down. 'Gabinius took it from ...'

Narcissus raised a hand, silencing him. 'I'm well aware of what happened, legate, and of why and how it happened, because I sanctioned it. As I'm sure you've both surmised, it made no difference to me who found the Eagle so long as it was found. When Callistus came to me in private, after you had left Rome, saying that he had information as to where it was hidden, I gave my permission for him to send Gabinius after it. It suited me to have two expeditions and it suited me to have my colleagues squabbling over who would gain the glory for finding it. What didn't suit me, however, was Callistus' little plan to have you killed because that reduced the chances of success; had I found out about it sooner I would have put a stop to it.'

Vespasian met Narcissus' eyes and, for once, believed him. 'We're very pleased to hear that.'

'That's gratifying but neither here nor there. What is relevant, though, is my other reason for not wanting you killed. As you know, I'd specifically instructed Gabinius that he was not to harm you if your paths crossed, and I also sent him a copy of your orders so he fully understood that you were under my protection.'

'Even if the Eagle had not been found?'

'Even if the Eagle had not been found.'

The brothers glanced sidelong at each other, utterly confused. Narcissus' face betrayed a rare hint of amusement. 'Believe me, that was not the case when we made our bargain; then I fully intended to have you killed, Sabinus, had you failed. But things change very quickly in politics and politicians must change with them if they are to survive.

'I will be frank with you. In the first few months of Claudius' reign it became apparent to me that I was not the major influence over my impressionable patron; I may have my mouth to his ear but, unfortunately, his very attractive young wife, Messalina, has hers to his cock and I think that we can all agree that is a far more influential position to be in.'

Vespasian was not about to argue the point as a vision of Caenis rocked his concentration. Sabinus grunted his agreement, no doubt contemplating Clementina's favours.

'Messalina, however, unlike me, does not have Claudius' best interests at heart; in fact she has no one's interests at heart other than her own and those of her brother, Corvinus. Now, that's not surprising in itself but what does concern me is that her interests are purely pleasure and power and that the Emperor's cock is not the only such organ that she has her mouth close to.' Narcissus steepled his hands and leant across the desk. 'She is starting to build a formidable network of ambitious young men tied to her in bonds of mutual gratification and lust for power; in other words, an alternative court.'

'Then why don't you tell the Emperor?' Vespasian asked, struggling to see what this had to do with him or his brother.

'I have, and so have Pallas and Callistus but he doesn't believe us, he won't believe anything against the mother of his new son; so I need to drive a wedge between them, and you are both to be a part of that wedge.'

'Why us?'

'Because I need men whom I can trust.'

The brothers looked at Narcissus in astonishment.

'You seem surprised, gentlemen. Of course I can trust you because I am the only person who can advance your careers as I have proved by giving you both legions to command. You both have a choice between me and obscurity – or worse. Do we understand each other?'

Of course they did. Vespasian and Sabinus mutely accepted the truth of the statement.

'Good. Now, I believe that Messalina's objective is to fill the top ranks of the army with her lovers, then rid herself of her husband and have Corvinus adopt her new son. The siblings will rule as co-regents until the child comes of age, or for even longer, supported by her network of loyal bed-sharers who will guarantee the loyalty of the legions. She canvasses Claudius regularly, seeking positions for men who have just left her bed as a thick-stripe tribune or auxiliary prefect or as a legate, as she did in Geta's case right at the beginning.'

'Geta's her lover?' Sabinus was shocked.

'One of the many.'

'But he was made a legate in Mauretania shortly before she gave birth.'

'He has specialised tastes, I would assume. But I knew they were having an affair whilst she was pregnant. What was strange, however, was Claudius appointing Geta without me or my colleagues suggesting it; most unusual. This is what first alerted me to Messalina using her influence over Claudius. Then, shortly after you left Rome, Claudius insisted on something that made no military sense whatsoever. We had already decided the makeup of the Britannia invasion force: three legions from the Rhenus, which is sensible, now that we have an understanding with the Germanic tribes; and then one of the legions from Hispania, which has been peaceful since the Cantabrian war, almost thirty years ago. However, Claudius vetoed this Hispanic legion and demanded instead that Corvinus' Ninth Legion should be sent from Pannonia, a province that is, to say the least, restless. He could not be talked out of it, saying that his darling wife's family deserved their share of glory.

'At that point I could only guess at her real motives but I knew that she would not insist on her brother being put unnecessarily in harm's way without a very good reason; I therefore began to counter her. I immediately began placing my people into as many positions in the other three legions as possible. Vespasian, you had already been appointed to the Second Augusta, which suited my purpose; but to strengthen my position I decided to overlook your part, Sabinus, in my patron's elevation and, due to your experience as legate of the Ninth Hispana, which I felt might be helpful in the future, give you the Fourteenth. But then, a couple of months ago, my nomination for the legate of the Twentieth was recalled by the Emperor and replaced by Geta, ostensibly as a reward for his part in the campaign in Mauretania and its annexation. That move confirmed my suspicion: Messalina was hijacking the invasion for her own purposes.'

Vespasian looked at Sabinus and then back to Narcissus, frowning. 'How come we're still here? Surely she would have persuaded Claudius to replace us as well.'

'Oh, she tried; she tried very hard, in fact, but one factor confounded her: the Nineteenth's Capricorn. By this time I had been forced to confide in my two colleagues my fears of what would happen should she get her nominations in all four legions. Pallas showed me the Capricorn that you'd sent him.' Narcissus paused and let his gaze pass between the brothers. 'That you'd sent *him*, not *me*; but I shall put that bit of disloyalty aside. Anyway, it was just what we needed. We presented it to Claudius saying that it was a gift from you two. He was thrilled and made a big public spectacle and propaganda coup as he returned it to the Temple of Mars. After that you were safe; Claudius will hear nothing against you. Not even Messalina can get him to replace his "two loyal Flavians", as he's taken to calling you.'

Sabinus ran his fingers through his hair. 'Why was the Capricorn so important to him when he already has the Seventeenth's Eagle?'

Vespasian took one look at Narcissus and understood. 'Because he doesn't know about the Eagle yet, brother; does he, imperial secretary?'

'The Eagle will be found at the appropriate moment.' Narcissus' tone showed that discussion of that subject was over. 'So, I knew that I still had two of the four legions going to Britannia under my control and not hers. I also managed to ensure that Asiaticus commanded the reinforcements; as you both know well, he's been of great use to the emperor before.'

Vespasian remembered the part that Asiaticus, whilst consul, had played when he and Corbulo had murdered Poppaeus, at the behest of Claudius' mother, the Lady Antonia, eight years previously. The murder had been planned by Pallas and Narcissus and had left Claudius fabulously wealthy. He blanched at the thought; it was not a deed to be proud of. 'I imagine that their shared past ensures his loyalty.'

Narcissus' hand gesture dismissed the notion. 'It's more the fact that Asiaticus helped Claudius to invest his windfall from the Poppaeus incident and has done very well out of it; in fact, he's recently purchased the Gardens of Lucullus. He's very grateful and I can rely on him as I can on you two. If all four legions and the reinforcements were commanded by Messalina's men, Claudius would not get his victory.'

'She would sabotage it?' Vespasian looked incredulous. 'But that would be madness; she needs Claudius to secure his position in order to safeguard hers.'

'Not if you look at the bigger picture. When Aulus Plautius was appointed to the command there was a debate about who would take over if he were to be killed. The obvious choice would be that fat pig Sentius but even Claudius recognised that that would be a disaster, and I wasn't foolish enough to try and persuade him otherwise. It would take too long to get a suitable candidate from Rome or one of the provinces, which is why I chose Asiaticus to command the reinforcements; he would only be a couple of days away. But to counter me, Messalina suggested, whilst no doubt working her feminine charms on her husband, that her brother should be nominated as the commander designate as he would be closer to the action, and Claudius agreed and cannot be argued out of it. Corvinus has an imperial mandate to that effect and I believe that he intended to make use of it.'

'He's going to murder Plautius?'

'He *was* going to murder Plautius; now he's not so sure. That worried look that you may have noticed pass between him and Geta was not concern for the success of the invasion, it was because their plans have been disrupted. Corvinus and

Messalina's original idea was for him to seize command once victory was assured. He would claim the glory, which, as the brother of the Empress, Claudius would not be able to deny him; Claudius' position would therefore be weakened by the invasion, not strengthened. So to counter that, I decided that Claudius should be present at the final victory and lead the army in person, even though I knew that it would mean bringing the timetable forward considerably and put a great strain on the logistics of the whole enterprise. Having never had the chance of personal military glory, he jumped at the idea and Messalina couldn't be seen to argue with it, although I'm sure that she'll express many a false concern for his welfare from beneath the sheets. So now if Corvinus was to decide to murder Plautius he knows that the Emperor will be coming to claim all the glory anyway, so what's the point?'

'None at all.'

'Yet he still may try, and then he and Geta will ignore the order to wait at the Tamesis and press on to a victory before Claudius arrives. So this is what I need you two for: keep Plautius alive and don't let Corvinus and Geta go too far before the Emperor arrives.'

'We should warn Plautius,' Sabinus suggested. 'He'll be easier to keep alive if he's watching out for himself.'

Vespasian shook his head. 'No, brother; I imagine that is something that the imperial secretary has already discounted for security reasons.'

Narcissus twitched an eyebrow appreciatively. 'Indeed, legate; Plautius must know nothing of this and I want your oaths that whatever happens, and I mean *whatever* happens, you will not go to him.' He turned back to Sabinus. 'If he were warned of this impending treachery he would do one or both of two things. He would write to the Emperor demanding that Corvinus and Geta are replaced and, with me not in Rome to filter Claudius' mail, that letter would get through. He would also perhaps confront them with their plan. Either way, Messalina would be alerted to the fact that I am on to her and that must never happen; my life would be in great danger and Messalina would be more careful in any future conspiracies. To get rid of this harpy I have to keep her feeling secure so that she becomes arrogant to the point of carelessness.' Narcissus' lips flickered in a mirthless smile. 'It may surprise you to learn that to add to her sense of security I've even been helping the vengeful bitch to prosecute old enemies of her family.'

Vespasian sighed. 'Nothing surprises me in imperial politics any more.'

Caenis wrapped her arms around Vespasian's neck and kissed him, pressing the length of her body hard against his. 'I've missed you, my love.'

Vespasian responded with equal fervour whilst Sabinus and Magnus looked around his tent as if the plain furnishings and sparse decoration were suddenly worthy of closer scrutiny.

'What are you doing here?' Vespasian asked, disengaging himself.

'Exactly what it looks like: I'm the secretary's secretary, and would you believe back in Rome I have my own secretary!'

Vespasian laughed. 'The secretary's secretary's secretary? That is surely taking bureaucracy to an extreme level.'

'Perhaps, but Narcissus, Pallas and Callistus love it; the more functionaries that they can cram into the palace and the more protocols that they put in place the harder it is for anyone but them to understand how things work.'

'But why are you working for Narcissus, rather than Pallas?'

'Claudius ordered me to and I can't disobey my patron and Emperor, can I? I think that it was Narcissus' idea with Pallas' connivance. They use me to communicate with each other without Callistus' knowledge.'

'Loathsome little shit tried to have us killed,' Sabinus spat.

'Yes, Pallas was as furious as I've ever seen him when he found out; he very nearly raised his voice. It shattered any little trust that he and Narcissus had for Callistus. Now they're trying to find or fabricate evidence that Callistus is working with Messalina so that he'll go down with her. Rome's not a good place to be at the moment.'

'How's our uncle coping with it?' Vespasian asked.

'He's keeping out of the way as much as possible, although his new domestic arrangements mean that he has to get out of the house more than he would like.'

'Mother's finally arrived?'

'Yes, two months ago, Artebudz escorted her; she and Flavia have differing views on how to look after children.'

Vespasian grimaced. 'I can imagine. I don't suppose they keep them to themselves either, do they?'

'I'm afraid not. I've got letters for you from both of them and one from your uncle, all no doubt complaining about each other.'

'It's as bad as Claudius' squabbling freedmen,' Magnus commented, pouring himself a cup of wine.

'Worse even,' Sabinus chuckled, 'at least they don't all live in the same house.'

Vespasian scowled at his brother. 'Perhaps I really should start thinking about getting my own house.'

'Don't come asking me for a loan, brother.'

'I'd wait a while, sir,' Magnus advised refilling his cup. 'Things ain't going to be too stable in Rome with Narcissus and his mates bringing down the Empress.'

'If they manage to get her.'

'Oh, I'm sure they will get her; but the trouble is when they do who's going to take her place? That'll be a position that will attract applications from some poisonous bitches.'

'We'll worry about one poisonous bitch at a time. Seeing as Narcissus seems to have involved us in this fight I see no reason for him not to involve us in the next.' Vespasian put an arm around Caenis' shoulder. 'In the meantime, I've got things to do.'

Magnus drained his cup. 'I thought you were going to join your lads practising for the invasion this afternoon.'

'I'm sure they can manage on their own.'

'Whilst you invade elsewhere, if you take my meaning?'

Caenis smiled. 'Something like that, Magnus.'

CHAPTER XIIII

'ARE YOU QUITE certain of this?' Aulus Plautius demanded of two Gallic traders standing nervously before him in his briefing room, now awash with flickering oil lamps.

'Yes, general,' the elder of the two replied, 'my son and I heard the news yesterday. We sailed from Britannia at first light this morning; they had begun to muster in the lands of the Cantiaci in the south-eastern corner of the island.'

'I know where the Cantiaci live,' Plautius snapped; his temper had not been helped by this news. 'How many tribes?'

'The Catuvellauni and all the tribes under their rule.'

'Who commands them?'

'Caradoc, or Caratacus as you Romans call him, and his brother Togodumnus of the Catuv—'

'I know which tribe they're from!' Plautius tossed a chinking purse at the older man. 'You may go.' The traders bowed and hurried out of the room as he turned to a huge long-haired man in his early thirties, with a ruddy complexion and a long, drooping moustache. 'How many men do you think, Adminios?'

The Briton answered immediately. 'If both my brothers are there then that would mean the Trinovantes, the Atrebates, the Regni confederation and the Cantiaci confederation at least; and then possibly the Dobunni and Belge from further west. That's a force of at least one hundred thousand warriors, possibly more, facing us on the beach. And I can assure you they will be waiting; it's their best chance of defeating us.'

'Not all the Atrebates and Regni confederation,' an elderly Briton, with greying hair and black moustache in the same style, interposed.

Plautius ran a hand through his close-cropped hair. 'What makes you say that, Verica?'

'My nephew, the King of Vectis, hates Caratacus; his sub-tribe won't be joining the army. Nor will all of my people, the Regni.'

'Even so, that's still going to be many more than faced Caesar and he had a hard enough time of it.' Plautius looked over to his legates seated on his right. 'Well, gentlemen, it seems that they have found out that we're coming early; the question is what do we do about it?' He could not disguise his alarm.

Vespasian glanced at his three colleagues, none of whom looked as if they were about to come up with an idea. 'We need to delay; a force that size can't live off the land for very long at this time of year. They'll have to disband soon.'

'I agree, Vespasian; that's the obvious thing to do, but politically it's impossible. I can see myself facing a treason charge if we leave harbour so much as an hour late. We have to go in two days' time, which means that we start embarking the troops tomorrow.'

'Change where we land, then,' Sabinus suggested.

'That's what I'm considering. Tribune Alienus, the large map.' Plautius stood and walked to his map table; his legates joined him. A young thin-stripe tribune unrolled a map showing the south and east coasts of Britannia and the Gallic coastline closest to the island. Plautius pointed to Gesoriacum and then to a point just northeast of the nearest part of the Britannic coast. 'I planned to land here, just as Caesar did, for three reasons: first because I didn't want to risk a longer voyage than necessary, second because we have Caesar's record of the landing place and these fucking tides that they're so fond of up here, and third it's the shortest crossing for our line of supply. From here I planned to cut up north to the Cantiaci's main town and restore Adminios to his throne.' He traced his finger up to a town just inland from an island on the eastern tip of Britannia. 'At the same time the fleet would take control of the channel between this island, Tanatis, and the mainland giving it access to the Tamesis estuary and the mainland. I would also send a secondary force south to secure the small natural harbour under the white cliffs here.' He pointed to the closest part of Britannia to Gaul. 'With our rear secure and a pro-Roman administration in place along our supply lines, we would force-march the thirty miles from the Cantiaci town, or Cantiacum as I shall now refer to it, along the estuary, keeping to the north of this range of hills to shield our flank, to seize the only bridge over this river, the Afon Cantiacii, which flows into the Tamesis estuary here. This route has two major advantages: we can receive support and supplies from our fleet in the estuary and we can take advantage of the hills, which Adminios tells me are only partially wooded, for feeding our animals.' Plautius traced his finger along a line almost parallel with the estuary. 'From here I would head west until this ford on the Tamesis, here, cross into Catuvellauni lands and then push east to their capital, the Fort of Camulos, so named after their patron god of war.'

'What happens if the Britons destroy the bridge before we get to it?' Vespasian asked, looking at the river that seemed to be the only major obstacle before the Tamesis ford.

'In all likelihood they would and will try to hold the river against us; in fact that's what I expect them to do. But we'll prob-ably have to fight them crossing the Tamesis so it's no bad thing to give the lads a bit of practice with this river first.'

'And we've got eight infantry cohorts and one cavalry ala of Batavians; I've seen them cross rivers, it's not a problem for them. We should play to our strengths, sir.'

'Oh, we will; we'll bring light boats in the baggage train to bridge the river, they won't expect that. But all this is going to have to change now if we've got a hundred thousand hairy-arsed savages covered in that hideous blue-green clay waiting for us on the beach, with bags full of slingshot and an unwelcoming demeanour.'

'Why not land near the Fort of Camulos itself,' Corvinus suggested, with a look in his eye that immediately confirmed to Vespasian that Narcissus' theory had some foundation.

'I can't take that without the Emperor.'

'Then land well to the north of it in the lands of the Parisi, with whom we have a peace treaty,' Sabinus said, pointing to an area well to the north on the east coast, 'and come down the coast; it all has to be conquered at some point.'

'That would be military madness, legate, putting our forces at the end of such a long sea route supply line; only a woman would think that feasible.'

Sabinus tensed at the insult.

'I apologise, Sabinus, that was unworthy of me; all possibilities should be discussed.'

Sabinus relaxed and raised his hand in acceptance of the apology; Corvinus, next to him, smirked.

'What if we should land further west?' Geta suggested, putting his finger on an island along the south coast. 'The channel between Vectis and the mainland would protect the fleet; or there's this natural harbour just east of it, which I believe is Verica's capital, so we may get a friendly welcome.'

Verica inclined his head in agreement. 'From my people, the Regni, you would, but they are just one sub-tribe of the Atrebates; you would have to fight your way north and before you did so you would have to defeat my nephew on Vectis.'

Plautius shook his head. 'And on the way north we wouldn't be able to receive support from the fleet. We'd have an overland supply line over seventy miles long by the time we got to the Tamesis and we would be open to attack from east and west as we went north; it's too risky. One reverse and we could be cut off and humiliated. So, bearing in mind that only a fool would split his forces in such hostile country before a decisive victory, we have to work out a way of landing the whole force in the southeast.'

Vespasian cleared his throat and pointed at the channel between Tanatis on the extreme eastern tip of Britannia and the mainland. 'Then do your original plan backwards, sir. Land here behind them and then come south and take them in the rear. We're going to have to fight them at some point so if they're going to oblige us by putting all their men in one place I think we should take advantage of it.'

'What are the beaches like here, Adminios?'

'Good for our purpose.' He pointed to a promontory on the mainland. 'We call this place "Rhudd yr epis" or "horse ford" in

Latin. It's a gently rising beach protected by the island and from it there's a good trackway for all of the ten miles to the Cantiaci town.'

'So we would need to land a force on Tanatis first to take that before the main body lands at this Rutupis, or whatever it's called, secures the bridgehead and then moves on to the town. Once we have that we turn south and deal with your trouble-some brothers. Will they fight us or try to run to ground of their choosing?'

'They'll fight, they'll have no option. They can't run west because of the great oak forest. No one lives there; an army that size would find it impenetrable, so they'll have to fight us either to defeat us or get round us.'

Plautius stared at the map for a few moments. 'Yes, that idea has merit, although no matter how effectively we do the job a goodly amount of them will escape. I'll leave Sentius with a small secondary force down where we would have landed to secure the supply line and press on northwest with the main force following the remnants of the Britons' army. They'll have no option but to cross the bridge and destroy it and try to hold the river against us; that will be a bloody day. Then, whatever's left of them will fall back across the Tamesis.' Plautius ruminated for a while weighing the matter in his mind. 'Yes, this would work and we could be across the Tamesis within a month and a half of landing, having destroyed this Britannic force in three battles.'

'And then we sit there with our thumbs up our arses for three months, waiting for my brother-in-law, whilst the Britons muster another army?' Corvinus asked, giving Plautius a questioning look.

'Legate, I would remind you that your brother-in-law is our Emperor and if those are his orders then I have to obey them.'

'They're not *his* orders; they came from that jumped-up freedman of his and you know it … sir.'

'It makes no difference; he spoke with the Emperor's authority.'

'We could have the whole of the southeast under our control by the end of June!'

'Do not raise your voice to me, legate; argue any more and, by the gods of my household, I'll remove you from your command

and write to your precious brother-in-law telling him that I suspect you of treason.'

'I'm sure my colleague was just expressing the frustration that we all feel at the delay,' Vespasian put in quickly, earning a confused glare from Corvinus. 'And I'm sure that he understands, as well as any of us, the political necessity behind that delay.'

Plautius grunted. 'I'm sure you're right, Vespasian; it is very frustrating for all of us but that's how it is. It won't do to have discord amongst us so we'll say no more about it, will we, Corvinus?'

Corvinus jutted his jaw out but then clearly thought better of continuing the argument. 'No, sir.'

'Good. The supply ships have all been loaded and moved out of the harbour. We begin the embarkation of the army at midday tomorrow; the men will spend the night on the ships and then we'll sail with the tide an hour after midnight. Any questions?'

The four legates shook their heads.

'Have your legions and attached auxiliaries parade in full gear, and with seventeen days' rations issued, in front of the camps at noon tomorrow. Dismiss, gentlemen.'

Vespasian saluted along with the other three legates and turned to march smartly out next to Sabinus; Corvinus followed with Geta.

'What are you playing at, bumpkin?' Corvinus drawled in Vespasian's ear as a slave closed the reception room doors behind them. 'I would have thought that it would delight you and your cuckolded brother to see Plautius try and remove me from my command.'

Sabinus spun around, grabbing Corvinus by the throat, slamming him against the corridor wall. 'What did you call me?'

Corvinus brought his right arm cracking up onto Sabinus', breaking his grip. 'Just what you are.'

Vespasian grabbed his brother by the shoulders as Geta stepped in front of Corvinus. 'Leave him, brother! Come away.' Sabinus struggled for a few moments as Vespasian pulled him back.

Corvinus smirked over Geta's shoulder. 'The truth hurts, doesn't it?'

Sabinus seethed. 'I will have you one day, you arrogant cunt; I'll bring you down.'

'I find that most unlikely with my sister in the Emperor's bed.'

'She won't be there forever, she—'

'Sabinus!' Vespasian shouted.

Corvinus scoffed. 'And just who is going to drag her out? You?' He abruptly stopped and then smiled knowingly. 'Or Narcissus? Is that what he kept you behind to discuss the other day? Is that why your bumpkin brother supported me just now? That was quite out of character. Why else would you want me to remain in my command unless it was to give the impression that everything was normal? That oily Greek is moving against my sister and you two are part of it.'

'Don't be so stupid, Corvinus,' Vespasian said, pushing his brother behind him. 'Why would he do that? He has the Emperor's best interests at heart.'

Corvinus raised both eyebrows. 'Really? I suppose that's true insofar as they coincide with his own; after that, I doubt it. Good evening, gentlemen; thank you for this little chat, it has been most enlightening.' He walked away; Geta followed him with a scowl at the brothers.

Vespasian turned on Sabinus. 'That was very—'

'Don't tell me, you little shit; I'm well aware of how stupid that was.'

Vespasian woke just before dawn to the sound of men striking camp. He felt Caenis' warm body nestled in the crook of his arm and spent a few moments listening to her soft breathing, knowing that it would be a long time before they would share such intimacy again; that night would be spent aboard the ship waiting to take them to the savage island across the sea.

Nuzzling his face into her hair he breathed in her scent and kissed her tenderly before easing his arm out from under her and slipping out of bed.

'Is it time to go, my love?' Caenis asked sleepily as he fastened his loincloth.

'My officers are reporting to me soon and then I'll be busy the rest of the day getting my men aboard.'

'Then we had better say goodbye now. Narcissus wants me to

travel back to Rome, with his personal despatches for the Emperor, as soon as you have embarked.'

Vespasian sat back down on the bed and took her in his arms.

'Will it be a very long time, Vespasian?'

'At least two years, probably more.'

'Little Domitilla will be three or four before she meets her father.'

'That's assuming that some clay-covered savage doesn't do for me first.'

'Don't talk like that, my love, it brings bad luck. You'll be fine, I know it.'

'I've got letters for Flavia, mother and Gaius for you to take back to Rome, if that's all right.'

Caenis kissed his cheek. 'Of course it is. Flavia and I are on very good terms, much to your mother's confusion; she even has little Titus address me as aunty. Although every time he does so I wish he was calling me mother instead.'

Vespasian held her tight, unable to reply. He was only too aware of just how much Caenis had sacrificed to be with him. 'Stay safe in Rome, try and keep away from the palace as much as possible. I imagine that Narcissus' scheming will escalate now that Sabinus has been so indiscreet.'

'I can't, I have to be there every day now that I'm working for him, even though he's remaining here. But even if he and Messalina are openly at war, she wouldn't be able to bring him down; Claudius relies on him too much.'

'She might try to have him murdered.'

'Narcissus is a very cautious man; he even has a slave taste his food. But even if she was successful I wouldn't be harmed because I'm no threat to her. And anyway, because I stayed hidden for so long during Caligula's reign, I doubt that she even knows my name.'

'Let's hope that is the case.'

'I'm sure it is. The person who should be worried is Sabinus; Narcissus was not at all pleased.'

'That is an understatement,' Vespasian said, thinking of the brothers' interview with Narcissus shortly after Sabinus' indiscretion with Corvinus. Narcissus had flown into a rage, which had expressed itself with a hardening of the eyes into an icy glare and his voice becoming very quiet and clipped as he tore into Sabinus. The humiliation of being so spoken to by a mere freedman had almost been too much for Sabinus to bear and Vespasian had had to place a calming hand on his brother's shoulder at the point when Narcissus called him incompetent and threatened to relieve him of his command. It was not until Vespasian had pointed out that Corvinus had absolutely no proof of his suspicions, which were based purely on assumption, that Narcissus calmed down and called for a Praetorian centurion to organise the interception of any courier leaving Corvinus' camp that night. It was, however, only a temporary measure and they all knew that Corvinus would find a way of alerting his sister to what he suspected. Narcissus had dismissed them with a curt warning that if he had not managed to get rid of Messalina by the time that they got back to Rome then they would find themselves choosing between the options of suicide or murdering the Empress and then being executed for the crime.

'You should go, my love,' Caenis said, kissing his lips. 'I can't bear long-drawn-out goodbyes.'

'Nor me.' Vespasian stood and slipped his tunic on over his head.

'Sir! Sir!' Magnus' voice shouted from the living area of the tent.

'I know, I'm coming.'

Magnus popped his head through the curtains dividing off the sleeping area. 'No, you don't know. Mucianus sent me to get you; we've got a massive problem: the lads are refusing to strike the camp.'

'What? That's mutiny. Who are the ringleaders?'

'That's just it, sir, there don't appear to be any; you see it's not just the Second Augusta, it's all four legions and all the auxiliaries. They're united. They realised that when they were ordered to strike camp that meant that it was the real thing, not training, and they don't like it. They say the island is watched over by powerful gods and full of strange spirits and they won't go. As the old saying goes, they have no desire for the unknown. The whole army has refused to embark; they won't go to Britannia.'

'I suggest that you assemble the army and speak to them immediately, general, or I'll see you going back to Rome in chains,' Narcissus threatened without any preamble, barging into Plautius' briefing room, his voice as brittle as ice. 'And yours is not the only career that will be curtailed.' He looked menacingly around the assembled legates, auxiliary prefects, tribunes and camp prefects of the army.

Plautius met Narcissus' glare with a calm countenance. 'That would be most unwise, imperial secretary.'

'Unwise? You think it's wise to let an army of forty thousand men refuse their Emperor?'

'I don't think that is wise but I do think it unwise to try to persuade them to embark … just now.'

'They have to get on the ships today if you are to sail tonight.'

'We won't be sailing tonight.'

Narcissus stared at Plautius, dumbfounded for a moment. 'Are you telling me, General Plautius, that you are also refusing to go?'

'No, we're just not going to go tonight; we'll let the men calm down for a while and then I'll address them in a few days' time and we'll go the day after that.'

'They're soldiers, they do what they're told to when they're told to; not at some time at their convenience once they've "calmed down".'

'I couldn't agree with you more, imperial secretary, but the fact of the matter is that this is not for their convenience but rather for yours and the Emperor's and everybody else who wishes to see this campaign pursued quickly and efficiently.'

Vespasian was forced to suppress a smile as he saw, for the first time, complete bafflement on Narcissus' normally unreadable face.

'I'm afraid you'll have to enlighten me, general, as to how delaying the invasion is going to make the campaign quicker; I'd have thought that it would have the exact opposite effect.'

'That's because you are not a soldier, Narcissus, you are a palace functionary who has as much understanding of military matters as I have of etiquette.'

'How dare you talk to me like that!'

'No, Narcissus! How dare you burst in here and threaten me and my officers, humiliating me in front of them. You may have the Emperor's ear and consider yourself to be of great substance but you are still a freedman, an ex-slave; without Claudius you are nothing and you know it. You are an irrelevancy who would be dead within hours of your master's demise, which if this invasion is not a success, will be very soon. I on the other hand come from the Plautii and I won't tolerate your arrogance any more. So you will listen to me, freedman; yesterday we heard from some Gallic traders that upwards of one hundred thousand warriors were mustering just across the straits.' He pointed an accusatory finger towards the window beyond which a calm sea gleamed in the morning sun; on it a ship under sail slowly receded. 'I don't shy from odds of three to one or even five to one when fighting undisciplined savages, but I think that even you'll agree that the fewer the enemy the better is a reasonable military maxim, especially when you're trying to disembark your army. Now tell me what you see out of that window, imperial secretary.'

Narcissus squinted against the glare. 'The sea.'

'And what's on the sea?'

'A ship.'

'A ship? But that's not just any old ship; that ship is going to make the difference between crossing the Tamesis in forty-five days or thirty days because that ship is going to disperse the Britannic army within a market interval.'

Narcissus' bafflement was complete. 'Nine days! How?'

'Because the very same traders who took my silver yesterday in exchange for information about the Britons are now returning to Britannia; this evening they will be taking Togodumnus and Caratacus' silver and telling them that our troops have mutinied and we won't be coming. Once the warriors hear that, they will disband and go back to their farms, which they won't do if we suddenly appear tomorrow. Now, I would have thought that even a non-military man like you can grasp that if your enemy's army splits up it will be much easier to defeat him and will cost fewer lives. So, imperial secretary, I suggest you leave the timing of this to me because this has nothing to do with politics; we'll go on the calends of May. And don't worry, the Emperor will still be called for in time for his glorious victory.'

'See to it that he is, general.' Narcissus glared at Plautius before turning and retreating from the room with as much dignity as he was able to summon in the circumstances.

Plautius turned back to his assembled officers as if nothing was amiss. 'Now, gentlemen, where were we? Ah yes, the landing beaches; we will still use the new site just in case they leave a force at the original one, although I doubt they will. We'll land in three waves; Legate Corvinus, you will have the honour of leading the first wave.'

Corvinus smirked with pride. 'Thank you, general.'

Plautius pointed with a stick to a map of Britannia nailed to a wooden board behind him. 'Your Ninth Legion and its attached auxiliaries will land on Tanatis and secure it. I shall command the second wave consisting of Legates Vespasian and Sabinus' Second and Fourteenth Legions and their auxiliaries; we shall land an hour later on the mainland at this Rutupiae, as I shall now call it. The Second will muster and then advance immediately to Cantiacum, ten miles inland, taking King Adminios with you. On the first night Adminios will meet with kinsmen who have pledged loyalty to him and take their oath on behalf of three of the sub-tribes in the area whilst his emissaries will negotiate the surrender of the town. If they're stupid, besiege it. Clear, Vespasian?'

'Yes, sir.'

'Good. You will also send your Batavian cavalry, under Prefect Paetus, west to see what's ahead of us.' Plautius searched out Paetus amongst the crowd of officers. 'But you are not to make contact, prefect, just scout, is that understood? I want no flamboyance in my army.'

Paetus mustered his most serious expression. 'No flamboyance, sir!'

Plautius stared at the young prefect for a moment, trying but failing to detect any insolence, before grunting and then carrying on. 'The Fourteenth will move south, sending out your Thracian and Gallic cavalry on long-range reconnaissance to see if any of the Britannic army remains down there. If it's clear, you are to leave a garrison at the natural harbour by the white cliffs and then rendezvous with us at Cantiacum no more than three days after we land. One hundred triremes will shadow you down the coast and base themselves in that harbour ready for use later on in the campaign for land and sea operations along the south coast. Whilst they wait their crews and marines will be put to work turning that harbour into a port fit for our purpose; I want warehouses, jetties and a lighthouse. We've come to stay, Sabinus, understand?'

'Yes, sir.'

'Any questions?'

'What if we find the whole hundred thousand-strong army down there?'

'Then you send to me for reinforcements at the speed of Mercury.'

'At the speed of Mercury, sir.'

Plautius nodded curtly. 'The third wave will be under the command of Legate Geta. It will consist of his Twentieth and their auxiliaries and the supply ships with the baggage, artillery and one month's rations. You will be twelve hours behind us to give us time to clear the landing area of transports. Once you're ashore, Geta, your men will construct a fortified camp in two days, big enough to hold the whole force should we suffer a reverse. This will be the basis of a permanent garrison with a port. Then you will join the Second and the Fourteenth at Cantiacum on the third day.'

Geta looked less than pleased to be given construction work.

'When Geta vacates the camp, Corvinus, you will bring your lads across the strait and occupy it and then put half the remaining navy to work building the port and send the other half north into the Tamesis estuary ready to shadow the main force west. Then we shall be ready for our advance, provided Sabinus has not found too much resistance in the south. I will issue general orders concerning that on the third day ashore once everything is in position and I have a better idea of the enemy's disposition. Any questions, gentlemen?'

Vespasian looked around the room; no one seemed to be about to ask the obvious question. 'Yes, general, I have one: what do we do about the mutiny?'

'Nothing, Vespasian. There are almost two market intervals until we go and there will be plenty more traders going to and fro across the Gallic straits. They have to think that we are at an impasse with our men. They'll believe it because they saw the same thing happen four years ago when Caligula tried to invade. I want nothing done to suggest to the Britons that we may come after all and cause them to re-muster their warriors. The supply ships will remain loaded but the men will remain in camp doing only basic fitness training. It will be down to me to persuade them onto the ships the day before we go; then we shall see. Dismiss, gentlemen.'

'I don't think he can do it,' Magnus informed Vespasian as they stood outside the gates of the II Augusta's camp.

'We shall see.'

'You reckon? Well, I reckon we'll see a fiasco. I've been talking to a lot of the lads and they don't want to go. They're shit-scared because they've been listening to some of the old-hands' stories, lads who re-enlisted after their first stint. More than a few of them in the Fourteenth Gemina were part of Germanicus' fleet when it got caught in the storm on the way back from Germania, twenty-seven years ago. They were wrecked on Britannia's shore and they've got tales of beasts half human and half fish and spirits and ghosts and all sorts. They don't fancy it, sir, not one bit.'

Vespasian looked at the faces of the legionaries marching in cohorts out of the gate to parade with the other legions and auxiliary cohorts on the flat ground between the port and the five massive camps that surrounded it – the fifth had been constructed by Asiaticus' newly arrived reinforcements of two Praetorian cohorts, four cohorts of the Eighth Legion and auxiliaries –

including elephants – that Claudius would technically bring from Rome with him. 'They do look sullen, to say the least.'

'Sullen! I'd say they look mightily pissed off and mutinous.'

'Perhaps; we'll see,' Vespasian muttered but agreeing silently with his friend.

He had no cause to disagree; in the first few days after Plautius' briefing, discipline in the camps had been on the verge of breaking down. The centurions and their optiones had been hard-pressed to keep their men from boiling over into outright rebellion. He had been obliged to order two executions, more than a dozen whippings and countless canings and it had seemed to him that there were more men on latrine fatigue at any one time than there were trying to fill them. Recently, however, the men had calmed down and discipline and a sense of unity had returned; punishments had decreased and basic training and kit maintenance had continued. However, although their morale had returned Vespasian was not sure that it had returned in sufficient quantities to give Aulus Plautius much chance of persuading them to embark in a few hours' time.

The one benefit of the delay had been the extra time with Caenis. Although they were both busy with their duties during the day, the nights were their own and they had taken full advantage of them. She had also been a valuable source of information as to Narcissus' mood, and it was plain that it would not be just Plautius who would suffer if the invasion did not go ahead; he would carry out his threat to curtail the careers of all the officers. What Caenis could not say for certain, though, was whether Narcissus' own career was at stake. She rather suspected it would be because she was sure that both Pallas and Callistus would use the failure against him; as would Messalina if and when her brother's suspicions were conveyed to her. It seemed to Vespasian that Narcissus had potentially as much to lose as Plautius if this assembly did not go well; now would be the appropriate time to find the Eagle.

It was with these thoughts going around his head that he watched his men march to their allotted place on the parade ground and form up in neat ranks and files next to the two cohorts of the

Praetorian Guard in the place of honour opposite the dais. Once they were in position and he had taken their salute he made his way to his place, next to Sabinus, with the other legates and auxiliary prefects, beside the dais from where Plautius would address the men – via many heralds placed around the field to relay his words.

Plautius arrived as soon as the last unit had taken up its position. As was his right as a proconsul he was preceded by eleven lictors, which made Narcissus, walking beside him, look rather foolish with just a retinue of two slaves following him. Leaving the freedman at the bottom of the steps he mounted the dais whilst his lictors formed up in front of it, displaying their fasces representing the power of Rome that he held in his hand: the power to command and to execute.

At a bawled order from somewhere amongst the lines of iron-clad men reflecting the warm morning sun a shout went up and they hailed their commanding officer – although not with as much enthusiasm as Vespasian had heard them do so previously.

After a few moments – and wisely before the accolade started to die down of its own accord – Plautius raised his hands and gestured for silence. 'Soldiers of Rome, I stand here before you not only as your general but also as your brother. As your general I will lead you, but as your brother I will share with you all the hardships that we may be forced to endure. As a soldier I know that hardship is as much a part of our lives as victory; and victory will be ours. However, we have to go out and earn it, which we cannot do by staying here in our tents.'

Plautius paused so that the heralds could relay his words throughout the vast crowd punctuated by standards and banners and fronted by four legions' Eagles. Vespasian studied the faces of those legionaries nearest him; their expressions did not fill him with hope.

'I understand your fears,' Plautius continued, 'you have no desire for the unknown. But Britannia is not unknown. Our armies have already been there almost one hundred years ago and they came back! And when they did it was not with tales of strange monsters and vicious spirits but of men, men who could be beaten. They came back with tribute and treaties.'

'I think he's going about this the wrong way,' Sabinus whispered to Vespasian as again the words were carried around the field. 'They don't give a fuck about tribute and treaties; they want plunder and women.'

'He can't promise them that; if we're to pacify the tribes we need to beat them in battle and then take their surrender and make them allies, or at least neutral, so we can work our way west without having to be constantly looking behind our backs.'

As if to confirm Sabinus' statement a low growl began to emanate from the massed ranks before them; they were unimpressed by tribute and treaties.

A nervous look flashed across Plautius' face as he carried on: 'So I appeal to you, soldiers of Rome; do not let unfounded fears get in the way of glorious conquest. I already know personally of the valour of the Ninth Hispana and their auxiliaries from our time together in Pannonia.' A half-hearted cheer went up from that legion and their supporting cohorts. 'And I know of the valour of the Second, Fourteenth and Twentieth Legions and attached auxiliaries in safeguarding our Empire along the Rhenus from the reports I read when I was appointed commander of this expedition, and I look forward to witnessing it at first hand.' There was no such cheer from the rest of the army, instead the growl began to grow and pila shafts started being thumped on the ground; centurions bellowed at their men to desist but to no avail. Only the Praetorians stayed motionless. Plautius glanced down at Narcissus with fear in his eyes and nodded to the freedman. Narcissus looked over to the Praetorian cohorts, raised up his hand and then headed for the dais steps; from within the ranks of the Praetorians two guardsmen walked forward carrying a large wooden box between them. Throughout the army the thuds of pila shafts regulated into a uniform beat.

Vespasian shared the tension of the officers surrounding him.

'What can that duplicitous shit do to help?' Sabinus muttered against the growing tumult.

'I think he's trying one last throw of the dice,' Vespasian replied as Narcissus joined Plautius in front of the army. 'The dice that we risked our lives for.'

The two guardsmen hefted their burden up onto the dais and retreated back towards their unit. The rhythmical pounding continued to grow and here and there shouts of 'No!' and 'We won't go!' could be heard over the din.

Narcissus knelt down to open the box and reached inside.

The army grew increasingly vociferous with more and more men declaring their refusal to go. Centurions and optiones, outnumbered as they were by forty to one, were unable to prevent the escalation, and stood glowering, furious at their impotence in the face of such mass disobedience.

Narcissus got back up, holding with both hands a wooden pole, one end of which remained hidden in the box; with an effort he swung the pole up and raised aloft the Eagle of the Seventeenth.

The front ranks of the central two legions gradually ceased beating their pila on the ground; their stillness radiated out to the two flanking legions and back along the files to the auxiliary cohorts behind. All eyes were soon fixed on the symbol of Rome held up before them.

'Your Emperor has raised for you Rome's fallen Eagle,' Narcissus almost shrieked as soon as he could be heard. 'He gives you back the Eagle of the Seventeenth!' The heralds echoed his words along the ranks of now silent soldiery. An eruption of cheers broke from the Praetorian cohorts to be taken up by the legions on either side, spreading in a wave from cohort to cohort and travelling through the army just a hundred paces behind the heralds' relayed cries, until every man knew what he was looking at and was voicing his approval as loudly as his comrades in front.

Vespasian and his fellow officers joined in the celebrations wholeheartedly, as much for the return of the fallen Eagle as for the theatrical way that Narcissus had turned around the situation. Plautius turned and saluted the golden image hovering over the invasion force, crashing his arm across his chest and stamping to a rigid attention. Centurions throughout the legions caught this gesture and roared at their men to do the same; within a few heartbeats forty thousand pila-clenching fists pointed towards the Eagle as the Praetorians chanted 'Hail Caesar!' Soon that chant was unanimous, in unison and deafening.

Narcissus let it ring out, pumping the Eagle in the air in sympathetic timing until men were becoming hoarse. As the chant began to wane he lowered the Eagle and with a melodramatic flourish handed it to Plautius, who kissed it and then held it with his left hand whilst holding up his right, appealing for silence. 'The Emperor's loyal soldiers thank him for his gift,' he called as the noise died away.

'The Emperor is pleased to bestow such a gift on his valiant legionaries and auxiliaries,' Narcissus replied, turning to the quietening ranks as the words were relayed. The final herald finished his cry and Narcissus carried on: 'The Emperor has done this for you; will you now do his bidding? Will you, free-born soldiers of Rome, now embark?'

There was complete silence as the whole army stared at the Emperor's freedman appealing on his master's behalf.

Vespasian felt his heart thumping within him.

'Io Saturnalia!' a voice bellowed suddenly from the crowd.

Vespasian felt two more beats in his chest and then heard laughter, rough and raucous, mingled in with more jovial shouts of 'Io Saturnalia!' that quickly spread, along with the hilarity, until every man present was laughing except for Narcissus, who was obliged to stand and be mocked as the slave or freedman allowed to wear his master's clothes and run his house for one day over the course of the Saturnalia. He looked at Plautius, appealing with his eyes for him to stop this; but Plautius knew better than to curtail the release of so many days of tension.

'So they have extended the Saturnalia without telling us,' Sabinus said through his mirth.

'Evidently!' Vespasian replied, enjoying Narcissus' humiliation as much as the army's change of mood. 'And it's put the lads in a holiday mood. I think that after this they'll be on for an outing.'

CHAPTER XV

'WHERE THE FUCK are we?' Magnus grumbled, peering into the thick fog that had greeted them upon waking an hour before dawn.

Vespasian took a bite from a hunk of bread. 'The same place as we camped yesterday evening, I would have thought, alongside a trackway about three miles from Cantiacum; unless of course some god of the Britons has swooped down and moved ten thousand men during the night to somewhere inconvenient.'

'Everywhere on this island's inconvenient.'

'Not true. This trackway is very convenient; it will lead us directly to Cantiacum. What *is* inconvenient is the fog and the fact that Adminios' emissaries haven't yet returned and he's not due back until the second hour of the morning. I need to know the mood of the town before I dare move forward blind in case we're attacked from the flank; I won't be able to send out covering patrols because just west of here the trackway passes through very wet land with marshes to either side.'

'There you go, then, they're inconvenient.'

'Not to the Britons they're not; Adminios warned me about feeling complacent if my flank was protected by marsh; the locals know their way through, even in fog. I wouldn't like to be taken in the flank with only a swamp to fall back on; remember what happened to Varus.'

'So we wait, then?'

'Yes, old friend, we have to wait for the fog to lift but every hour we delay is another hour's warning for the Britons. Hopefully Adminios' emissaries will be back soon and we'll know more. I'll see you later.' Vespasian turned and walked back through the marching camp's gates.

He threaded his way through huddles of cold legionaries taking a miserable breakfast, fires being impossible in the conditions. Grumbling to one another about spending the night under a heavy sky with no more than a blanket each to protect them from the elements, they did not lower their voices as he passed. Vespasian disdained to notice the complaints but resolved to chase up the mule train with their leather tents that had arrived at Rutupiae with the third wave of the landings.

The landing itself had been an anti-climax in that it was unopposed and uneventful; which is exactly what the prayers at the numerous sacrifices made before the fleet sailed at midnight had asked for. Although the livers indicated that the gods seemed to favour their endeavour and the sacred chickens had pecked at their grain in an auspicious manner, there had been a time when every man thought that they may have been deserted by the divine. Mid-voyage the wind had got up and had started to blow them back to Gaul; the light from Caligula's massive lighthouse at Gesoriacum, made in imitation of the Pharos at Alexandria, had started growing in size again for a couple of hours no matter how hard the rowers strained at the oars. Their minds were eventually put at rest, however, by a dazzling shooting star streaking across the night sky heading west in the direction that they would conquer. The wind had soon died, easing their churning stomachs as they squatted on the vomit-slick decks, and as dawn broke the coast of Britannia was in full view; and it had been empty. Plautius' hunch had proved correct: the Britons had disbanded their army and there was no dark horde shadowing them north along the coast to oppose their landing.

Plautius had been the first man ashore, keeping the promise he had made to his men once they had finally mastered their mirth the day before. Being unaware of how the politics in Rome were developing, the experience of the Emperor's wishes being conveyed to them by his freedman had seemed so upside-down to them that when Plautius made a final appeal to their honour they had acquiesced to him with a mighty series of cheers. Vespasian had supposed that this had been mainly because they were pleased to have the established order of things returned in the shape of a general of high birth commanding them – although they had been visibly impressed by the resurrection of the Eagle as well as Plautius' offer of a bounty of ten denarii per man.

They had struck camp and begun the embarkation immediately – an efficient operation owing to the months of practice – and the first wave had sailed twelve hours later as the tide turned. Vespasian and Sabinus' wave left an hour after that in the hopes that they would be at the landing area soon after dawn. But the wind had delayed them and it was midday by the time the II Augusta clattered down the ramps onto the beach and formed up on the crunching shingle just as they had done in training, so many times before. Vespasian had allowed his men to eat a cold meal of bread and dried pork whilst remaining in formation as Paetus' cavalry patrols ranged out. They had returned an hour later to report nothing between the beach and Cantiacum except a few deserted farms with fires still glowing in the hearths; the Britons had pulled back and Plautius ordered the advance.

Sabinus had taken his legion south and Vespasian had led the II Augusta, accompanied by Adminios and his fellow exiles, along a well-used trackway west as the third wave of ships had appeared on the horizon beyond the island now occupied by Corvinus and the VIIII Hispana.

After three hours' marching, Vespasian had, on Adminios' advice, called a halt on the last dry ground before entering an area of low-lying marshland between two rivers, to give them time to build the huge marching camp, necessary for so many men, before nightfall. Adminios' emissaries had continued on to Cantiacum to ascertain the mood of the town and, if possible, negotiate its surrender, whilst Adminios himself went to the meeting with his loyal kinsmen to the north close to the estuary. Vespasian had hoped that the emissaries would be back by nightfall, but now, twelve hours later, they had still not returned; it was the only thing of concern in what had been otherwise a remarkably smooth operation, Vespasian thought, as he headed for the practorium – that and, of course, the fog.

'Good morning, sir,' Mucianus greeted him as he entered the praetorium, which was, naturally, just an area marked out on the ground because their baggage was yet to catch up with them; the legion's Eagle and cohort standards stood at one end guarded by a *contubernium* of eight men. 'I've just received the verbal reports from all the senior centurions from each cohort both legionary and auxiliary: we are less than a hundred men down from our full strength and the mood of the lads is good apart from being cold, damp and in need of a hot meal.'

'And a hot woman, no doubt?'

Mucianus grinned. 'Well, there's always that, sir; it seems pointless wasting your time reporting it to you.'

'Thank you for your consideration, tribune, I shall be sure to mention that in my report to Plautius. Tell Maximus to bring Adminios to me as soon as he returns to camp.'

'Yes, sir.'

As Mucianus left the praetorium, Vespasian sat down on the moist blanket that had been his only shelter during his brief few hours of sleep, pulled his cloak tight around his shoulders and chewed on his hunk of bread as he contemplated his options should Adminios' men not return.

Maximus, the prefect of the camp, approached what would have been the entrance to the tent with Adminios and snapped to attention, bringing Vespasian out of his thoughts. 'Permission to enter, sir?'

Vespasian beckoned them through, standing. 'Did your kin submit, Adminios?'

Adminios waved a dismissive hand. 'Yes, but they only count for a couple of thousand warriors.'

'That's a couple of thousand swords fewer pointing at our backs.'

Adminios grunted a reluctant assent. 'But it was good to see them after five years of exile.'

'I'm sure. So, what do you think about your emissaries?'

'They'll be back very soon, legate, they would have left shortly after dawn.'

'What's taken them so long?'

'They've been drinking.'

'Drinking?'

'Yes, they've evidently negotiated the town's surrender with the elders otherwise they would have come back – or been killed; it's our custom to seal a deal like that with an all-night drinking session.'

'How do you know they haven't been murdered?'

'One would've been sent back alive with his tongue cut out if the elders had decided to kill them, to emphasise that negotiations were over.'

'Then we're safe to approach the town in column seeing as the marsh prevents us from deploying in battle order?'

The exiled King nodded.

Vespasian's mind was made up. 'Maximus, have Paetus send a couple of turmae along the trackway and report back within the hour. The men will strike camp; I want them ready to move as soon as the fog lifts enough to see a hundred paces ahead. We're already behind schedule; there's not a moment to lose.'

Maximus turned and barked an order at the bucinator on duty outside the praetorium; he lifted his horn to his lips and blew a call of five notes. The call was taken up by his fellows in each cohort, invisible in the fog, and was then replaced by the shouts of centurions and optiones rousing their men from the remains of their cold breakfast; soon, from all around, Vespasian could hear the fog-dulled sounds of a legion preparing to march. 'Adminios, come with me back to the gate, I want to talk to your men as soon as they're here.'

Magnus was still there, chatting with the centurion of the watch, when they arrived. 'I thought you weren't going to move until the fog lifts or you knew whether the town was ours or not, sir.'

'It's a calculated risk that I have to take; Plautius will tear me apart if I'm not at Cantiacum soon, I'm late enough as it is.'

'Yeah but that ain't your fault; we were late landing and couldn't make it all the way last night, and then this.' He waved a hand in the swirling air.

Vespasian looked at Magnus with raised eyebrows.

'Ah, stupid of me. This is the army. Of course it's your—'

A challenge shouted by one of the sentries cut him off. Twenty paces away along the trackway silhouettes slowly materialised.

'Is that your men, Adminios?' Vespasian asked, feeling a deep relief.

'Yes, legate; I'll speak to them.'

Adminios walked forward to greet his followers as two turmae of Paetus' Batavians, led by Ansigar, rode out of the gate; the decurion saluted Vespasian and gave Magnus a cheery wave before disappearing into the fog.

Adminios' men dismounted and, after a few words with their King, they approached Vespasian with bloodshot eyes and reeking of alcohol.

'We may walk into the town, legate,' Adminios informed him, 'the elders will open the gates.'

'I'm relieved to hear it.'

'There's just one problem.'

Vespasian's face fell. 'What?'

'Yes, a lot of the young warriors didn't like the elders' decision. About a thousand slipped away during the night in the fog to join Caratacus in the Atrebates' main township southwest of the Afon Cantiacii. By tonight he'll know that we're here.'

Vespasian closed his eyes. 'Plautius will crucify me.'

'Why the fuck didn't you stop them and kill them, legate?' Plautius exploded as Vespasian reported the embarrassing news to his general upon the latter's arrival at Cantiacum, two days later.

Vespasian winced at the ferocity of the question. 'We didn't have time to get to the town on the first day, sir. With two hours until sundown I had a choice between making camp or leading my men through three miles of marsh that the tail of the column wouldn't have cleared until well after dark.'

'But you would have been on schedule! And you could've had the town surrounded and killed any long-hairs that decided they didn't like us. But instead you do the worst possible combination of things: you leave the town open but send a delegation to announce that we'll be arriving tomorrow and get the elders to declare for us, leaving time for all the young fire-eaters to piss off west to fill the ranks of Caratacus' army. Idiot!'

'Yes, sir,' Vespasian admitted, burning with shame inside, due as much to realising now the magnitude of his mistake as to the amused looks on the faces of Corvinus and Geta as he received this very public dressing-down. Only Sabinus remained neutral as Plautius paced up and down his tent. Rain drummed on the roof, increasing and decreasing in intensity with each gust of wind. The musty smell of damp woollen clothing pervaded the atmosphere.

'In war delay can be fatal, legate,' Plautius continued once he had collected himself somewhat. 'Just read Caesar again if you want to understand the importance of seizing the initiative with quick action.'

'Yes, sir.'

'Why didn't you send cavalry out after them as soon as you were told?'

'The fog was—'

'The fog! We all had fog; you're going to have to get used to the fucking fog in this damp arsehole of the world. If you'd sent cavalry immediately they could have at least been closer to the bastards by the time the fog lifted; they were on foot, for fuck's sake!'

'Yes, sir; I'm sorry, sir.'

Plautius glared at Vespasian for a few moments before letting out a huge sigh. 'Well, it's done now and a thousand men is not such a great number in the scheme of things. But let that be a lesson to you, Vespasian: next time I order you to do something, you do it unless you can show me the evidence that Jupiter himself came down and personally gelded you and put out your eyes in order to stop you; because if you can't, that's what I'll do to you. Do you understand me?'

Vespasian winced again. 'Yes, sir!'

'Good. Sit down.'

Vespasian sat back down next to Sabinus as Geta and Corvinus exchanged an amused glance.

'Stop smirking,' Plautius growled at them as he sat at his desk.

'I expect it's not the last mistake that will happen on this trip but I'm sure it's the last that Vespasian will make. Now, to business, gentlemen.' He unravelled a scroll and perused it for a few moments before looking back up at his subordinates. 'So far it's gone reasonably smoothly. To sum up: Sabinus found no one to the south worth mentioning, we've seized the harbour by the white cliffs and the navy has started work on it. We have a large squadron in the Tamesis estuary to our north and Rutupiae is secure and work has started on the port. The Ninth has occupied Geta's camp and has already laid two miles of temporary road from there towards us. Adminios is in place as our puppet and has received the loyalty of the local sub-tribes and a civil admin-istration favourable to us is being created under the watchful eye of Sentius. Our cavalry patrols report that there is no large enemy force between us and the Afon Cantiacii and the bridge is still standing. So with our rear and flanks secure we start our push west immediately. I want your legions ready to march two hours after this briefing ends; is that understood?'

'Yes, sir!' all four legates replied simultaneously.

'Good. That was the easy part; from now on we've lost all elements of surprise and the Britons know the land far better than we do. We shall move forward on a broad front, quickly, but taking care not to damage too much of the farmland; I want a good harvest growing behind us as I don't intend that either our lads or the tribes that surrender to us should go hungry this winter. Sabinus' Fourteenth will be my centre; it's mainly undu-lating ground between here and the river so there's no need to deviate unless the enemy appear. Your auxiliaries will act as the army's forward scouts.

'Geta, your Twentieth will take the right flank. You will keep to within two miles of Sabinus. Your task is twofold: firstly to stop anything getting around that flank, and secondly to keep in contact with the squadron in the estuary who will be supplying us. Your auxiliaries will be busy.

'Vespasian, your Second will be our left flank. You will advance along the north side of these downs with your auxiliaries taking the high ground. I want regular reports from the south side; it wouldn't do to have an army sneak past us that way.

'Corvinus, the Ninth will guard our rear. Two of your auxiliary cohorts will stay in Rutupiae making the camp a permanent structure. Another two will carry on constructing the road; I want nothing fancy, we'll build a proper one when we have the time and slaves to do it. Just make it so that it can take wheeled transport. I want your cavalry alae patrolling the south making our presence felt amongst the locals so that they get used to us. The legion and the rest of your cohorts will follow half a day's march behind us just in case something slips behind our backs.

'You will all take your own baggage with you now that it's caught up; the siege train and other heavy stuff will advance with the Ninth. Any questions, gentlemen?'

'Will the Ninth always have to tag along in the rear?' Corvinus asked with more than a hint of derision in his voice.

'You will address me as sir or general, legate!' Plautius snapped, slamming his fist down on the desk top. 'Being the Empress' brother does not put you above me here. This is an army in a war zone not a dinner party on the Palatine; do you understand me, lad?'

Corvinus all but recoiled at the vehemence of the put-down and the insult. The muscles in his cheeks tensed and re-tensed. 'Yes, general,' he answered eventually.

'That's the second time you've questioned my orders recently; there'll not be a third. The Ninth will do as it's told; it will be our rearguard for this river but it'll be the freshest legion when we come to the Tamesis and then it'll see hard fighting. Once we've secured the Tamesis crossing and whilst we're waiting for Claudius, your legion will head south and place Verica on his throne and then take Vectis in preparation for the push west next season; so you'll have plenty to do. I know from our time in Pannonia together that you're up to it, Corvinus; that's why I didn't object when you were made a part of this army.' Plautius pointed his finger threateningly at Corvinus' face. 'Don't give me cause to regret it.' He rolled up his scroll and then stood and addressed the other three legates. 'We march in two hours; that gives you four hours before you'll need to build camps for the night. By then I want Vespasian and Geta's legions in the positions I've given you either side of Sabinus ready for a hard day's march tomorrow. I intend to be at the Afon Cantiacii by dusk the following day; let's hope that we don't find it held against us. Dismiss, gentlemen.'

The sun warmed Vespasian's face for the first time since arriving in Britannia as he and Magnus, accompanied by a turma of the II Augusta's legionary cavalry, rode up the grass-covered northern slope of the hills on the left flank of the army's advance. With the sun out, the landscape took on a completely different aspect. Gone was the gloom of dripping vegetation and rain-spattered puddles on mud-churned ground, all pressed down upon by a heavy, grey sky that seemed so low as to be touchable. In its stead was a lush, green countryside of pasture, woods and freshly sprouting wheat fields; the air was clear and fresh, and with the warmth returning to his body Vespasian felt that it might not be such a miserable land after all.

It had been two days since Plautius' briefing and the advance had been as fast as it had been uneventful; the only obstacles to their progress had been the weather and the occasional enemy cow or sheep, which invariably found its way to the cooking fires of whichever century claimed the honour of tackling such a fearsome foe.

'I'm beginning to think that a plague has wiped out almost every living thing west of Cantiacum,' Magnus commented as they passed yet another deserted farmstead. 'And judging by the freshness of the sheep shit it must have been very recent.'

'But where are the bodies?' Vespasian asked, smiling at his friend's hypothesis. 'Perhaps Paetus can tell us; we should come across him soon.'

'I don't understand why you didn't send a message ordering him to come to you instead of traipsing all the way up here.'

Vespasian pulled up his horse and turned it around. 'That's why,' he said, extending his arm to the view.

Below them the country was speckled with marching columns, eight men abreast, arranged in an almost straight line north; the three legions in the middle were advancing in a broader formation, each forty men abreast in two long columns of five cohorts and trailed by endless pack-mules and wagons. Between Vespasian and his II Augusta, just three miles distant, tramped his seven infantry auxiliary cohorts, the closest one, the archers of I Cohort Hamiorum, was a hundred paces just down the slope from them. In front of the three legions the XIIII Gemina's eight cohorts of Batavian infantry scouted ahead to spring any ambushes set, in order to protect the more valuable lives of the Roman citizens in the legions. A cavalry turma galloped past them returning from a patrol to the west. The low, booming sound of cornua floated up from the army as it advanced with the sun reflecting off countless helmets.

In the distance, ten miles away to the north, the supporting squadron of triremes and supply vessels appeared like small dots on the glittering Tamesis estuary. Then to the east, bringing up the rear five miles behind the last of the columns, was the dark shadow of the siege train and heavy baggage followed by the almost square formation of the VIIII Hispana flanked by auxiliary cohorts.

'What a sight that is,' Vespasian said after a few moments of admiration. 'That is a very big army.'

Magnus was unimpressed. 'I've seen bigger.'

Vespasian was disappointed at his friend's reaction but hid it; he had forgotten momentarily that Magnus had served with Germanicus in Germania with armies almost twice the size. 'I suppose you must have,' he mumbled, turning his horse and kicking it on up the hill towards the woods that crowned it. 'Anyway, the main reason is to see for myself the lie of the land ahead of us.'

'Of course, very sensible.'

'And to see what Paetus' situation is at first hand.'

'Indeed.'

Paetus' situation was similar to every other commander's in the army: quiet. 'We've seen hardly anyone,' he told Vespasian and Magnus once they had caught up with him amongst the trees. 'Occasionally we come across small family groups, without any men of fighting age, hiding in the woods with their livestock. I don't let the chaps touch them, not even take something for the pot. All my patrols from the south have come back in with nothing to report apart from the occasional hostile deer that demonstrates its martial prowess with a consummate display of running away. Nothing's here, and no one is moving.'

'I've a feeling that we'll find them soon, Paetus.' Vespasian looked out over the thickly forested country to the south. 'How deep have you sent patrols into there?'

'Ten miles in, sir. We've found nothing but a few charcoal burners. It's thick forest; you could hide an army in there but it wouldn't be able to move very fast.'

'Thank you, Paetus, keep your lads at it.' Vespasian turned to leave.

'You know of course where they all are?' Magnus said as they rode out of the trees.

'Where?'

'All together.'

'I've worked that out. The question is: are they waiting for us at the river, or are they trying to get around behind us, or are they going to do something that we just don't expect?'

Magnus' face fell. 'I think it's the latter, sir, look.' He pointed west to a hill just beyond the advance of the Batavian infantry.

Vespasian followed his gaze; over the hill came a dark smudge, blurred by the dust rising from it. Then came the distant roar of massed voices raised in hatred. 'They must be mad! They can't take us head on.'

Thousands of warriors, led by hundreds of two-horse chariots careering over the grass, were swarming for the XIIII Gemina and the II Augusta. The Batavians had evidently had warning from advance scouts and the eight cohorts had formed into line and closed up forming a protective shield for the legions as they too manoeuvred into battle order.

'I think it's time you got back to the legion, sir.'

CHAPTER XVI

'IT SEEMS THAT we're facing about thirty thousand, sir. Plautius has ordered us to send forward cohorts one to four of our Gallic auxiliaries to support the Batavians,' Mucianus reported as Vespasian and Magnus pulled their horses up to a skidding halt at the II Augusta's command post between the two lines of its ten cohorts, now in battle formation. 'I've sent them; they made contact with the Batavians not long ago. The fifth I've had move on to our left flank along with the rest of the legion's cavalry.'

'Good; what are our orders?'

'Form two lines to give us as broad a frontage as possible but remain in open order, which we've done, and then wait.'

'Wait?'

'Yes, sir, wait.'

'All right. Send a messenger to the First Hamiorum telling them to come in range of our left flank; I want archer support when it comes to it. And send another to Paetus; he's to stay on the hill in case they try to outflank us. You can rejoin your first and second cohorts when that's done.'

'Yes, sir!'

Vespasian looked over the heads of his front rank cohorts and up the slope ahead; two hundred paces away, the auxiliaries were formed up four ranks deep in a line almost a mile long. Beyond them, at the top of the hill, a mass of thousands of naked and half-naked tribesmen bellowed war cries, whilst capering and brandishing weapons as hundreds of chariots skitted around on the cropped grass before them. Skilled drivers brought their vehicles close enough for the single warrior in each to hurl a couple of javelins at the shielded auxiliaries before veering their stocky ponies off back up the hill to be replaced by another wave and then another before coming around again. Occasionally a warrior, carried away by battle-lust, jumped from his chariot to charge single-handedly into the front rank of the auxiliaries – with the inevitable consequence. His brisk and bloody death earned raucous roars of approval from the mass of tribesmen watching on.

One man in particular caught Vespasian's eye: tall and powerfully built, his broad chest and muscular arms daubed in swirls of blue-green vitrum and his hair spiked high with lime, he stood proud in his speeding chariot, punching a sword into the air, urging each wave on down the slope towards the Roman lines. 'That chieftain must be either Caratacus or Togodumnus.'

'Running around in circles in chariots isn't going to get them anywhere,' Magnus observed. 'Why don't he just order them to charge?'

'I think that their noble warriors in the chariots have to have the honour of being the first to engage the enemy. They're expecting us to send a few champions forward for some single combat. According to Caesar it's how they like to start battles.'

'Well, they're going to have to get used to our way now. Our lads haven't even bothered to waste any javelins on them.'

A rumble of cornua relayed along the line; the auxiliaries' standards dipped one by one, ordering the advance. The Batavians and Gauls, whose great-grandfathers had so fiercely opposed Rome and her conquests, now marched forward to conquer in her name.

The chieftain jumped from his chariot and, facing back up the hill to his massed warriors, extended his arms, sword in one hand, shield in the other, as if embracing every man. The chariots hurtled away, leaving their warriors on the field with their chieftain as slowly he turned to face the oncoming enemy.

The Britons charged.

It was a charge unlike any Vespasian had seen or heard before: wild, unco-ordinated, and fearsome in its recklessness. With a roar that would shake the dark realm of Pluto himself and with no thought for maintaining lines for mutual support, thousands of warriors, smeared in outlandish blue-green designs, waving long slashing swords above the spiked hair on their heads, ran pell-mell down the slope, each trying to outdo his comrades for the honour of being the first to draw blood. They were oblivious to danger as hundreds were punched down by the first javelin volley that scythed through them, fifty paces out. They hurdled their skewered dead and wounded, who crashed to the ground in sprays of crimson, splintering the shafts that impaled them, and came on as a second volley tore through their massed, unprotected flesh, thumping them off their feet, backs arched, teeth bared, screaming their last.

With their javelins thrown the auxiliaries halted, weight on their left legs, bracing their oval shields before them and readying their swords; the rear ranks closed up to support the men before them as the shock of impact shuddered through the mile-long line.

Vespasian held his breath; the cohorts buckled slowly in places and then straightened as centurions bellowed their men forward, leading by example, fending off the slashes and downward cuts of their opponents' long swords and dealing out death in return with their spathae, jabbing and cutting before them as the Britons strove to cleave through the line.

But the superior number and weight of the Britons did not tell; their long swords were not designed for close-quarters work and once they had crashed their shields into those of their opponents and swiped at their heads they pulled back so as to be able to work their weapons properly: slicing down or across from above their heads as if in single combat, not as part of a shield wall. The line settled; the charge was absorbed and cornua rumbled over the screaming: Plautius had signalled the II Augusta and XIIII Gemina to advance and relieve the auxiliaries.

'Advance in open order!' Vespasian shouted at the command-post *cornicen*. A series of rumbling notes was repeated throughout the legions' cohorts. Standards dipped and the II Augusta advanced for its first taste of combat with this new and savage foe.

Vespasian eased his horse forward to keep pace with the advance, feeling a pride that he had never known before as it came home to him that he was commanding a full legion in a set-piece battle. His whole life had come down to this moment and now he would find out if he was worthy of it. He steeled himself, determined not to give Plautius cause to rebuke him; there would be no more mistakes.

'This is going to take some timing,' Magnus muttered from behind him.

'What are you still doing here?'

'I was wondering that myself.'

'Well, if you're staying don't distract me because yes, you're right, it is going to take some timing.' Vespasian turned his concentration back to the advance of the five cohorts in the front line. They were in open order with every second file of four men removed and placed alternately in the file next to it, leaving man-wide gaps.

Thirty paces before the II Augusta reached their hard-pressed auxiliaries Vespasian looked down at his cornicen marching alongside him. 'Prepare to release!'

The man blasted out three notes, which were taken up by his fellows in the front rank cohorts; standards signalled and the first four men of each line pulled back their right arms, feeling the weight of their pila. With ten paces to go the two rear men of each of the auxiliaries' files broke off and sprinted down the gaps in the II Augusta.

'Release!' Vespasian shouted.

With a deep note from the cornu the centurions bellowed the order and more than a thousand pila soared over the heads of the auxiliaries to slam down, with lead-weighted impetus, onto their adversaries, crunching through skulls, sternums and shoulders with brutal and sudden violence.

The neighbouring XIIII Gemina's volley struck an instant later as the Hamorians started pouring their arrows in from the flank, felling hundreds; the Britons all along the line wavered for a moment. It was all that was needed. The remaining auxiliaries turned and headed down the gaps in the relieving legions' lines, which were closed by every other man in the file of eight rushing to fill them as soon as their auxiliary comrades were through.

Here and there Britons managed to break into formations causing little pockets of havoc within the regimented ranks and files of the cohorts; but these were soon dealt with.

Vespasian glanced down at the cornicen. 'Rear ranks, release.'

Another few notes, repeated throughout the legion, and the rear two men of each file hefted their pila over their comrades' heads as they began their mechanical sword work stabbing at the vitals of the howling enemy.

Barbed pilum heads on the end of thin iron shafts, designed to maximise the penetrative pressure of the weighted weapon, again rained down on the Britons, sheering through many, causing the ground beneath them, already churned with blood, urine and faeces, to become even more treacherous.

Fresh to the fight and having not seen proper action for over two years, the legionaries of the II Augusta went about their business with vicious and enthusiastic efficiency, the body-count before them escalating as they stabbed and stamped their way forward supported by rapid volleys from the Hamorians that spat into the rear ranks of their foes and any that tried to slip around the flank.

The combined weight and tactics of the two legions in unison was too much for warriors used to fighting as individuals and they began splintering off, firstly in ones and twos, then in scores and hundreds, until what was left of the army was running back up the hill with almost as much speed and noise as it had descended it, leaving thousands lying still or writhing in the foul-smelling mud.

'Sound halt!' Vespasian ordered.

The cornu blared out and its call was echoed. The II Augusta came to a stop and jeered its vanquished enemies as they raced away having learnt what it means to face a legion of Rome.

But the jeers soon faded as a new force, as large, if not larger, appeared on a hill two miles to the north, facing the XX Legion; it would now be their turn to show their mettle.

'Relieve line!' Vespasian called.

Another rumble through the legion caused the rear five cohorts to advance, allowing their tired and bloodied comrades through their formations and replacing them as a fresh front line, should the legion be called upon again that day. Behind them the Gallic and Batavian auxiliaries had begun re-forming and receiving fresh javelins from the quartermasters' mule-drawn carts stationed in the rear.

The II Augusta watched as the new arrivals began to work themselves up into a battle fever, bellowing courage into their hearts.

'What's happened to their chariots?' Magnus asked once he noticed their absence.

'I don't know,' Vespasian replied, shaking his head. 'But the real question is: why didn't they attack together? They could have thrown sixty thousand men at us at once.'

'Still wouldn't have been enough, though.'

'No, probably not. They were idiotic to face us in the open; why didn't they just wait at the river? It can't be more than three or four miles away.'

'I'm sure they're going to oblige us by doing that very thing; as will that lot once the lads of the Twentieth have introduced them to their iron.'

From out of the middle of the new arrivals strode a single warrior; although he was far away and it was impossible to discern any of his physical attributes, Vespasian understood from the roaring of the tribesmen that this was a man of great importance and smiled coldly. 'My guess is that's the brother of whoever was leading our opponents; I think that I detect a sibling rivalry.'

'Ah, that's why they didn't wait; nothing worse than sharing the glory with your brother – and it looks like yours is going to outshine you today.'

To their right the XIIII Gemina were preparing to support the XX next to them as the horde of Britons on top of the hill began to fan out into a wider frontage. The Gemina's two lines of cohorts had already exchanged places and now their auxiliaries were being brought forward to take up again the first shock of the wild charge.

They did not have to wait long. With a roar that was blood-curdling even at two miles distant, the dark shadow of warriors began to flow down the hill with a viscous, ever-changing front, like molten pitch being poured from a tub onto an enemy below.

On they came as the cloud of a first volley of javelins from the XX Legion's Spanish and Aquitanian auxiliaries darkened the sky above them to dissipate quickly into a sharp-pointed rain. Vespasian watched with silent admiration; the charge refused to falter as the first and then the second volley hailed down on it.

'Sir!' a young voice shouted as the charge hit home with a marked increase in volume.

Vespasian looked around to see the thin-stripe tribune from Plautius' staff, sitting on a sweating horse, saluting.

'Yes, Tribune Alienus?'

'The general compliments you on your actions so far and asks that you move your auxiliaries forward to threaten the enemy's flank. He believes that will cause them to break; once they do you are to follow them up with all possible haste and try and catch them as they cross the Afon Cantiacii.'

'Thank you, tribune, you may tell the general that it will be done.'

Alienus saluted again before galloping off as Vespasian issued the orders for Maximus, the camp prefect, to relay to the waiting messengers of the legion's cavalry detachment and then to oversee the manoeuvre.

The horsemen sped off and Vespasian turned his attention back to the fighting on his right. The auxiliary line had held and, with a rumble of cornua, the XIIII and the XX were advancing to relieve them.

Magnus gave a wry smile. 'You have to hand it to the army, when it comes to tactics they don't win any prizes for innovation.'

'If something works then why change it?' Vespasian replied, admiring the precision of the manoeuvre as the rear ranks of auxiliaries broke off and filed back through their legions' lines.

By the time both legions were fully engaged the II Augusta's auxiliaries, still smeared in fresh blood, were jogging past Vespasian, equipment jangling and feet pounding, in columns eight abreast and on through the gaps created between the front rank cohorts of the legion. As they emerged onto the open ground the columns fanned out to either side in a fluid motion of precisely drilled soldiery to form a four-deep line, each unit abutting its neighbour. The shouts of their centurions and optiones as they dressed the ranks were lost beneath the battle's bellows, screams and clanging, metallic clashes, as if herds of cattle were being slaughtered simultaneously to the accompaniment of thousands of blacksmiths maniacally ringing down blows upon their anvils.

With the ranks straight, the auxiliary line began its advance from the left, co-ordinated by Maximus, wheeling until it was at forty-five degrees and then moving forward at the double towards the Britons' exposed flank.

Vespasian glanced up the hill ahead; there was no sign of the defeated force. 'Slow advance!'

Again the cornu sounded and again the II Augusta moved forward steadily up the hill in support of their auxiliaries as they closed with the enemy. The sight of a fresh force closing in on the battle put heart into the men of the XIIII and XX Legions and they renewed their efforts as, simultaneously, the Britons wavered; the faint-hearted turned to flee back up the slope rather than take on the new enemy. Panic began to spread through the mass of warriors and more and more turned to run until only the most blood-hungry were left to face the mechanical sword work of the legions; they were soon despatched with merciless and violent efficiency.

And then suddenly it was over.

Maximus recalled the II Augusta's auxiliaries; they had not even needed to charge, their presence alone had been enough to turn the battle. They moved swiftly across the path of the advancing legion and took up position two hundred paces to its front.

To Vespasian's right, the XIIII and XX both relieved their front rank cohorts and allowed their auxiliaries through to form a protective line ahead of them before continuing their advance so that the three legions were at a slant with the II Augusta in the lead.

Vespasian sat bolt upright on his mount, his heart thumping in his chest. 'Advance at the double!' he called down to the cornicen, revelling in the pride he felt as his legion led the way west, chasing a beaten but not yet defeated foe.

The message rumbled out and within a few heartbeats the legion had quickened its pace, their footsteps pounding the already trampled grass. Ahead, the auxiliary cohorts responded and started to jog up the last hundred paces of the hill as a lone warrior appeared at its summit. Within moments the warrior was joined by a multitude of figures, silhouetted by the afternoon sun, stretching across the length of the hill-brow. The auxiliaries halted and for the third time that day dressed their ranks for combat.

'Halt!' Vespasian ordered.

'Bastards haven't run away like they should,' Magnus complained as the cornu's notes brought the legion to a stop.

'We'll have to keep beating them until they do,' Vespasian muttered as he tried to assess how many men could be hidden behind those already visible.

The XIIII Gemina and the XX carried on until they were level with the II Augusta before they too halted, and for the first time that day silence descended over the field as the two forces faced each other.

Vespasian looked over his shoulder to Plautius' command position behind Sabinus' legion; messengers were being despatched. He turned back to the enemy; they were still. The two sides continued to stare at each other for a few more quickening heartbeats until the lead warrior began to walk forward towards the II Augusta; after he had covered ten paces he raised a branch in full leaf in the air and the men behind him followed.

'They've had enough already,' Magnus exclaimed as all along the Roman lines cheering erupted.

'I don't think so; look.' Vespasian pointed to the slowly advancing Britons. No one appeared over the hill behind them. 'It must be just one tribe and a small one at that. I'm going to talk with them.' He kicked his horse forward as the Britons slowed and then as one threw their weapons to the ground before walking backwards a few paces away from them and then falling to their knees.

Vespasian galloped through the ranks of his legion and on past the auxiliaries to draw his horse up in front of the lead warrior, the only man still on his feet.

The Briton looked up at him. His face was long and ruddy with lines of care etched from the corners of his eyes and frown creases across his brow, which, combined with his downward-drooping silver moustache, gave the impression of a world-weary man burdened with troubles. 'I am Budvoc, King of the Dobunni, subject of Caratacus and master of nothing but my own fate,' he said in passable Latin. 'Today I and my warriors have done all that honour requires of us and now, having shed our blood, we choose our fate. If we are to remain a subject tribe we will do so out of choice and we would rather be subject to the might of Rome than to our neighbours the Catuvellauni. What is your name, general?'

'Titus Flavius Vespasianus, but I am no general, I am a legate.'

'No matter, legate; it was this legion that we fought following Caratacus and it was this legion that defeated us and it is to this legion that we yield.' He took his sword from its scabbard and dropped it on the grass in front of Vespasian's horse's hooves and then placed his branch over it, covering it with its leaves. 'We are your people now, do with us what you will.'

'What's going on here, legate?' Plautius shouted, pulling his horse up.

'I've just accepted the surrender of Budvoc of the Dobunni, sir.'

'Have you now?' Plautius looked down at the King. 'Well, Budvoc, your men fought bravely even though they were led by men with as much military sense as a mule. I imagine that you have nothing to thank Caratacus or Togodumnus for in the way that they behaved this day.'

The King shook his head. 'Regretfully Caratacus wanted to claim the glory of defeating you for himself and would not wait for his brother even though his army was in sight. I understand honour and I understand the need to die for honour's sake but I will not sacrifice my men for the vainglorious honour of a fool.'

'And on your honour do you swear that your men will submit to Rome?'

'I will take my own life if any of these men here raises a hand against you.'

'In that case your lives will be spared and you will remain free. You will stay here under the guard of the reserve legion. If you try to escape or break your word in any way one half of you will die on crosses and the other half will become slaves.'

The King bowed. 'That will not be necessary, general.'

'I hope not. Vespasian, have two cohorts of your auxiliaries remain with them until the Ninth arrive, they shouldn't be long, they're already in sight, and then let's get on; we've got a river to cross.'

The sun glowed golden, falling into the west, bathing the grassy summit of the final hill before the Afon Cantiacii with soft, warm light. Vespasian rode ahead of his legion and auxiliaries with Mucianus, Maximus and Magnus, escorted by sixty of the legion's hundred and twenty cavalry. The other half was away patrolling the river, having reported that the Britons had crossed to the west bank and destroyed the bridge behind them.

Suppressing an elated grin at the way he and his legion had conducted themselves that day, Vespasian looked back at his men trudging wearily up the hill behind him. 'We must make sure that the lads get a good meal and a good night's rest, Maximus. Give them permission to have half as much again of their food ration once we've built the camp; but not their wine ration. I don't want them hungover in the morning; I've a feeling that we're going to have a hard day of it.'

'The food I can do, sir, but as to getting a good night's rest, that's unlikely for all of them; I expect that you'll want a lot of patrols out as I'm sure the long-hairs will try a few raids across the river.'

Vespasian cursed himself inwardly for letting his elation cloud his professionalism. 'You're right, of course, Maximus, but try and spread the duties.'

'I'll see to it that only one century from each cohort has a broken night's sleep.'

Feeling foolish at having been reminded of a simple precaution by his prefect of the camp, however tactfully it was done, Vespasian vowed to himself to be more level-headed after the rush of battle. Maximus would not have cause to correct him again; but then, he reflected, that was part of his role. The prefect of the camp was by far the most experienced soldier in the legion; he would have joined up as a raw legionary recruit and worked his way up through the ranks to become the most junior centurion in the tenth cohort. He then would have risen through the centurionate, eventually becoming the primus pilus of the first cohort before being promoted to the highest rank a legionary could aspire to. With that much combat and administration experience he was there to keep an eye on his less experienced social betters and superiors: the legate and the senior tribune.

It was a good system, Vespasian considered, as they ascended the last few feet to the hill's summit, provided that the legate was not so arrogant as to dismiss the advice of a man of a far lower social status, which was a fault all too common in society. He swore to himself that he would never make that mistake; better to look a bit foolish and be safe than to try and save face and be dead.

Such musings were immediately driven from his head as he crested the brow of the hill. 'Mars Victorious, hold your hands over us,' he whispered as he looked down the half-mile slope to the river and the broken, wooden bridge and then beyond.

On the far bank and up the hill beyond, stretching left and right for almost a mile, were more men than he had ever seen gathered in one place other than in the Circus Maximus back in Rome. They were camped haphazardly in groups and clusters and as he looked more were arriving over the hill and swarming down to join their countrymen. As the Roman legions appeared on the brow the entire British army got to their feet and roared their defiance; it was deafening.

'There must be over a hundred thousand of them.'

Maximus drew his horse up next to him and surveyed the scene for a few moments. 'Yes, that would be about right; maybe ten thousand or so more or less than that and their numbers are growing all the time. If I was Plautius I wouldn't wait for tomorrow; there's still four hours of daylight left; plenty of time to bridge a river.'

Magnus whistled softly in admiration. 'Now that's what I call a big army!'

CHAPTER XVII

AULUS PLAUTIUS GRINNED at his legates and auxiliary prefects assembled around a table in the open air. 'We go immediately, gentlemen, to take advantage of the careless way that they've camped – before one of them shows some initiative and throws up defence works.' He unrolled a roughly sketched map of the Afon Cantiacii, spread it on the table and put his finger on the river. 'We're here; just to the north of us the river does a dog-leg and for a half-mile stretch it's out of sight of the Britons' camp behind this hill.' He pointed to the map and then at the 200-foot hill to their north, about a mile beyond the wrecked bridge. 'I want the eight cohorts of Batavian infantry to swim across as soon as possible.' He looked at a bearded auxiliary prefect. 'Civilis, as the prefect of the first cohort, I'm placing you in command; as soon as you're across, take that hill. That should wake them up. My hunch is that the undisciplined rabble will swarm all over you but with the high ground in your favour you should be able to hold long enough for us to almost achieve our objective before they notice what we're doing; then the pressure will be off you and onto the Second Augusta. Any questions?'

Civilis frowned. 'What is the objective that we're acting as a diversion for?'

'The Second Augusta throwing a bridge across the river, of course. You're to keep that high ground at all costs. Now get going, there's not a moment to lose and may Fortuna, or whichever god you Batavians hold dear, look to you.'

'Fortuna will do, sir.' Civilis saluted sharply along with his seven colleagues and jogged off to muster his men.

Plautius' gaze ranged around his officers. 'We've got two great advantages here: the Britons don't know that we've got eight

cohorts of eight hundred men each who can swim a river in full
armour and they also don't know about pontoon bridges. They
think that we're going to wait for the tide to go down and then start
sinking piles into the river bed and start building a proper bridge,
so let's not disabuse them of that. I want you all to go through the
motion of building camps to lull the long-hairs into a false sense of
security and to draw their attention away from Civilis' men
heading north; but just do the earthworks, leave all the tents
packed with the baggage.' Plautius' eyes rested on Vespasian. 'The
carts carrying the boats should be with us imminently; have them
unloaded and ready in amongst your camp's building works.' His
attention passed to Sabinus. 'As soon as the Batavians appear on
that hill, Sabinus, I want your legion to advance to the destroyed
bridge and make as if you're going to try and rebuild it. The Britons
will then be split between trying to dislodge the Batavians and
hurling slingshot at your lads to keep them off the bridge. I'm
afraid you'll take some casualties but it's vital that you stay there.'

'Yes, general.'

'Vespasian, as soon as the Britons are preoccupied to the
north you get those boats into the river, here.' He pointed to a
stretch of river, one mile to the south of the broken bridge. 'The
hills curve away from both banks at this point so you won't have
to be fighting uphill once you're over there. You'll have an hour
to get across and secure enough of a bridgehead for Geta's legion
to cross behind you.' He looked up at Geta. 'I want your legion
to form up right here where we are as soon as the Batavians
appear on their hill; then I need you to march north to confuse
Caratacus and his brother, they'll think that you're trying to cross
where the Batavians did and that will keep their attention away
from Vespasian. After an hour you double-back and cross the
Second's bridge at dusk. Once you're across I'll have the bridge
towed up to the Fourteenth's position under the cover of night,
as soon as the moon has set; it'll be ready by dawn. Then we
attack, with the Second on the low ground along the river and the
Twentieth on the high ground, both heading north to link up
with the Fourteenth; we'll then roll the long-hairs back and crush
them against the Batavians.'

'What about the Ninth, general?' Corvinus asked, visibly affronted that his legion had not been mentioned.

'I was coming to them, legate. Keep them hidden from view on the other side of the hill and then bring them over at dawn tomorrow and cross the bridge after the Fourteenth. Once the Britons break the survivors will head to the Tamesis. Just north of here it is less than a mile wide and apparently almost completely fordable at low tide; if you know the paths, there's only a couple of hundred paces where you have to swim. We'll try to stop them getting there and the fleet will try and pick them off in the water but I'm sure many thousands will escape across. Whilst we're mopping them up I want the Ninth to head west with all possible speed and seize the north bank of the ford upriver; hold it until we arrive. If you have to fight your way across then so be it. Is that a task commensurate with your dignitas, Corvinus?'

Corvinus scowled, unsure of how to answer without appearing foolish, and instead just nodded dumbly.

Plautius gave a thin smile. 'Good, I'm pleased to have found something worthy of you. Now, gentlemen, I'll leave the battle orders for your legions and auxiliaries up to you; do what I have ordered in whatever way you see fit. Are there any questions?'

Vespasian looked around the other officers: most were looking at the map, mulling over the plan in their minds, their nods and sounds of agreement a testament to their finding it precise and workable. He caught a look of complicity pass between Corvinus and Geta and realised that the time that Narcissus had foreseen was fast approaching. He glanced at Sabinus, who nodded; he had also noticed the shared look and understood its significance.

After a few moments Plautius grunted in satisfaction. 'Good. In the first contacts with the enemy I expect all of you to fight in the front rank. It's imperative that the men know that their officers aren't afraid of the sheer numbers of the clay-smeared bastards. Now return to your commands and start pretending to build camps; the Batavians should appear on that hill within the hour. I shall make sacrifices to Mars Victorious, Fortuna and

Jupiter on the army's behalf; let us hope that they hear me because this is going to be a very close-run action. Dismiss, gentlemen.'

'Right, my lovelies, let's get these bastard boats offloaded,' Primus Pilus Tatius bawled at two centuries of legionaries, trained in assembling the pontoon bridge, looking unenthusiastically at a train of twenty ox carts each holding two fifteen-foot boats.

'Don't bother, primus pilus,' Vespasian called, riding up the slope as fast as his dignitas would allow. 'I've just had a look at the ground between here and where we'll put the bridge across, it's flat grassland; it'll be much quicker to unharness the oxen and manhandle the carts down to the river.'

'If you say so, sir.' Tatius turned back to his men, some of whom were already obeying the last order. 'Put those bastard boats back where you found them! Why are you taking them off perfectly good carts on which we can roll them down to the river?' The legionaries looked confused at their primus pilus, but knew better than to ask questions. 'That's better; now unharness these oxen and take them away; and don't eat them, they're army property and need to report back to their rightful commander.'

'Are the officers gathered at the praetorium, Tatius?'

'Yes, sir, I left them there to come and sort out these boats.'

Vespasian kicked his horse forward through the carefully choreographed industry of constructing a marching camp and on towards the centre with Tatius following, having left the pontoon detail in the hands of the centuries' optiones.

All of his tribunes, prefects and centurions from the legion and the attached auxiliary cohorts were waiting for him as he dismounted at the camp's heart and handed his horse to a waiting slave.

'I'll be brief, gentlemen, as we should be on the move in a little over half an hour. Tatius has united the fifth and sixth centuries from the tenth cohort, both trained in pontoon construction, with the boats.' He looked at his prefect of the camp. 'Are the planks here, Maximus?'

'Yes, sir. The first century of the second cohort is being issued with hammers and nails as we speak.'

'Excellent. I've just been down to the river; the tide is on its way out but it is still a good fifty paces across, that's thirteen or fourteen boats to span it, so we have enough to make a double span.' He picked out Paetus from the crowd. 'As soon as we make our move, Paetus, I want your lads to get down to the river and swim it in double quick time.'

The young prefect grinned. 'I've already had them empty their water-skins and issued them with ten javelins each.'

'Good. Once you're across you're to delay anything that tries to come and stop us finishing the bridge.'

'Yes, sir.'

'The Hamians will give you archer support from this bank.' Vespasian looked for the prefect of the I Cohort Hamiorum. 'How many arrows have your lads been issued with?'

'Fifty apiece and twice that many on the reserve carts.'

Vespasian nodded. 'That should last the day. I want all the legion's bolt-shooters attached to the Hamians, Maximus.' The prefect of the camp nodded. 'Once the bridge is down – and let us pray to Janus that we can do it in half an hour – then the first cohort will lead the way over the right-hand bridge with Tatius and myself in the front rank. You will all follow our example, gentlemen, and fight in the front ranks of your units, even the young gentlemen.' Vespasian cast his eye over the five youthful faces of the thin-stripe military tribunes, their shining eyes and earnest faces betraying excitement and apprehension in equal measure, and prayed that none of them would succumb to the mindless battle-frenzy that used to plague him in his youth; there was no place for that in the disciplined ranks of the legions. 'Once across, the first cohort will form up facing north with the river right on their flank. They will be followed by the second with Mucianus in its front rank and then other cohorts in order. We'll form up in three lines with four cohorts in the second line. The left-hand bridge will be for the auxiliaries; I want the Gallic cavalry ala over first to seize the high ground on our left flank as quickly as possible and hold it until the five Gallic infantry cohorts arrive. They should form up on the hill, maintaining contact with the legion's left flank; the cavalry will then act as a deterrent for any attempt to outflank us up there. The legionary cavalry will be the last to cross and will act as a reserve. The Hamians and the artillery will stay on this bank and move forward with us, so the *carroballistae* should stay on their carts and shoot from them. However, today we will not move forward as our orders are to hold the bridgehead and wait for the Twentieth. Any advance we do make will be short and tactical and will be signalled by the first cohort; you will move to support it. Is that all clear, gentlemen?'

Murmurs of agreement from the assembled officers answered Vespasian's question. 'I very much doubt that we will be allowed to deploy unmolested but the quicker we do this thing the more chance we have of taking the Britons by surprise. But they will come for us, be assured of that, and they will try to push us back across the river.' He looked out towards the horde of tribesmen on the hill opposite, less than a thousand paces away; they had given up their jeering and now seemed preoccupied with cooking their supper and drinking. Their voices were a constant background drone. 'We mustn't allow that to happen, so we will have to fight hard against odds of five or six, maybe even seven to one. Our objective is to secure a bridgehead by dusk; then the Twentieth will come over and join us, relieving our auxiliaries on the high ground. After that we will have a hard night of it, remaining in formation, sleeping briefly by rotation after what has already been a tiring day. In the morning we advance north and that, gentlemen, will be a bloody path.'

As the truth of his words was contemplated by his officers the timbre of the drone of the thousands of voices from across the river changed, gradually at first and then quickly, to become another roar of defiance.

Vespasian looked north and smiled grimly as he felt his pulse quicken and a churning in the pit of his stomach. 'The Batavians have made it; so it begins, gentlemen. Return to your units, have them stop this pointless camp construction and form them up in column. I'll give the order to move as soon as I think that the

Britons have their attention sufficiently engaged elsewhere; the Batavians, Hamians, artillery and the bridge party will go first. I'll go with them, Mucianus; once we've reached the river, move the men out. Dismiss.'

With a jangling of equipment the officers saluted their legate, turned smartly and marched away to rejoin their commands. Vespasian gazed back across the river; the Britannic horde was starting to swarm north with an oddly fluid swirling motion.

'Just like a flock of starlings changing direction,' Magnus commented, coming up behind him.

'I don't think I've ever seen so many starlings flocking together.' Vespasian turned and looked at his friend and started in surprise. 'What are you doing dressed like that?'

'Well, I'm wearing this chain mail tunic in order to make it harder for one of them savages to examine my entrails; as for the helmet, that's quite good for preventing your head being split open, and the shield is a far more effective device for deflecting a sword blow than just your left arm, if you take my meaning?'

'I do indeed; does that mean you're determined to fight?'

'I did contemplate making myself a nice little picnic supper and sitting up here on the grass to watch the whole affair but then I thought that I might get rather chilly, so it would be better to be tucked up nice and snug in the front rank next to you. Oh, and I brought this for you.' Magnus handed Vespasian his shield.

'Aren't you getting a little old for this?' Vespasian asked, taking the shield with a nod of thanks.

'I'm fifty-one this year, plenty of fight and fuck left in me; besides, I ain't never fought a Briton – should be interesting.'

Vespasian shook his head, knowing that he would be unable to talk Magnus out of a fight that, as a civilian, was not his. He realised that he did not want to either; he would feel much better with his friend at his side. He looked back across the river; the Britons were moving north en masse. As he watched the dark shadow of humanity cloud the grassy hillside, a limb of it suddenly split off and headed down towards the river; the XIIII were approaching the broken bridge. Vespasian offered a silent prayer to Sabinus' god Mithras to hold his hands over his brother as, half a mile to his right, the XX started to move north behind the XIIII in their feint to the Batavians' crossing point.

'That's got them interested,' Magnus observed as the volume of the Britons' shouting rose appreciatively at the sight of a new threat on the move.

'It has indeed, almost all of them are moving away from us; time to go.' He looked at the duty bucinator waiting by the praetorium. 'Sound the advance.'

The notes rang out, high and clear, and immediately the throaty rumbling of cornua boomed out. To his left the two bridging centuries began to push their carts down the hill with mounting speed as Paetus' cavalry galloped away, followed by the Hamian archers at a jog and then the sixty mule carts carrying the legion's bolt-shooters.

Vespasian took a deep breath and steeled himself for what he knew would be one of the most testing few hours of his life. 'Let's get this done, my friend.'

'I was hoping you'd suggest that.'

Vespasian and Magnus began to walk down the hill in the wake of the carts as, all around, the cohorts of the II Augusta and its auxiliaries prepared for combat against an enemy that far outnumbered them. Vespasian knew that the struggles of that afternoon would seem as nothing compared with what awaited the II Augusta on the far bank of the Afon Cantiacii.

'Don't just look at them, float them!' the centurion of the sixth century of the tenth cohort bawled at four of his men who were momentarily resting after the exertion of lifting a boat from its cart; behind him, men pounded sledgehammers down upon eight thick stakes, ramming them into the drier earth up the bank. The legionaries hurriedly tipped the boat over onto its bottom and manhandled it through the tall reeds on the riverbank and onto the mud beyond. With a real sense of urgency, enhanced by their centurion's malevolent glare, they untied the two oars secured to the benches inside and then pushed it into the river; all four of them jumped in, with muddied sandals, once it had achieved buoyancy.

Vespasian watched, occasionally glancing nervously north, past the artillery carts forming up in three ranks of twenty behind the Hamians and on to where the Britons were swirling towards their perceived threats; along the bank the unloading procedure was repeated until all the boats were bobbing in the slow-flowing river.

The pounding ceased when the optio in charge of that detail was satisfied that the eight stakes, four for each bridge, were secure enough to begin fastening the four long coils of rope waiting on the ground; beyond them, the boats of the second bridge waited in the water. Slightly further south, on the opposite bank, Vespasian could see the last of Paetus' men scramble out of the river to join the ala, already forming up in four lines. So far there was no sign of the enemy moving against them.

'We might just get away with this,' Vespasian said, looking past Magnus, up the hill to where the II Augusta was doubling down towards them.

Magnus spat and clenched his thumb between his fingers and muttered a prayer, warding off the evil-eye.

'Sorry.'

'First boats!' the centurion roared; his colleague on the second bridge bellowed the same order.

Five boats immediately started rowing into position, fanning out into the river. As the first boat came in line with the stakes two legionaries grabbed it, holding it steady, whilst a couple more passed the coils of rope, each secured to two stakes, to the men not rowing, one in the bow, the other in the stern. They quickly fed the rope through large metal eye-holes screwed into each end of the vessel and secured them before passing them onto their colleagues in the second boat as it came alongside. The oarsmen held the boats together as the ropes were threaded through, knotted and then passed onto the third boat, the outside oarsman always working his blade in the water keeping the line stable, withdrawing it only as the next boat came into position. Beyond them a mirror image of this operation was taking place with the second span.

Vespasian looked back to the hill in the north; a mass of chariots was speeding up the grassy slope towards the Batavians arrayed along its summit. A thin, dark cloud suddenly soared up from the auxiliaries and arced in the sky to descend into the chariots' midst; any screams resulting from the volley were drowned out by the general background roar of tens of thousands of raised voices, but even at this distance he could make out scores of chariots immobilised on the slope with their ponies lying still before them.

'Next five!' the centurions called out as the last two boats were secured, drawing Vespasian back to the matter in hand.

Five more boats, on either side, headed out into the river; on the bank, a century equipped with hammers and nails jogged down past the stakes, followed by mule carts full of planking. Ousting the former occupants of the boats, the four lead legionaries made their way forward along the secured boats; a work-chain formed behind them relaying the two-foot-wide planks to them. As the planks arrived they were laid down across the boats' thick, horizontal gunwales and secured into place with long nails hammered through into the wood below. Working from the centre out, a twelve-foot-wide wooden road began to take shape, and was soon extended back to the bank by more planks overlapping those already laid. By the time the final planks were secured the next five boats were in place, stretching two-thirds of the way across the river, and the whole process began again as the last of the boats headed out towards their positions. On the far bank Paetus' ala advanced past the line of the bridge as two boats landed a contubernium of legionaries equipped with sledgehammers and stakes to secure the bridges to the western bank.

Camp Prefect Maximus crashed to attention next to Vespasian with a jangle of *phalerae*, his military decorations, and gave his crispest salute. 'The Second Augusta and its auxiliaries are formed up in column ready to cross, legate!'

'Thank you, prefect.' Vespasian turned to see the ten thousand men under his command extending up the hill in two columns, each eight men abreast. The warm westering sun glowed on their tired, grim faces and played on the burnished iron cladding them, front-lighting the standards that they would follow to death itself.

The shrill call of a long *lituus* cavalry horn from across the river startled Vespasian, not by its volume but by its significance. He did not bother to look at its source but instead turned his head to the north and saw what he had been dreading. The movement of the II Augusta had not gone unnoticed – how could it? A sizeable force had broken away from the Britannic horde and was now heading along the flat, riverside meadow towards them, led by a large formation of chariots. Paetus' ala had dressed its ranks and broken into a trot towards the oncoming enemy, just a mile distant.

'Speed this up, Maximus, or we'll get caught before we've got the first cohort across.'

The prefect of the camp took a look at the last two boats on each bridge still to be positioned and ran off bellowing for more haste.

Magnus frowned. 'That ain't going to do much good, the lads are going as fast as they can; I've never seen a river bridged so quickly.'

Vespasian ignored him and signalled over to the I Cohort Hamiorum's prefect to report to him.

'Shadow our cavalry north, sprint if you have to, but I want there to be eight hundred arrows every ten heartbeats supporting them when they come into contact; and shoot at the horses.'

The prefect saluted and rushed away; within moments the Hamians had turned and were doubling north along the river in pace with the trotting Batavians.

Despite Magnus' reservations, the appearance of Maximus at the end of the bridge had inspired the men to even greater efforts and the last two boats were now being lashed into position. Vespasian retreated a few paces up the hill and took his place in the front rank of the first cohort, next to Tatius; Magnus took his position on the other shoulder. Behind them the Eagle-bearer of the II Augusta, resplendent in his wolfskin, stood erect, ready to hold his sacred standard aloft with both hands in the coming battle whilst those around him fought to keep it safe from the enemy. Vespasian needed all his willpower not to fidget as the ropes were secured to the stakes and the final lengths of the wooden road were laid and nailed. A glance to the north told him that half a mile away the Batavians were less than two hundred paces from contact and the Hamians were sprinting in a ragged formation to keep up with them.

'Don't look at them, sir, there's fuck all you can do about it,' Magnus muttered in his ear.

Vespasian gripped his sword hilt and checked that the weapon was loose in its scabbard in an effort to keep his mind from the excruciating tension. He reflected that this was the first time he had used the Lady Antonia's gift of her father Marcus Antonius' sword in combat since the Jewish riots in Alexandria almost five years previously. He had missed it in Germania; the longer auxiliary spatha was not—

'Clear the bridge!' Maximus shouted.

The work parties dashed back down the wooden construction's length, causing it to undulate unevenly.

'Let's move, primus pilus!' Vespasian ordered before the last men were clear.

'The first cohort will advance at the double.'

The cornu blew, the standards dipped twice and eight hundred men of the five double-strength centuries of the first cohort moved forward.

'Break step!' Tatius ordered just before the bridge.

With a series of small jumps they broke step so that their regulated pace would not cause the pontoon bridge to bounce itself to destruction as they pounded along the wooden road.

Vespasian restrained himself from racing across, keeping instead to the speed set by Tatius; hobnails thundered down behind him, amplified in the hollows of the boats below like a constant rumble of thunder in the darkest of storms. His anxiety grew with every step as his eyes continually flicked to the north where Paetus' men were now engaged in a series of skirmishes with the elusive chariot force. Unwilling to make contact head on, the chariots had veered away at the last moment, their warriors hurling javelins into the Batavian ala, which returned the compliment, bringing many of the ponies crashing down, sending their wooden vehicles and their occupants hurtling through the air and causing dozens of obstacles in front of the cavalry line when they crunched to the ground. To break formation would have been disastrous; the Batavian line had been forced to stop and they were now fighting hand to hand with the few chariots they had caught and the dismounted warriors who had crawled from the wreckage. A couple of hundred chariots now swirled back at the pinned Batavians, under a continuous rain of arrows from the Hamians on the east bank, to deliver two or three javelins apiece into the stationary ala, felling many in a chorus of agony both human and bestial.

Suddenly Vespasian's footsteps made no sound, nor did the ground move beneath him; the front rank was over. Half a mile to the north, Paetus' ala broke and fled, unable to withstand the catastrophic losses dealt to them by a mobile enemy they could not fully engage. The Britons in turn were suffering grievously under the hail of Hamian shafts pouring from the sky, but they pursued their broken foe in the knowledge that they would soon outdistance the arrows of their tormentors. Behind the chariots, thousands of warriors surged forward in their wake in an undisciplined but determined mass.

The first cohort poured onto the west bank, Tatius increasing the pace as he realised they were in imminent danger of being caught in the open whilst forming up. He counted the paces aloud as they raced across the meadow, already trampled by Paetus' cavalry in their sacrificial charge north. Next to them the Gallic cavalry ala thundered forward towards the hill, equally aware of the need for speed in this very tightly fought affair; behind them their infantry compatriots followed with all haste with their centurions and optiones bellowing encouragement. As Tatius reached the count of fifty the Batavians were no more than five hundred paces away, riding their foaming horses for their lives, outpacing their slower pursuers who in turn had outdistanced the Hamians' extreme range. Their arrows were now turned onto the surging infantry behind the chariots, which began to pay with their lives for their compact formation.

At seventy paces Vespasian nervously glanced sidelong at the primus pilus but refrained from saying anything, knowing that the seasoned veteran knew just how much frontage his eight-hundred-man cohort needed to form up. With his heart thumping within his chest he pushed himself forward; Magnus grunted with exertion next to him.

'Right wheel!' Tatius shouted as he passed one hundred.

The front rank wheeled to the north with the fleeing Batavians now less than three hundred paces away. After twenty more excruciating heartbeats Tatius raised his arm in the air. 'Halt and form line!' He gradually slowed his pace to prevent a disastrous concertinaing of the cohort and then finally stopped; behind him the column fanned out, slotting lines of four men into position on either side with the ease and precision that come only from endless drill, turning the column into a line, four men deep. To their rear, the Gallic auxiliaries pounded on towards the high ground and the second cohort cleared the bridge as the Batavians, to their front, swerved to get around their comrades revealing the chariots and massed warriors beyond.

Tatius gave a questioning sideways look at Vespasian.

Vespasian nodded. 'It's your century, primus pilus, you give the orders until I decide that the legion should be doing something else other than holding its ground.'

'Sir! Present pila!'

Throughout the cohort, cornua rumbled, his subordinate centurions repeated his order and all along the front rank, rippling out from either side of Tatius' central position, left legs stamped forward, shields snapped to the front and the long, barbed-ended shafts of pila protruded over their tops. Although the pilum was not designed as an overarm thrusting weapon, Tatius knew, with his long years of experience, that presenting a solid wall spiked with wicked iron points at the ponies' eye height would prove to be a savage deterrent to the stocky beasts thundering towards them just a hundred paces away.

Vespasian glanced over his left shoulder. Above the heads of grim legionaries he could see the second cohort's standard level with him; they had extended the line. The third cohort could be glimpsed as figures flicking past the gaps in the formation; beyond them Paetus' cavalry were rallying and the Gauls had begun the ascent of the high ground. He turned back to the oncoming terror, now just fifty paces away, and realised that the third cohort would be caught mid-manoeuvre.

A very quick succession of sharp twangs and heavy thumps caused his eyes to flick right as the faint traces of sixty carroballista bolts flashed low across the river with a resonating hum to slam into the chariots, causing high-velocity carnage. Men, beasts and vehicles were punched away in a heartbeat of violence; just in front of Vespasian, a pony was thumped into its neighbour, a bloodied ballista bolt through its neck, skewering the two animals together as the driver of the chariot next to them was bodily lifted from his kneeling position and thrown, impaled, against the belly of the thrashing beast; there he stuck, gaping-mouthed. The whole tangled mess skewed around, with blood spraying, to crash to the ground in shrieking agony. All through the Britannic charge chariots flipped over, splintering apart, wheels, wickerwork and wood shards flying back up into the faces of those coming behind, as yet untouched; they swerved to avoid the wrecks before them, trampling the prostrate bodies of the wounded and felling half-dazed survivors as they staggered to their feet, all the time slowing as their drivers and warriors looked with fear at the II Augusta's artillery across the river that was capable of wreaking so much havoc. Within a few moments of the volley's impact the charge had come to a grinding halt; more than fifty chariots lay in shattered ruins, either as a direct result of the heavy missiles or from collisions with the wreckage that they had caused.

Vespasian knew that now was the time to take the initiative. 'The Second Augusta will advance!'

Cornua sounded; the Eagle and the first cohort's standard both dipped and, as one, the eight hundred men moved forward. The second cohort followed their lead as the third cohort, with Maximus in the front rank, finished forming line on the last piece of flat ground before the hill. Behind them more legionaries and auxiliaries doubled across the bridge, all the time adding to the

legion's fighting strength. Before them, the now stationary chariots, their impetus lost, turned and fled, to triumphant Roman
jeers, back towards the mass of supporting infantry, just four
hundred paces away, extending in a dark swarm from the river up
to the hill's crest.

'Halt!' Vespasian cried as they approached the first of the
many wrecks that peppered the field.

The line drew up just short of the first tangle of dead or
writhing ponies and men in amongst the smashed remnants of
three chariots as the third cohort, now in formation, doubled
forward to complete it.

'That was the easy part,' Magnus muttered, looking at the
horde flowing inexorably towards them.

'Really? I'd say getting ten thousand men across a river, almost
without casualties, under the eyes of the enemy was less than
easy. Look.' Vespasian indicated to his left.

Up the hill the Gallic cavalry were silhouetted by deep golden
light on its brow; the first of the auxiliary cohorts had almost
reached them. The next two were close behind whilst the final
couple were moving into position to form a reserve. As they
watched, the lead cohort reached the crest and began to form
line; the cavalry gave up the ground and disappeared over the
hill. The next two cohorts also manoeuvred to face the enemy
before all three jogged forward until the shoulders of the nearest
cohort abutted the legion's left flank, creating a solid line with a
file of four men per pace extending for more than half a mile.

As the last two Gallic cohorts moved forward to complete the
second line Magnus grunted and turned back to the Britons.
'Silly me, I didn't realise that the easy bit was to hold our ground
for an hour until sunset against five or six times our number.'

Vespasian watched the massed warriors coming on and
noticed that they were slowing. On their left flank, along the
riverbank, hundreds of slingers were now engaged in a missile
duel with the Hamians; the unshielded archers were having the
worst of it as the rounded shot from their shielded opponents
cracked into them and scores were already down with the rest
retreating, under the pressure, out of reach of the shorter-ranged

slings, back to their supply carts to restock their arrows. In the distance beyond, the Batavian infantry still held the high ground, fending off repeated uphill charges. What was happening with Sabinus' legion at the bridge was obscured by the multitude before him, who now came to a halt just two hundred paces away.

Again a chieftain stepped forward from the middle of the Britons' line, tall and proud. Turning to face his followers, he raised his arms and shouted, loud and clear, in his native tongue.

'That's not the same one that we faced this morning, sir,' Tatius said, 'so he must be Togodumnus.'

A roar went up and, from within the enemy horde, scores of carnyxes, long upright horns with animal mouths, were raised and began a blare of sounds ranging from shrill, staccato notes, like fox calls, through wavering mid-range trills and on to deep rumbles resembling the cornu. The din grew, drowning out the reports of the carroballistae as a volley of bolts streaked with deadly accuracy into the Britons, carving bloody gaps that were soon filled.

Togodumnus ignored the deaths of such a small percentage of his men and turned to face the invaders, raising his sword in the air; it flashed golden in the evening sun, and, howling his hatred, he slashed it down.

The Britons charged.

With Togodumnus leading from the centre the charge bulged forward. It was unlike the one that Vespasian had witnessed only that morning; it was far more measured. No warriors were racing ahead in search of personal glory and, although there were no dressed ranks as such, there was a feeling of order; Vespasian realised that this time they had come to try to overwhelm the legion with their sheer weight of numbers.

He looked to Tatius. 'Your cohort, primus pilus.'

Tatius nodded. 'Prepare to release, then receive charge!'

Again his orders were relayed through the silent cohort and eight hundred right arms went back. All along the Roman line the centurions took their lead from the senior cohort and the legionaries prepared themselves for the impact of the horde as they came on, brandishing flashing iron and bulging considerably now from the centre, flowing across the field like quicksilver.

Again the artillery sent sixty lightning-fast bolts into the mass, skewering scores whose screams were drowned by the battle cries of tens of thousands. The slingers now turned their shot to the artillerymen as they strained to re-tension their carroballistae. Twirling their leather slings over their heads as they ran, they sent hundreds of stones clattering into the carts, cracking the bones of men and mules, felling many, driving some beasts to bolt with their loads and sending men scuttling for cover.

Vespasian felt his bowels churn as the Britons came on and he comforted himself with the thought that every man in the Roman line must be feeling the same fear; he could smell it all around him.

Without a pilum, he loosened his gladius in its scabbard and prayed silently that he would wield it with the martial prowess of its long-dead former owner. Still the Britons came, now less than fifty paces away, the swirling vitrum designs clearly visible on their naked torsos and arms, and long, drooping moustaches flowing back in the wind to reveal snarling mouths howling death. He tensed his shield arm.

With the clash of metal and the resounding blows of shield against shield, the head of the bulge crashed into the third cohort; Vespasian glanced left as the second cohort's pila flew skywards. Up the hill the Gallic auxiliary cohorts emitted dark shadows of javelins in turn as the bulge flattened against Roman shields, rippling out each way from its first point of impact.

'Release!' Tatius thundered as the breaking wave of humanity crashed onto the furthest shields of the second cohort.

With a communal growl of exertion, the eight hundred legionaries of the first cohort launched their pila forwards, stamped down on their left feet and drew their swords in one much-practised motion. Vespasian felt the shield of the man behind him press firmly onto his back as the deadly volley swept silently towards the baying host.

For a moment time seemed to still and the world was silent; and then screams rent the air, shrill and sudden, as the lead-weighted pila swept into the onrushing warriors, kicking them back in arcs of blood, howling, impaled, faces pulped by lead balls, shields smashed and arms pinned to chests or bellies. Back they were hurled in their hundreds, legs buckling beneath them, weapons flying up from outstretched arms, blood spraying with their death-roars, eyes wide with pain, flattening comrades behind, as those untouched by the volley sped past, suddenly seeming to accelerate because of their opposite trajectories.

Vespasian gritted his teeth and, hunched behind his shield, tensed, as the human wave broke upon the first cohort, from left to right, with a racing, ever-nearing succession of pounding blows along the line. And then his body shuddered with the shock of a collision of such velocity that his right leg almost buckled behind him. The shield pressed against his back punched him forward, exploding the air from his lungs, as he fought to stay upright.

Instinct took over.

Gasping for breath, he jerked his shield upwards, cracking its rim on a descending arm, shattering it before it could deliver a downwards cut. He felt a sword clatter down his back as he stabbed his gladius at an angle through the gap between his and Magnus' shields; yielding flesh ripped open and an instant later warm blood slopped onto his left foot. His ears rang with howls, metallic clangs and clashes and the pounding of bodies onto leather-faced wood. Twisting his blade, he pulled it free and raised his eyes to stare into those of the man he had just gutted, pinioned upright against his shield by the press of blood-hungry warriors behind; his mouth was slack under a long moustache flecked with mucus and dirt and he tried to draw a choking breath. The Briton's ribs had already cracked from the punch of Vespasian's shield boss, and now being compressed against the same, he struggled to inhale; raising his chin, his eyes rolled, the whites bloodshot, as the pressure from behind grew. Vespasian responded and heaved forward against him, the men behind adding their combined weight. The stench of fresh faeces filled his nostrils, blanking out the iron tang of blood. To either side, Tatius and Magnus, bellowing every known curse, were also hunched behind their shields, straining with all their might, along with every other man in the Roman line, to halt the concerted drive from so many tens of thousands of men.

Weapons were now pointless as the whole line became one long scrimmage; even if a gap in the shields could be found the flesh on the other side was already dead, either from a sword thrust or crushed to death by the enormous pressure, providing a barrier to the Britons' swords; they no longer flashed down. The pressure suddenly increased on Vespasian's back and he realised that the second line of cohorts had added their weight to the scrum. He kept his shoulder pressed at an angle to his shield, pushing against it also with his head, the fist of his right hand and his left knee, knowing that to use his whole body would mean a slow and painful crushing of his ribcage. The gutted warrior's head lolled on the shield rim, bloody drool from his dead mouth trickled down the wooden board in front of Vespasian's eyes. The yelling had died down to be replaced by the straining grunts and growls of a mass of men heaving against each other with every ounce of their strength.

Even with the added weight of the second line the force was proving too much and the II Augusta was slowly and inexorably being pushed back. The leather thongs of Vespasian's sandals were cutting into his feet from the pressure coursing down through his body and, despite the hobnails' purchase, he felt them sliding backwards inch by inch, ripping up grass as they went. Back and back his feet slid, ploughing small furrows in the giving earth and the longer those grew the more his hope faded. He had calculated that they had retreated at least ten paces and knew that the force would soon tell somewhere along the line and it would break and disaster would ensue, when suddenly the pressure eased; they were no longer going back. He risked raising his eyes over the shield's rim, using the gutted man as cover, and glimpsed chaos in the Britannic line: the Hamians were shooting low into the legs and buttocks of their rear ranks.

Despite the slingshot barrage that they were receiving, the eastern archers were showing their mettle by concentrating their aim on the threat to the whole legion and not the massed slingers that pounded them. Many were going down but they kept shaft after shaft thumping into the Britons closest to them, those directly facing the first cohort.

Vespasian knew that this was their one opportunity. They had to take it now before the Hamians were forced to withdraw. He looked at Tatius. 'Forward!'

The primus pilus turned and bellowed the command left and right; it was taken up not just by his subordinate centurions but by the whole cohort in a rough, growling chant.

Vespasian heaved on his shield, feeling the combined pressure of the men behind, and forced his left foot forward a half-pace; next to him Magnus and Tatius managed the same. That first, small gain in ground was enough to inspire the cohort and quickly the chant changed from a growl to a loud and clear statement of intent. With another muscle-bulging push his left foot progressed another pace; and then another.

'The bastards are slipping,' Magnus shouted at him.

'What?'

'They've churned all the blood, shit and piss into mud, they can't grip.'

With another concerted shove they regained an additional couple of paces back towards their original line and the pressure on their shields eased; the gutted man slithered to the ground along with a few hundred other crushed or stabbed warriors, forming a small wall of dead bodies beyond which the Britons were now in total disarray. Many had slipped in the mud produced from noisome fluids squeezed from the dead and dying in the crush, and more had tripped over the wounded brought down by the Hamians' arrows as they had been forced back.

Vespasian glanced at Tatius; they nodded to each other and stepped over the line of dead taking the front rank with them; now they could use their swords.

Although disorganised, those Britons still on their feet scrambled to their own defence, leaping individually at the line of blood-smeared shields.

Cracking his shield boss up into the naked chest of a giant of a man in front as he raised his long sword for a killing blow,

Vespasian jabbed his gladius forward, low, slicing the point of its finely honed blade deep into the warrior's groin as, beside him, Magnus narrowly avoided an overarm spear-thrust to his face, which cracked against the shield of the following legionary. In a swift double motion, Vespasian jerked his sword free and cracked his shield rim up under the now screaming giant's chin, shattering his jaw and silencing him momentarily as Magnus, bellowing, stamped his hobnails down onto the spear-wielder's foot; howling with pain the warrior yanked his broken foot back, pulling Magnus' leg with it by a hobnail caught in the boot's strapping. Caught off balance on a slimy surface, Magnus crashed onto his back, twisting his left leg under him. Despite his injured foot, Magnus' opponent seized his opportunity and stabbed down with his spear, but the second rank legionary quickly straddled Magnus, lowering his shield to deflect the thrust into the ground. Pulling his gladius back, level with his face, he rammed it forward, straight and true, into the warrior's throat, punching the Briton back so that he could take his place at Vespasian's side, filling the gap.

Not knowing what had become of Magnus, Vespasian worked his blade and concentrated on staying on his feet as the Britons who had slipped or tripped regained theirs and, covered in vile mud, hurled themselves forward. But there was no speed in their charge and they had reverted to fighting as individuals, so they stood little chance against the ruthless killing machine that moved relentlessly forward. A few score more of them sacrificed themselves on the dripping blades of the first cohort. Here and there they claimed a Roman life, but never the time to celebrate it. Soon they realised that there would be nothing to boast of around the campfires that evening; they turned and fled.

'Halt!' Vespasian cried as the first cohort found itself unopposed.

The legionaries needed no second invitation and they stopped, gasping for breath, aching with exertion, physically and mentally exhausted.

Looking to his left, Vespasian could see that things had not gone as well in other areas of the battle: the second cohort had also benefited from the archer support of the Hamians and had almost beaten off their opponents, but the third was in deep trouble and it had evidently only been the timely intervention of one of the third-line cohorts, plugging the gap as the second moved forward whilst the third was being forced back that had prevented the line from breaking. However, it was the situation up the hill that caused Vespasian the most concern: the two auxiliary cohorts on the left flank had been turned and, despite the reinforcements from the two in reserve, they were being slowly pushed back down the hill. The Gallic cavalry ala harrying the Britons' flank and rear was the only thing stopping them from building up enough momentum to break the auxiliaries entirely.

Vespasian pointed to the last few hundred Britons still in combat with the second cohort. 'Tatius, take the first and clear those bastards away and then start rolling up their flank with the second. I'll leave the fourth and the fifth here behind you to cover this ground. I'm sending the other cohorts to relieve the auxiliaries.'

Tatius nodded his understanding, military formality being the last thing on anyone's mind at that moment. Vespasian turned and made his way quickly down the files, patting gasping men on their shoulders as he went, knowing that speed, now, was everything.

'I'm going to take the civilian's prerogative and sit the rest of this out, sir,' Magnus said, limping up to Vespasian. 'I've satisfied my curiosity and nearly got myself killed in the process.'

Vespasian nodded to the II Augusta's baggage, rumbling over the bridge and mustering to the rear of the legion. 'I imagine that you'll find a skin of wine over there that'll put up much less resistance than a Briton.'

Magnus grinned and then winced with pain. 'Yes, that's what I need, an enemy that doesn't fight back when you try to empty it of its guts, if you take my meaning?'

Vespasian watched his friend hobble away from the battle and felt a weariness settle upon him now that the tense excitement of conflict was wearing off. But he knew that he would get very little rest until victory was in Roman hands; and that would not be until tomorrow.

He turned back to the battle. The screams of the maimed and the dying and the clamour of combat had not let up; Vespasian, however, was now inured to the cacophony. From the vantage point of his horse at the head of the legion's four cavalry turmae, he watched the eighth, ninth and tenth cohorts double away up towards the hard-pressed Gallic auxiliaries; they had already been forced halfway back down the hill leaving a trail of dead in their wake. To his right the first cohort had swept away the remaining warriors opposing the second; and now, together, they had engaged the flank of the mass of Britons still pressing the centre of the crooked Roman line. He had sent a message to the Hamians to remain on the far side of the river, with the artillery, to discourage another attack along its body-strewn bank by the routed Britons who were now rallying on their comrades opposing Sabinus' legion, which continued to demonstrate at the ruined bridge as if preparing to rebuild it, crucially keeping many thousands of the enemy occupied. Beyond them the Batavian infantry could just be seen in the dimming light still in position on their hill. There was, however, no sign of the XX returning from their diversionary march. But then, he reflected, it was less than two hours since the Batavians' arrival on the hill had set the battle in motion and not even an hour since he had crossed the bridge, although it felt like a day at least. He looked up at the sky; night would be upon them soon, much to his relief. The battle-field was now in full shadow; they did not have long to hold before darkness would force the Britons to withdraw.

Having given his orders clearly and succinctly to the reserve cohorts he could now only wait to see the results, since he had decided to stay with the legion's cavalry to plug any gaps.

Paetus rode over to him from his rallied but depleted ala. 'My chaps are down to just under three hundred effective, legate, but they're ready and keen for another go. They didn't like being routed in front of the whole army, especially as many of them have kinsmen in the infantry up on that hill. We'll fight hard to make up for the shame.'

Vespasian studied the young prefect for a few moments; blood-soaked dressings on his right thigh and around his helmetless head told clearly of the ferocity of the action that had bought the legion the extra time it had needed to make the crossing. 'Well done, Paetus, and thank you. Have your ala form up next to me and tell your lads that they shouldn't be ashamed; we'd still be struggling to make it across if it hadn't been for their sacrifice.'

Paetus saluted. 'It'll be a pleasure, sir.'

Vespasian watched his long-dead friend's son canter back to his troops, hoping that he would not have to give him another order that would again put his life in such peril.

An unmistakeably Roman cheer jerked his attention away from such morbid thoughts and he turned to see the central mass of Britons begin to disintegrate. Hundreds were now streaming away to the north to escape the relentless blades of the first and second cohorts as they turned the Britons' flank, compressing their unarmoured bodies against the third cohort, which, led by Maximus in the front rank, knew that their ordeal was almost over and began to fight with renewed vigour. The only auxiliary cohort not to have been turned also took heart despite their visibly dwindled number. More and more Britons turned and fled, flowing away across the field until a mere thousand or so warriors remained, in reasonable order, giving ground gradually, marshalled by the chieftain in their midst.

'Togodumnus!' Vespasian whispered to himself. He watched the Britons fall back in the face of the concerted Roman onslaught. From within their ranks carnyxes blew the same short, high refrain as their front rank steadily disengaged. In answer to the horns' calls chariots raced towards them from the north, weaving through the warriors in flight as, up the hill, the Gallic auxiliaries finally broke. Togodumnus slowed his retreat, watching his right flank swarm down after the beaten Gauls, hewing at their rearmost with their slashing swords as the auxiliaries pelted towards the safety of the reserve cohorts just thirty paces down the hill. Vespasian saw the British chieftain pause and look back at his erstwhile opponents who now had warriors threatening their rear as if assessing whether the breakthrough on the right flank was worth exploiting. The reserve cohorts opened their ranks and the Gauls streamed through; with breath-taking precision they closed again just before the first of the Britons threatened to break through, leaving only a few auxil-iaries stranded and doomed. Seeing the space blocked, Togodumnus continued his retreat, taking his men with him, steadily back, pace by pace, swords pointed at their foes who were now using the respite to relieve their lines. At fifty paces they simply turned their backs and jogged away towards the oncoming chariots.

The Roman centurions obeyed their orders and stood firm. There was no follow-up, not that close-formation heavy infantry would have been able to catch lighter Britons.

Vespasian stared at the retreating back of Togodumnus; to have a chance of breaking the retreating formation and perhaps capturing the greatest prize of the day he had to act immediately. A quick glance back up the hill confirmed that the reserve cohorts had checked the Britons' advance and that the remnants of the Gallic auxiliaries were rallying behind them; the flank was secure for the time being. 'Advance in column!' A lituus cavalry horn blew behind him and he kicked his horse forward, waving an arm at Paetus to signal that he should do the same.

Accelerating into a canter he led the legion's four cavalry turmae towards the small gap in the Roman line created by the first and second cohorts' flanking move. The retreating Britons were no more than two hundred paces away, their backs still turned and their attention concentrated on reaching the chariots coming to cover their retreat.

Funnelling through the gap, the turmae slowed slightly as they changed formation from column to line, giving Paetus' ala time to catch up. Without waiting for the ranks to be dressed, Vespasian drew his spatha and brandished it in the air. 'Let's have them, lads!' The turmae roared, kicking their mounts into a gallop, clasping the reins with their left hands, shields strapped to the forearm, and feeling the weight of the javelins in the right.

The wind ripped at Vespasian's cloak, whip-cracking it as his horse's hooves accelerated out of the foul mud that delineated the extent of the recent bloody combat and onto firmer, open ground. After so long in the frightful confines of a compressed front rank, he found himself grinning at the exhilaration of the charge and turned, bellowing encouragement to his men, urging them on, in anticipation of facing the Britons' chieftain.

The litui shrieked their high-pitched calls and were answered by those of the Batavians following close behind, anxious to have their revenge for the humiliation of retreat.

The blare alerted the Britons to their presence on the field; the panic felt by infantry at being caught in the open by cavalry shuddered through their ranks. Those closest to the relieving chariots, under a quarter of a mile away, broke into a sprint, fragmenting the body as Togodumnus bellowed at his followers to form up and face the threat. But the order had come too late and a few hundred were already away whilst the rest, confused and disorganised, attempted to form some sort of line.

'Release!' Vespasian cried as the enemies' features became discernible. The turmae's javelins soared into the air, with a velocity greatly increased by the speed of the charge, and hammered down in a hail of death onto the unformed lines. Slender, pointed missiles pummelled into naked flesh, throwing men back, skewering them to the ground, shafts vibrating with the sudden deceleration. Confusion heightened, panic escalated and gaps widened. Vespasian steered his horse directly at a warrior standing alone, attempting to fill an opening five paces wide, raising his sword two-handed over his head, his eyes widening with terror. Vespasian punched his spatha forward, horizontally, over his mount's muzzle as the long blade flashed down, deflecting it with a ringing report. As if yanked simultaneously by the hair and ankles the warrior disappeared beneath the hooves of Vespasian's horse as he broke through the line with troopers to either side of him, pressing home their advantage. On he drove, slashing down to his right into a neck, hacking it open in a spew of blood, on towards Togodumnus who stood, foursquare, facing him behind a barrier of warriors.

Another shudder went through the Britons' formation; the Batavians' javelin volley seared into them, followed by the massed weight of the ala crashing fresh holes through the line, bent on vengeance and rejoicing in its sensation as they slew. More and more warriors turned in flight but Togodumnus stood firm. His eyes oozed hatred and a sneer graced his ruddy, round face. With a roar, he barged through the barrier of his followers, sword raised, and leapt towards Vespasian, who slewed his horse to the right, taking the vicious slash clean on his shield. Togodumnus' followers threw themselves at the troopers to either side of Vespasian in a blur of sudden movement; iron flashed, horses reared, blood sprayed and limbs fell, but Vespasian only had eyes for the Britannic chieftain. Pulling his high-stepping horse back to the left he drove it at Togodumnus; the Briton jumped backwards, lowering his sword, and with both hands clenched around the hilt he powered it into the beast's broad chest. With a shrill whinny it reared up, yanking the weapon from Togodumnus' grasp and hurling Vespasian from the saddle to land, with a lung-emptying crash, on unforgiving ground. Ducking under the thrashing forelegs, Togodumnus bounded through the air at Vespasian, drawing a sleek knife from his belt. With his vision clouded, Vespasian just made out the shape leaping towards him and rolled to his left; the chieftain landed with a jolt where Vespasian had been an instant before as the horse's hind legs buckled; the beast tipped back and, with a final snort, it collapsed. Togodumnus turned his head and screamed as the dead weight of horse flesh descended upon him; with a cracking of bones it smashed down onto his prone form, bouncing up slightly on first impact, its flaccid body rippling back down with a secondary, crushing blow, pulverising the chieftain's chest and leaving him staring with unseeing eyes at the darkening sky.

Then the chariots hit.

Heavy-shafted spears whipped into the melee followed by fresh warriors, running up the poles of their vehicles and leaping, using the extra height, straight at the troopers, knocking them from their saddles as their stocky ponies powered into their mounts, in a desperate attempt to rescue their chieftain.

Vespasian jumped to his feet, still gasping for breath, and, dodging an onrushing chariot team, looked around in the deepening gloom for a loose horse in amongst the chaos. Thrusting his sword into the back of a Briton hacking into a trooper's throat he grabbed the reins of the dead cavalryman's mount and, using the corpse as a step, hauled himself into the saddle. Knowing that the objective had been realised with Togodumnus' death and with night falling fast he reared his mount up. 'Break off! Break off!'

The troopers nearest him heard the cry and those who could began to disengage, passing the command on to their comrades further along the line. With most of the Britannic infantry now safely behind the chariots, the fresh warriors found themselves outnumbered and had already begun to seek the safety of their vehicles. It was almost by common consent that the combatants gradually parted, pulling back wearily, dragging their wounded with them, until the field was still and the two sides faced each other in the fading light. From the far side of the river came the sound of thousands of marching feet. The XX Legion had doubled back.

'I can see that you've had a hard time of it, Vespasian,' Gnaeus Hosidius Geta acknowledged, slipping from his horse as the cohorts of the XX marched over the bridge. 'You've done well to hold a bridgehead against such numbers, even if they are barbarian savages.'

Vespasian managed to conceal his surprise at being complimented by a man who was normally antagonistic to him, if not openly hostile. 'Thank you, Geta; the lads have fought well all day.' He looked back over to the Britons' lines; they had disengaged from the Batavians, leaving them in possession of the hill, and had pulled back from the ruined bridge now that the XIIII Gemina had retired. The whole army seemed to be concentrated upon lighting fires, thousands of which flickered golden in the half-light, and were paying no attention to the XX crossing the river. 'It looks like they're more interested in cooking their supper rather than trying to stop you crossing.'

Geta waved a hand dismissively. 'Rabble, that's all they are; brave enough but no discipline and badly led.'

'They've got one leader less now; I killed Togodumnus earlier. Or rather my horse did by dying on him; crushed him to death.'

Geta looked at Vespasian, concerned; behind him his legion marched past and on up the hill. 'That might not have been such a good thing to do.'

'Why not? One less chieftain is one less point of focus for resistance.'

'Granted, but today we've been helped by the fact that the brothers have seemed incapable of working together – they split their forces this morning and again this afternoon. If there had been one overall commander don't you think that he would have left a holding force in front of the Batavians, ignored the Fourteenth and thrown everything he had against you and pushed you back over the river?'

Vespasian frowned. 'Yes, you could be right, I suppose.'

'I know I am; and tomorrow they'll have just one commander, so we'll have a harder time of it. Perhaps you should have thought of that before allowing your horse to kill Togodumnus.' Geta turned and led his mount away, following his command up the hill.

Vespasian watched him go, his expression strained, as he contemplated his words and then dismissed them: although he conceded that Geta had a point, both Caratacus and Togodumnus would have to die or surrender for Rome to triumph and he felt sure that his actions that day had helped to hasten that event.

By the time night had fallen and a near-full moon shone over the field, the XX Legion had taken their position on the II Augusta's left flank. Lines and lines of soldiers of Rome stretched from the river to the summit, preparing to stand to for the night; the moonlight played on their helmets, which glowed like regimented ranks of pearls. The last of the baggage crossed the bridge and then came the sound of the engineers splashing in the water, attaching ropes to the structure, ready to haul it north once the moon had set. Vespasian offered a prayer to Mars, knowing that tomorrow there could be no retreat back across the river.

CHAPTER XVIII

THE FIRST GLOW of dawn touched the eastern horizon to the sporadic accompaniment of birdsong. Vespasian was just finishing a tour of the five cohorts standing to, praising the men for their gallantry the previous day and encouraging them to face the perils of this new one with the same resolution. Maximus had rotated the ten cohorts allowing each four hours' sleep under the clear sky that had burst forth with stars once the bright moon had set. Supper had been bread and salted pork eaten standing in formation; no fires had been lit so as not to provide light for the Britannic slingers and few archers to aim by. The slingers had come on a couple of occasions, unnoticed in the dark until their deadly shot clattered into the unsuspecting ranks, felling a few in the moments before shields were raised properly. After the first such attack only the very weary or reckless allowed their shields to drop, earning a sharp, hissed tirade from their centurions.

The II Augusta suffered no other attacks during the long night; however, the prolonged noise of battle from over the hill in the early hours implied that the XX Legion's auxiliaries had encountered a night outflanking move by the Britons. The fact that no alarm had been raised had led Vespasian to conclude that they had been successfully repelled and a messenger from Geta had confirmed this shortly before he had begun his tour of inspection.

Vespasian drew a deep breath of fresh, early summer dawn air as he surveyed the spectral ranks of legionaries; he wondered how many, that day, he would be sending either to their deaths or to lives of limbless misery relying upon the charity of strangers. He knew that it was a morbid subject to contemplate but the weight of command lay heavy upon him after the battles of the previous day. Although he thought that he had acquitted himself well – the praise, albeit double-edged, from the far more experienced Geta had confirmed that – he was well aware of just what a close-run thing the securing of the bridgehead had been. The margin between victory and defeat had been fine, to say the least, and the thought of failure in front of the whole army had gnawed at him ever since his public dressing-down by Aulus Plautius for his neglecting to advance quickly enough to Cantiacum. Even though it had not had disastrous consequences it had been a salutary lesson to him and he now knew that a cautious general could be as much of a liability to the army as a rash one. Sometimes it was essential to make a decision without knowing all the facts; therefore the key to a successful decision was sound judgement. But that could only be gained by experience; and experience was something he was lacking.

As the other five cohorts, recently woken from their brief sleep, marched smartly back into position in the second line, he looked at the centurions' weathered and hardened faces. He could see that each one had far more experience than he with his four years' service as a military tribune and two years, so far, as a legate; and yet he was their superior by chance of birth. What did they think of him for his delay at Cantiacum? Did they trust him with their lives now after yesterday's action when his timely reinforcement of the left flank narrowly saved the legion from being surrounded; or did they consider him to be another inexperienced commander placed over them because that was how the system worked and they were forced to make the legion function in spite of him? He did not know and he could not ask anyone. He smiled ruefully and reflected that this was the lot of a commander: loneliness. There was no one with whom he could share his thoughts and doubts, not even Magnus, because doing so would make him appear weak, and that was a quality that was universally despised in every soldier from the newest recruit to the most seasoned general.

A cornu rumbled from over by the ruined bridge and in the dim half-light he could just make out figures jogging across the newly positioned pontoon bridge upriver from it. Plautius was not waiting for dawn; he was seizing the initiative whilst the enemy was still rousing from sleep. Grateful for another lesson in decisive action, Vespasian consoled himself with the undoubted fact that if he survived this campaign he would be one of the most battle-hardened and experienced legates in the legions and he was learning from a general whom, despite his political slipperiness, he was coming to admire. He strode towards the II Augusta's command point in the gap between the two lines of cohorts, where his new horse awaited, determined not to make any mistakes of judgement this day and steeling himself for hours of noise, blood and death. His confidence grew as he mounted up and surveyed the might of the legion all around him; they would triumph this day because Rome accepted no other result.

Vespasian drew another deep breath, tightened the chinstrap on his helmet and then looked down at the cornicen standing close to him. 'The Second Augusta will advance!'

The Britons had, quite literally, been caught napping. The small force that they had left by the ruined bridge had not noticed the pontoon being towed soundlessly downriver in the complete darkness of the moonless part of the night. The first they knew about it had been when the lead cohorts of the XIIII Gemina, with Aulus Plautius and Sabinus in their front rank, had suddenly stormed across a bridge that had appeared, seemingly, out of nowhere. By the time any of them had worked out how it had been done they were facing the mechanical blades of the Gemina's first cohort and the question was driven from their minds by the pain that they inflicted. Within a few moments those who were not lying dead or wounded were fleeing back to the main body of their countrymen further up the slope, who broke into a roar of anger so loud that it would have disturbed the peace of Hades itself.

The II Augusta marched steadily on, with the XX beside it; their auxiliaries followed behind. This was to be a day for close-quarters butchering; Vespasian had decided to use the lighter auxiliaries to chase the Britons once they had been broken into a defeated rabble. The legionaries knew that it was down to them to break the horde that was rapidly arming just a mile ahead of them. They thumped their pila slowly but rhythmically on their shields as they advanced, singing the hymn of Mars in low, sonorous voices to the beat, stirring courage into their hearts.

The men of the XX took up the song, doubling the volume; ten thousand voices now boomed out the ponderous hymn praising the god of war and asking him to hold his hands over them as they marched, rank upon rank, towards their enemies in the half-light.

Vespasian looked up and down the lines of iron-clad heavy infantry advancing steadily towards a fearsome enemy, many times their number; their expressions told that each man was determined to play his part to the best of his ability in the coming battle, to fight for himself and the men next to him in the spirit of camaraderie that glued a legion together, each man equally as important as the next. He pulled back his shoulders and sat bolt upright in the saddle, his heart swelling with pride; his self-doubt, which had been eating at him only moments earlier, dissipated to be replaced by a certainty: he would command his legion to the best of his ability. To doubt his ability would be to let down the men surrounding him. Rome would conquer and he would play his part in that victory and Rome would remember his name for his actions on this day.

More than half of the XIIII Gemina's cohorts were across the bridge when the attack came. A multitude of disembodied voices rose out of the gloom, brewing into a shrieking of war cries, and the shadow of massed warriors rolled down the hill. Individual figures were indistinguishable in the dim yet waxing light, but their intent was clear: they were all heading in one direction, towards the XIIII to throw them back across the river before the II and the XX could link up with them. With all of their Batavian auxiliaries still occupying the high ground to the north the XIIII Gemina's strength was just five thousand legionaries; five thousand against almost a hundred thousand. The weight pressing against their shields would be intolerable; they could not resist for long.

'Advance at the double!' Vespasian called to the cornicen over the tumultuous bruit of charging Britons and the rousing hymn of his men.

Within a few heartbeats the order was relayed throughout the legion; the pace increased but the song remained the same.

On the eastern bank the Hamians and artillery carts, shadowing the legion, also accelerated, knowing that, although their shafts would make little impact on the numbers of such a vast horde, every death they caused would count in some small way to the legion's preservation.

In the growing light, individuals could now be made out, pelting down the slope towards the cohorts forming up beyond the pontoon bridge; the first line of five, with Sabinus in the front rank, had been completed and the rear line consisted now of two cohorts with the rest streaming over behind. The formation was a pitiful sight when compared to the mass surging towards it and Vespasian was under no illusions that it would not be swamped, having nothing to protect its flanks.

Judging the distance in the ever-growing light Vespasian reckoned that they were five hundred paces away; they could cover that ground in half as many heartbeats. Sabinus must hold for that time.

A dim pall soared from the XIIII Gemina: pila. An instant later another volley followed; both were absorbed by the Britons as if they had been cast, instead, into a river: the deaths of a few thousand of that multitude made no impact on their intent.

Then the charge carried home. The line shuddered, almost buckled and then gave a few paces before settling. Then it disappeared, engulfed. Above, the first rays of the sun hit high-altitude cloud with a deep red glow as if the sky itself was bleeding.

The only evidence of the legion's existence was now the clamour of battle rising from within the packed mass of warriors. The last two cohorts crossed the bridge and disappeared into their midst proving that the legion still held, adding their weight to what would be, Vespasian knew from the previous day, an horrific heaving match of rib-crushing intensity.

With two hundred paces to contact, a goodly proportion of the Britons swirled away from the XIIII Gemina and turned to face the II Augusta, easing the pressure on Sabinus' legion; they had held for those vital first few moments, they could surely hold a while longer against fewer enemies. The warriors still up the hill also changed their direction and made towards the XX, further reducing the threat to the beleaguered legion. On the eastern bank the Hamians began releasing volley after volley into the fray, felling hundreds, whilst the artillery carts' crews levelled their weapons and frantically began the loading process.

Vespasian put his fear for his brother from his mind and concentrated on the timing of the signals. All around him the hymn to Mars soared to the sky, drowning out the clanking of equipment and the doubled footsteps of the legionaries but not the din of the battle raging deep within the howling enemy, who were now almost close enough to receive the first of the legion's deadly weapons. He gave the order and the pila flew. More than two thousand of the cruel barbed points swept into the front ranks of the Britons, reaping a bloody harvest of ripe young lives and sowing terror into the hearts of their comrades behind as they leapt the skewered bodies seeping their lifeblood into the earth.

But they came on. Vespasian ordered the charge and the legion accelerated for the final few paces to the rumble of cornua. The hymn faltered as the long line of front rank shields, each with the weight of four armoured men behind it, powered into the Britons. A massed communal gasp burst from the lungs of both sides. The Roman shield wall drove forward with the impetus of the charge; the regimented discipline of the heavily armoured legionaries thrust the more numerous but lighter and less cohesive Britons back with grinding inevitability.

Then came the clash of iron; then the screaming started.

The legion gradually lost momentum and the battle settled. Much to Vespasian's relief the Roman line remained firm, but it was perilously thin. Shouting over the tumult he ordered the second line of five cohorts forward to add their pila and their weight to the fight. Still singing the hymn at the tops of their voices the other half of the legion advanced; each soldier hurled both their pila in quick succession over the heads of their comrades and then joined the heaving files, pressing their shields into the backs of the men before them.

The extra weight of half a legion driving into the Britons broke whatever loose formation they had. Hundreds crumpled dead and hundreds more were punched back, blood pulsing from mortal wounds, as the legion regained momentum and ploughed on. The men in the first line who had stopped singing at first contact took up their comrades' hymn again as they slew, praising the god of war as they savagely worked their blades.

A new terror then scythed into the warriors as the artillery shot weighty wooden bolts into their flank in one torsion-powered, devastating volley, clearing swathes of them away in a sudden acceleration of blurred motion as men just disappeared from sight to reappear again ten paces away with a bolt sideways through their chest and surprise in their dead eyes.

The men of the II Augusta sang on, blades slick with gore and faeces, stamping their feet forward over fallen Britannic warriors. The front rank straddled the bodies; the second rankers ground their swords into them, whether they looked alive or dead; wary of an upward thrust of a knife into their groins, they took no chances.

Pushed steadily back and back, pace by pace, tripping over corpses, the Britons' resistance gradually waned as the sun rose. Vespasian had no way of knowing how long they had been fighting, time had become meaningless and he could only measure it in the regular artillery volleys; he thought that he had counted eight but could not be sure. What was sure, however, was that the deadly bolts had cleared the riverbank of the enemy and the first cohort was now almost unopposed. Through the gap he could see the left-hand cohorts of the XIIII Gemina; they still held. With one concerted effort the II Augusta could link up with them and the line would be complete.

Another artillery volley hissed into the Britons, plucking yet more from their feet in showers of blood and dropping them back down with their limbs at impossible angles, like puppets with their strings severed. This time the Britons wavered and the men of the II Augusta sensed it. Taking advantage of the momentary lull they surged forward with renewed vigour, stabbing their swords, punching their shield bosses, stamping their feet, stab, punch, stamp, stab, punch, stamp; the rear ranks still singing, the front saving their precious breath for the struggle.

The Britons began to fall back with greater urgency as the unstoppable Roman war machine increased its pace, dealing out death to all in its path. The first cohort now slewed, wheeling to the left, blocking the artillery's direct line of fire, but closing on the left flank of the XIIII Gemina. More and more Britons were backing away, allowing the II Augusta more ground, which it gratefully accepted as it closed in on its sister legion.

The sun rose over the hill in the east, bathing the field of battle with morning light to the accompaniment of the long rumble of cornua and the blare of litui; massed horns crying from the top of the hill. The Britons looked up as they backed away, their faces falling in despair; at that instant the first man turned and ran.

The rout began.

Vespasian looked up to his right; along the hill's crest was lined the VIIII Hispana and its auxiliaries, silhouetted against the golden, newly risen sun. On they came, marching in battle order over the hill and down, another deadly Roman war machine, fresh and ready to do the work that justified its existence. Having just faced three legions and been pushed back at great loss, the sight of a fourth was too much for even the most reckless warrior and the rout spread like fire through a field of wheat stubble.

The first cohort's shoulders touched the flank of the XIIII Gemina; the line was complete. Vespasian ordered the auxiliaries and the legion's cavalry up. Now was the time to finish it.

A deep booming from the cornua told the cohorts to open their ranks; gaps appeared between each unit. Taking his place at the front of the legionary cavalry, Vespasian kicked his horse forward and led them, along with Paetus' ala and the Gallic ala, through the gaps towards the exposed backs of the fleeing warriors; behind them came the infantry cohorts. As they sped across the body-strewn ground more horns blared, this time from the hill occupied by the Batavian foot; Vespasian glanced up to see all eight cohorts charging down the slope towards the chaotic, porous flank of the broken horde. Vengeance for the hot and bloody time they had endured the previous day would soon be theirs and, as Vespasian's sword slashed open the first exposed back that he came across, the Batavians carved into the other side of the rout with deadly intent.

The cavalry broke formation to sweep through the fleeing warriors, hacking and stabbing at them as they pounded back up the hill for their very lives. Here and there they came across little pockets of roughly organised resistance, men banded together for safety in clumps of a hundred or more retreating in tolerable order; these they avoided, not wishing to fall at the very moment of victory, concentrating instead on the plethora of individuals. They went down in their hundreds, shrieking curses as the invaders' blades ripped the life out of them and they crashed to the blood-soaked earth of their homeland that Rome would now claim for its own.

Vespasian showed no mercy as he weaved his horse left and right, picking off as many of the vanquished as possible. He took care, however, that he and his cavalry did not venture too far into the main body of the Britons and risk being isolated and surrounded and, no doubt, subjected to a vengeful death. Further up the hill the XX Legion's cavalry had broken out to reap their share of easy lives in amongst the more dense formation of the rout. A quick glance behind told him that the XIIII Gemina had moved aside and the first units of the VIIII Hispana were preparing to cross the bridge and begin their lightning march west to the Tamesis crossing point. Closer to him a group of Roman cavalry galloped in his direction with Aulus Plautius, resplendent in his general's cloak and helmet crest, at their head.

'Legate!' the general shouted as he approached. 'Pull your cavalry back before they get cut off. We'll follow up with the auxiliary infantry; we'll push them north into the Tamesis and hopefully a few thousand will drown trying to cross.'

'Yes, general.' Vespasian shouted at the nearest *liticen*, 'Sound the recall!'

The man raised his horn and the order was sounded.

'Your legion has served Rome and the Emperor well, Vespasian; I shall make sure that the right people know that. Today has been a good day for all our careers.'

Vespasian looked at Plautius; under the veneer of his cloak he was blood-splattered and cut and there were huge dents in his cuirass. 'The Fourteenth had the hardest time, I should think; how is my brother?'

Plautius frowned, dislodging scrapings of crisp, dried blood from his forehead. 'He'll survive; he took a spear-thrust in his right shoulder just before the Britons broke. The bleeding has been stopped but he won't be fit for command for a couple of days or so. I've got my personal doctor looking after him.'

'Thank you, general.' Vespasian struggled to keep his mount steady as, all around, the cavalry was rallying; frisky horses with the smell of blood in their nostrils stamped and snorted. 'I'm sure he's had worse. What are your orders for the Second, general?'

The high-pitched call of a lituus from further up the hill sounded before Plautius could reply; everyone recognised its meaning.

'They're in trouble,' Vespasian said, looking in the direction of the call. About half a mile away he could see that a small group of the XX Legion's cavalry had been sucked into the retreating mass of Britons.

Plautius spat, 'Fucking idiots, that's exactly what I didn't want to happen. I've got few enough cavalry as it is, I can't afford to lose those fools if we can avoid it. Legate, bring your men and follow me.'

Plautius flicked his reins on his mount's neck and the beast took off up the hill. Vespasian charged after him, yelling at his men and Paetus' ala to follow as the II Augusta's auxiliary infantry caught up with them on their way to harry the enemy's retreat.

Galloping up the hill they soon caught up with the rearmost stragglers; they ran them down if they could but made no attempt to chase them, such was their haste to come to the rescue of the isolated cavalry. The little pocket was surrounded by hundreds of warriors, herding them further away from the

Roman lines and picking them off one by one. The lituus let out another shrill call that was abruptly terminated with a squeak, testifying to the demise of its owner.

Plautius crashed into the rearmost tormentors of the isolated cavalry, trampling two and bowling a few more aside with shattered bones. His horse reared, forelegs thrashing, raining down blows on skulls and shoulders as he swiped the head clean off a warrior; the man's astonishment showed on his face as his headless body stood for a moment, emitting a fountain of blood, and then collapsed onto his severed head as the last of life faded from his eyes.

Vespasian followed his general in, his cavalry to either side, cleaving a bloody path through the Britons, who had been too intent upon their prey to notice the threat from behind them. Plautius' wrath, aimed as much at his cavalry for getting themselves into this position as it was at the men who were trying to kill his precious mounted troops, drove him on in a fearsome killing spree that none dared oppose. Vespasian hunted in his wake, cutting down any who had managed to avoid the mounted terror scything its way through them, urging his mount on, its flanks drenched in blood, sticky beneath his calves.

Having already broken once that day, the Britons swiftly yielded up the prize they had surrounded and fled on up the hill. The eighty or so survivors of the XX Legion's cavalry were left, shocked by their losses at the very close of the battle, facing their irate general.

Plautius rounded on the nearest decurion. 'Get up the fucking hill after them and restore some pride!' He turned to Vespasian. 'Take your lads with them and make sure they don't behave like raw recruits again. Just kill the stragglers and stop at the hill's crest. Five each and that's a thousand less of the bastards next time we face them.'

'Halt!' Vespasian shouted, raising his sword arm in the air; blood trickled down the blade onto his fingers and wrist. On the ground to his right lay the body of the final warrior he had killed in the harrying of the retreat. Grass was entwined with his drooping moustache and his bottom teeth were sunk into the ground; his eyes stared blankly at the gory crown of his skull that lay upright before him like a ghastly chalice.

As the cavalry rallied behind him, Vespasian surveyed the scene from the hilltop. To the north the bulk of the defeated army streamed towards the Tamesis, glittering in the warm sun just ten miles away. They were pursued, in good order, by the Batavian infantry and the II Augusta's auxiliaries, picking off the rearmost but making no attempt to make contact with the main body as they drove them north. The rest of the Britons were heading west; a few chariots could be seen at their head a couple of miles distant and the lucky stragglers, who had narrowly escaped the cavalry spathae, were no more than two hundred paces away.

'The sight of an enemy running always warms the heart, eh, legate?' Plautius observed, pulling his horse up next to Vespasian. 'A decent day's work; we must have killed nearly forty thousand of the buggers. It's ironic that after such a victory I have to write to the Emperor requesting his help.'

'You've left him a few to deal with.'

'Yes, a few too many for my liking; there must be twenty thousand heading west and another forty thousand making for the river.'

'Why don't you try and finish it, general?'

'Because I don't have enough fucking cavalry. They're not stupid enough to turn and face legions again, but if I had fifteen thousand cavalry I wouldn't need them to turn, I could just mop them up. But never wish for what you don't have, it takes your mind away from using what you do have to full effect. I've sent orders to the auxiliaries to let the river and the fleet's catapults do the rest of the day's killing and I'm sure that they'll be happy to leave it that way; the Ninth will follow the others west and take the Tamesis crossing point. And then Caratacus and Togodumnus will have to decide what to do.'

'Togodumnus is dead, sir, I saw him die.'

'Really? Who killed him?'

'My horse.'

Plautius looked at the beast beneath Vespasian with an appreciative eye. 'Quite an animal you've got there.'

'It wasn't this one, it was another; Togodumnus killed it and then managed to get underneath it as it hit the ground.'

'Very careless of him. But I'm grateful for your horse's sacrifice, that'll make things a lot easier politically. Caratacus rules in the west but Togodumnus' realm was to the north of the Tamesis based in Camulodunum, the capital that Claudius wants to enter himself. If they're defeated and leaderless and we hold the north bank of the Tamesis I think that we could get them to see sense, provided that we don't give them any more cause to hate us. Well done, legate, your horse might just have saved thousands of lives.'

Vespasian was tempted to ask Plautius to tell Geta that, but refrained. 'Thank you, sir.'

Plautius nodded with satisfaction and turned to the remnants of the XX legion's cavalry. 'Which one of you unsponged arseholes is responsible for losing so many of my cavalry?'

The decurion who had been the object of Plautius' wrath earlier ventured a reply. 'It was our legate, sir.'

'Geta? Where is the idiot?'

The decurion indicated down the hill with his head. 'Back there, sir; he fell just as you broke through to us. I think he's dead.'

Vespasian and Plautius retraced their steps down the hill littered with corpses and stained with blood in every direction. Vespasian stared about him aghast at the magnitude of what had happened: thousands upon thousands of dead Britannic warriors lay sprawled on the battlefield from the Batavians' hill in the north, along the line of the XIIII Gemina's stand by the pontoon bridge – which the VIIII Hispana was now traversing – and on to the line of the II Augusta's first combat, the previous day in the south. They lay singly, in groups or in long rows, like driftwood marking the extent of high tide, showing where they had taken on the might of Rome, head on, with little hope of victory. There were Romans too amongst the dead, not nearly as many, probably one for every forty Britons, Vespasian estimated. It had been a decisive victory at relatively little cost but its aftermath was a sombre sight: endless corpses of young men cut down in their prime as they defended their homeland from an invasion that, as far as Vespasian could make out, was motivated not by any strategic necessity but by the desire of three freedmen to keep their unmartial, drooling master in power so that they could enjoy its benefits. He quickly banished the bitter thought from his mind, knowing that unless he retired back to his estates and forewent a career in Rome he would always be a witness to the selfishness of politics.

'Apart from the Fourteenth's defensive line this must be one of the few places on the field where more than twenty or so of our lads lie together,' Plautius reflected as they approached the point where the cavalry had been rescued.

Vespasian surveyed the tangle of troopers and their mounts, nearly forty in all; their comrades were working their way through them looking for any signs of life as the auxiliaries of the VIIII Hispana marched by, acting as the vanguard for their legion. 'My Batavians also took heavy losses buying us time to form up across the bridge.'

'Yes, I watched that, it was bravely done; I shall see that Paetus comes to the Emperor's attention when he gets here. And Civilis of the Batavian Foot, the diversionary action on that hill was the key to the battle. Did you know that he's the grandson of the last Batavian King?'

'No, I didn't.'

'His men treat him as if he was the King himself, they'd follow him anywhere.'

'General!' a trooper shouted from the midst of the corpses. 'It's the legate, he's still breathing.'

Vespasian and Plautius dismounted and picked their way through the dead to where Geta lay. Blood seeped from under his breastplate; it was pierced just below the ribcage. He was unconscious but definitely breathing.

Plautius looked down at him with a mixture of regretful disapproval and sorrow. 'Get him to my doctor, trooper, you'll find him in a tent across the river.'

The trooper saluted; he and three mates began to prise the wounded legate out of the tangle of dead flesh.

Plautius shook his head. 'He's a fine soldier but why he made such an elementary mistake is beyond me. Everyone knows that you don't take cavalry too deep into an enemy rout; it's asking for trouble.'

'Perhaps he saw Caratacus, and tried to get to him.'

'We'll find out, if my doctor manages to save him. You should get back to your legion now; I want a full report of casualties first thing in the morning. We'll march west at dawn the following day once I'm sure that Togodumnus' men are either dead or across the river; I wouldn't like to have a force that size come and bite my arse. I want your legion to lead the way, seeing as you'll be the only fit legate left to me.' He looked at the first cohort of the VIIII Hispana now marching by with its Eagle at its head. 'It's their turn now.' He spotted Corvinus sitting proudly on his horse riding to the side of the column and rode over to him. 'March your lads hard, legate, it's down to speed now and you've got thirty miles to go; I want you at the Tamesis by tomorrow afternoon.'

'We'll be there, general.'

'I'm sure of it. The fleet will be following you in support once they've dealt with the Britons trying to cross the river. And remember, take the north bank and hold it; do not go further.'

Corvinus smiled thinly and saluted. 'Of course, sir. Goodbye!'

The tone of the last word struck Vespasian as having a finality to it as he watched Corvinus riding away and, thinking of Narcissus' suspicions, he wondered whether to confide in Plautius. 'Do you trust him, sir?'

'Trust him? I have to. Narcissus suggested to me that I should send him forward, just before we left for Britannia. He thought Claudius would appreciate me sending his brother-in-law to be the first Roman to cross the Tamesis since Julius Caesar; it would reflect well on the imperial family and the gesture would not go unnoticed by the Emperor. For once I agreed with that oily freedman.'

'But he didn't seem very keen on waiting for Claudius.'

'He'll obey his orders.'

'What if he doesn't?'

'He will. Narcissus pointed out that he and his sister both have everything to gain from Claudius' supposed victory.'

Vespasian stared, incredulous, at Plautius' profile. 'Are you sure he said that?'

'Of course I'm sure, legate! I'm not deaf.'

'I apologise, sir. I'll return to my legion now.' Vespasian gave a salute and turned. Riding away, he looked back up the hill at the VIIII Hispana and, in a moment of clarity, he realised what Narcissus had done and why: he had made his first move towards the removal of Messalina.

CHAPTER XVIIII

'WHAT DO YOU mean you can't warn Plautius?' Magnus asked, struggling to make sense of what he had just been told.

Sabinus shifted slightly in his campbed, lifting his head and grimacing with pain. 'My brother's right, Magnus, Narcissus made us promise that whatever happens we must not go to Plautius.'

'But why? He could stop Corvinus now; the Ninth are less than a day's march ahead of us.'

Vespasian held a cup of steaming wine to his brother's lips and Sabinus sipped from it gratefully. 'He doesn't want Corvinus stopped; he knew that this would happen because he set it up. He wants Plautius to see for himself Corvinus' treachery; that way he'll have solid evidence to present to Claudius when he arrives, not mere suspicions. Claudius doesn't believe his freedmen's warnings about Messalina and her brother but he might just believe the evidence of his own eyes if Plautius presents it to him.'

Magnus looked around the dimly lit tent, evidently exasperated. 'So what will you do?'

'Do? Why, nothing for the time being. Narcissus asked us to keep Plautius alive and not to let Corvinus and Geta go too far. We thought that he meant not to let them go further than the Tamesis but he didn't; he meant not to let them go too far north of the Tamesis. In other words stop them once they've damned themselves but before they get all the way to Camulodunum.'

'Well, Geta's not going anywhere in a hurry; he's lucky to be alive according to one of the orderlies, who's a mate of mine. He says Geta's put himself out of commission for the foreseeable future, so that's half the threat gone.'

'And, more to the point, that's something that Corvinus won't know because he was too far away to see Geta being taken from the field. So if Geta was the one who was meant to deal with Plautius whilst Corvinus goes north, it won't be happening soon.'

Sabinus lay back down with a sigh. 'True, but Priscus, his thick-stripe, is now in command of the Twentieth, and who knows where his sympathies lie.'

Vespasian placed the cup down, next to the only oil lamp in the tent, on the rough bedside table. 'We've got to keep an eye on Plautius, somehow. Meanwhile we'll march west tomorrow. The Second Augusta will be the vanguard because I'm the only legate on my feet at the moment, so it'll be my cavalry scouting.'

Magnus chuckled. 'And Paetus will only see what he's told to see.'

'Something like that.'

'And how will you stop Corvinus?'

'That's where Narcissus' forward thinking sometimes just leaves me breathless with admiration.'

The severely wounded had been despatched back to Rutupiae in a long train of wagons, disappearing east through the smoky haze issuing from the scores of pyres disposing of the fallen. The battlefield had been partially cleared by the Dobunni but many bodies still remained lying out in the sun and the tribesmen laboured amongst the dead, piling the corpses of their former allies onto the pyres under the supervision of just two auxiliary cohorts; Budvoc had been true to his word and his men worked willingly.

Vespasian turned away from the sombre sight and rode towards his legion, formed up in column on the hill, ready to begin the march west. Apart from a visit to Sabinus the previous evening and a couple of periods of brief but sound sleep, his time had been taken up with the aftermath of battle. He had received the lists of casualties from each cohort and had been relieved by their comparative lightness: just under three hundred dead and twice as many wounded, of which almost a hundred would never serve again. Dead or severely wounded centurions, optiones and standard-bearers had to be replaced and promotions were made under guidance from the surviving officers of each cohort. Finally, the few centuries that had been badly mauled were temporarily disbanded and the survivors used to bring others up to a respectable strength. All this had been achieved in haste on the day after the battle so as to bring the legion and, more importantly, its chain of command, back up to battle readiness.

And battle there would be; Vespasian was sure of it. As Plautius had predicted, the bulk of the Britons had crossed the Tamesis, despite the best endeavours of the fleet, which had massacred thousands in the water. The auxiliaries had tried to follow them through the marsh tracks to the river, but without local knowledge they found it all but impossible and many foundered, sucked into the slime, weighed down by their chain mail. A couple of Batavian cohorts did manage to find a way through and foolishly swam across, only to be repulsed with heavy losses by a few thousand tribesmen who had rallied on the north bank, despite receiving artillery support from the ballistae mounted on the bows of the fleet's triremes.

Vespasian reached the front of the column. He raised his arm in the air and, with a slight flourish, swiped it down; a deep horn sounded, the signal was relayed and the II Augusta moved forward. Before them, two auxiliary cohorts scouted ahead in open order with two more on either flank; behind followed the XX and XIIII Legions, both without their legates – although Sabinus had been pronounced fit enough to travel in a covered wagon. Geta, however, although conscious, was very weak from loss of blood and had been despatched to the hospital tents at Rutupiae, along with the other wounded.

As he rode, Vespasian contemplated Narcissus' skill in engineering a situation whereby from a safe distance back in Gaul he could force an enemy to expose himself for what he was and thereby set in train a sequence of events that might well topple an empress. Again, he knew that he was being used as a small piece in a bigger game; but it was ever thus in the murky world of imperial politics whose fringes he felt he would be always destined to inhabit – unless, of course, he retired to his estates. But, then, would he be happy to live out his life quietly as he had once wanted? A life in which his only excitement would be, as Sabinus had described it so disparagingly, to see if this year's wine would be better than the last. He thought back to that conversation two years previously in Germania: at the time he had genuinely considered retirement as a way of avoiding being caught up in imperial politics, but now he realised that his brother had been right, he would be bored. Now that he had commanded a legion in battle and received the praise of his commanding officer for his conduct; now that he knew he was capable of such command and that there would be more battles ahead from which to learn, how could he possibly retire to a farm and watch the changing of the seasons? He looked back at the legion at whose head he was riding and exalted in the pride that he felt. There would be no retirement – at least not yet – he would continue his career and the price would be his involvement with politics.

He consoled himself with the fact that this time his role was more crucial in that he now had to judge how long it should be before he reported to Plautius what he was sure his scouts would be telling him in just a few hours. He knew that it was imperative for Corvinus to have enough time to damn himself completely in Plautius' eyes; it was not so much that he cared about Narcissus' power struggle with Messalina – although he realised that in the choice of the two evils he was better off with Narcissus winning that struggle – it was the chance of revenge for Corvinus' abduction of Clementina and deliverance of her to Caligula for violent and repeated rape. He smiled coldly, his eyes set with satisfaction, as he contemplated the sweet sensation of delivering vengeance upon a man who had so wronged his family.

'You're looking pleased with yourself,' Magnus said, pulling his horse up next to him. 'Did you have a particularly good shit before we left?'

'I did, as a matter of fact. Where've you been? I was looking for you earlier to tell you all about it.'

'Oh, I'm sorry to have missed out on that treat; but don't worry, I've been down to see Sabinus and he made up for it by easing one out in his wagon whilst I was there. More to the point,

I saw my orderly mate again and he told me that he had over-heard a mightily displeased Plautius ask Geta to explain to him why he made the elementary mistake of letting his unit probe too deeply into the routing enemy and allowing forty of his precious cavalry to go absent without leave across the Styx.'

Magnus paused; Vespasian waited for a moment and then looked at him. 'Well, go on then, tell me what he said.'

'He didn't really have a reason, he just said that he'd been fired up with enthusiasm and it would never happen again.'

'Did Plautius accept that?'

'Apparently; he shouted at Geta for a short while, until the doctor advised against it for medical reasons, and then he left, seemingly satisfied with the explanation, and with no more than a warning about not being a reckless arsehole in his army again and a vague threat concerning his testicles, a weighty hammer and an anvil.'

'It doesn't make sense. Whatever you might think about Geta, he's got a reputation as being an excellent soldier; just take the Mauretanian campaign, for example – from all accounts his conduct was exemplary. He's not the sort of person to make a stupid mistake like that.'

'We all do, now and again.'

'If you're alluding to my failure to advance quickly enough on Cantiacum, it's not the same; I'm not nearly as experienced as Geta and yet I know not to lose my head and go chasing off into the heart of a horde of very angry Britons with just my legion's cavalry.'

'Fair point; but there was a time when you might have lost your head.'

'I'm over that now.'

'Thank the gods; I always thought that that would be how you'd get yourself killed. But I agree, Geta wouldn't do that. Anyway, who gives a fuck? He's done it now and pissed off Plautius into the bargain.'

'You're right, I suppose, it's just a pity he didn't get himself killed along with all the other poor sods he did for. How's Sabinus?'

'Oh, he's much better, the wound's healing up like a Vestal's gash; the doctor says he can ride tomorrow, so he'll be fine for your little chat with Corvinus.'

'I'm pleased to hear it,' Vespasian replied, looking ahead to where Paetus was riding towards him. 'Here it comes.'

'Here comes what?'

'Decision time.'

'My patrol has just returned from the Tamesis crossing, sir,' Paetus reported as he slowed his mount.

'And apart from a century on either bank there was no sign of the Ninth?'

The young prefect looked momentarily astonished. 'How did you know, sir?'

'That doesn't matter; send that patrol out again, I don't want that to be public knowledge.'

'But Plautius—'

'Will be told when the time is right; I'll take the responsibility for it, Paetus, you've just got to trust me. As far as you're concerned the Ninth is making itself nice and comfy on the northern bank of the Tamesis and if you say otherwise to anyone I think that you'll find yourself on the wrong side of Narcissus.'

Paetus raised his eyebrows. 'I'd rather not find myself on any side of Narcissus, sir. I'll report back when I've got news that the Ninth have finished building their camp.'

'Thank you, prefect, I'll be very interested to know just how long it takes them.'

Paetus grinned and saluted.

Magnus looked dubious as Paetus rode away. 'This is a very dangerous game that Narcissus has got you playing, sir. When Plautius finds out it won't just be Geta's testicles that will be feeling the weight of the general's hammer, if you take my meaning?'

'I'm rather hoping that it'll be Corvinus' balls that'll receive Plautius' kind attentions.'

'There's room for more than one pair on the general's anvil.'

*

The inevitable delay of one day after the battle forced Plautius
to drive his army on as fast as possible and the march west was
an arduous affair for the weary legionaries. The going, however,
was easy, over gently undulating farmland that, with the
VIIII Hispana so close behind, Caratacus had mainly left
untouched. It was through fields of ripening wheat and barley or
arable land that the column made its way and not a landscape
blackened and destroyed by a retreating army intent upon
denying its pursuer the ability to forage.

The morning of the second day saw them descending a hill
into a basin through which the Tamesis, now just a mile to the
north, wound in a ponderous, looping fashion, forcing the part of
the fleet shadowing their advance to row harder in order to keep
pace with the column.

In the distance, five miles or so to the west, Vespasian could
see the ships that had supported Corvinus' advance, bobbing at
anchor at what he guessed must be the Tamesis ford. He knew
that his hoodwinking of Plautius could not go undetected for
much longer. A smudge on the horizon, well to the north of the
river, caught his eye and he pulled his horse to one side, allowing
the men of the first cohort to tramp past, as he scrutinised it carefully. After a few moments' deliberation, chewing on his bottom
lip, he turned his mount and headed back down the column.

'Take command, tribune,' he shouted at Mucianus, at the
head of the second cohort, as he sped past. 'And keep the pace
up. I need to report to the general.'

Galloping past the ranks and ranks of marching legionaries he
eventually came to the legions' six hundred pack-mules, one for
each contubernium, and the wagons and artillery belonging to
each century. Behind these rode the army's command group, just
ahead of the XIIII Gemina.

Vespasian slowed his horse and drew a deep breath as he
approached Plautius. 'General, I need to speak to you urgently
and in private.'

'He's done what!' Plautius exploded.

'Carried on towards Camulodunum, sir.'

'What makes you so sure?'

Vespasian pointed to the north. 'Look at the horizon over there; what do you see?'

Plautius squinted. 'I'm afraid that my eyes aren't as good as they used to be; what is it, legate?'

'Smoke, sir, a lot of it.'

'That doesn't mean that it's Corvinus.'

'Corvinus never stopped, he never intended to.'

'But that's miles from the ford; how did he get there so quickly? Your report last night said that he had built a camp on the north bank by the ford.'

'That wasn't true, sir.'

Plautius glared at Vespasian, outraged. 'If you're telling me that you knew about this all along and covered it up then that's treason, legate.'

'I know, sir; but if I had told you earlier then that could have been construed as treason as well.'

'Vespasian, I fail to see how preventing Corvinus from going against the Emperor's explicit orders can be seen as treason.'

'Because they're not the Emperor's orders, they were given only in his name. The Emperor doesn't rule, he's just seen to be ruling; the real power is—'

'Don't patronise me! I know who the real power is, but it comes to the same thing: Narcissus speaks for the Emperor.'

'No, sir, that's not true; Narcissus speaks for himself but from within the Emperor's shadow. In fact, he *is* his shadow. He uses Claudius in order to wield the power that he couldn't be seen using in the full light of day and he guards him jealously in order to hang on to that power. But because the Emperor is a cunt-struck fool he doesn't see – or won't believe – the threat to his position from within his inner circle.'

'The Empress?'

'Exactly.'

'But she's nothing without him.'

'Not so; she's the mother of the Emperor's son.'

'But he's too young to rule without a regent and no one would accept a woman in that position.'

'Granted, but they would accept a man and a woman, the mother of the young Emperor and her brother.'

Plautius' eyes widened in comprehension. 'That woman being the mother of a true Caesar and the man being the conqueror of Camulodunum and the founder of the new province of Britannia; a couple who couldn't start their own dynasty because they are siblings and therefore are no threat to the Emperor's line but, rather, the guardians of it. Perfect, until something happens to the child, at which point the regents are secure enough in their positions for the Guard to continue in their support.'

'Exactly, and we know that the imperial family are capable of anything; Claudius' sister, Livilla, was already poisoning her son, Tiberius Gemellus, before she in turn was starved to death by her mother, Antonia. If anyone should realise what is possible it should be Claudius; but the fool can't be made to listen.'

'So therefore he must be made to see.' Plautius touched his hand to his forehead and closed his eyes. 'Oh, I see it now. That bastard Narcissus manoeuvred me into giving Corvinus the opportunity to disobey the Emperor so that I would be the one to expose the plot to Claudius, along with the hard evidence to convince him that his brother-in-law and wife are moving against him. You did right not to tell me until Corvinus had made contact with the enemy, Vespasian, I would have stopped him before he damned himself.'

'No, he would have killed you. In fact I believe that you would be dead now if Geta hadn't got himself wounded.'

'Geta!'

'Yes, I think that he was meant to have you killed in a way that wouldn't look suspicious.'

'Like leading his cavalry into an impossible position just in front of me.'

'That seems a little extreme, sir; after all, he nearly got himself killed doing that.'

'Only through bad luck. I had that decurion brought to me after I saw Geta yesterday because I couldn't believe that someone with Geta's experience would have made such a stupid mistake through "fired-up enthusiasm", as he put it. The decurion told me that Geta wasn't leading them, he was right in the middle of the unit as safe as he could be, which I found very strange. But now, looking back at it, think of the timing. I'd come up the hill to recall you, then, when I'm just a few hundred paces away Geta suddenly takes his men into a mass of retreating and pissed-off Britons knowing full well that I would try and save them because I've so few mounted troops. I charge in, taking you and your lads with me, and could well have been killed and no one would have suspected a thing. As it was I was so angry at the situation that nothing could stop me. We broke through to Geta's men, as he knew we would, but, unfortunately for him, not before a stray spear dismounted him and he got trampled upon. The little arsehole deserves it; forty of his lads killed for nothing.'

'That would explain it, I suppose.'

'Too fucking right it explains it. I'll have that bastard when he's recovered. Why didn't you tell me that they were going to try and kill me?'

'Narcissus would have seen me dead.'

Plautius gave a mirthless smile. 'Well, Narcissus will see us both dead if we don't stop Corvinus now. How do you halt a rogue legion without bringing it to battle and causing the invasion to collapse?'

'Narcissus has already thought of that; I can do it with just Paetus' cavalry and my brother.'

Plautius looked at Vespasian quizzically. 'Very well,' he said after a few moments, 'I suppose I have to trust you seeing as you seem to understand Narcissus' mind. Take what you need – and hurry. I'll be close behind you; I'll try and get two legions across the river at low tide later this afternoon. Now that Corvinus has started hostilities in the north I'm forced to finish off what the treacherous little sod started; not to do so would be seen as weakness by the Britons. It may be that Claudius won't have a battle left to fight after all.'

'So long as he can be the first to enter Camulodunum, it might not be such a bad thing, general.'

'No, it wouldn't.' Plautius paused for another moment of thought. 'And Claudius will still get what he needs without the possibility of being exposed as an incompetent commander.'

'I wonder if Narcissus has already thought of that too.'

'Yes, the oily little freedman! I wonder.'

'I've got orders not to let anyone across, sir.' The centurion of the century of the VIIII Hispana stationed on the south bank of the Tamesis was adamant; he pulled his shoulders back into a more rigid attention as if to emphasise the point.

Vespasian leant down from his horse, placing his face close to the veteran's. 'I'm sure you have, centurion, but I have orders to cross; mine are from Aulus Plautius and yours are from Legate Corvinus. So tell me, which one has precedence?'

The centurion swallowed. 'It would be the general, sir, but Corvinus told me that he was dead and that he was in command now and no one was to cross until Legate Geta arrives.'

'Is that what he said? Well, I can assure you, centurion, that Plautius is very much alive, so alive, in fact, that he will personally execute you when he arrives here in three hours or so and finds us still debating who's in charge of the army.' He jerked his thumb over his shoulder. 'And what's more, there's a legate, a cavalry prefect and three hundred troopers who will testify to him that you obstructed me in obeying his orders.'

'And a civilian,' Magnus added.

'Yes, and a civilian.'

Sabinus moved forward. 'Centurion Quintillus, isn't it?'

'Yes, legate; it's good to see you again, legate,' Quintillus barked, attempting to force his body into an even more rigid state of attention.

'And you, centurion. It would be a shame if this was to be our last meeting.'

'It would, legate.'

'So what's it to be?'

Quintillus glanced nervously around, swallowing hard again. 'Well, I suppose that in the circumstances I'd better let you cross.'

'That was a very sensible decision.'

'But you'll have to wait at least a couple of hours for the tide to fall; it's too high at the moment.'

Vespasian swung off his horse. 'Not for these lads, it isn't. Now, tell me, Quintillus, which way did the Ninth go?'

The centurion pointed to two small hills covered with a smattering of trees, next to each other on the far bank, over a quarter of a mile away. 'They disappeared between them hills, heading northeast, sir. Be sure to go between them not over them; a local farmer told us that one of them, and I don't know which, has a shrine on it sacred to a god called Lud and you wouldn't want to piss him off, apparently.'

'Thank you for the warning, centurion, I'll be sure to mention to the general just how co-operative you've been. Right, Paetus, it's time your lads got wet.'

'I'm going to have to stop soon,' Sabinus said through chattering teeth after they had travelled only three or four miles from the twin hills. 'If I don't I'll pass out.'

Vespasian looked up at the sky; the sun was falling towards the horizon and beginning to deepen in colour. 'All right, we'll stop here; we won't catch up with them tonight anyway. Paetus, have your men build a camp.'

The Batavians set to their task and by nightfall the camp's three-foot-deep ditch was dug and its resulting embankment topped with a palisade of stakes interwoven with hazel plashing, making a defendable wall half as high again as the height of a man. By necessity it was small and cramped, there being just enough room for the three hundred troopers and their horses, who remained saddled in the event of an alarm; it was also cheerless as Vespasian had, for obvious reasons, forbidden the lighting of fires. The still damp Batavians shivered in their cloaks and many of them lay beneath their mounts for extra warmth, risking a gush of urine from above that would add to their misery.

'Plautius should have reached the ford and be camping on this side of the river tonight,' Vespasian said, rubbing Sabinus' shoulders, trying to get some heat back into his brother's blood-depleted body. All around them men hunched against the cold, eating a cheerless supper and talking in hushed tones.

Magnus bit a chunk from a slice of salted pork. 'What do you think he'll do tomorrow?'

'He'll leave one legion north of the river and one on the south bank and then come after us with the remaining one,' Sabinus suggested, 'in case we're not successful stopping Corvinus.'

'You mean he'd attack the Ninth if they refused to stop?'

Vespasian shrugged. 'He'd at least threaten to as a last resort, he'd have no option; he knows that his life is now at stake. If Narcissus can't give Claudius the personal victory he's promised, he'll distance himself from it; Plautius will take the blame and will receive a nice polite note, in the Emperor's name, requesting that he do the decent thing.'

Magnus chewed thoughtfully for a moment. 'And I would guess that he won't be the only one to get such a note.'

'I think you'd be guessing correctly; Sabinus and I know too much. Our grandmother warned me about this, years ago; she told me not to get involved with the schemes of the powerful because ultimately all they want is more power and to get it they use people of our class as disposable tools. We're very handy when things are going well, but an embarrassment when they don't because we know too much. We therefore need to be discarded.'

'She never said that to me,' Sabinus said, aggrieved.

'That's because you never listened to her; you were too busy terrorising me and then you joined up and never went back. But I used to talk to her, or, more to the point, listen to her, and most of the things that she told me have begun to make complete sense as I've grown older. Magnus said it: in the Rome that you and I live in we can never rise to the top because those positions are reserved for one family; but we carry on our careers despite that because what would we do otherwise? Look forward to tasting next year's wine? So we have no choice; there're always going to be people more powerful than us and they're always going to be using us and one day they'll be the death of us. Unless we're successful tomorrow, that day might be very soon and Plautius knows it.'

'Perhaps I should do more listening in future.'

Vespasian smiled in the dark. 'The day you start listening will be the day I ask for a loan.'

'Sir,' Paetus hissed, walking quickly towards them through the tangle of resting troopers. 'I think that you should come and see this.'

'What is it, prefect?'

'A fire, some distance off; it's just been lit.'

Vespasian followed Paetus to the northern defence. Looking out into the night he could see a point of flame that grew appreciably as he watched it. Then shadows appeared around it and a faint chanting drifted through the cold air. 'Can you make them out, Paetus?'

'Just, it's very strange; they don't seem to be wearing trousers like the Britons do; when they bother to dress at all, that is.'

Vespasian squinted; as he did so two of the figures lifted a small bundle into the air. 'You're right; they're wearing robes almost down to their ankles. What are they?'

'Shall I send some men to find out?'

'Better not, it might be a trap; we're safer staying in here.'

Magnus joined them peering at the group, which seemed to consist of half a dozen of the strangely garbed figures. The bundle was laid back onto the ground and the chanting stopped to be replaced by an infant's wail. 'I think we're being cursed,' he muttered darkly as a figure knelt down over the bundle. 'I've heard stories about this lot, and none of them were good. I'd wager that you'd rather have that nice polite note from the Emperor asking you to relieve the world of the burden of your life than run into them.' The wail was abruptly cut off; Magnus clutched his thumb between his fingers and spat. 'They're priests; they're called druids.'

Vespasian felt his throat dry as the acrid fumes from the still smouldering burnt-out village rasped into his lungs. It was not the first such sight that they had come across but it was certainly the largest since leaving the camp at dawn two hours before and riding past the gutted remains of the tiny infant. He surveyed the dismal scene of charred bodies and timber for a few moments and then turned to Sabinus. 'This must be what caused the smoke I saw yesterday, it's big enough.'

'Then the Ninth can't be too far off.'

Vespasian pointed to the half-burnt body of a young girl. 'Corvinus isn't going to make matters easier by doing this. It's one thing to beat an army and kill as many fighting men as possible, but murdering women and children for no reason other than you've come across their village isn't going to induce that beaten army to surrender. They'll be bent on revenge.'

'If you beat them often enough they'll surrender because they fear you.'

'Yes, but if they hate you as well then how long will they submit before rebelling? As Plautius said, we've come here to stay; incidents like this will just cause resentment that we'll pay for in Roman lives later.'

'I wouldn't worry about it; a few lives here and there aren't going to make much difference in the long term. There's a lot of hard fighting ahead before we completely subdue this island and many more children are going to go the way of that little girl, and you and I will be responsible for our fair share of them. We need to keep going whilst I've still got the energy.' Sabinus flicked his reins and moved off, leaving Vespasian to contemplate the dead child.

Magnus joined him. 'He's right, we should get going, sir. Forget about her, she was lucky to reach the age she did. At least she had the chance to know that she was alive unlike that baby them druids sacrificed last night.'

'I suppose you're right, Magnus.'

'Of course I'm right. It don't do to dwell on death: too morbid. It comes to all of us and the timing is in the hands of the gods.'

'And in the hands of their priests, evidently,' Vespasian retorted, urging his horse forward and signalling to Paetus to move his men out.

Vespasian led the column on at a canter, northeast across flat semi-wooded land, following the trail of the VIIII Hispana, passing burnt-out farmsteads and villages, each one adding to his growing sense of urgency; now that Corvinus had damned himself he had to be stopped before he did irreparable damage to the chances of an honourable surrender.

As the sun climbed towards its zenith, rising through a blue sky punctuated by scudding, high clouds, the column crested the first low hill they had encountered and Vespasian, Sabinus and Paetus simultaneously drew up their mounts.

'Shit!' Sabinus exclaimed. 'He's fighting Claudius' battle for him.'

Vespasian punched his thigh hard, causing his horse to step nervously. 'Narcissus will have me for this, I've totally mistimed it.'

A mile or so before them, the VIIII Hispana and its auxiliary cohorts were engaged with an enemy force of at least twice their number. The legion's line was broad and thin with only two cohorts held in reserve in front of the gates of the marching camp in which they had spent the night. The left flank seemed to be anchored to marshy ground to the north, preventing any attempt by the Britons to move around it in any great numbers; but the right flank was hard-pressed and had buckled round in order to prevent an outflanking move by combined chariotry and cavalry.

'What are your orders, legate?' Paetus asked, controlling his frisky mount with a couple of sharp tugs of the reins.

'Sir,' Magnus shouted. 'Look behind us.'

Vespasian glanced over his shoulder; from this vantage point he could see for some distance over the Tamesis basin. Less than three miles away was a fast-moving column. 'Cavalry! That must be Plautius' forward ala riding ahead of the legion. Paetus, send a messenger down to them and order them, in my name, to hurry. And send one to Plautius to tell him what's happening.'

'Yes, sir! And what do we do?'

'What we have to: charge the Britons threatening Corvinus' right flank and hope that we can hold until that ala arrives. Form line!'

Within moments the riders had been despatched and the shrill blare of the lituus filled the air as the column, bridles jangling, horses snorting and decurions shouting, changed formation into a four-deep line.

Vespasian pulled his brother to one side. 'I don't care what you say, Sabinus, but there is no way that you'll be fit enough for this.'

Sabinus went to protest but Vespasian cut him off. 'You go down and get into the camp, and see if you can find anything of interest in Corvinus' praetorium. That would be much more useful than getting yourself killed because you're too weak to punch a sword hard.'

Sabinus grasped his brother's forearm. 'Just this once I'll listen to you and take your advice, brother.'

'You're going to have to ask for a loan now, sir,' Magnus chuckled as Sabinus rode off, 'Sabinus just listened to someone.'

'Well, you go with him and make sure he doesn't do it again, I wouldn't want to ask for two loans in the same day. You'll be of much more help with him than getting in everyone's way complaining about fighting on horseback.'

'I can't argue with that,' Magnus affirmed, following in Sabinus' path.

The line was formed and Vespasian took his place between Ansigar and Paetus, drawing his sword, glancing at the young cavalry prefect and giving a brief, business-like nod.

'The First Batavian Ala will advance!' Paetus roared, sweeping his spatha from its scabbard and raising it in the air.

The lituus sounded and the three hundred surviving Batavian troopers kicked their horses forward, holding their reins in their shielded hands and brandishing javelins in the air with their right.

Down the hill they came, breaking first into a trot and then a canter at Paetus' signal; the thunder of hooves drowned out the clamour of the battle before them as they pounded across the ground towards the legion's threatened right flank. As they closed the distance, Paetus ordered the charge; the troopers roared the battle cry of the Batavians, deep and guttural, and urged their willing steeds on. Vespasian's calves gripped the sweating flanks of his mount, feeling its huge chest rise and fall, sucking in vast gulps of air as it drove its legs forward over the rough grass, head stretched forward, ears back, the muscles and ligaments in its powerful neck straining beneath tight skin.

A force of a few score British cavalry and some chariots broke away from the hard-fought melee that had infiltrated the Roman line and turned to face the newcomers to the field; but it was not enough. Many of them went down to the hissing volley of sleek javelins that broke their already ragged formation and panicked more than a few of their mounts.

With the enemy's cohesion gone, most of the Batavians' horses willingly carried the charge home, crashing through the large gaps in the Britons' unsteady line, with only a few shying at the last, unwilling to charge straight into a fellow beast, even though they were of smaller stature.

Slicing his spatha in a sideways cut, Vespasian severed the sword arm and opened the naked chest of a young mounted warrior, almost half his age, sending him howling to the ground in a spew of blood as his mount bolted in terror. Vespasian's horse and those of his comrades slowed suddenly of their own accord as they penetrated deep into the Britons' formation, turning the combat into a static affair. Many troopers wheeled their mounts on the spot, hacking at any enemy brave enough to attempt to hold his ground, clearing the areas around them with bloody efficiency before moving on towards fresh foes. Working with Paetus and Ansigar's turma, Vespasian cleaved a path towards the rear of the Britons still engaged with the extreme right auxiliary cohort of the Roman line.

The auxiliaries, with weight of man and beast pressing against them greatly reduced, roared their war cry and renewed their bloody endeavours. Punching their swords up into the eyes of the stocky ponies and hacking at the dangling legs of their riders, they forced them back from within their formation and gradually began to lock shields again, cohering the unit together once more into an effective fighting force determined to avenge the dead comrades beneath their feet.

With the blades of the vengeful auxiliaries before them and the honed iron of the new, terrifying force bearing down upon their defenceless backs, the Britons wavered for a few moments and then, as if by immediate mutual consent, broke. Chariots and cavalry turned and fled back towards the bulk of their army around the corner of the buckled flank. Vespasian and Paetus led the Batavians in a haphazard pursuit, slashing at the backs of the enemy and the rumps of their horses. With only a few javelins flung by chariot-mounted warriors to harm them, the Batavians took to their merciless task with relish, shedding as much blood as possible without venturing too far and risking engulfment by the horde of foot warriors that were still very much of a mind to break the Roman will. Behind them the auxiliaries followed, led by their centurions and pushed forward by the long poles of the optiones to their rear, arcing back round to straighten the line.

'Halt!' Vespasian cried as their quarry diverted around the flank of the main body of foot warriors, who began to turn and face the Batavians.

'Fall back and rally!' Paetus shouted, knowing that they were too disorganised to risk an encounter with infantry.

The lituus blew and the Batavians retired, melting around the side of the oncoming auxiliaries who continued at a brisk jog, shield to shield, increasing in pace as they closed with the enemy until, in an act of brave opportunism, they swung round and crashed into the Britons' flank.

Vespasian surveyed the scene as the decurions dressed the Batavians' ranks a hundred paces behind the auxiliaries. The VIIII Hispana held as the Britons attacked and then retreated, only to charge again, repeatedly. This was not the mindless shoving and heaving in a press of bodies in an attempt to break through by sheer weight of flesh, this was hand-to-hand combat in waves; flowing forward, with long swords flashing and spears jabbing, making contact and then disengaging and pulling back as if sucked by an undertow before surging forward again. The effect rippled up and down the line, so that there was always contact at various points, in a strangely fluid motion; except where the auxiliaries had pinned the flank. Here the Britons were forced against the shields of the rightmost legionary cohort and the legionaries were thankful for it. Their unseen blades were working bloody death in the press of front rank warriors, who shrieked in gutted agony as the moist coils of their intestines slopped to the churned ground to be stamped upon by hobnailed boots as the legionaries pressed home their advantage.

Caught on the anvil of the legion by the heavy blow from the auxiliaries hammering into their flank, panic began to spread through the massed tribesmen and the tone of their cacophony changed, rising in pitch, becoming shriller and more terrified.

The legionaries pressed on whilst the auxiliaries continued to squeeze and the warriors fell in droves, unable to pull back from the cruel blades. And yet they held, as if the will of their gods forced them to stand and die on the sacred earth of their homeland; their screams and death-shouts rising to the sky in homage to the deities that watched over them but could not, ultimately, protect them.

And then came a new sound: a low groan of despair. Vespasian looked to his left; along the crest of the hill, mounted figures were arriving. More and more appeared, ranging along the entire length of the crest. As their number increased so did the hopes of the Britons lessen, for they knew that behind this second, larger unit of mounted troops would surely be another legion of Rome and the blare of its horns would herald their certain deaths.

Sensing the growing hopelessness in their opponents, the legionaries went on the offensive, urged on by their centurions, attempting to maintain contact all along the line, engaging the enemy on their own terms and increasing their kill rate. The Britons, forced back and suffering dreadful casualties, wavered. Then, as the second mounted force to appear on the hill that day advanced, they began to break and run; the tide had turned.

Away they flowed to escape the relentless blades of the legion, leaving their many dead and wounded behind them, sprinting east for their lives.

Vespasian turned to Paetus. 'Join up with this new ala and pursue for a mile or so; kill as many as you can.'

'My pleasure, sir. Won't you be joining us?'

'No, Paetus; I'm going to find Sabinus and then together we'll confront Corvinus. If we're dead when you get back you must ride to Plautius and tell him that we've failed.'

Paetus saluted as Vespasian turned his horse and rode towards the camp.

Riding at speed behind the ranks of cheering cohorts, Vespasian quickly reached the southern gate of the marching camp and then followed the deserted Via Principalis to the praetorium at the camp's heart. Dismounting, he tethered his horse and then passed through the unguarded entrance.

'You took your time, brother,' Sabinus said from the depths of the tent.

'There was the small matter of an army of Britons to defeat. Where are the guards?'

'They wouldn't co-operate so Magnus and I were forced to relieve them of their weapons. They'll be fine, apart from having sore heads.'

'Did you find anything?'

'Very much so; it's in the sleeping quarters with Magnus.'

Vespasian followed his brother through an entrance at the rear of the tent to see Magnus sitting by a figure lying prone on the bed. As his eyes got used to the dim light he could make out long grey hair and a drooping black moustache. 'Verica! What's he doing in here?'

'It's not of his own accord,' Magnus informed him, 'he was unconscious and tied up when we found him; he only started to come to just before you arrived.'

The old King slowly opened his eyes and groggily focused on Vespasian, then said: 'They came to surrender.'

'Who did?'

'The Catuvellauni and the Trinovantes. They arrived this morning and Corvinus formed the legion up in front of the camp; their leaders came forward to speak with him under a branch of truce and I translated for them. They said that they had come to lay down their arms; once Togodumnus died they had no chieftain in the east who was still willing to resist the invasion and they would therefore submit to Rome. Corvinus sneered at them for being weak and said that he wanted to win Camulodunum, not have it given to him; he had them executed in front of their men. I protested and he knocked me cold when the Britons charged – when they saw what Corvinus had done they abandoned all thoughts of surrender. That's all I know.'

'Well, he's had his victory, and a bloody one at that; the road to Camulodunum is open.'

Verica looked bitter as he eased himself up to sit. 'It was open this morning and not awash with blood.'

'Will they still be willing to surrender?'

'Yes, they're truly beaten now; but resentment for this will run deep and many of the warriors will go west and join Caratacus; Rome will have a long hard war against him.'

Sabinus shrugged. 'We were always going to have a hard fight against him; a few thousand more warriors won't make that much difference.'

Vespasian shook his head. 'It's not so much that; it's the fact that the news will spread that we don't accept surrender. The tribes will think that they have no choice but to fight to the death; Corvinus has just cost us many Roman lives.'

'When those guards are found I want the skin off their backs, primus pilus,' a voice growled, entering the tent.

'Yes, sir!'

'In the meantime a cup of wine to celebrate a good morning's work, gentlemen?'

'Thank you, legate,' three voices replied.

The brothers looked at each other. 'Time for our chat with Corvinus,' Vespasian whispered. 'Magnus, stay here and only come out if there's a fight.'

Magnus nodded as the brothers walked through to the main part of the tent.

'Bumpkin! And the cuckold!' Corvinus exclaimed, outraged. 'How dare you come into my praetorium uninvited!'

'How dare you ignore the Emperor's orders!' Vespasian strode to within a pace of Corvinus. 'And how dare you not accept the surrender of two tribes when it was freely offered!'

Corvinus' nostrils flared; his three officers tensed and put their hands on the hilts of their swords. 'What honour or glory would I have had in taking their surrender when my legion hasn't seen any part of the fighting so far? But then you wouldn't understand that, would you, coming from a grubby little family whose taste for glory has never been whetted because it has conspicuously failed to achieve any honour.'

'Whereas you consider it honourable to steal the glory that the Emperor has reserved for himself?'

'The Emperor's a fool!'

'Whatever the Emperor is, he's also your brother-in-law; and the people surrounding him know full well how you intend to use that position and what you plan to do with his stolen glory.'

Corvinus' dark eyes narrowed. 'Supposition. No one can prove that I was not acting in Claudius' best interests.'

'That would be the case if Plautius were dead, but he's not.' Vespasian enjoyed the look of surprise that Corvinus did his best to conceal. 'When you said goodbye to him with such finality, thinking never to see him again, what you didn't know was that your friend Geta was lying only fifty paces away. He'd tried to lure Plautius to his death by sacrificing his cavalry but the general survived; no doubt Geta would have tried to murder him some other way had he not been severely wounded and sent back to Rutupiae. We'll never know; but what is certain is that warrant that you hold from the Emperor giving you command of the invasion in the event of Plautius' death is no more than an unexercised warrant. You're not in command, Corvinus, therefore you have committed treason and Plautius has sent us to take you into custody.'

Corvinus went to draw his sword from its scabbard. Vespasian's left hand clamped around his wrist, arresting the motion, whilst his right swept his *pugio* from his belt and pricked it under Corvinus' chin, forcing his head back. Corvinus' three officers were not so impeded and three glinting blades flashed up to threaten Vespasian's throat.

'I would consider your positions, gentlemen,' Sabinus advised, walking forward, his gaze falling on two of the three men; behind him Magnus rushed from the sleeping area, his sword drawn. From outside came the good-humoured clamour of a victorious legion returning to camp. 'Vibianus, I'm pleased to see that you're still primus pilus, and Laurentinus, I imagine that you're on your last few months of service and the Ninth will be needing a new prefect of the camp soon.' He looked at the youngest of the three. 'Scaevola, I'm sure you feel you owe loyalty to Corvinus for making you his thick-stripe tribune but I would advise you to put that aside for the moment and listen.' The young tribune's eyes flicked nervously over to Sabinus for an instant and then back to Vespasian; his sword stayed firm as did those of his fellows. 'Plautius will be here very soon with at least one legion. You three have only two choices: try to kill us and then carry on being a party to your legate's treason or hand Corvinus over to us. Choose the first option and you will find yourselves leading your legion against fellow Romans, as Plautius will have no option but to use force to ensure that the Emperor's orders are obeyed. But choose the second and you'll receive the thanks of a grateful emperor.'

Scaevola pressed his blade harder against Vespasian's throat. 'Why should I trust you?'

'You've got no reason to; but Vibianus and Laurentius, you know me and you know the pride that I have in the Ninth Hispana, my first legion when I was a military tribune and my first as a legate. Do you think that I would want to see this legion disgraced? You both served under me for a couple of years; did I ever do anything that would make you doubt my word? Narcissus has set this up to expose Corvinus' treachery; but at the same time he made me legate of the Fourteenth so that there would be somebody whom you trust to reason with you, someone whom you know has your best interests and those of this legion at heart. Believe me, gentlemen, your new legate has lied to you and has put your lives in danger.'

Vibianus and Laurentius looked across Corvinus into each other's eyes; after a moment they both gave the slightest of nods. Their swords slowly moved from Vespasian's throat and pulled back to Corvinus'.

Scaevola's face tightened with indecision and sweat formed on his battle-grimed forehead.

'They'll be in here, sir,' Paetus shouted, bursting through the entrance, causing the young tribune to start; his sword jerked and Vespasian pulled his head back, blood trickling from a straight cut on his throat.

'What the fuck am I going to tell the Emperor and Narcissus?' Plautius roared, storming in after Paetus. 'You said that you'd stop this treacherous shit before he did too much damage.'

Vespasian looked down in horror at the blood on the sword blade; as he did Scaevola's hand released the hilt and it clattered to the wooden floor. Over Corvinus' shoulder Scaevola's eyes glazed and blood seeped from between his lips. Vibianus and Laurentius held a rigid Corvinus motionless with their swords pressed to his throat; Scaevola slid to the floor with a knife protruding from the back of his neck.

Vespasian checked the wound to his throat and found to his immense relief that it was superficial; he moved his hand down and eased Corvinus' weapon from its scabbard and chucked it away. 'I'm sorry, general, we arrived too late.'

'Too fucking right you did.' Plautius marched over to Corvinus and, without hesitation, slammed his fist into the centre of his face, crushing his nose and sending him collapsing onto Scaevola's body. 'That feels much better.' He stared furiously, neck ligaments bulging, at Vibianus and Laurentius. 'Get that dung heap out of my sight and keep him secured until the Emperor arrives to sentence him to death.'

'Yes, sir!' they replied, simultaneously snapping to attention.

'Which one of you killed the tribune?'

'I did, sir!' Vibianus barked.

'Put yourself on a charge, primus pilus.'

'Yes, sir!'

'Charge dismissed; now fuck off out of here.'

Vibianus and Laurentius crashed salutes and hurried from the tent dragging Corvinus with them. Vespasian nodded his thanks to Vibianus as they left.

Plautius turned his malevolent gaze onto the two brothers.

'I saw what happened; I was with the cavalry on the hill. It seems that we have them beaten; they'll probably ask for terms tomorrow.'

'They tried to surrender this morning but Corvinus had the envoys murdered,' Verica said, hobbling out of the sleeping area.

Plautius looked in shock at the old King and then slumped down onto a folding stool and wiped the sweat from his brow. 'What a fuck-up this is and none of it will be Narcissus' fault. What's Claudius going to do now when he gets here apart from have Corvinus executed and march into an already occupied town?'

'Don't occupy it, then,' Vespasian suggested. 'If it surrenders tomorrow that doesn't mean we have to march in immediately.'

Plautius paused, frowning, and then broke into a grin. 'Of course, the fool has never been to war, he won't know what it looks like. We could just dress up a few prisoners, like Caligula did when he pretended to invade Germania, kill them as we march into the town and then have Claudius take its surrender and he'll feel that he's done something glorious. He'll be happy, Narcissus won't be able to complain and, more to the point, I'll be in the clear. I'll send for him to leave Rome right away.'

'What do we do in the meantime, sir?'

'I'll despatch envoys from the Britons who've already come over to us to all the tribes and ascertain which chieftains will be willing to pledge themselves to the fool. Sabinus, I want prisoners for Claudius' triumphant entry into Camulodunum; take your legion west for a month making our presence fully known and then return here with some captives. The Ninth will now remain here where I can keep an eye on them. I've left the Twentieth building a bridge across the Tamesis and securing the southern bank from Caratacus. The Second I've left the other side of the river ready to head south. So, Vespasian, it now falls to you and not Corvinus to take Verica back to his capital and then secure the Isle of Vectis so that there's no threat in your rear next season when you start to push west along the coast; do it by negotiation with the King if you can – we need to preserve our troops. But if that fails then invade.

'I expect Claudius to arrive soon after the calends of September. I want you back here by then with Vectis secure, Verica in place and your legion established as the main force in the south of Britannia.'

CHAPTER XX

'MY NEPHEW WILL yield,' Verica assured Vespasian, 'and once he does he will be completely loyal to Rome.'

Vespasian tightened his grip on the rail as the trireme was again buffeted by a gust of wind in the choppy channel between the mainland and the Isle of Vectis. 'Do you think so? He's shown no inclination to be so in the last month of negotiations.'

'Once honour has been satisfied he will accept Rome.'

'But to satisfy his honour a good many of my men will have to die?'

Verica shrugged and wiped the drops of salty spray from his face. 'It's always been the way of things. Many more of his warriors will die for his honour than will legionaries.'

'I'm sure they will; but why do it? Why didn't he just capitulate when I sent envoys offering good terms?'

'Because I told him not to.'

Vespasian turned to the old King, startled. 'You did what?'

'I did what I knew to be the best for everyone as I intend to make Cogidubnus my heir. My people's blood has been shed fighting for Caratacus at the crossing of the Afon Cantiacii; Cogidubnus and his warriors weren't there because of his and Caratacus' hatred for each other. If Cogidubnus were to surrender to Rome without a fight my people would never accept him.'

'They accepted you back and you came with us.'

'True, but they did so only grudgingly. Now that Caratacus has been defeated and has fled west the Atrebates and Regni confederation are no longer under his dominion. They have accepted me back as their rightful King who was usurped by Caratacus. However, they resent the fact that I came with Rome and didn't stand with them against her.'

'So to secure your position you will make your nephew a hero for resisting Rome and then adopt him as your heir and fuck all the lives that will cost.'

'Yes, you could put it like that; but the important issue is that my kingdom will be stable and when I die, which will be very soon, there will be a strong successor who will be supportive of Rome. You wouldn't like the Atrebates and the Regni revolting next year or the year after, cutting off your supply lines as you move west, would you?'

'No, I wouldn't.'

'If this battle doesn't happen then that's what you'd have. Both my sons are dead, legate, and my natural heir is my sole grandson, named after me, but he is only in his teens; he's too young and, besides, he's lived with me in Rome for the last three years so he doesn't know my people and they won't accept him.'

'Doesn't he mind being passed over for his cousin?'

'I haven't told him yet; but I hope that he will see that it's for the best. I think he'll try to make his way in Rome. Along with me, he was given citizenship and equestrian rank and now speaks fluent Latin. At the moment he's serving as a thin-stripe tribune on Plautius' staff, perhaps you've come across him? Tiberius Claudius Alienus is the Latin name he's taken.'

'Alienus? Yes, I've seen him; he is young.'

'And obviously not strong enough to hold my people together under Rome.'

'And Cogidubnus will be if he can demonstrate that he stood up to Rome?'

'Yes; this small battle and small loss of life is a price worth paying for that, don't you think?'

Vespasian looked round at the hundred and fifty men of the first century of the depleted first cohort, kneeling on the deck, wet with spray, looking in apprehension at the island's shore, now less than a mile away, which, even in the thin dawn light, was visibly defended by a large force. Behind them, clutching their bows, knelt the two contubernia of Hamian auxiliaries that Vespasian had allocated to each ship. How many of these men would be dead within the hour to secure Verica's kingdom? After a few moments contemplating the hardened faces he realised that, pragmatically, it did not matter how many would die now so long as the goal was achieved and Verica's chosen heir could be seen as a man who bowed to the superior might of Rome after testing that strength for himself. Rome's position in Britannia would be stronger for it.

Verica was right, Vespasian mused, as the wind tugged at his cloak: his welcome had been less than enthusiastic. In the month after Corvinus' arrest, Vespasian had led his legion south, in stages, down through the Atrebates' heartland; every hill fort, township or village they had come to had opened their gates and submitted to Rome. The warriors had laid down their weapons but Vespasian had permitted them to take them back up so long as they acknowledged Verica as their King who would rule in the Emperor's name; indeed, he even bore the Emperor's name, Tiberius Claudius Verica, having been granted citizenship by Claudius whilst he was in Rome. This fealty, however, had not been granted immediately and Verica had been obliged to enter into protracted negotiations with the elders of each settlement before they would consent to accepting back their former King. The pacts had inevitably been settled with a long night's drinking, each successively taking their toll on the ageing Verica's health, and in the mornings there had always been fewer warriors coming to reclaim their swords than had deposited them the previous day. Some warriors had been waylaid heading west to Caratacus and they had been sent in chains to Plautius for use in Claudius' mock victory but a significant number had slipped away to swell the ranks of the defiant chieftain's growing army.

Verica's arrival at his power base, Regnum – a port within a natural harbour on the mainland, just to the east of Vectis – had been more triumphant as he was welcomed by his kin of the Regni. The II Augusta's welcome, however, had not been so warm and both Vespasian and Verica had been forced to work hard at smoothing over relations between the two sides during the following month as the legionaries built a permanent camp and the navy modernised the port. It was at this point that Vespasian had entered into negotiations with Cogidubnus, King of Vectis, for the peaceful surrender of his kingdom, but his overtures had always been thwarted, despite the honourable terms offered and the presence of a large Roman fleet in the Vectis channel.

Now he had been forced to use that fleet to take what Rome demanded he realised why it had not been given freely. He looked sidelong at the wily old King. 'Why didn't you tell me that you'd told Cogidubnus not to surrender without a fight? I've wasted almost a month in negotiating with him.'

'I had to have my people see that you were prepared to try and talk peace; had I told you at the beginning you would've invaded immediately and Rome would've looked like an impetuous aggressor.' Verica turned his rheumy eyes to Vespasian. 'You have to understand, young man, that if Rome is to stay here and doesn't wish to keep four or five legions constantly tied up keeping the tribes subdued, then you must rule with the broad consent of the people and to get that Rome must be seen as powerful and inclusive. And besides, had I told you, you might have had me executed.'

'That would've been a very unwise move.'

'Yes, it would've been, and I'm pleased that you can see that.'

'Brace yourselves, my lovelies,' Primus Pilus Tatius roared. 'This won't hurt – too much.'

The double-strength century slammed their shields down on the deck and crouched behind them; sailors ran forward to man the two corvi. The hollow thwacking of slingshot thumping into the hull from the beach, just over a hundred paces away, started in earnest. The now familiar sight of massed, clay-daubed tribesmen bellowing their defiance and brandishing their weapons to the blaring of carnyxes sent a shiver of fear down Vespasian's spine; he felt his left hand go clammy as it grasped his shield grip. He offered a silent prayer to his guardian god to spare him this day from falling in a battle that was unnecessary in the short-term but whose long-term political implications he now fully understood.

The hiss of a speeding lead shot passed close to Vespasian's head and he too knelt down behind his shield. 'You'd best get below, Verica.'

The King nodded and walked away towards the stern, erect and seemingly oblivious to the stones and lead that now flew all around. Vespasian glanced to either side; the forty ships of his invasion fleet were all in a line, with no more than five-pace gaps between their oars, and would hit the beach simultaneously; behind them on the right flank were six ships in reserve, carrying Paetus' cavalry.

At a shouted order from the trierarchus the oars were brought rasping in and Vespasian knew that they would hit the beach in a matter of moments. With a sharp cry of pain one of the sailors stumbled back and collapsed at the foot of a corvus, clutching a shattered arm. A roar from the trierarchus sent two more men forward to take his place. Only one man made it to the bow; his mate lay on the deck with blood seeping from his mouth, his forehead shattered by the direct hit of a high-velocity missile.

The hail of shot intensified, ricocheting off shields, the rail and the mast with sharp staccato cracks. Hunched tight behind their leather-clad wooden guards the men of the first cohort grimaced, gritting their teeth as the unrelenting salvo clattered about them and spent shots rolled up and down the heaving deck. Vespasian's ears sang with the report as his shield jolted back and a rounded stone, half the size of a fist, rebounded off and slammed into the shin of a kneeling legionary, cracking the bone and puckering the flesh. The man screamed and clasped his right hand to the wound but kept his shield up knowing, even in his agony, that to lower it would mean death.

The shots trailed off as the ships neared the beach, making the angle impossible for the slingers but bringing them into the range of hand-hurled weapons; javelins and spears rained down and the legionaries raised their shields into an interconnecting roof, but not before two soldiers fell, pierced and bleeding, to the deck.

With the grating rasp of wood on shingle the trireme ground up the beach, decelerating violently. The impact sent many of the legionaries sprawling forward, dismantling the protective roof with catastrophic consequences. Almost a dozen failed to obey Tatius' screamed order to stand and move forward as the two corvi arced down, with a rattle of pulleys and a squeal of hinges, onto the shingle, crushing one warrior who was unable, owing to the press of comrades behind, to move out of the way. As the legionaries ran forward to the ramps the javelin barrage was supplemented by renewed efforts from the slingers, who once again had a direct line of sight. Vespasian raised his shield, deflecting a heavy spear, and, drawing his sword, barged his way into the third rank as they began their descent down the right-hand ramp with a volley of pila. With shot pounding in from the front and sharp iron hissing down from above, the first cohort surged down the vibrating wooden planking, front ranks with their shields forward and the rest raising theirs once they had loosed their pila, knowing that the sooner they closed with the enemy the sooner the heavy hail of missiles would lessen as close contact made their usage nigh on impossible.

Down they coursed into the warriors clustered nine or ten deep at the base of each ramp.

'With me!' Vespasian shouted over his shoulder to the men in the fourth and fifth ranks as the lead legionaries exploded onto the first of the Britons. He jumped off the side of the corvus, taking the men behind him with him, and hurled himself onto the warriors below, punching his shield down as he landed, knocking the sword from a snarling, naked man's hand and following through with his shield boss to split open his face and send him crashing to the shingle. Vespasian landed with a heavy jolt on top of the unconscious warrior and rolled to one side, bringing his shield up over his face as the wicked point of a spear thrust down at him. With an arm-juddering impact, the iron tip embedded itself in the solid wood as a couple of the legionaries who had followed him regained their feet. Vespasian felt the pressure on his shield ease and smelt fresh faeces, suddenly, next to his head. He kicked his shield up and twisted around, getting to his knees as the spear-wielding Briton fell forward, shrieking, his belly slashed open, spewing forth its reeking contents. With no time to acknowledge the man's killer and straining with the added weight, Vespasian forced himself to his feet; he slammed his spear-encumbered shield forward, catching the shaft of the weapon on the shoulder of the next warrior as he endeavoured to close the gap. The impact dislodged the spear; it fell at the warrior's feet, entangling them, and he stumbled, pitching forward onto Vespasian's sword-weighted fist. Then, with a dull crunch of a shattered jaw and teeth, he slumped back. Vespasian moved forward, giving a lightning jab at the throat of the downed tribesman before joining the comrade who had probably saved his life in close combat sword work as more and more legionaries crashed down onto the beach behind them, forcing the Roman line ever wider. Then came what he had been waiting for: a fletched shaft suddenly materialised in the forehead of a warrior in front of him; the Hamians were now shooting into the enemy's ranks, sowing terror amongst them and causing the less steady to back off, relieving some of the pressure on Roman shields.

Although he could not see further than the little bubble of death and violence that encompassed him, Vespasian prayed as he worked his blade that the same scene was being played out in front of each of his vessels: if the Hamians were now shooting from the bow that meant all the legionaries were off the ship.

Feeling the weight behind him steadily increase, he disengaged and ducked down to one side allowing the next man to take his place. Pushing his way back, he made his way to the corvus and clambered back up to the deck. Looking up and down along the beach he saw that most of the ships had disgorged their martial cargo and in a few places centuries from neighbouring vessels had linked up, forming the beginnings of one long front. All the Britons were engaged in clumps around the beached ships; now was the time to seize the initiative.

'Raise the signal flag,' Vespasian called to the trierarchus.

After a brief scurrying of bare-footed sailors, a large, square black flag was hoisted up the mainmast. Within a few moments the reserve ships responded and set a course to land on the extreme right flank. Praying that Paetus would be able to land his cavalry quickly and unhindered, Vespasian barged his way between two Hamians at the bow and returned his attention to the fighting in front of his ship. The first century had pushed the Britons back a few paces, thanks to the earlier archer support. However, to counter this, the Britons had withdrawn slingers behind their line and they had now entered into a missile duel with the Hamians, two of whom were already sprawled on the deck. Deprived of the limited but crucial archer support the first century was now struggling to make any headway in linking up with the second century on their left and the sixth century to their right; fighting in isolation they ran the serious risk of being swamped.

Vespasian turned back to the trierarchus and bellowed: 'Get me twenty or so sailors or oarsmen, with as many javelins as they can carry!' The trierarchus acknowledged the order and Vespasian pulled on the nearest Hamian's shoulder. 'Fall back!'

The archers retreated to the mainmast, the angle of the ship taking them out of the slingers' line of sight; within a few moments the rag-tag crew had joined them and broached the weapons box beneath the mast. They retrieved half a dozen javelins each.

'On my command,' Vespasian shouted over the battle's clamour to the javelinmen, 'run to the bow and get as many shots into the midst of the Britons on the left as you can. The archers will come with you and take care of the slingers. Understood?'

The scratch unit nodded nervously and mumbled the affirmative; the Hamians, more positive, nocked arrows ready to give cover.

Vespasian grabbed a couple of javelins. 'Right ... now!' He sprinted up the sloping deck with his men following; reaching the bow he hurled his first missile into the Britons facing Tatius and then, within an instant, let fly with the second as his men did the same. The Hamians shot a volley at the slingers who, caught unawares, did not reply until the swift archers had released another, bringing down more than half a dozen as javelin after javelin hurtled down into the press of warriors with shocking effect. Slingshot took two of the oarsmen back, blood exploding from ghastly head wounds, before they could release their full complement of missiles; but the rest completed their task and it was enough. The Britons gave ground, such were their losses; Tatius urged his legionaries forward. As he pulled his men back to the mast to rearm, Vespasian glimpsed the extreme left of the first century link up with their comrades from the second next to them.

'We do this once more,' he said as his men emptied the remaining javelins from the weapons box, 'but this time to the extreme right.'

Drawing his sword, Vespasian again raced forward; however, he did not stop at the bow but continued down the ramp, jumping off to the right and running along the rear of legionaries as javelins rained down from the ship. Reaching the last file, who were struggling thigh-deep in blood-red water to prevent the century being outflanked, Vespasian splashed around them and, roaring incoherently, crashed his shield into the side of the first Briton he came to, punching him away from the legionary facing him. Pushing forward to the next man he halted suddenly as a javelin passed just over his shoulder and seared into the tribesman's chest, throwing him back with outstretched arms and shocked dead eyes.

Encouraged by their legate's intervention and the missile barrage from above, the legionaries pressed forward, finding that the weight against them had lessened considerably. Flashing their blades, whilst struggling to keep their footing on the treacherously slippery stones beneath the water, they edged on as the rear ranks of Britons fell to the javelin storm and their resistance began to peter out. Stabbing his sword hard and low into an unprotected thigh and receiving a spray of arterial blood up his arm, Vespasian reached the water's edge; two rear rank legionaries pushed past him to extend the line, stamping on the wounded warrior as he clutched his thigh on the shingle and finishing him with a thrust to the throat. With one final flurry of punching shields and thrusting sword tips they slew or beat off the last few tribesmen between them and the fifth century.

The line was complete.

Vespasian pulled back, breathing in ragged bursts, and stared with wild, combat-hardened eyes up and down the beach; there was no break in the Roman formation, all the cohorts had successfully landed and linked up and were now fighting at least four deep against a much depleted enemy. However, there were scores, maybe hundreds, of Roman dead sprawled in the shallows and on the shingle and he knew that the II Augusta would need a new draft of recruits before it could start its push west the following spring.

A new sound broke over the cacophony of battle, a sound not heard since the first blows had been struck: the call of massed carnyxes. A hundred paces beyond the Britons a group of warriors blew a single note repeatedly on their strange, upright horns. As the note continued the Britons began to pull back. Vespasian sighed in relief; that call could mean only one thing: Cogidubnus' honour was satisfied. He looked around for the cornicen and shouted: 'Disengage!'

Four deep notes rumbled out to be taken up by neighbouring cohorts and soon the soldiers of both armies were stepping away from one another, exhausted and relieved that the ordeal was over. Here and there pockets of violence continued where blood-lust overruled self-preservation until the combat was stopped either by death or the intervention of comrades.

Eventually all hostilities had ceased, the carnyx and cornu calls faded and an eerie quiet descended over the beach, broken only by the moans of the wounded, the lapping of waves and the creaking of ships.

As the Britons withdrew in a line to the carnyx players, one man stayed facing the II Augusta.

Vespasian sheathed his sword and walked forward. 'Keep them formed up, Tatius,' he said, slapping his blood-covered primus pilus on his shoulder as he passed through the ranks. 'And have Verica come and join me.'

Tatius barely acknowledged him, his chest heaving with exertion.

Crunching his way across the shingle, Vespasian approached the solitary man; even given that he was higher up the beach than him, he could see that Cogidubnus was huge, at least a head taller with a bull-like neck around which was wrapped a golden torc as thick as a thumb. Silver arm rings, just as thick, bound bulging biceps as if they needed to be restrained from bursting through the skin.

Vespasian stopped five paces distant and, saying nothing, waited.

Cogidubnus smiled knowingly, inclined his head and approached. 'I am Cogidubnus, King of Vectis.'

'Titus Flavius Vespasianus, legate of the Second Augusta.' To Vespasian's surprise, rather than bowing in submission Cogidubnus held out his arm for Vespasian to grasp as if they were equals. He did not take it but, rather, indicated with his head at the blood encrusted upon it. 'Your honour comes at a very high blood-price, Cogidubnus.'

The King wiped some of the crust away. 'Today is the first time that Roman blood has soiled my skin but not the last time that Britannic blood will soil yours, legate; take my arm in friendship and I swear by Camulos, god of war, that today will also be the last time I shed Roman blood.'

Vespasian looked up into Cogidubnus' pale green eyes; they burnt with pride but showed no hatred nor sign of desire for vengeance. Verica had been right: this man would be Rome's friend and the sacrifice of his men this day to ensure that had been worth it. He grasped the proffered arm with a firm grip; it was returned with more than equal measure.

'You may keep your sword, Cogidubnus.'

'And my crown? Do you have the power to promise me that?'

'No. I'll not lie to you; it's something that's only within the Emperor's gift, but I can—'

The shrill blast of a lituus, from behind the Britons, cut him off. Vespasian jerked his head up in its direction: half a mile away, on a knoll to the right of the Britons' line, glinting in the warm morning sun, appeared Paetus' Batavian ala, formed up ready to charge.

Cogidubnus released his grip and wrenched his arm free. 'Is this Roman honour to take a surrendering enemy from behind?'

The rear rank Britons began to turn to face the new threat, growling their disgust at the perceived treachery.

'Trust me and come with me, Cogidubnus,' Vespasian entreated, looking the towering King in the eye. 'They're not aware of your surrender; they must be assuming that we're at a standoff and that their intervention will make the difference. We can stop this – but we'll have to sprint around your men.'

Cogidubnus held Vespasian's look briefly. 'No, it'll be quicker to go through.' He turned and ran back towards his warriors; Vespasian signalled to Tatius to remain where he was and then followed, pumping his shorter legs ferociously so as not to be outpaced.

As Cogidubnus reached the first of his warriors he slowed to a walk; Vespasian tried to pass him but was restrained by the King's massive hand clamping onto his shoulder.

'We pass through slowly, legate, together.'

Vespasian looked up; Paetus' ala had already begun to move forward. 'But we'll be too late.'

'My men haven't yet laid down their arms; there are many here who would kill you, so stay close.'

Unable to do anything but comply, Vespasian walked forward with the King into the mass of his bloodied and battle-scarred warriors, cutting across them towards the right-hand corner. They parted grudgingly, their mouths set grim beneath their long moustaches, their eyes hard. As Vespasian passed through they closed behind him, towering over him, pressing in on him so that he was engulfed by the stench of their sweat and their hot breath; he kept his head held high, looking neither left nor right, refusing to be intimidated by their height. Cogidubnus spoke soothingly to his people in their own tongue whilst all the time keeping a firm grip on Vespasian's shoulder, emphasising that the Roman was under his protection. Growing shouts of warning and alarm from the rear of the formation told of the approach of Paetus' cavalry but Vespasian could see nothing over the heads of the warriors.

They reached the tribesmen who had turned to face the charge and Cogidubnus moved with more urgency, pushing through, raising his voice to make them move aside. Suddenly the warriors before them extended their spears forward and went down on one knee. Vespasian's heart pounded; Paetus' men were at full charge, almost a javelin throw away. Cogidubnus roared a command to his men and pushed him forward. Shouting for all he was worth Vespasian ran out into the open, holding his right hand, palm out, aloft.

But the volley had been released.

More than three hundred javelins soared through the air towards him, followed by a high-velocity wall of horseflesh. He stopped abruptly, still bellowing at Paetus to stop, and raised his shield. Three evilly sharp points appeared a thumb's breadth through the board before his eyes; the weight of their impact buckled his legs and he collapsed onto his knees, twisting his right hand back to support himself as the burden of the javelins pulled his shield aside leaving him totally exposed.

He stared in horror at horses; nothing but horses: black, bay, dun, brown, grey horses. Eyes wild, mouths foaming, teeth bared, heads tossing, flanks sweating, forelegs kicking, all he could see was horses, horses. Noise suddenly broke into his consciousness: neighing and whinnying; the shouts of men in languages that he could comprehend and in those that he could not; hooves thumping the ground, metal jangling. A confusion of sound, as confusing as the images before him: horses rearing, horses scraping their forelegs through the air, horses everywhere – but not trampling him.

Suddenly he realised he could see their bellies; they were rearing; they were stationary.

And then in twos and threes they came down, snorting, prancing, high-stepping, onto four legs and now he could see their riders, bearded, chain-mailed, helmeted with the same wild eyes as their mounts as they looked fearfully beyond him.

'Stop,' Vespasian shouted hoarsely, as if he could not believe that they had really come to a halt.

'We have, sir, and rather abruptly so.'

Vespasian blinked repeatedly and eventually focused on Paetus looking down at him from a very skittish mount.

'And judging by the fact that these barbarians aren't trying to hack us off our horses, I take it that they've surrendered and that's why you rather foolishly stood in front of our charge.'

'And that's why I ordered my men not to return the volley,' Cogidubnus said, walking forward, 'despite the fact that a score or more have been killed. But many more would have died had it not been for the legate.' He stood over Vespasian, contemplating him with a confused expression for a few moments as if trying to decide just what was kneeling on the grass. He held out his hand and helped Vespasian to his feet.

'Take your men back to the beach, Paetus,' Vespasian ordered, still reeling from the terror. Feeling the weight of the javelins embedded in his shield he threw it down and winced; there were four heads piercing it, not three, and one was bloodied. He turned his arm over to reveal a seeping puncture just below the elbow; a shock of pain suddenly hit him and he clasped his hand to the wound.

Cogidubnus pulled his hand away to examine the injury. 'It's not deep and it'll heal well; it was honourably received. It was a brave act that saved many lives, both Roman and Briton. My crown may not be yours to give, legate, but I would rather accept it from your hand than from an emperor who expects men to die for him whilst he sits in his palace.'

Verica emerged from the ranks of Britons. 'There is no choice in the matter, nephew; it is only the Emperor who has the power to grant your kingdom. However, he is imperfectly formed and cannot fight.'

'Then Rome has the wrong emperor. What is an emperor if he does not lead his men in battle?'

'An emperor is power; power to which you and I must now submit. He is on his way here to lead the army into Camulodunum. When we go there and bow before him we will act as if he has personally achieved the greatest victory and we will laud him as the supreme man on earth, even though he is a fool that drools.'

'And this is the man I must serve, rather than the warrior who defeated me and then saved the lives of many of my men?'

Vespasian kept his face neutral. 'Yes, Cogidubnus, we all must serve him.'

CHAPTER XXI

VESPASIAN STOOD AT the stern of the trireme, next to the trierarchus as he guided the ship into the port of Verica's capital. Sweltering in the hot, late August sun burning down from a cloudless sky, he watched an electrical storm rumble and flash its way along the range of downs, not five miles inland, and marvelled at the strange weather that afflicted this northerly island.

'Taranis, the god of thunder, often visits the southern downs to watch over us,' Verica informed him, clutching the golden, four-spoked wheel pendant around his neck. 'He will require a sacrifice.'

'What sort of sacrifice?'

'Well, it is normally the druids who decide, and they would burn a virgin alive in a tub. However, they've fled west, cursing me as a blasphemer because of my support of Rome, so it's up to me instead.'

'We consider human sacrifice abhorrent.'

'I haven't lived in Rome for three years without realising that; I'll choose a chariot and two horses. I intend to wean my people off the more extreme practices of the druids.'

'What exactly are druids?'

Verica sighed, long and slow. 'They're the priestly class, exempt from taxes and military service; they think they have a monopoly on the will and desires of the gods and so the people both fear them and stand in awe of them at the same time. They do not fear death because they believe that the soul lives on and is transferred into another body; that makes them very dangerous. I'm pleased to have got rid of them because they meddle like women and plot like younger sons; but I'm sure they'll be back, seeking to regain their power over my people, and the first thing they'll try to do is kill me. They belong to no tribe and have no loyalty other than to themselves and the gods of our fathers and of this land.'

'They're different?'

'Yes. When my people came to this island – the bards deem it to be about twenty-five generations ago – the people we supplanted worshipped different gods; they had built great henges in their honour, ancient beyond reckoning. The druids dedicated these places to our gods but still the presence and power of some of the island's gods persisted and they demanded worship.' Verica's face darkened and his voice fell low. 'The druids took on that responsibility and uncovered their dark secrets and rituals; they keep the knowledge to themselves and they're welcome to it; but what I know of it fills me with dread.'

Vespasian felt chilled by the old King's evident fear. 'What is it that disturbs you?'

Verica looked into Vespasian's eyes; his gaze intense. 'Some of these gods have a real power; a cold power that cannot be used for good.'

Vespasian grimaced. 'In the hands of priests?'

'In the hands of fanatical priests.'

'My experience of priests hasn't been good.'

'No one's experience of priests is ever good, unless you happen to be one. My advice to you is to kill them all otherwise Rome will never hold this land. The druids will always be able to rouse the people by putting the fear of the gods into them; they know that there is no place for them under Rome so they will have nothing to lose by being your most implacable enemy.'

Vespasian looked over to Cogidubnus leaning on the rail, watching the approach of the newly built wooden jetty. 'Would your nephew agree with you?'

'Ask him yourself, but yes, he would. He understands, as I do, that if we are going to bring our people into the modern world and share in all the prosperity that that entails then we have to look forward; the druids only ever look back.'

Vespasian contemplated this as the ship slowed, nearing the jetty. His experience of Rhoteces, the duplicitous Thracian priest, and Ahmose, the lying priest of Amun, as well as the self-serving Jew, Paulus, who had usurped the Jewish sect he had once persecuted and had begun moulding it into an unnatural religion based upon redemption in some theoretical afterlife, had left him fully aware of the power religion had to stir men into fighting, and how susceptible that power was to abuse. 'We shall have a hard journey west, then.'

'With the druids opposing you, yes, you will. But you will also find men like me out there who have no love for them and would rather be subject to Rome than to priests.'

'I'd hope that given the choice all men would choose Rome over priests.'

Verica smiled. 'Knowing their love of power, I think that the day the priests realise that will be the day that they start plotting to take over Rome.'

Vespasian shuddered at the thought as the trireme gently docked to an accompaniment of nautical orders and hurling ropes.

'You'd better hurry, sir,' Magnus' voice shouted over the noise.

Vespasian looked up to see his friend climbing up the gangplank. 'Why? What is it?'

'It would seem that the Emperor is anxious to get his victory. Sabinus sent a message saying that Claudius' reinforcements have just arrived at the Tamesis bridge in preparation for his arrival. He's inspecting Gesoriacum and then he's going on to Rutupiae and after that he's sailing up the Tamesis; he'll be at the bridge in two days.'

Vespasian and Sabinus snapped to attention as a fanfare rose from the imperial quinquereme upon whose deck stood over a hundred senators, resplendent in their purple-bordered togas. Festooned in purple and complete with an imperial tent at the stern, the vessel was docked at a jetty on the southern side of the newly constructed wooden bridge across the Tamesis. Aulus Plautius marched to the foot of the gangway and saluted as it was lowered. The fanfare broke off and, apart from cawing seagulls flitting on the light breeze, an expectant silence fell over the two Praetorian cohorts and the four from the VIII Legion and their auxiliaries formed up along the riverbank with Decimus Valerius Asiaticus at their head.

After a pause of imperial proportions the tent flaps were drawn back and a silhouetted figure stood in the entrance.

'Imperator!' cried a single voice from within the Praetorian ranks.

The cry was taken up by all present, soaring to the sky, scaring off the gulls, as the acclamation of 'imperator' was heard for the first time on the island of Britannia.

'He hasn't even seen a Briton and he's already being lauded as a victor,' Sabinus shouted in Vespasian's ear.

'And the men lauding him haven't even done any of the fighting,' Vespasian observed before joining his brother in the accolade.

As the chant grew, Claudius, complete with laurel victor's crown and wearing full, imperial military uniform – purple cloak, gold-inlaid bronze cuirass and greaves, a purple sash around his waist and with a purple-plumed, ornate helmet under his left arm – shambled forward, head twitching with excitement and right arm jerking as he acknowledged the crowd: a comic parody of an emperor.

Vespasian was relieved that he could shout, otherwise he feared that he would burst into unrestrained laughter at the sight of such an unmartial man in such military attire. A sideways glance at Sabinus, who caught his eye for an instant, confirmed that his brother was having the same thoughts. For once in perfect accord, the siblings feted their Emperor.

Narcissus and Pallas then appeared from the tent and walked hurriedly to catch Claudius up before he attempted to descend the gangway unaided. They each took an imperial elbow and guided their master down onto the jetty. Aulus Plautius brought his arm down from across his chest and, standing to attention, head and shoulders back, bellowed with the rest. Claudius approached him and, with much ceremony and saliva, embraced and kissed him.

The chant turned into cheers as the Emperor held the general in his arms for a few moments before turning to face the troops. Claudius gestured for silence as Plautius stared straight ahead, trying to ignore the drool on his cheeks.

'S-s-soldiers of Rome,' Claudius declaimed, once the cheering had died away, 'my g-g-gallant general has asked for his E-E-Emperor's assistance and advice in defeating the Britons.' He paused and gestured to the senators. 'The Senate of Rome begged me to heed his call, saying that General Plautius has g-g-g-got so far but has r-run into fierce opposition of the kind that only I, your Emperor, can overcome.'

The senators all nodded sagely, twisting their faces into expressions of theatrical relief. Vespasian cast his eyes along their number as Claudius stumbled on and was pleased to see the corpulent form of his uncle; Gaius shrugged as he caught his eye and carried on listening with exaggerated concentration to the Emperor.

'So follow me, soldiers of Rome, f-f-follow me and I will lead you to a glorious victory, a victory that will be remembered for generations as the triumph of your Emperor Claudius over the barbarian hordes. I have come, I now see, I will c-c-conquer!'

Claudius turned to Narcissus, Pallas and the senators, who all laughed obligingly at this pathetic paraphrase; Vespasian noted that his uncle seemed to find it the pithiest line ever uttered. The legionaries once again cheered their Emperor, pleased, no doubt, to have an excuse not to have to make an overt display of enjoying Claudius' feeble wit.

Vespasian and Sabinus joined in the cheering; only Plautius did not. He stood rigid, his neck bulging in anger, staring at the quinquereme.

Vespasian followed his gaze: at the entrance of the tent stood the copious figure of Sentius Saturninus, which did not surprise him; what did surprise him was the man standing behind him: Geta. Vespasian nudged Sabinus and indicated to the tent. 'How in Mars' name did he get here?'

'Ah! So that's where the little shit has got to,' Sabinus muttered. 'I should have guessed. Soon after you went south,

Plautius sent for him; he never came, disappeared in fact. He must have heard about Plautius detaining Corvinus and his guilty conscience told him that he was liable to share the same fate.'

'So he ran to the Emperor to put his side of the story first.'

'And a very heroic side it will be, I'm sure.'

'The bastard!'

'Maybe, but he's a sensible bastard.'

Narcissus pointed at the horn-blowers and another fanfare blew, silencing the cheering.

Claudius walked along the jetty towards the two brothers with Narcissus and Pallas following. 'Ah! My loyal F-F-Flavians, the returners of the Nineteenth's Capricorn.'

The brothers bowed their heads. 'Princeps.'

'You have been outshone by P-P-Publius Gabinius who recently returned the Eagle of the Seventeenth to me. But no matter, your feat was useful; let your Emperor embrace you.'

Vespasian tried not to wince as he was clasped to the imperial bosom and received an overly moist kiss on both cheeks.

'Will you follow me as I drive the enemy from their strong-holds?' Claudius asked, having subjected Sabinus to the same treatment.

'Yes, Princeps.'

'We shall have a f-f-fine time of it.' Claudius twitched and stepped back; he looked the brothers up and down apprecia-tively and then frowned. 'What's that?'

Vespasian followed his gaze and put his hand on his sword hilt. 'That's my sword, Princeps.'

'I know that weapon.'

'Yes, Princeps, it was your grandfather Marcus Antonius' sword.'

Claudius' eyes probed Vespasian's. 'And then it was my father's and after him it went to my brother, Germanicus.'

'That's correct, Princeps.'

'I know it's c-c-correct! I know my own family's history. I also know that when Germanicus died Agrippina wanted to give it to her eldest son but my mother, Antonia, refused her, saying that she would decide; but she never did. After she died I looked for it but it was nowhere to be found. I asked P-P-Pallas but he denied all knowledge of it.'

Vespasian glanced over Claudius' shoulder to Pallas; the Greek freedman's normally neutral faced betrayed a vague flicker of anxiety.

'So how did you come to own it?'

Pallas caught Vespasian's eye and shook his head a fraction.

Vespasian swallowed. 'Caligula gave it to me, Princeps.'

'D-d-did he now? And how did he come to have it?'

'I don't know, Princeps. Antonia must have given it to him.'

'I doubt it. It w-w-was common knowledge in my family that Antonia was going to give it to the person she thought would make the best Emperor; she didn't by any chance give it to you, did she, Vespasian?'

'No, Princeps; as I said, Caligula gave it to me.'

Claudius studied him for a short while, twitching frantically and dribbling from the corner of his mouth. 'Well, he had no right to.' He held out a shaking hand. 'Seeing as I've come to wage war it is only right for me to do so with my family sword; give it to me.'

Without hesitation, Vespasian unclipped the scabbard from his baldric and passed it to Claudius.

'Thank you, legate. I wouldn't like to think that my mother gave it to you; you haven't got the b-b-blood of the Caesars in you.'

'Indeed not, Princeps.'

'G-g-good. We'll say no more ab-about it.' Claudius drew the sword and examined the blade, tracing the engraved name of his grandfather. 'A noble blade now back where it belongs.' He lifted it above his head with ridiculous theatricality and addressed the troops. 'With the sword of my sires I lead you to war.'

To cries of 'Hail Caesar!' he lurched off towards a quadriga, harnessed to four white horses, waiting for him on the bridge.

'Did our master catch you fibbing, colleague?' Narcissus enquired of Pallas.

'Never, my dear Narcissus, it must have been exactly as Vespasian said; wasn't it, Vespasian?'

'Exactly, Pallas.'

Narcissus raised an eyebrow at Pallas. 'I do hope so; you know how nervous he is about plots against him. We wouldn't want Claudius thinking that *your* protégé harbours any unrealistic ambitions.' With a courteous inclination of the head to the two brothers he followed his master.

'Never let the truth be known, Vespasian,' Pallas warned as he passed. 'Messalina has Claudius seeing threats everywhere to distract from herself. He's becoming irrational; executions have already started.'

'What was that all about?' Sabinus asked as Pallas walked away.

'That, brother, was about people reading too much into a simple gift.'

'So Antonia did give it to you, despite her saying that she would only give it to the person she thought would make the best Emperor?'

'Yes.'

'Well then, what if she was right?'

'How could she be? We don't have the blood of the Caesars.'

'The blood of the Caesars? How long is that going to last?'

As Claudius began to lead his army across the bridge Vespasian watched the heir to Gaius Julius Caesar follow in the great man's footsteps to the northern bank of the Tamesis and was struck by just how much the bloodline had deteriorated. How long could it last? And when it finally failed whose would replace it?

Again, the ludicrous thought that he had tried to suppress came to his mind. 'Why not?' he muttered to himself. 'Why not indeed?'

'Dear boys,' Gaius Vespasius Pollo boomed as the senators filed off the ship, 'I'm relieved to see you with all your limbs in place.' He slapped an arm around each of their shoulders, led them away from the crowd and lowered his voice. 'Thank the gods this ghastly affair is almost over; it's been almost insupportable listening to that drooling fool going on about how grave the situation must be if Plautius felt it necessary to call for him.'

Vespasian frowned, curling his lip in disbelief. 'You mean he actually believes this farce, Uncle?'

'Believes it? He's convinced that only he can save the whole endeavour from becoming an even worse defeat than Teutoburg. He's been going on about how fortunate Rome is to have an emperor who has read every military history and manual written and has a complete understanding of the strategy and tactics of warfare.'

'Is that why he's brought half the Senate with him, so that he can show off his martial prowess to a flock of sycophants?'

'Don't be such a hypocrite, dear boy; I've seen you practise the life-lengthening art of sycophancy with tremendous skill. But to answer your question: no; at least that's not the main reason. We're here to ensure our good behaviour; Claudius' insecurity means that he wants to keep the people that he distrusts the most, closest.'

'So why are you here? You've never done anything but enthusiastically support whoever's in power.'

Gaius laughed without humour. 'I know, but you're both commanding legions; I'm here to remind you of the fact that your families are at Claudius' mercy back in Rome, should you think of misusing your legionaries.'

'But Narcissus—'

'Dear boy, this has nothing to do with Narcissus; this is purely Claudius, he's got a taste for power and blood and he enjoys savouring them both to feed his paranoia. He's executed more senators and equites in his first two years than Caligula did.'

'If he's so worried about his position why did he leave Rome?'

'It's a gamble, I agree; but every senator who has been left behind has a kinsman here under Claudius' eye. And he's left Lucius Vitellius, who was his colleague in the consulship for the first part of this year, nominally in control of Rome – although in practice Callistus will make the decisions as he's the only one left in the city who understands how the enormous bureaucracy that he and his fellow freedmen have created works. Claudius feels that he can trust Vitellius because he's a favourite of Messalina; so the Venus only knows what that little whore will get up to whilst her husband's away and Vitellius turns a blind eye.'

'Is she as bad as that?' Sabinus asked, evidently interested. 'Narcissus mentioned that she was rather willing, to say the least.'

'Rather willing? She's a female Caligula; anyone who spurns her advances finds themselves accused of treason. She's got her husband so obsessed about the Senate plotting against him that they're almost invariably convicted.' He waved a hand at the passing senators. 'She's sucked the cock of every one of these men under the age of fifty and Claudius won't see it. I can only thank the gods that I am past my prime otherwise I would be subject to the intolerable ministrations of that harpy. You watch yourselves when you come back to Rome or she'll have you in her web; but if you're sensible you'll both stay away for as long as possible.'

Vespasian cast a questioning look at his brother, who, understanding, nodded his agreement. 'I think that Narcissus has plans for her—'

Gaius' hand moved from Vespasian's shoulder to his mouth, clamping it shut, with surprising swiftness. 'I don't want to know! I want to live out the few years remaining to me in blissful ignorance of imperial politics as I intend to die in my bed and not in my bath with my blood swirling around me. The only reason that I attend the Senate any more is because of the intolerable situation at home.'

'Flavia?'

'Yes, she and your mother do not see eye to eye and both look to me to adjudicate their petty female squabbles; unfortunately I don't have enough correspondence to keep me in my study all evening so I'm forced to face them for an hour or two each day.'

Sabinus laughed as they watched the last of the troops cross the bridge. 'It looks like you're going to have to take on the expense of a house, brother, for the sake of our uncle's sanity.'

'Thank you, Sabinus, but I'll make my own decisions about where my family live.'

Gaius looked at him, his eyes suddenly hard. 'No, Vespasian, you must get Flavia her own home; until she has her own household to terrorise she will make my life a misery.'

He was serious; deadly serious. Vespasian had never heard him use that tone before. 'I'll do it as soon as I get back to Rome, Uncle, I promise.'

'No, dear boy, *I'll* do it for you as soon as *I* get back to Rome; this situation cannot continue.'

'But what shall I do for money?'

'You're commanding a legion subduing a new province: slaves and plunder, dear boy.'

'I suppose you're right.'

'I am; now let's go and watch our glorious Emperor-General show everybody how it should be done.'

'G-g-gentlemen, that army is all that stands between us and C-C-Camulodunum,' Claudius announced, pointing an unsteady hand at the poorly armed ragged mass of prisoners lined along the far bank of a stream. 'How many would you say there are, Plautius?'

Plautius scanned the paltry number. 'At least ten thousand, Princeps,' he replied, doubling what he knew to be the truth.

Claudius twitched with excitement. 'Excellent. I shall crush them within the hour. Plautius, what were my battle orders?'

Plautius flicked a subtle glance at the officers present. 'I believe you wanted the Praetorian cohorts in the centre with the four cohorts of the Eighth and then the Fourteenth on the right, the Twentieth on the left and the Ninth held back in reserve.'

'My b-b-brother-in-law's legion in reserve? That won't do. Corvinus must be on the right flank in the place of honour; the Fourteenth will be my reserve.'

'Corvinus no longer commands the Ninth, Princeps, he's awaiting trial by you for disobeying orders.'

'Disobeying what orders? That's the first I've heard of it. Why didn't you tell me about it, Narcissus?'

Narcissus cleared his throat. 'I didn't know, Princeps.'

'You're meant to know everything and keep me informed. Plautius, why didn't you tell him?'

Plautius shot the freedman a venomous look. 'I er ... I sent a despatch but it must have gone astray.'

'Indeed it must have, because I'm sure that had Narcissus known about it he would have ordered my brother-in-law released, whatever he had done.'

'But he tried to take Camulodunum without you, Princeps, and leave you nothing to conquer.'

'That is most serious, Princeps,' Narcissus interjected, with a rare look of exaggerated shock on his face. 'Why would he have tried to steal your victory? Was he trying to set himself up over you?'

Claudius chuckled. 'No, he's not like the jealous senators who are always plotting; he's family. He was just being impetuous like my darling wife; you can tell that they're brother and sister. Well, no matter, he didn't succeed and there still is an army for me to beat and a town for me to capture, otherwise I wouldn't have been sent for, would I, Narcissus?'

Narcissus was momentarily lost for words.

Despite enjoying the slight twitch at the corner of Narcissus' mouth as he realised that to damn Corvinus he would have to admit to Claudius that this battle was a farce and Camulodunum had already surrendered, Vespasian felt a chill. 'The idiot's going to let him go,' he whispered into Sabinus' ear.

Sabinus chewed on his lip. 'And I don't suppose our part in arresting Corvinus will go unnoticed.'

'Well, Narcissus?' Claudius pressed. 'Has Corvinus stolen my victory?'

'It would seem not, Princeps.'

'Then why is a member of the imperial family being detained? Have him brought here immediately, Plautius; the Ninth will take the right flank and my Messalina's brother will command it and share in my glory. The rest of you, get to your posts, I'm eager for battle.'

With no legion to command Vespasian sat watching the farce with Magnus, at the head of Paetus' cavalry, which had escorted him from the coast. To the right of them the senators sat on chairs viewing the proceedings as if at a race day in the Circus Maximus.

'It just goes to show that you can be too devious for your own good,' Magnus commented as they watched the lead cohorts of the VIIII Hispana advance across the stream and make contact with the fraudulent army of Britons beyond, 'and everybody else's, for that matter.'

'Except for Corvinus' good,' Vespasian reminded him as the first screams of the wounded echoed over the field. 'He'll come out of this as a wronged hero in Claudius' eyes.'

'And he'll be after you.'

Vespasian shrugged. 'We'll be far apart; once Claudius leaves I'll go back south to the Second, and the Ninth will stay here and then head north up the east coast next season.'

'That's if Plautius stays in command.'

'Oh, he'll still be in command,' Pallas affirmed, riding up behind them and once again taking Vespasian by surprise. 'I'm sure that Claudius would like to get rid of him at the moment but he'll soon see sense once Narcissus and I explain to him that appointing another general would mean two men requiring public acknowledgement back in Rome; best to keep praise limited, don't you think? After this, Claudius can return to a triumph and then when Plautius comes back, in four years or so, Claudius can show the people that he's an inclusive emperor by magnanimously awarding an ovation to someone who's not a member of the imperial family; for obvious reasons, that's not something that one would want to do twice.'

Vespasian shook his head with regret. 'Won't you ever stop scheming, Pallas?'

'How else can a mere freedman wield power? I'm nothing without Claudius; my fortune is bound up in him remaining emperor, and with this battle we've secured that for the near future.'

'At the cost of the lives of a few thousand British prisoners,' Magnus muttered as the Praetorian cohorts drove the centre of the British line ever back.

'I'm told that they were given the choice between crucifixion and chancing their luck with a weapon in their hand. It's a small price to pay for having the Senate witness the Emperor lead legions in battle; and an elderly emperor at that.'

'Ah! So that's your next worry,' Vespasian said, 'Claudius dying. Surely you just attach yourself to Claudius' son?'

'That would be a foolish move; the boy's only two and will lose his mother as soon as we can contrive it. If Claudius is lucky with his frail health he might live another ten or so years but he'll die before his son reaches manhood; so who would be regent? There are no acceptable choices left; the bloodline is almost dry. The Senate will never accept being ruled over by a child and Republican sentiments will come to the fore again, which will put them in direct opposition to the Praetorian Guard, leading to chaos. I'm afraid the boy is destined to be a Tiberius Gemellus; he will never be emperor and will be killed by whoever succeeds Claudius.'

'And you know who that will be, I suppose.'

Pallas raised a knowing eyebrow. 'If Claudius is lucky and lives for ten years, then yes, and you would do well to follow my lead when you return to Rome because I intend to pick the winning chariot in this race. I'm telling you this as a friend: when Messalina dies watch whom I cultivate and you'll understand.'

'You're as mysterious as ever, Pallas.'

'I learnt from my late mistress Antonia that it doesn't do to be too open with your plans.' A huge cheer erupted from the Roman formation, which quickly transformed into a chant of 'imperator'. 'Well, that was quickly done, come gentlemen, it's time to join our glorious Emperor on his victorious entry into Camulodunum.'

The legionaries of the XIIII Gemina stood to rigid attention, lining the sun-hardened-mud main street of Camulodunum, keeping the local population back as Claudius entered their town.

Although not big by Roman standards, Camulodunum was the largest settlement in the south of the island and even boasted a scattering of brick-built public buildings. Its few thousand inhabitants lived mainly in round huts in family groupings and, similar to Mattium in Germania, there did not seem to be much thought put into civic planning away from the main street and marketplace.

Surrounded by a sturdy palisade, three times the height of a man, almost a mile in circumference and protected on its northern side by a navigable river – its lucrative trade route to the Northern Sea and on to the Rhenus – it would have been a formidable town to take by storm and Vespasian, riding behind Claudius, felt a certain relief that they had not been obliged to.

The local populace gasped in awe as Claudius entered their town; two massive beasts, the likes of which had never been seen before in Britannia, pulled their new master's chariot. Large and lumbering and draped in purple cloth, with huge ears, long swaying proboscises and fearsome tusks sheathed in gold, the elephants impressed the people of Camulodunum more than the display of military might that followed behind them.

The legionaries of the XIIII Gemina hailed their Emperor as he passed with yet another chant of 'imperator', drowning out the townsfolk's rumble of astonishment at the contrast between the magnificent animals and the malformed man whom they drew. No amount of purple or gold could make Claudius look imperial; standing unsteadily in the chariot as it bumped along the rough street, with one hand grasping its side whilst the other was held aloft, palm out, acknowledging his ovation, he struggled but failed to control all the tics that afflicted his twisted body.

Immediately behind the imperial chariot rode Narcissus and Pallas between Aulus Plautius and Sentius Saturninus, both of whom smouldered with indignation at being publicly accompanied by freedmen. Vespasian and his fellow legates followed behind them in icy silence. Then came the senators, walking with sombre dignity, ignoring the stares and the pointing that their attire elicited as the people of Camulodunum caught, what was for many, their first sight of a toga. Finally, in marched the Praetorian cohorts followed by the senior cohort of both the XX Legion and the VIIII Hispana, joining in the chant of their comrades lining the way.

Vespasian glanced to his left at Corvinus; his face was set in the same expression that he had worn for the last two days since Claudius' mock victory: smug, self-satisfied.

'Worried are you, bumpkin?' Corvinus sneered, catching Vespasian's look.

'Why should I be? I was just protecting the Emperor's interests.'

'The Emperor's interests? Bollocks. Since when was Narcissus the Emperor? I know exactly what you were doing; and I know exactly how to prevent you from meddling again next time our paths cross.'

'Thankfully that won't be for a while, Corvinus; you'll be in the north and I'll be in the south.'

'Wrong, bumpkin, I'll be in Rome. I've got what I need from this campaign and have no desire to carry on commanding the Ninth when my officers are so untrustworthy, so I've had a quiet chat with my dear brother-in-law, a couple of quiet chats, actually; he's agreed that I should return to Rome to look after his business in the Senate and be close to the family. Talking of family, in that second chat I had with Claudius I made a suggestion – as a concerned uncle, you understand – about the future wellbeing of his son. I think you'll find it very amusing.'

'Nothing that you do amuses me.'

'We'll see, bumpkin, we'll see.'

Vespasian turned away and edged his horse closer to Sabinus. Up ahead the imperial chariot had reached the marketplace, again lined with legionaries. The mahouts steered their charges to one side, revealing, at the far end, eleven British Kings and chieftains, amongst them, Verica and Cogidubnus, kneeling in submission in front of an empty curule chair; their swords lay on the ground before them.

Pallas and Narcissus dismounted and hurried over to their master as the mahouts brought the elephants to a halt; helping him down, they guided him to the chair.

'Follow me, gentlemen,' Plautius ordered, swinging off his horse and handing the reins to a waiting slave. He walked over to stand behind Claudius, facing the men who were about to pay homage to the physical embodiment of Rome's power.

Vespasian took his place beside Plautius with Sentius and the other legates; the senators gathered behind them as the Praetorian cohorts marched in and filled the remainder of the marketplace, leaving the legionary cohorts backed up along the road.

A hush fell.

Vespasian stood, waiting for something to happen; eventually Narcissus cleared his throat, meaningfully, looking at Claudius.

'Ah, y-y-yes,' Claudius spluttered, sitting as upright as he could in the backless chair, 'of course. Who speaks for the Britons?'

Verica raised his head. 'Every man here speaks only for himself and his tribe but our words are the same: we accept Rome and we bow to her Emperor.'

'C-c-come forward and receive Rome's friendship.'

One by one the Britons came forward, shuffling on their knees, their swords held out before them resting on the palms of their hands. Claudius bade each in turn to rise and confirmed him in his position of king of his tribe or chieftain of a sub-tribe under Rome.

Vespasian read the shame on each face. The ceremony was a public humiliation of these proud men. Cogidubnus caught his eye, as he rose to his feet before the Emperor, with a look of bemused disbelief at the form that the power of Rome took. Vespasian inclined his head fractionally and the King of Vectis, shaking his, backed away and returned to his place.

Verica was the last to subject himself to the ordeal; once he had submitted there was a stir amongst the Praetorians off to the left. Claudius struggled to his feet, helped by Pallas and Narcissus, and turned to face the senators as a Praetorian centurion approached him holding an imperial Eagle.

Claudius gave a lopsided smile and taking the shaft held it aloft for the senators to see. 'Members of the Senate, do you know what Eagle this is?'

There were mutters but no replies.

'This is the E-E-Eagle that none of you would have seen for thirty-four years. This is the Eagle that just three months ago I presented to my loyal troops in gratitude for the suffering that they were willing to undertake in coming to this island. This, Conscript Fathers, is the Eagle of the Seventeenth. I, Claudius, have raised the last fallen Eagle of Rome and I ask you to return to Rome with me and place this Eagle where it belongs: in the Temple of Mars.'

The senators burst into loud and enthusiastic cheering and applause.

Vespasian looked at his brother. 'And what were we doing whilst Claudius was bravely raising this fallen Eagle?'

'Surviving, brother.'

'We return to Rome together,' Claudius continued, 'but first we must organise this new province that I have won for Rome, the province of Britannia. This shall be its capital and here I shall build a temple in my honour. For his help in aiding me in this great victory, I name Aulus Plautius as the first Governor of Britannia and I award him the right to wear Triumphal Ornaments. Come forward, Plautius, and once again receive your Emperor's thanks.'

Stiff and formal, Plautius approached Claudius and was again embraced; this time Claudius whispered a few words in his ear and when he turned away the general was clearly burning with indignation. Plautius paused and then held his head back. 'Conscript Fathers, I must offer my thanks to you for persuading our Emperor to make this long journey and come to my aid. Without his leadership and strategic and tactical abilities our cause would have been lost and we would have been thrown back into the sea.'

The senators applauded this sentiment, enjoying the implication that they had played a decisive part in the conquest of Britannia, whilst neglecting the fact that it was very far from over.

Vespasian glimpsed Pallas and Narcissus exchange a look between them; although it was fleeting it hinted at the immense satisfaction that they were both feeling. 'They'll have made Claudius the darling of the people when all this is reported back in Rome,' he muttered to Sabinus. 'And the Senate get to reflect in his glory because they're the ones who begged him to come.'

'And they're the ones who will return the Eagle with him; it makes me feel queasy.'

'Yes, it's terrifying; if a man like Claudius can be kept in power by his freedmen, who knows what we might get next?' Vespasian's mouth twisted in distaste.

Claudius handed the Eagle back to the centurion. 'I shall also award the right to wear T-T-Triumphal Ornaments to C-Corvinus, the brother of my darling wife, whose role in the conquest has been crucial throughout.'

Vespasian's shook his head in disbelief. 'Crucial?'

Corvinus went forward; his face was a picture of subservient gratitude as he received the Emperor's embrace.

'How did he go from treason to Triumphal Ornaments?' Sabinus muttered, not bothering to hide his outrage.

'By coming from the right family, brother. Magnus was right: people from families like ours are wasting their time.'

'And Triumphal Ornaments will also go to the three subsidiary legates; firstly, Hosidius Geta whose bravery at the Afon Cantiacii saved his cavalry from capture by the enemy. Despite being surrounded and severely wounded, he led his men to safety.'

Aulus Plautius did little to conceal his opinion of this version of the events that Claudius had been given, and Geta did little to conceal the fact that his general's opinion did not concern him in the slightest as he returned from Claudius' embrace.

'And then my loyal Flavians, hard-working, honest and happy to toil in the shadow of greater men for little reward, come forward.'

Vespasian submitted to Claudius' clutches, receiving yet more unwelcome kisses. 'Thank you, Princeps.'

Claudius held his shoulders and looked him in the eye. 'I hope that I will still be able to refer to you as my loyal Flavian when you return to Rome.'

'Always, Princeps.'

'I've been told that you have an infant daughter and a son a few months older than mine?'

'Indeed, Princeps.'

'And I believe that you have no house of your own and that your family is lodging with your uncle, Gaius Vespasius Pollo.'

'That's correct,' Vespasian replied hesitantly, wondering why Claudius had all of a sudden taken such an interest in his domestic affairs.

'Then that's perfect. When I get back to Rome I will arrange for your wife to move into an apartment in the palace; I'm sure she would appreciate her own home and I'm sure that my darling Messalina would love her company. And then, of course, our two boys can be playmates.'

Vespasian felt sick as Claudius released him from his grip. Playmates? Forcing down the horror that welled inside of him, he kept his face blank as he walked away from the Emperor, past Corvinus, who smiled, broad and innocent.

Flavia had got her wish, a home of her own.

But whilst he served the Emperor in Britannia, his wife and children would live or die in Rome at the whim of Corvinus and his sister, the Empress, Messalina.

AUTHOR'S NOTE

THIS WORK OF Historical Fiction is based on the writings of Suetonius, Tacitus, Cassius Dio and Josephus.

Josephus gives us the most detailed description of Caligula's assassination and Claudius' elevation and I have kept to the basic facts; however, for the sake of the narrative I have compressed the time-line somewhat. Milonia Caesonia and her daughter, Julia Drusilla, were murdered by Lupus the following day, not immediately after Caligula's death in a covered passage; the young girl's head was, however, dashed against a wall. The deliberations of the Senate and the toing and froing between them and the Praetorian camp, where Claudius was being held, went on for a couple of days. Herod Agrippa did play a major role in the transition of power, which explains why Josephus recounts the episode in such detail.

The plot to kill Caligula was far more wide-ranging than I have shown but I have kept the numbers of conspirators down for simplicity's sake. Callistus is mentioned by Cassius Dio, who also gives us the pleasing detail of the Consul, Pomponius Secundus, kissing Caligula's slippers whilst watching the entertainment. Suetonius tells us that a farce called *Laureolus* and a tragedy by Cinyras had been performed that morning and in true Suetonius style he points out that the same tragedy had been performed at the games at which Philip II of Macedon was assassinated. Not having access to either of these two pieces I used *The Pot of Gold* by Plautus translated by a fellow alumnus of Christ's Hospital school, E. F. Watling.

Sabinus being involved in the conspiracy is my fiction, although his brother-in-law, Clemens, is mentioned by Josephus and was executed, along with most of the others, for his part in the plot. A couple of the conspirators were allowed to commit suicide, Cornelius Sabinus being one of them, but I have taken the liberty of having them all executed for dramatic effect.

The influence that Claudius' freedmen had over their master is a subject for debate. In this fiction I have chosen to emphasise it. However, the fact that they all became immensely wealthy before their various demises shows that their influence must have been considerable.

We do not know when Vespasian's father died; in all likelihood it would have been earlier than this but I kept him hanging on, firstly for the plot and also so that there could be a farewell.

Artebudz's mention of his memorial to his father, Brogduos, is a reference to one of the only two surviving inscriptions in the Noric language that, coming from Noricum, Artebudz would have spoken. Rather pleasingly Artebudz probably translates as 'bear penis'; I wonder how he would get on at school nowadays!

Suetonius tells us that it was through Narcissus' patronage that Vespasian received the command of the II Augusta.

The future Emperor Galba was Governor of Germania Superior at this time so Vespasian would have met him when he arrived there in AD 41. Galba did indeed repel a Chatti raid in this year.

Corbulo being the legate whom Vespasian takes over from is, of course, fiction; as an ex-consul he was far too senior for such a post but it is not entirely unfeasible for Caligula to have given him the post as a humiliation. However, I wanted him there so that we could have a scene with him and Lucius Paetus; later in life they were both generals out in the East and the steady and reliable Corbulo had to come to the aid of the flamboyant Paetus. Their mutual loathing did not help the conduct of that campaign.

Publius Gabinius is credited by Tacitus and Cassius Dio with the retrieval of the lost Eagle of the XVII from the Chauci in AD 41; Vespasian and Sabinus' part in it is my fiction, as is the role of Thumelicus. Thumelicus and Thusnelda were sent to Ravenna after starring in Germanicus' triumph; Tacitus tells us that Thumelicus was trained as a gladiator and promises to tell us his fate at the appropriate time in his narrative. The fact that he never does probably means that Thumelicus died in one of the gaps in *The Annals*, most likely between AD 29 and 31. However, it is not impossible that it was during the later gap between AD 37 and 47, in which case I felt justified in having him alive for this fiction.

Adgandestrius was King of the Chatti at this time and had offered Tiberius to poison Arminius; the offer had been declined. Arminius' Germanic name may well have been Erminaz, and I have added the 't' to make it Erminatz to get closer to modern German pronunciation.

As to the invasion of Britannia: we know very little about it from the primary sources, Tacitus' account being lost, Cassius Dio's being short and Suetonius being dismissively brief in his biography of Claudius and sketchy in that of Vespasian. In fact, the only legion that we can say with some certainty that took part was the II Augusta, as we know that Vespasian was the legate at the time and he is attested as being a part of the invasion by both Suetonius and Cassius Dio, who also mentions Sabinus and Geta; Corvinus being the fourth legate is my fiction. Archaeological evidence places the VIIII, XIIII and XX Legions as part of the force and that is now accepted so I have gone with it, although it is by no means certain.

The operation itself was massive and nothing was seen on that scale again until the Normandy landings – a conjecture that will no doubt leave me open to many letters. To appreciate the huge logistical undertaking I thoroughly recommend John Peddie's masterful *Conquest: The Roman Invasion of Britain*. Brigadier Peddie approaches the subject from a military as well as a historical point of view and fills in the gaps of our knowledge with practical military hypotheses. With the Romans being both military and practical I found Peddie's analysis of what might have happened the most convincing that I have read, and therefore based my account of the invasion and a good deal of the battle of the Medway on his work. I have also used his research into the auxiliary cohorts that may have taken part in the invasion and his calculation of when the invasion must have taken place in order to get the Emperor back across the Channel before the autumn equinox. Thank you, John.

The troops did at first refuse to embark and Cassius Dio tells us that it was the bizarre sight of a freedman, Narcissus, attempting to address free soldiers of Rome in the Emperor's name that caused such amusement with cries of 'Io Saturnalia!' that they decided to follow Plautius willingly. I have embellished this somewhat, and the use of the XVII's Eagle is my fiction, as is Caenis becoming Narcissus' secretary.

Romans held their markets every eight days, but because they counted inclusively a 'market interval' was reckoned as being nine days.

I have discounted the theory of landing at Chichester Harbour due to the unsupportable nature of an advance north to the Thames and the exposure of both flanks of the column to hostile territory. Likewise I have discounted the fanciful idea that Sentius Saturninus took the VIIII Hispana in at York and then came south; firstly the supply lines would be so long over the treacherous North Sea as to make it an exercise in madness and secondly because Saturninus had been consul two years previously and therefore was very unlikely to have been a legate. I have also discounted the idea of three separate landings because it would seem foolish to divide one's force before one has secured a safe amount of territory and, seeing as the major objective was Camulodunum, the obvious way to get there seems to me as I have described in the narrative. The three separate forces that Cassius Dio mentions I have chosen to interpret as three waves.

I have placed the landing at Richborough, or Rutupiae, because to me that makes most strategic sense. Thanet was a proper island at that time and the main part of the fleet probably landed in the strait between it and the mainland that has now become the Wantsum channel. The shooting star that Cassius Dio mentions travelling from east to west in the direction that they were sailing is taken as proof by some that Chichester was the landing site, as to get to Richborough from Boulogne one sails south to north. On a modern map one does but on ancient ones the position of the British Isles is somewhat flexible! Ptolemy's map, to which Cassius Dio would have had access, actually places Chichester very much to the southwest of Boulogne rather than due west, whilst Richborough is northwest rather than north. I've therefore chosen to interpret the direction as the one in which they would conquer.

We do not know how the Roman army would have effected a beach landing at this time; Caesar mentions an Eagle-bearer jumping from the ship into the sea in his narrative. I have placed ramps in the bows of the ships because it is possible that almost a hundred years later this innovation may have happened, seeing as the corvus had been in use for a couple of centuries in naval battles. With little or no evidence either way I felt free to include them in order to give the invasion a more immediate feel with echoes of Normandy 1944.

Cassius Dio also mentions the Britons' careless camping at the battle of the Medway – if it was indeed at the Medway – not expecting the Romans to force a crossing without a bridge. He then goes on to say that some German auxiliaries, most likely Batavians who were renowned for this feat in full armour, swam the river and took the Britons by surprise. The rest of the battle is vague but it did last two days, and Vespasian and Sabinus distinguished themselves crossing the river and Geta gets a mention for soundly defeating the barbarians after nearly being captured. Well, I put a different spin on that and my apologies to his shade for doing so.

The Thames was much wider and therefore shallower at the time of the invasion and, we are told, the estuary was fordable close to the mouth of the Medway. Where Aulus Plautius' legions crossed is a matter for dispute but I have placed it around Blackfriars Bridge just opposite Ludgate Hill.

We have no firm idea of how the Romans relieved their front ranks; unfortunately the ancient sources never mention it as it was probably deemed too obvious to write about. I have used one theory out of a handful.

As to what Claudius actually did when he arrived we do not know for sure. Suetonius tells us that he fought no battles; however, Cassius Dio tells us that he took command of the legions waiting near the Thames – but not which side of it. He then goes on to say that Claudius crossed the stream – not the river – and then engaged and defeated the barbarians and took Camulodunum. These conflicting views leave Claudius' role open to all sorts of interpretations and so I felt that I had a free hand in my fiction.

It is mentioned that he brought elephants but it seems unlikely that they would have been used in battle and so I attached them to Claudius' chariot – something not unknown in Rome.

We know from an inscription in Antioch that Publius Anicius Maximus was camp prefect of the II Augusta during the invasion and was decorated for his services.

I have kept to the same method of signalling with the cornu for the battlefield, the bucina in camp, the lituus for cavalry, and ignored the tuba because of its modern-day connotations.

We do not know what Cogidubnus' position was before he inherited Verica's throne; there is no evidence to suggest that he was King of Vectis but neither is there any to say he was not. Suetonius tells us that Vespasian subdued Vectis. What relation Cogidubnus was to Verica, if he was one at all, is also not known.

Vespasian's son, Titus, was educated with Claudius' son, who became known as Britannicus; but more of that in future volumes. The arrangement starting when and how I have portrayed it is, of course, my fiction. I am also indebted to John Grigsby for his help with the Celtic language of the time and for his particularly ingenious theory of how Rutupiae could possibly have come from Rhudd yr epis. Any mistakes in Celtic place names and character names are my own. John's website is www.johngrigsby.co.uk.

My thanks, as always, to my agent, Ian Drury, at Sheil Land Associates for his help and advice and his explanations of the publishing world. Thank you also to Gaia Banks and Virginia Ascione in the foreign rights department. To Sara O'Keeffe, Toby Mundy, Maddie West, Corinna Zifko and everyone at Corvus/Atlantic, a big thank you for putting so much energy behind the Vespasian series. Thank you to my copy-editor, Tamsin Shelton, for her thorough work in cleaning up the manuscript, especially with reference to my erratic use of capital letters!

And finally thank you to my editor, Richenda Todd, who has once again managed to coax out all the points that I had in my head but had neglected to share with you, dear reader.

Vespasian's story continues in *Masters of Rome.*